The Hemlock Falls Mysteries
1 pretty little town in upstate New York
1 picturesque inn overlooking Hemlock Gorge
2 talented sisters better at solving crimes
than they are at their day jobs
1 (or more) murders

A WINNING RECIPE FOR MYSTERY LOVERS
Don't miss these Hemlock Falls Mysteries . . .

A Carol for a Corpse . . .
Having the Inn featured in a magazine and on a television show chases away the holiday blues for Meg and Quill—until a slope-side slayer strikes . . .

Ground to a Halt . . .
Murder doesn't stop the Inn's pet food conventioneers from fighting like cats and dogs—but it does bring business to a grinding halt.

A Dinner to Die For . . .
Less-than-friendly professional competition. A serious case of cold feet. And, oh yes, a local murder. Could things go worse on Meg's wedding day?

Buried by Breakfast . . .
The leader of a raucous group of protestors turns up dead—and the Quilliams must quell fears and catch a killer before another local VIP is greeted with an untimely RIP.

continued . . .

A Puree of Poison ...

While residents celebrate the 133rd anniversary of the Battle of Hemlock Falls, the Quilliam sisters investigate the deaths of three people who dined at the Inn before checking out.

Fried by Jury ...

Two rival fried chicken restaurants are about to set up shop in Hemlock Falls—and the Quilliams have to turn up the heat when the competition turns deadly.

Just Desserts ...

There's a meteorologist convention coming to the Inn, and it's up to Quill and Meg to make sure an elusive killer doesn't make murder part of the forecast.

Marinade for Murder ...

The Quilliams' plans for the future of the Inn may end up on the cutting room floor when a group of TV cartoon writers checks in—and the producer checks out.

A Steak in Murder ...

While trying to sell the locals on the idea of raising their own herds, a visiting Texas cattleman gets sent to that big trail drive in the sky. The Quilliams set out to catch the culprit and reclaim their precious Inn ... without getting stampeded themselves!

A Touch of the Grape ...

Five women jewelry makers are a welcome change from the tourist slump the Inn is having. All that changes when two of the ladies end up dead, and the Quilliams are on the hunt for a crafty killer.

Death Dines Out . . .

While working for a charity in Palm Beach, the Quilliam sisters uncover a vengeful plot that has a wealthy socialite out to humiliate her husband. Now the sleuths must convince the couple to bury the hatchet—before they bury each other!

Murder Well-Done . . .

When the Inn hosts the wedding rehearsal dinner for an ex-senator, someone begins cutting down the guest list in a most deadly way. And Quill and Meg have to catch a killer before the rehearsal dinner ends up being someone's last meal.

A Pinch of Poison . . .

Hedrick Conway is a nosy newsman who thinks something funny is going on at a local development project. But when two of his relatives are killed, the Quilliam sisters race against a deadline of their own.

A Dash of Death . . .

Quill and Meg are on the trail of the murderer of two local women who won a design contest. Helena Houndswood, a noted expert of stylish living, was furious when she lost. But mad enough to kill?

A Taste for Murder . . .

The annual History Days festival takes a deadly turn when a reenactment of a seventeenth-century witch trial leads to twentieth-century murder. Since the victim is a paying guest, the least Quill and Meg could do is investigate.

DEATH IN TWO COURSES

CLAUDIA BISHOP

BERKLEY PRIME CRIME, NEW YORK

THE BERKLEY PUBLISHING GROUP
Published by the Penguin Group
Penguin Group (USA) Inc.
375 Hudson Street, New York, New York 10014, USA
Penguin Group (Canada), 90 Eglinton Avenue East, Suite 700, Toronto, Ontario M4P 2Y3, Canada
(a division of Pearson Penguin Canada Inc.)
Penguin Books Ltd., 80 Strand, London WC2R 0RL, England
Penguin Group Ireland, 25 St. Stephen's Green, Dublin 2, Ireland (a division of Penguin Books Ltd.)
Penguin Group (Australia), 250 Camberwell Road, Camberwell, Victoria 3124, Australia
(a division of Pearson Australia Group Pty. Ltd.)
Penguin Books India Pvt. Ltd., 11 Community Centre, Panchsheel Park, New Delhi—110 017, India
Penguin Group (NZ), 67 Apollo Drive, Rosedale, North Shore 0632, New Zealand
(a division of Pearson New Zealand Ltd.)
Penguin Books (South Africa) (Pty.) Ltd., 24 Sturdee Avenue, Rosebank, Johannesburg 2196,
South Africa

Penguin Books Ltd., Registered Offices: 80 Strand, London WC2R 0RL, England

This is a work of fiction. Names, characters, places, and incidents either are the product of the author's imagination or are used fictitiously, and any resemblance to actual persons, living or dead, business establishments, events, or locales is entirely coincidental. The publisher does not have any control over and does not assume any responsibility for author or third-party websites or their content.

PUBLISHER'S NOTE: The recipes contained in this book are to be followed exactly as written. The publisher is not responsible for your specific health or allergy needs that may require medical supervision. The publisher is not responsible for any adverse reaction to the recipes contained in this book.

PRINTING HISTORY
Berkley Prime Crime trade paperback edition / July 2010

Library of Congress Cataloging-in-Publication Data

Bishop, Claudia, 1947-
  Death in two courses / Claudia Bishop.
    p. cm.
  ISBN 978-0-425-23562-1
  1. Quilliam, Meg (Fictitious character)—Fiction. 2. Quilliam, Quill (Fictitious character)—
Fiction. 3. Hemlock Falls (N.Y. : Imaginary place)—Fiction. 4. Women detectives—
New York (State)—Fiction. 5. Sisters—Fiction. I. Title.
  PS3552.I75955D43 2010
  813'.54—dc22   2010009415

PRINTED IN THE UNITED STATES OF AMERICA

10 9 8 7 6 5 4 3 2 1

CONTENTS

A Pinch of Poison

1

Murder Well-Done

233

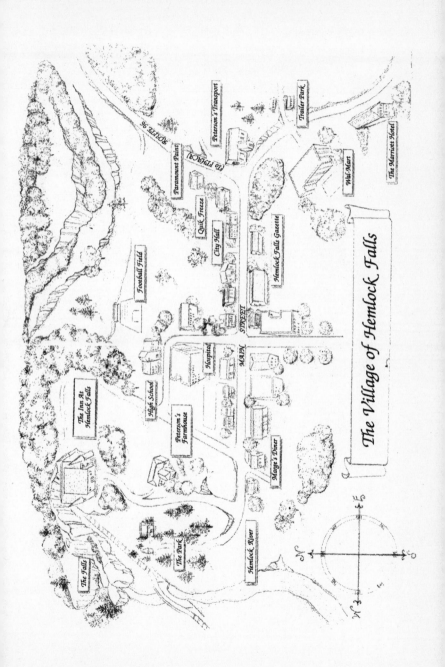

The Village of Hemlock Falls

ROUTE 96

(to IDAHO)

Peterson's Transport

Trailer Park

The Marriott Hotel

Wal-Mart

Paramount Point

Quik Freeze

City Hall

Hemlock Falls Gazette

Football Field

STREET

MAIN

Hospital

High School

The Inn At Hemlock Falls

Peterson's Farmhouse

Marge's Diner

The Park

Hemlock River

The Falls

N
W E
S

A PINCH OF POISON

For Helen and Les,
with love

THE CAST OF CHARACTERS

THE INN AT HEMLOCK FALLS

Sarah Quilliam	owner-manager
Margaret Quilliam	her sister, gourmet chef
John Raintree	business manager
Doreen Muxworthy	head housekeeper
Dina Muir	receptionist
Kathleen Kiddermeister	waitress
Axminster Stoker	guest
Lyle Fairbanks	president, the Rudyard Kipling Condensation Society
Lila Fairbanks	his wife
Jerzey Paulovich	member, the Rudyard Kipling Condensation Society
Aurora Kent	member, the Rudyard Kipling Condensation Society
Georgia Hardwicke	member, the Rudyard Kipling Condensation Society
Toshiro Sakura	former director, Sakura Industries
Motoyama	his chauffeur
Kenji Sakura	his son, professor of art appreciation at Cornell University
Marco DeMarco	owner, DeMarco Construction
Eugene	engineer, DeMarco Construction

MEMBERS OF THE CHAMBER OF COMMERCE

Elmer Henry	mayor
Harvey Bozzel	president, Bozzel Advertising

Howie Murchison	town attorney and justice of the peace
Freddie Bellini	director, Bellini's Funeral Home
Miriam Doncaster	public librarian
Marge Schmidt	owner, the Hemlock Hometown Diner
Betty Hall	her partner
Esther West	owner, West's Best dress shop
Dookie Shuttleworth	minister, the Hemlock Falls Church of the Word of God
Pete Rosen	publisher/editor, the *Hemlock Falls Gazette*
Mark Anthony Jefferson	banker, the Hemlock Falls Savings and Loan
Harland Peterson	president, Agway Farmer's Co-op
Petey Peterson	his cousin, owner of Peterson's Septic and Floor Covering
Norm Pasquale	principal, Hemlock Falls High School

. . . among others

THE SHERIFF'S DEPARTMENT

Myles McHale	sheriff of Tompkins County
Dave Kiddermeister	deputy

CHAPTER 1

Margaret Quilliam flipped another page in the tabloid-sized news-paper, bolted upright, and shrieked, "My *God!*" She shook her head. "This is outrageous. Like discovering Martha Stewart's had a sex change operation, or that Julia Child binged on Twinkies. I can't believe I didn't take a look at this when it was published a week ago."

"We've been busy," said Quill shortly. "The new restaurant's taking up more time than I thought it would."

"Yeah, but, Quill. There's no excuse. With Doreen so annoyed with you—"

"Doreen is *not* annoyed with me."

"She's annoyed at both of us," said Meg comfortably. "Which is why she didn't let us know about this outrageous newspaper, I expect. I wish I'd gotten down to the diner for the gossip this week. It must be fierce. And, by God, it says the next issue's due out today. I'll bet everyone's all of a doodah. Well, you needed a mur-der to solve. Sure as heck somebody in town will knock this bozo off. Detecting will be good for you. It'll pull you right out of this depression you're in."

Sarah Quilliam ignored her sister, concentrating instead on the Arriving Guests list. She penciled "Query: Sashimi?" next to the names Sakura Kenji and Sakura Toshiro, then wondered where they'd find fresh fish. Ken Sakura taught art commentary at Cor-nell. Toshiro must be his father. She didn't really paint anymore, and it was too much to expect that someone like Ken Sakura had heard of her, but still. Sushi would be nice. A gesture.

She dropped the list onto the wrought-iron tabletop and sighed. Meg's comment about depression was an exaggeration, like her reaction to the newspaper. If she, Quill, was a little down, it was because it was Friday and the Inn would be full by tomorrow. On the other hand, since a capacity crowd was unusual for the summer, it was probably the heat that was making her feel cross-wise.

It was hot even for August. When the kitchen thermometer in the Inn the sisters owned together hit eighty-eight (with a rise of ten degrees forecast for the afternoon), they'd headed outside to the gazebo by the waterfall to finish their weekly meeting over menus and the guest list. Quill scanned the items on her written agenda: review food to be served at their new boutique restaurant; assess inventory process improvements; verify menus and activities list for the upcoming week; discuss special menu requests from the customer survey results. Meg wasn't going to like that last one. Quill sat back and sighed. Even her elbows were sticky from the muggy weather.

The temperature had brought most of the Inn's guests out onto the lawn. Temporarily abandoning special menu requests, which was Meg's job, anyway, she wondered for the fourth or fifth time if they should air-condition the building. The Inn was situated high over Hemlock Gorge, and a breeze from the falls and the river usually cooled the Inn from the ground floor to the eaves. The heat was intolerable only two weeks out of the summer.

Maybe it wasn't as hot as it felt. Quill was wearing a light cotton skirt, sandals, and a flowered gauze blouse with full sleeves. Most of the guests had on less than that. Meg was in shorts, and she'd knotted her T-shirt above her waistband, but sweat trickled down her temples and her face was flushed. Quill lifted her own mass of hair to let the breeze from the gorge cool her neck. It didn't work. It was as hot as it felt. She thought about the things she should be doing instead of sitting in the gazebo. She should grab the newspaper away from Meg and force her to plan her own bloody menus. And she should either talk to Mike the groundskeeper about deadheading the roses or do it herself. The heat had forced an early petal drop, and things were looking shaggy. What she really wanted to do was go swimming in the clear water of the gorge and let the gardens, the Inn, the menus, and the guest list take care of themselves. She looked at the building, the grounds, and the garden filled with people whose relationship to her was defined by the limits on their credit cards. She sighed. Meg was right. She was depressed. Which was undoubtedly making her feel the heat even more.

Quill tried to convince herself that the Adirondack chairs placed at strategic intervals throughout the gardens were filled with guests drawn irresistibly outside by the sound of the falls and the scent of the roses, and not the muggy temperatures. A large elderly lady next to a four-foot-high bush of Apricot Nectar fanned herself with a copy of *Vogue*; her sigh of annoyance drifted accusingly across the lawn. Quill looked again at the estimate for air-conditioning, then grabbed an ice cube from her iced tea and ran it around the back of her neck. Now she was both hot and wet. She pulled a curl from behind her ear and looked at it. "Should I go blond?"

Meg glanced up, scratched her bare leg with one hand, and waved Quill's question away with the other. "It's been red since you were born. It's still red. Leave it alone."

"I'm going gray and I'm not even within spitting distance of thirty-four."

"That's not gray, that's Gruyère from the quiche at lunch. You're gorgeous, okay? Now, I wouldn't say you looked happy, or even pleasant, not for the past couple of weeks, at least. But gorgeous? Absolutely."

"Be quiet," said Quill crossly. "Put that thing down. I want to get to work."

"In a minute. You've got to see this after I'm through. Hedrick Conway never claimed he was going to publish a good newspaper. But this is ridiculous. It's not a newspaper, it's a joke."

"It looks like a newspaper to me. And I don't care what it is, anyway. How do you feel about sushi?"

"Sushi?"

"We have the Sakuras coming in. Do you know who they are? The father just retired as managing director of Sakura Industries, which is this huge multinational company."

"What's the former managing director of a billion-dollar business doing in Central New York? Need I ask. My cooking, naturally."

"His son teaches art appreciation at Cornell. He's Ken Sakura, the critic."

"Oh." Meg affected an air of unconcern. "We could unpack some of your paintings, maybe? He might want to take a look."

"I've quit."

"Quill . . ."

"My point was that it might be nice to offer a special Japanese menu."

"I don't know a thing about Japanese cooking except that you have to be licensed to serve fugu."

"Fugu?"

"It's a fish. The liver's poisonous. Kills you in something like two seconds." Meg mimed swallowing, clutched her throat, rolled her eyes, and made a sound like a garbage disposal with a fork in it. "You have to pass a test in cutting the liver away from the fish part." She looked thoughtful. "I wonder how they can tell when you've flunked? Now, there's a worthy subject for one of the nutty statistical studies you've been messing with recently. The morbidity rate in fugu inspectors on the island of Honshu."

"I would really appreciate it," said Quill stiffly, "if you'd cut the crap and give me a hand here."

Meg raised her eyebrows, said nothing for a moment, then saluted. "Yes, ma'am."

Quill flushed. She was willing to admit to a slight—very slight—depression over her breakup with Myles McHale, but it was not making her—what had been John Raintree's adjective? *Touchy.* Or was it *bitchy*? Maybe it had been a little bitchy to tell John to stick to minding the general ledger. Now, telling him he was not the Inn's resident shrink and to butt out of her private life would qualify as bitchy, since John was a friend of long standing as well as being their business manager. She didn't think she'd gone as far as that. At least not in so many words. Anyway, business was business, and the sooner everybody at the Inn figured that out, the better off they'd be. "Which," she said aloud—and to Meg's slight confusion—"we came out here to do, anyway, so we should get back to it."

"If you're talking about next week's menus, let me finish this newspaper first, and then I'll be your willing slave. How much do you suppose Hedrick Conway and his family invested in it anyway? He's going to lose his shirt."

Quill, perversely, found herself in sudden sympathy with the Conways, whom she had never met. She dampened her fingers and scrubbed at the gray strand in her hair. "You remember what everyone said about us when we opened up six years ago." Having determined that the gray was in fact Gruyère, she interrupted herself, considered a haircut, and bunched her hair together at her chin line. "You think I should go short?"

"No," Meg said without looking up. "It's nice the way it is. And yes, I remember what people said when we moved here and opened the Inn. Nothing. Nobody talked to us for a year."

"Well, when we *did* start making a few friends, they wanted to know why we were wasting our time and money on this junk heap and were we made of money or what?"

"What's that got to do with anything?"

"Nothing would ever get accomplished if people didn't take risks. Make sacrifices. Make tough personal decisions. Like my deciding to quit painting for the time being. And . . . other things. I'm getting the same kind of negative reaction to my efforts to improve the way things are done around here that the Conways are getting to their newspaper. 'You stick to what you do best. What do you want to mess around with stuff for when the Inn practically runs itself?' Runs itself, hah! I'd like to see some people run this Inn and find out how easy it is."

"So Doreen *did* talk to you this morning! She told me she'd had it up to here." Doreen, their head housekeeper, was a fiftyish widow whose three husbands had not, as occasional opinion would have it, died from being nagged to death. "She's got a right to be mad at you. I'm a little annoyed with you myself over this sudden immersion into all this quality improvement stuff." Meg tapped the agenda in a way loaded with significance. "Doreen's got her own case of . . . what's your euphemism for your lousy mood? 'Slight irritability,' that's it. Anyhow, ever since that miserable Axminster Stoker took up residence in the Shaker suite and the two of you started harassing her about how he can help her be more efficient, she's been more than slightly irritable, she's been pissed."

"It wasn't just the process improvement stuff," Quill said in gloomy agreement, "it's the boutique restaurant. Despite the fact that we've been planning it for months and included the staff every step of the way, Doreen hates the idea. She was complaining about the restaurant again this morning."

"Did you tell her she could put her Amway catalogs near the

cash register? As soon as you do that, she'll come around to our way of thinking. You haven't changed your mind about the boutique, have you?"

"No."

"Good. I think it's terrific. And the mall design is neat. The town needs the tax revenues. I'll be able to try some snazzy little dessert thingies that aren't right for the main dining room. I need the creative space that a little restaurant like that can give you. I can improvise. I can—"

"If you need creative space," Quill interrupted, "why don't you start with some Japanese food? The feedback from this new customer survey Mr. Stoker suggested says that people like to eat the things they're familiar with. And the Japanese are familiar with sushi."

"If people want familiar, they can stay home." Meg's face flushed with more than the heat, well past the ninety-degree mark now. "This sort of thing is exactly what Doreen was complaining about. You're brooding over Myles and making the rest of us jump through hoops. Process improvement for Doreen. Menu changes for me. Investment projects for John. No painting for you. I was sympathetic for a while, but you were the one who decided not to marry him."

"I am not brooding over Myles," Quill said carefully.

Meg opened her mouth, caught her sister's eye, and closed it. "I'm sorry. I didn't mean to . . . never mind. Why don't I get us some more iced tea? Stop thinking about the Inn. Forget Myles. Take three deep breaths."

Quill sat very still.

"Are you breathing?"

"Yeah."

"Really, truly just sitting there and forgiving me for being a tactless jerk?"

"Yes." Quill cleared her throat and wiped carefully under each eye with the back of her hand. There'd been a family saying for years when they were little, and she used it now. "It's just so hot my eyeballs are sweating."

Meg laughed a little, squeezed her hand hard, and released it. "One of the many advantages of having an older sister is they never completely let you forget your childhood. Here. Read this. I'll be back in a minute and we can talk about your next project. It'll be a real community service. Trust me."

Determined to be diverted, Quill took the paper.

The village of Hemlock Falls (population three thousand four hundred and fifty-six) had two newspapers for the first time in its three-hundred-year history. The venerable and conservative *Hemlock Falls Gazette* had carried hog and cattle prices and covered birthdays, weddings, graduations, and funerals to the exclusion of news stories for over seventy years. If anything so cataclysmic occurred that even Dookie Shuttleworth (the amiable but absentminded minister of the Hemlock Falls Church of the Word of God) was aware of it, the *Gazette* would refer to it in terms so elliptical that no one could possibly take offense. Natural disasters such as the Blizzard of '88 were usually apologized for: QUITE A BIT OF SNOW IN TOWN had been the headline reporting forty-eight inches. Man-made disasters, such as the murder investigations into which Quill and Meg had been involuntarily drawn several years before, were alluded to indirectly, if at all: UNFORTUNATE INCIDENT INTERRUPTS HEMLOCK HISTORY DAYS AND PAINT FACTORY PRODUCTION SLOWS were the *Gazette*'s response to a total of five corpses. Town opinion had it that the *Gazette* was more properly a medium for amiable social exchange than an organ designed for the balanced analysis of events.

The town had been in shock when Pete Rosen had put the *Gazette* up for sale. When Hedrick Conway, his mother, Louisa, and his sister, Carlyle, purchased the vacant Nickerson Hardware building (the hardware business had fallen victim to the new Wal-Mart on Route 15) and announced the successful purchase of the *Gazette*, Hemlockians had been dubious. The old newspaper had an editor-publisher related to half the folks in town. A man, moreover, who knew that real news was published at Marge Schmidt's diner over Sunday breakfast. Best thing that could happen was the flat-land foreigners get their clock cleaned and return to wherever they had come from, flat broke.

Meg had rolled the paper into a cylinder with the address sticker uppermost. Quill read: Mrs. Sarah Quillam, Manageress, Hemlock Falls Inn, One Hemlock Road, Hemlock Falls, New York 14562.

At least the ZIP code was right. Quill and Meg had both retained their maiden names after Quill's divorce and the demise of Meg's husband; they both preferred to use *Ms.* although *Miss* would do in a pinch; they spelled their name with two '*i*'s; the Inn was named the Inn at Hemlock Falls; and the term *manageress* had gone out with World War II, if not Warren G. Harding.

Even Dr. Watson could deduce quite a bit from something as simple as an address label. She frowned thoughtfully at it. The Conways were probably sweet, certainly elderly, obviously retired. Hedrick was probably fulfilling a lifelong dream of running a hometown paper in the Eden-like setting of Hemlock Falls. Hedrick's mother undoubtedly had pure white hair and a bravely wielded cane.

Quill decided to take out a subscription, maybe even an ad. People (like, for instance, Myles McHale) were unreceptive to those who tried to change the course of their daily lives. Especially if that person was a thirty-three-year-old artist turned Inn manager who preferred to remain single. Who wasn't sure she was tough enough to have a husband whose job took him into dangerous, life-threatening situations at all hours of the day and night. Especially a husband who wanted children. Not, Quill thought, the paper crumpled in her lap, her eyes on the water cascading over the rocks to the Hemlock River below, that babies weren't a pretty good idea in the abstract. She just wasn't sure about the particular.

A red-tailed hawk swept the narrow ledge of the gorge and shrieked, hunting to feed its ravenous young.

She shook herself, smoothed the tabloid over her knees, and read:

THE TRUMPET!

Premier Issue no. 1 vol. one
FREE COPY ONE TIME ONLY!!!

Underneath the banner was the headline:

DOG'S RUN WILD IN THE STREETS!!!

"Holy cow," said Quill.

Meg, back from her trip to the kitchen, set a fresh pitcher of iced tea on the table and settled into her seat. "Told you."

"Dog's run wild in streets?" said Quill. "In Hemlock Falls? A dog's what, anyway? Good God, listen to this! 'It was a dark and stormy night when this reporter took to the streets and alleys of our fair village. . . . '"

"Tuesday, I should think," said Meg with a judicious air. "That's when it rained last, three nights ago."

"'A dark shape followed this reporter as this reporter patrolled the muddy alley. A ferocious growl made menacing noises.' A ferocious growl?" Quill peered around the paper's edge. "Behold my wild surmise."

"I think he must have been behind Esther's shop. That's the first place in the village to get muddy when it rains."

"Got it. And the ferocious growl?"

"Buddy, Esther's poodle. She lets him out at seven-thirty for what she discreetly refers to as his constitutional. Doesn't fool a soul. Turn the page."

Quill turned the page. A photograph of "this reporter" filled the upper right quadrant. A banana-nosed man in his early thirties held the bottom of his loafer toward the camera with an expression of extreme distaste.

Quill shrieked.

"He stepped in it." Meg's grin was reluctant. "The editorial's about leash laws. He wants the town council to enforce leash laws—"

"No!"

"As you see. But that's not the worst part."

"Does it get worse?" asked Quill, fascinated. She skimmed the rest of the story. "Of course it gets worse. He wants the sheriff's office to issue citations for canine 'infractions.'"

"Now that's a good thing," said Meg. "It might make more dog owners aware of heartworm. August is a terrible time for heartworm. But that's still not the worst part."

"How do you know that about heartworm?"

"Andy told me."

"Andy's a people doctor, not a vet."

Meg shrugged, the slight blush with which she was liable to greet mention of the Falls' best-looking (and only) internist. "He's a dog-loving people doctor. Read on. See page four?"

Quill was cheered at the prospect, however remote, of six-foot-four Myles McHale chasing Esther West's yappy poodle to give it a ticket; Buddy was a notorious ankle-biter. She turned to page four. Her amusement faded. "Oh, no! He's printed the police blotter!"

"Cute, huh?"

"It's awful! As if there weren't enough gossip in a town this size. 'A juvenile, aged ten, of 256 Maple Drive, was arrested on a charge of petit mal larceny at the Wal-Mart store on Route Fifteen.'" Quill threw the paper on the table. "Honestly. Everyone knows it's just Benny Pasquale swiping gum. He's done it since he was eight years old. His parents make him give it back and work it off at the store. I think he just likes to stack cartons. And petit mal larceny? What the heck is that?"

Meg shrugged. "Not quite as funny as the 'infarction-infraction' mistake. Half the town is going to think Bennie's an epileptic and the other that he's kiting bad checks or stealing cars."

"This is too bad. His poor parents. That poor kid."

"There's more. Look at the bottom of the page. Pete Rosen would *croak* to see what's happened to the good old *Gazette*. I wonder if anyone's sent him a copy in Florida."

Quill picked the paper up and peered at the boxed item under the police blotter. "'Next week. Mini-Mall or Mighty Mess? Is the Entire Chamber of Commerce on the Take?! The *Trumpet!* has uncovered the true facts behind the construction—or should this reporter say *destruction*—of Hemlock Falls' most expensive venture in town history. Mayor denies cover-up!'" Quill dropped the paper on the table, and stared at her sister, astonished. She fished the lemon slice out of her tea and bit into it. The sour taste helped pull her scattered thoughts together. "This is just cheap gossip! Have you met these people? These Conways? Hedrick and Louisa and what's-her-name? Carlyle, his sister?"

"Nope."

Quill spit a lemon seed into her hand. She felt like throwing something. Not a large something. Just a gesture of disapprobation. Mike the groundskeeper had edged the gazebo with Old Spice sweet peas. It'd been a hot, wet summer, and the plants grew lushly cream, pink, scarlet, rose, and lavender around the latticework. She tossed the seed into the heavy foliage and pitched the rind in after it. "This is ridiculous. When I think of all the work that's gone into that stupid mini-mall—and the hours of time I've spent at Chamber meetings taking endless notes." She stopped. "There can't be anything in this. Can there?"

Meg shrugged. "Who's to say? On the face of it—or maybe I should say the sole of it, given that stupid picture—he's more likely a Geraldo Rivera wannabe. I'll tell you who would know if there's anything criminal going on at the mall."

Quill, who knew quite well whose name was about to surface, since he was the only real law in town, tore the paper into three long strips and said firmly, "Dookie Shuttleworth is head of the Mall Committee, as you very well know. And he couldn't be involved in anything crooked to save his soul. He's a minister, for Pete's sake."

"What about Harvey Bozzel?" asked Meg.

Quill pulled her lip. Harvey was Hemlock Falls' premier (and only) advertising executive. While Harvey's basic honesty was undeniable, his cupidity was problematic. With the best will in the world, Harvey had an eye for the main chance. "Nah. Marge Schmidt's on the committee. I could see Harvey getting involved with something crooked out of sheer dumbness, but Marge would put her size nines flat on his sweaty little neck. She's shrewder than the entire bunco squad at the FBI."

"Oh, sure," said Meg. "There's a superior comparison. If you're talking about the guys who didn't know their chief liked to wear a dress and bet mob money on the horses. What about the fact that nobody, but nobody in town is actually working at the site? The carpenters and electricians are all from out of town."

"Bull. We checked out DeMarco Construction thoroughly. At least, the committee did."

"And who was on that committee? Harvey Bozzel. And the Mayor. Neither of whom are up for Nobel prizes in investigation."

"So was Howie Murchison. And he's no fool. The best thing to do with this rag is ignore it. It's obvious, isn't it? Conway's a yellow journalist. He's trouble."

"Right here in River City," Meg chanted. "With a capital *T* and that rhymes with *P* and that stands for—"

"Poo!" they shouted together. Quill smiled and shook her head. "This is low-grade, bottom-of-the-barrel schtick humor, Meg."

Meg smiled back. "Whatever it takes. That's the first time I've actually heard you *laugh* since you packed up your paintings and decided to give Myles the boot."

Quill balled the paper up and stuck it under the chair. "Let's forget about it. We need to get through this agenda. Then I want to go swimming. It's been a tough week."

"No-no-no-no-no! Look. We got most of the full-time employees involved in this new restaurant of ours, right? One of your ideas about how much more appreciated they'd feel if they were truly a part of the business."

"You thought it was a good idea!"

"I still do. But what if there *is* something behind this mini-mall exposé? We have a clear responsibility to ourselves and our staff to find out the truth. My goodness, Quill, all our savings are in this project."

"Good God. You don't think there's something funny going on, do you?"

Meg shrugged. "Wouldn't hurt to find out. And who better than you to do a little discreet investigation?" She waved her arms dramatically. "Who was it that captured the Paramount Paint murderer? Confronted the History Day's killer? You're secretary of the Chamber of Commerce. Everyone in town likes you. It's perfect. So you'll do it? Maybe start with a quiet little interrogation of the Horrible Hedrick?"

"Well. You may be right."

"So you'll do it?"

"It's probably worth a look."

"And you'll start right now?" Meg's glance at the To Do list, which was uppermost on the stack of files on the gazebo table, was artfully innocent. "No time like the present. Can't hurt to start right now. Think of how cheerful you are when you're detecting. And how few lists you make."

"We'd have utter chaos without the To Do list. And there is absolutely nothing wrong with my moods."

"Well, let's talk about that. Before we get to the list."

Quill frowned, her hilarious mood evaporating as quickly as it'd come. "Okay, okay, maybe I've been a little—dour—lately."

"Dour! Try surly, cranky, tetchy."

"Not that bad," said Quill, startled.

"Let's stick with grouchy. We can all live with that. It's the hyperactivity that's tough. You throw yourself into all this useless work. I mean, look at this stuff." Meg pulled a file from the stack they'd brought from the kitchen and opened it with a dramatic flourish. 'Order Entry Process for Inventory.' What the heck is that? All these stupid little boxes showing Doreen how to do a job she's done perfectly well for the last five years."

"Axminster Stoker's been helping me. He was a process manager for a Fortune 500 company before he took early retirement."

"And you wonder why Doreen's been telling you to mind your own business? With you and this boob Stoker zooming all over the Inn with your slide rules and these dopey charts? Come on, Quill. It's impossible to have a decent conversation when you're depress—sorry, grouchy and defensive at the same time."

"I am *not* defensive!" Quill shouted. Then subsiding to a less bellicose tone, "Keep your voice down. Mr. Stoker's sitting right over there. It's not a dopey chart, it's a process chart. It's supposed to make us more efficient. Reduce costs. Improve profitability."

"My sister the Wizard of Wall Street. What about this other stuff?" Meg tossed the Order Entry Process for Inventory to the gazebo floor and fished another file from the stack. "Customer surveys. 'Rate your satisfaction with the quality of dinners during your stay at the Inn. a. Very Unsatisfactory. b. Unsatisfactory. c. Satisfactory. d. Very Satisfactory.'"

"We received an eighty-six percent 'Very Satisfactory' rating from that survey. Axminster says that's extraordinary for a business that's just getting into Total Quality. You should be proud. I've told you that, already."

"Fine. Swell. Good. Pretty nice," said Meg in an apparent—and in Quill's opinion—lame attempt at Total Quality humor. "So what did you do about the fourteen percent who thought my food was awful?" Her expression, innocently inquiring, didn't fool Quill at all. She was conscious of trepidation. Her sister's temper, serene only when she was cooking well, was volcanic when aroused.

"They didn't think your food was awful. They had suggestions for improving the menu, that's all. Some very, very small suggestions."

"So you asked the fourteen percent what I could do to improve," said Meg with a dangerous calm. "And why they hated my cooking. All you had to do, Quill, was ask me why they hated my cooking. You want to know why? I'll tell you why . . ." Meg, her face pink, began to tug at her short, dark hair with both hands—a bad sign.

"They didn't hate your cooking. They loved your cooking. A basic quality principle, according to Mr. Stoker, is that everything can be improved. They loved your cooking so much, they had ideas for it to get even better. It's not a criticism, Meg. It's feedback. It shows the customers are involved."

"Oh. I see. Of course." She picked up a survey response at random and read: "'Herring no good.' Silly, silly me, to have no-good herring. Dammit! I don't serve herring at all!"

"You have to know how to interpret these things," said Quill wisely. "That may sound like our herring was no good, but what it means is that it wasn't good that we didn't have herring. I'm pretty sure that this was from the reunion meeting of the Finns Who Found God. They eat a lot of herring, Finns do, and which was just the point I was making about our Japanese guests. People like it when you serve food familiar to them."

"Oh? What about this one?" Meg's nostrils flared. She read: "'We want tits!'"

"Well, that one . . . you remember?"

"The Society of Swamp Reclamation Engineers—the ones who wanted to know how come there were no topless joints in Tompkins County? How could I forget?" Meg's face got pinker. Her eyes narrowed. Her voice rose. "I am *not*, I repeat *not* going to change a. my cooking, or b. my menus, or c. remove my T-shirt to suit *anybody*! And that includes the President of the United States himself! Do you hear this? If the President himself showed up and asked for herring I would refuse! This quality stuff sucks!"

"Will you hush, Meg? Mr. Stoker—"

"Who cares!?"

"Okay," said Quill cautiously. Then, "I'm sorry. You have a point about the T-shirt."

"You bet I do."

"But not about the herring."

"Jeez!" Meg said. Her hair began to resemble bedsprings.

"Just think about adding a few specials to the menu to make the guests feel more at home. Not every day. Not all the time. Just once in a while. Like maybe sushi. It'll give you creative scope. I admit, I can see your point about the feedback—"

"Stuff the feedback. It's not the feedback. It's the fact that you think these people have the right to change the way I cook that's driving me bananas. All these dopey statistics tell you is that the Swamp Reclamation Engineers should have gone to Atlantic City and the Finns to Nantucket. You want feedback? I'll give you feedback. You and Mr. Stoker can take these statistics and—"

"Will you keep your voice down, please? The poor man can hear you. The entire town can hear you. I'm changing my mind about spending money on air-conditioning. At least we can argue in the kitchen, where nobody can hear us."

"Pooh! I'm not saying a single thing to you that I wouldn't say to that fussy little process gearhead myself."

"Airing these differences can be a good thing," said a dry voice in Quill's ear, "but only when the parties involved share a common vision for excellence." The clipped precise speech was an aural representation of a lawn mowed within an inch of its life.

Quill closed her eyes, turned in her seat, and opened them to see Axminster Stoker standing at the entrance to the gazebo. "Hi, Mr. Stoker."

Mr. Stoker was small and sinewy with a buzz cut and a stiff blond-gray mustache. He looked as though he wore khakis even when he didn't. His eyes were the color of little blue marbles. "Margaret? I can tell you what you are feeling now. You're feeling threatened. This is a normal response to those unacquainted with

Total Quality principles. I am, however, always glad to have the opportunity to enlighten the uninformed."

"It's enlightening enough to know somebody who's been named after a carpet," said Meg tartly. "We have an Axminster in the conference room. Were you born on one?"

"My family," said Mr. Stoker, with the air of someone who has had to explain this before and is rather pleased to do so, "came from the village in England. I sense that you are feeling offended as well as threatened. This, too, is a common reaction to my ideas for process improvement. Made worse, I might add, when inadequately explained." The birdy-blue eye fixed itself on Quill in impersonal accusation. "I do apologize for the intrusion, but I couldn't help but overhear the lamentable interpretation of Total Quality principles. May I sit down?" He stepped into the gazebo, settled onto the bench facing Meg and Quill, and drew a deep breath. "To begin with, there is no human activity that cannot be flowcharted."

"Terlits," said Doreen Muxworthy.

Quill jumped. Their head housekeeper, skinny and tough as a piece of barbed wire, placed both freckled hands on the gazebo railing and glared at Axminster Stoker. Quill wondered why voices carried in the humid air and footsteps didn't. She decided, crossly, that Doreen had crept up on them on purpose. "What is it, Doreen? I didn't hear you come up."

"D'ja hear me now?"

"Of course I hear you now. Anybody within a mile could hear you now. What about the toilets?"

"The maintenance of toilets," said Axminster Stoker, "lends itself in particular to a process flowchart. All it takes is an initial commitment to doing things right the first time."

Doreen's eyes narrowed, but she said nothing. Quill cleared her throat and said brightly, "What about the toilets?"

"Backed up." Although her mouth moved, Doreen's regard of Axminster Stoker's face was otherwise totally motionless, reminding Quill of a National Geographic Special she'd seen on lionesses stalking in the Kalahari. "Ground floor. Second and third floor like to go as soon as this lot sitting out here goes back to their rooms. Which'll be pretty soon. They been drinking iced tea like it's going out of style."

"Oh, dear." Quill got to her feet with a guilty sense of relief. She fully appreciated Axminster Stoker's advice, but it was advice that benefited from coffee with a high caffeine content and cooler temperatures. Otherwise it made her sleepy. "I suppose I'd better go. Doreen, did you call Petey what's-his-name?"

"Peterson," said Doreen. "From Peterson's Septic and Floor Covering. I already done that. So you can stay right here."

Her steady gaze was beginning to discomfit Quill, who couldn't imagine why it wasn't unnerving the apparently nerveless Mr. Stoker. "And leave you to deal with this on your own? I'd be a pretty poor manager if I did that." Familiar with the opinion Doreen seemed about to express, she hurried on, "Is Petey coming soon? It's Friday, you know, and I'm pretty sure I mentioned that we've got twelve people checking in this afternoon. Those Japanese guests, and the members of the . . . the . . ." She scrambled hastily through the file on guest preferences. "Rudyard Kipling Condensation Society. Now, that might interest you, Mr. Stoker. Do you like Kipling? You look as if . . . I mean with your family background and all."

"'Though I've belted you and flayed you, by the living God that made you, you're a better man than I am, Gunga Din,'" said Axminster unexpectedly. "Yes. I like Kipling."

"Dina Muir, our receptionist, should be able to tell you all you need to know about them. The Society sent ahead some literature. They give recitations on request, I guess, wherever they go." Drawing on six years' experience of managing guests prone to an astonishing variety of behaviors, she guided Axminster out of the gazebo and onto the lawn. Doreen swiveled her head to follow them, rather like the gun turret on a tank.

"I'm quite interested in Kipling," said Axminster, "but wouldn't you say that I was needed here? Prioritization is a key quality concept. Toilets are too critical to be left to chaos—"

Behind her, Doreen made a sound Quill hadn't heard before and was pretty sure she didn't want to hear again. "I wouldn't dream of asking you to use up your precious vacation time on plumbing problems. You've already been far, far more helpful than necessary. We are all in your debt. Will you be eating here tonight? If you decide not to, there are a number of places I can recommend.

Or what about taking the wine tour? The van leaves this evening at six-thirty from the foyer."

"I have already signed up for the wine tour," said Axminster, a little pathetically. "It will be my fourth such foray. You feel it would be worthwhile to go again?"

"You learn something new every time," said Quill firmly, "especially on the all-day tour. You can catch that one tomorrow."

"I sense that you may be backing off from your leadership commitment, Sarah. I am disappointed. Ladies? Good day to you."

Quill watched him march off with dismay. "I think I hurt his feelings."

"I think you saved his life," said Meg, her eye on Doreen.

Quill turned to Doreen, "No," she said.

Doreen's eyes widened in cagey innocence, which gave her the look of a startled rooster. "No terlits?"

"You know what I mean. No mops left jammed under Mr. Stoker's door in the morning. No slippery puddles of soapy water on the bathroom floor. No foreign substances in his food. And don't you dare call any religious organizations to convert him. Understood? Now. What about the plumbing?"

Doreen blinked. "Petey says we gotta pump the septic."

"How long will it take? When will he get here? The Kipling people are due to check in at four o'clock. And most of them are booked into the first-floor rooms." She thought a moment. "Maybe we can move the Kipling people to the third floor."

Doreen brightened. "We could throw out this Stoker. He's in the Shaker suite. Put a couple of the Kiplings in there."

"Mr. Stoker booked the Shaker suite for three months. And paid in advance. We can't afford to offend a guest like *that* Doreen."

"Up the proletariat," muttered Doreen. Quill groaned. Marx, after Amway, would be too much. "Doreen!"

"If they're into Kipling, they at least have pretensions to the literary," Meg intervened. She waved the tattered *Trumpet!* "We can search the trash cans all over town and get them copies of this rag. They'll be laughing so hard they won't think twice about toilets. Come to think of it, it'd be a good investment for you, Doreen. Benny Pasquale's dad has probably thrown most of them into the incinerator by now. They'll be collector's copies by next week and worth a bunch. I can't believe the guy will have the nerve to publish another issue."

"Oncet a week," said Doreen.

"Petey's going to have to come once a week?" said Quill, once again preoccupied with plumbing. "How much is this going to cost us? I'm seriously thinking of getting the air-conditioning people in this afternoon. And they want half of the payment for the installation up front."

"That thing." Doreen pointed a calloused thumb in the direction of the *Trumpet!* "Comes out oncet a week. Mr. Conway told me that himself."

Meg raised her eyebrows. "Hedrick Conway? The publisher of this piece of junk? I didn't know you knew him. Have you met him before?"

"You ain't?"

"Nobody's met him, far as I know." Quill thought a moment. "Howie Murchison must have. He handled the real estate closing for the Nickerson building."

Doreen shrugged. "He came out here to look for you a while ago."

"Hedrick Conway did? Then where is he?" Quill scanned the Adirondack chairs. She was familiar with all the guests and they all belonged there. Hot, but registered.

"Right here, Mrs. Quilliam." A very tall, banana-nosed man unfolded from behind the mass of sweet peas like a stork coming up for air. A lemon seed stuck to his forehead like an afterthought. "Ladies? Can I quote you on why you refuse to serve the President?"

CHAPTER 2

Meg gripped the sides of her wicker chair, threw her head back, and screamed. Judging from the cheerful look on her face, it was a satisfying scream. "And," said Meg, "you can quote me on that." She stood up, brushed off her shorts, and retied her T-shirt, exposing another few inches of flat stomach. Hedrick's pale blue eyes bulged. "Quill? I'll take this stuff back to the kitchen. Doreen and I will take care of the menu planning. I'll turn the guest list over to Dina. That leaves you"—Meg gave her a look loaded with significance—"to handle things here." She nodded briskly to Hedrick Conway, swept the files off the table, and marched out of the gazebo, trampling the tattered remnants of the *Trumpet!* underfoot.

Quill, trying to recall just when she'd pitched the lemon seed over the side of the gazebo, had come to the reluctant conclusion that Hedrick had heard all; it had occurred far too early in their derisive discussion about the *Trumpet!* to make social niceties credible. With a baleful eye, she watched her sister cross the lawn: the same conclusion had obviously occurred immediately to Meg. At least, her own decision to discover what lay behind Hedrick Conway's promised mini mall exposé had been thoughtful, determined, and unvoiced. Just like Lew Archer, the least verbal of all the great detectives.

"Quite a place you got here." Conway shifted from one very large foot to the other, crushing a particularly vivid spray of crimson sweet peas. The heat had plastered his coarse blond hair to his forehead. He was thin, except for a round ball of stomach. A white cotton shirt laundered far past its useful life fitted badly over his sloping shoulders. Baggy pale brown chinos and soft white suede shoes made him look like a marshmallow handled by too many Boy Scouts.

"Yeah," said Quill laconically, in true Archer style. "I'm Sarah

Quilliam. That's Quilliam with two *i*'s. What's up?" This, Quill realized even as she said it, was rude even for Lew Archer. And, to paraphrase what one vice presidential candidate had once said to another, she was no Robert Mitchum, she was the manager of a public hostelry, and constrained to be hospitable. "It's very nice to meet you. Can I offer you something cool to drink?"

"Wouldn't mind a glass of iced tea." Ignoring the graveled path that ran parallel to the sweet peas, he trampled through the plants to the gazebo entrance, thudded into the shelter itself, and sat in the chair Meg had so sensibly vacated minutes before. "The glasses are dirty," he pointed out.

"Well," said Quill inadequately. "This is . . . is there . . . I mean, did . . . Let me get you a fresh glass." She turned and looked for Kathleen, who was nowhere in sight. "The waitress will be out in a bit."

A brief silence reigned. Quill, momentarily discomposed, and in search of a conversational gambit, remembered that Hedrick wasn't solely responsible for the *Trumpet!* "Are your mother and sister with you today?"

"Nope, nope. They went to Syracuse. Shopping. You know gals. I was just roaming the streets of the village, looking for news. Carry this with me, at all times." He rummaged in the pocket of his chinos and withdrew a thick red spiral notebook. "It's all in here. The goods book. Not the Good Book, y'see, but the goods book. Get it?"

Quill got it. She eyed the book with a high degree of interest. "You keep your story ideas in there?"

"It's my bible." He descended to the practical with an abrupt change of manner. "Also, I stopped by to see if you got your free complimentary issue. Thought I'd better introduce myself, seeing as how people probably would like to know the person that runs something like the *Trumpet!*"

"Um," said Quill. Under her feet the *Trumpet!*'s second page fluttered in the breeze from the Falls, the picture of Hedrick's disgraced loafer flapping back and forth like a small flag. Hedrick *tsk'd* in distress and picked it up.

"This didn't happen in delivery?"

"The wind," Quill improvised, "blew it under the chair."

"You probably didn't read the old *Gazette* until now." He

smoothed the paper with a loving hand. "I told Ma, we're going to make some changes. Time this town had a real paper, tackling real issues. Take this f'instance." He began to read aloud. "'It was dark and stormy when this reporter—'"

"Yes," said Quill. "The leash law issue." She smiled in what she hoped was a winning way, and perjured herself without a qualm, something Archie Goodwin did frequently in the pursuit of justice. "I was just fascinated by the paper. This whole approach is such a departure from the way Paul Rosen used to run the *Gazette*. Especially the story you're going to write about the mini-mall."

Hedrick smiled complacently. "Made you sit up and take notice, huh? That's the mark of a good story. I suppose they know who I am in this town, all right. You see the police blotter?"

"You're going to make that a usual practice, are you?"

"It's Hemlock Falls first. That sheriff, what's his name?"

"Myles McHale."

"Yeah. Gave me a little lip about printing it. But I know my rights." He shook his head and laughed genially. "These small-town police. You gotta know how to handle 'em."

"I don't know that I'd call Sheriff McHale small town, precisely. Did you get the small-town impression because of his reaction to the story you're going to write about the mini-mall?"

Hedrick ignored this gambit. "Well. You been around a bit, like I have, you'd know what I mean." He narrowed his eyes at the sprawling building. "How big is this place, anyway?"

"This place? You mean the Inn? Twenty-seven rooms."

"Occupancy rate?"

"I'd have to ask John Raintree about that," said Quill, a little stiffly, "our business manager."

"Reason I asked is, with twenty-seven rooms, you'd probably want a good slug of papers every week. What can I put you down for, say, forty copies a week?"

"Forty?" Quill decided it wasn't the heat, but Hedrick's goat-like leaping from crag to conversational crag that was making her dizzy.

"Good business like this—if it is a good business, and you're not just blowing smoke like a lot of small-timers do—you'd want a copy for each room plus lobby copies, plus one for you and a couple of the staff."

"Well," said Quill cleverly, "we might think about a subscription—maybe even two—if we had an idea about upcoming features. For example, this story about the mini—"

"Quill? Meg sent out some refreshments." Kathleen Kiddermeister stepped into the gazebo, tray in hand. "And she said to tell you she'll think about the sushi, but she's got another way to impress this art critic guy."

Quill, normally glad to see Kathleen, was frustrated at this interruption of her subtle interrogation. She jumped to her feet and grabbed at the tray. "Thanks, Kath. You didn't need to do this. I'll take care of it."

Kathleen held on to the tray and dropped one eyelid in a surreptitious wink. Clearly, Hedrick Conway and his lunatic journalism had been a topic of discussion in the kitchen. "You just sit down, Quill, and let me clear this for you." With the deft efficiency that made her one of the Inn's best waitresses, she put the pitcher and the used glasses on the tray, folded the remains of the *Trumpet!* into her apron pocket, and set down a bowl of strawberries, plates, and a fresh pitcher of tea.

"So," said Quill. "Thanks."

Kathleen, curiosity all over her freckled face, said, "About the plumbing?"

"Mr. Peterson's here. He's taking care of it. So. Thanks."

"You know the toilets in 101 and 102 are like totally backed up."

"Plumbing problem?" said Hedrick alertly. "Toilets, huh?" He began scribbling and muttered, "Inn at Hemlock Fall Evacuated." He repeated this with a pleased air, then regarded the waterfall. "Any chance the sewage'll flood the gorge? Sure there is. 'Will Environmental Disaster Close Inn?'"

"Jeez," said Kathleen.

Quill raised her eyebrows at Kathleen and sent her a fierce mental message—an activity recently promoted by the Reverend Dookie Shuttleworth, who was currently experimenting with extrasensory-perception sermons—to beat feet. She braced her feet against the footer at the base of the gazebo with an assumption of careless ease. "Thanks for bringing the tea and fruit out, Kathleen. I'll be in after Mr. Conway is finished here."

"Nothing else I can do for you here?"

"Not a thing."

"Wait a minute, there, girlie." Hedrick took in Kathleen's soft peach uniform, her starched apron, and the loaded tray. "You a waitress?"

Kathleen, bridling over the "girlie," said rather tartly that, no, she was a shortstop for the New York Jets.

"Before you were a waitress?"

Quill stated the obvious. "The Jets don't take women players, Mr. Conway. Kathleen's been a waitress for six years, ever since we opened the Inn."

"Thought so. Hang on a bit, Mrs. Quillam. I got something to ask this little lady." Hedrick reopened the red notebook with a flourish. The pages were much-thumbed and filled with small, surprisingly neat writing. "Got a report I'm following up on here, ma'am, about policies regarding the serving of guests. You ever been instructed not to serve some people? You know, like some political figures?"

Kathleen blinked at Hedrick. "Refuse to serve some people?"

"F'instance, did Mrs. Quillam here ever tell you to kick some folks out? Not to serve them?" Kathleen's bemusement seemed to register on him and he added in an explanatory way, "Say, f'instance, the President comes to Hemlock Falls. Not that he has or anything. But say that he does. Mrs. Quillam here let you serve him?"

Quill intervened, "Mr. Conway, you've misinterpreted something you overheard a few minutes ago from my sister. Meg frequently overstates—"

Hedrick held up a fleshy palm. "No fair coaching. So, Katherine, say you got the President wanting to eat in your dining room."

"The President's coming to dinner?" said Kathleen. "Our President? You're kidding! Does Davy know?"

"Davy?" asked Hedrick with a clever air.

"My brother. If it's true, he'll need to know right away."

"Your brother, huh?" Hedrick licked the end of his pencil. "Local political activist? What's his name and address?"

"The Inn's full," said Kathleen with dismay. "Where are we going to put the President?"

"So you'd let your brother know, first thing," said Hedrick. "He's what they call a subversive, your brother?"

"*Stop!*" shouted Quill. Behind her the low murmur of the guests in the Adirondack chairs came to a sudden halt. Quill controlled her voice. "Mr. Conway, Kathleen's brother, David Kiddermeister, is Myles McHale's chief deputy. He'd be busy with security matters if the President visited, which, Kathleen, he *isn't* scheduled to do. Go back to the kitchen." Kathleen began to straighten the dishes on the table. Quill ignored her. "Mr. Conway, would you like some strawberries?"

"Strawberries?" He peered suspiciously at the bowl of fruit. "They're not canned, are they? I never eat canned food."

"We've made our reputation on the quality of our food," she said with determined cheerfulness. "Now. You were just about to tell me all about the mini-mall story. I read all about it in this week's *Trumpet!* and I can't wait to hear more."

"Well, now." Hedrick frowned. "My information's confidential of course, but . . . Quillam, Quillam," muttered Hedrick, paging through his notebook. "Sure. Here we go. Mini-mall. Chamber of Commerce. Payoffs to Mayor." He looked up at Quill alertly. "You're the alleged secretary of the Chamber of Commerce? Would you care to comment on the stories circulating in town about fraudulent activity in the mini-mall project?"

"Alleged? Alleged? I *am* . . . Mr. Conway, there is *nothing* fraudulent about the mini-mall project. What are your sources of information?"

"Quillam . . . denies . . . involvement . . ." muttered Hedrick, scribbling.

"Involvement in what! Are you referring to something specific?"

"I'm referring to the truth, ma'am. That's all I'm after. You involved in this mini-mall investment all by yourself?"

"We all are," Kathleen interrupted nervously. "Quill and John Raintree gave all us employees the chance to invest in the new boutique restaurant. Is there something wrong? Did somebody steal our money? You know what? I'll see if I can find John. He knows all about our new restaurant there. That sound like a good idea?"

"No," said Quill. "Kathleen, please—"

"Raintree, Raintree, Raintree . . . now where did I hear that name? Aha!" Hedrick held up a minatory hand, read to himself, lips moving, then looked at them with an expression Quill found incredibly sly. "He have something to do with this deal?"

"John Raintree is our business manager. And yes, we made the decision together to invest in the mini-mall project."

"Raintree? That a white name?"

"I beg your pardon?"

Kathleen coughed nervously. "Quill. John's going over the supplier bills in the office. I'll be back with him in two seconds." She hurried across the grass, the glasses on the tray jingling.

"Raintree. Doesn't sound like a white name." He raised his eyebrows expectantly. "It's important for a newspaperman to be accurate. First thing they teach you."

"John's a member of the Onondaga tribe. He has an MBA from Cornell and he's been with us four years. He handles our accounting and all the finances."

"So you don't have a hand on the checkbook. That's very interesting." Hedrick made a small finicky note in his book. "Can't say as I blame ol' John. Don't like to let either one of my ladies out of hand myself."

Quill stared at him, open-mouthed.

"Hello? Hello?" Hedrick rapped on the table. "Are we communicating here?"

"We're certainly exchanging words, Mr. Conway. But I have to say, I don't in the least understand what you're doing. Now, if you could just explain a bit more about this mini-mall story."

Hedrick leaned forward. His breath was unpleasant. "I've got the most important job there is. To publish the best paper I can. I'm a newshound, first and foremost. Like Eddie Murrow and Ernie Pyle, which is why I have to be on the alert for news all the time. Walking the streets of this town day and night, finding the news." He sat back, with that wild veer into the pragmatic Quill noticed before. "And I'm a publisher, which is why I have to find out about subscriptions, at least until I can find a circulation manager. You wouldn't know anyone who'd be interested in the job, Mrs. Quillam?"

"It's spelled Q-U-I-L-L-I-A-M," said Quill tartly. "And I am not married. I'm sure you'll agree that the first obligation of a good reporter is to get the facts straight." She fanned herself and took a deep breath. The first rule of innkeeping, she and Meg had agreed long ago, was not to belt guests in the mouth, even under the severest provocation. A change of subject was in order, if she wasn't going to violate rule one. "I'd be fascinated to know where you got your ideas about how to run a newspaper. I know Syracuse has a fine program. The S.I. Newhouse graduate program?"

"You mean did I go to journalism school? Nah. I guess I could teach so-called professors a thing or two about what sells papers. Nope, this issue of the *Trumpet!* is my first."

"You're not an experienced newspaperman, then?"

Hedrick lowered his notepad and gave her a look compounded equally of incredulity and hurt. "I guess maybe you didn't mean that the way it sounded."

Quill apologized, then hoping further digression would result in a more sensible conversation, said pleasantly, "Is there a reason why you chose Hemlock Falls for your first venture?"

"That him coming? The Indian?" Hedrick interrupted. "Got that brown skin and black hair. Must be."

Quill twisted around in her seat. "Yes, that's John." She waved. John smiled, his long legs covering the distance between the Inn and the gazebo with easy athleticism. He nodded to Hedrick as Quill made the introductions.

Hedrick, brow furrowed, mouth lightly agape, burrowed in his book like a mole after a grub. "Heard about you." He flipped the pages. "Here it is. Thought so. Got a record, right? Arrested on suspicion of murder a couple years ago. Served time for murder before that." He tucked the notebook into his shirt pocket with a nod of satisfaction. "Thing is, I was thinking maybe of doing a series of stories with a punch. Y'know, human interest. 'Will I Kill Again?' That kind of thing. Grabs the reader."

Quill's breath went short. She felt as though she were encased in glass, as if there were a transparent, sound-proofed barrier between Hedrick, herself, and the rest of her world. The skin on her scalp contracted and her fingers curled into fists. "Out." Her voice just above a whisper, she got to her feet. "Get out."

"Quill." John's voice was quiet, removed from her by that glass wall of rage.

"You heard me," said Quill to Hedrick Conway. She picked up the iced tea pitcher and pulled her arm back. She thought of Darryl Strawberry.

Hedrick smirked and waved the red-covered book as he left the gazebo and shambled across the lawn to the Inn's parking lot.

"Quill."

The world righted itself. She smoothed her hair. Her hands were shaking, and she sat down hard, bumping her head on the latticed wall of the gazebo.

"Hey." John squatted next to her chair. His coppery skin was redder than usual, but his expression was calm. "It's true."

"It's not true. Not the way he said it. It made you sound . . . guilty."

"I was guilty."

"Of manslaughter, John. No one in their right mind could blame you for what you did. That little muckraking *toad*! Has the *nerve*! I could just kill him!"

"No offense, Quill. But I can take care of him myself. And if I don't want to rearrange his nose down to his socks, why should you?"

"You don't?"

"Well . . ." The skin around John's eyes wrinkled in amusement. "Maybe a little. But what can he do to me now? Everyone in town knows what happened. If he reprints the story, so what? It's a nine-day wonder, and then it's over. You know Hemlock Falls."

"I guess I do. And you're right. But—! What a little twerp!"

"I'll buy that. Come on." His hand was warm in her own. He pulled her to her feet, "You'll be glad to know that Petey Peterson's pumping the septic tank and the toilets will be functioning again. That sounds like a tongue-twister, doesn't it? And the Kipling Society's due momentarily. We'll go back to the kitchen and see if we can talk Meg out of some of the *sorbet* she's made for tonight while we're waiting for them to check in."

"There's something wrong with this picture," Quill complained as she followed him across the lawn.

"Wow!" John cocked his head to one side, a funny note in his voice.

"I should be comforting you, and as usual, John, you end up comforting me. Wow, what?" She squinted. "My goodness. Does that look like an advance party of the Kipling Condensation Society to you?"

"If it is, I'm joining."

Two women emerged from French doors that led from the Tavern Bar to the flagstone patio. The younger wore a pink halter top that just barely contained a generous pair of breasts. They looked exactly like a pair of giant rolls in a wicker breadbasket. Even at this distance, Quill could tell she was chewing gum. Her sister was older, slimmer, and better-dressed. Even at this distance, the two women's sexuality was as blanketing as the August heat. Quill poked John in the side, hard. "Stop that."

"Stop what?"

"Drooling over that pair of sisters. They're poking holes in the lawn with their stiletto heels. You know how Mike hates that."

"I never drool. Except when it's deserved. It's deserved." John chuckled. "And they aren't sisters."

The women walked toward them like peacocks picking their way through a barnyard.

"Mother and daughter?" said Quill dubiously. "You're right, that's a heck of a face-lift on the mother. I wonder who they are?" The younger blonde was carrying a large paper shopping bag that read: SAKS FIFTH AVENUE AT THE SYRACUSE MALL! "Oh, nuts. More Conways."

"There's more?"

"Sure. You remember what Marge told us last Sunday. Louisa's the mother, the daughter's . . ." Quill frowned. "I keep thinking Thomas, but that's not right."

"Carlyle."

"That's it." A wave of heavy perfume hit Quill before the women came within hearing distance. "Giorgio. Phew! At one o'clock in the afternoon?"

John slipped her a sideways grin. "Snob."

They stood and watched the Conways wind their way through the rosebushes. Mrs. Conway wore a white linen suit—probably Armani, Quill thought—possibly Ungaro. Her daughter's halter, short skirt and gold-trimmed handbag were definitely Escada. Mrs. Conway's shoes would have paid Doreen's salary for a week. Although neither of the women looked directly at John, Quill knew in her bones that the animated conversation between them was for his benefit. They subsided into self-conscious silence as they neared the gazebo, then the elder extended her hand. "Ms. Quilliam? I'm Louisa Conway. My daughter Carlyle. We have to apologize for the gum; she's trying to quit smoking." Louisa Conway's hand was cool and firm, the nails buffed, not polished, the skin well-cared for. "Carlyle, this is Sarah Quilliam—you're familiar with her work? She's the artist?"

"The flower studies?" Carlyle shifted the gum from one cheek to the other, and said rapidly, "You did that terrific series of roses a while back. I saw the show in New York. They called you the heir to O'Keeffe, didn't they?"

"Just O'Keeffe's flower work, Cay. Ms. Quilliam's work is nothing like the desert studies." Mrs. Conway, with the air of a script prompter in a bad play, gave her a nod.

"Thank goodness for that, I say. O'Keeffe terrifies me. Do you hang any work here at the Inn?"

Quill blinked, opened her mouth, and said, "Not really."

Up close, the Conway women resembled nothing so much as heavy cream. Neither had a beautiful face; Quill could see the resemblance to Hedrick in both of them, especially around the mouth and eyes. But they had something: both had thick translucent skin, heavy-lidded eyes, full mouths, and hair the color of bronze, thinly beaten. Like plush cats with glossy fur, Quill thought. Except that she liked cats, and she didn't like these women at all.

"And you," said Louisa, "must be the famous Mr. Rain-tree." She widened her eyes and wriggled her shoulders. John's answering grin irritated Quill profoundly. "We've heard about you from some friends of ours who stayed here last year. The Ferragamos? No relation to the luggage people, but just as nice as can be. Theobold said you truly know your wines. When Cay and I eat here, you'll have to give us your personal attention."

John said, "I'll be happy to show you around the Inn, if you've got a little time. Excuse me, Quill. I'd like to show Carlyle and Louisa the koi pond."

I'll just bet you would, Quill thought, resisting the impulse to kick him. "We've got a fairly large party checking in in about twenty minutes, Mrs. Conway, but I could take you on a quick tour of the first floor." She patted the curl behind one ear, hoping she'd scrubbed off all the Gruyère, vowing she would not, under any circumstances, fluff her hair or check her lipstick.

"We've come at a bad time," said Louisa, raising and lowering her long lashes at John.

"You must be terribly busy, John," said Carlyle.

"I'll be happy to give you all the time you need. You go on ahead to the kitchen, Quill." In his haste to brush by her, John stepped on her foot.

"Thank you so much!" Quill's sarcasm might have been bird droppings, for all the notice John took.

Louisa's large blue eyes looked directly into John's. She smiled slowly, and—as Quill told Meg later, if she hadn't actually seen it with her own eyes she never would have believed it—ran her tongue around her lower lip. "We'd love to take the time, wouldn't we, Cay? Although, actually, we stopped by to find my son. Has he been here?"

"Yes," said Quill.

"He's so proud of that darn newspaper. Cay and I fully support it, of course, but it's definitely Hedrick's baby."

"You aren't going to be involved in it, then?"

"Oh, goodness, no. Cay and I travel quite a bit, and we've just established a home base in Hemlock Falls. We won't be here much at all."

"And Mr. Conway, your husband, I mean? Is he going to be joining you?"

"Aren't you sweet," said Louisa. "Mr. Conway died six years ago, unfortunately. Leaving me to bring the children up by myself."

"Mother," said Carlyle, "as though you didn't have a raft of nannies and servants to do it for you."

They laughed, like slow-breaking china: Hah-hah-hah.

"He was a dear, dear man, my Connie." Louisa's tone was absent-minded in the extreme, as though she had trouble recalling his name. Quill would have bet a quarter's income that she knew his estate to the nickel. "HC Pharmaceuticals, you know. *Big* money, I'm afraid. Cay and Heddie loved him as though he'd been their real father, and he loved them. It was truly a love story, Ms. Quilliam. All four of us, together. It was so sad when he died."

Quill, who couldn't think of any tactful way to inquire who'd fathered the horrible Hedrick, asked if they intended to make their permanent home in Hemlock Falls.

"God, no!" shrieked Carlyle.

"Not that we don't love it here," said Louisa. "But Cay and I are used to a little more activity at night than we've found here so far."

"I wouldn't mind a little nighttime activity with that sheriff," said Carlyle with a full-lipped smile at John. "My brother's asked us to make some calls around town, just while he's starting into the business, you know, and we stopped by the courthouse yesterday, and ran into him. Myles McHale. Mummy, didn't he remind you of that gorgeous banker we met in Saint T.?"

"Jean-Paul? Cay, you're right. He did!"

They both gave a little shriek.

"Saint T.?" asked Quill, who found she had to make an effort to unclench her teeth.

"Saint Tropez," Carlyle tossed over her shoulder. "Mom, this heat! Could you take us out of the sun, Mr. Raintree?"

Louisa leaned toward John, placed her lips near his ear, and said ruefully, "Daughters!"

"Just trying to save you money, Mummy. We could buy this place with what I spend on the dermatologist. I'd far rather spend the money at something more fun than repairing sun damage."

"Anything for you, precious. Although I claim seniority, and the right to this darling hunk of maleness." Louisa slipped one hand through John's elbow, the other through Carlyle's. The three of them ambled back to the Inn. Quill, trailing like a neglected puppy, was so astounded at the sudden transformation of her business manager that she tripped on the flagstone patio. At the French doors leading to the Tavern Bar, John stepped aside to let the women precede him. "God, your painting's gorgeous!" said Carlyle as they stepped into the warm shade. "Look at the lily, Mother."

"Actually, that's a print of O'Keeffe's," said Quill. "One of her most famous. When your average, everyday art lover thinks of O'Keeffe, that's what they think of. The lily."

"Quill's work is in storage," said John. "Although we're set up to display them anytime she cares to bring them out. We painted the north wall deep teal to set them off."

"This floor's terrific," said Carlyle. "It's so shiny!" Her thin heels clicked on the wood. She stepped daintily, like a chicken looking for worms.

"So shiny!" Quill mouthed behind her.

"Mahogany," said John, "like the wainscoting and the bar itself. All of this dates from the mid-nineteenth century, when the Inn was owned by General C. C. Hemlock."

"I'll just buzz on into the kitchen," said Quill loudly. "If you'll excuse me." She waited a moment. John gave her an absentminded nod. Louisa ignored her altogether. Quill walked through the Bar to the foyer, from there to the dining room, and into the kitchen, planting her sandals with loud, definite slaps. Meg was bent over the butcher block counter, peeling grapefruit. She looked up as Quill came in. "There you are. Good grief! What's the matter?!"

"Not the least little thing. No, ma'am."

Meg looked dubious. "If you say so. I can't find Dina, by the way, so I sent Doreen to look for her. The Kiplings are due to check in at any minute. It's not like her to take off in the middle of a shift."

"Maybe some muscle-bound cretin in a sleeveless T-shirt came slouching through the front door with a cigarette hanging from his lower lip and sweat rolling off his biceps and seduced her away."

"What?"

"Nothing. It's hot. It's August. I feel . . . witchy."

"So what's new? Did the Horrible Hedrick Reveal All?"

Quill decided she was too mad to answer the question. She settled onto a stool opposite her sister and picked up a section of grapefruit.

"Do you want to answer my question?"

"No."

"You want to sample the *sorbet*?"

"No."

"Just no? Not 'Your *sorbet*, Meg? Your fabulous sherbet! I would kill to get a teeny bit'? I've got blueberry, strawberry, banana, and grapefruit. And I've been sweating in this kitchen for hours and hours making it, so you owe me."

"It is hot in here," Quill conceded. "I'm going to call the air-conditioning people."

"Oh, it's all right. The breeze usually comes right through there." She nodded at the long row of windows lining the far wall of the kitchen. "I can take a little heat. And you know what they say, if you can't take the—"

"Stop. I'm in no mood."

"So was Hedrick as horrible as he looked?"

"Worse."

"As bad as his paper?"

"Worse than that." Quill swallowed the grapefruit.

"Worse than that," mused Meg. "Did you find out what's behind the mini-mall scandal?"

"No."

"Quill. This attack of taciturnity is *most* unlike you. What'd he do?"

Quill told her.

Meg frowned. "This little red book—"

"Great minds think alike. If we could get our hands on it, we could find out just what the heck he thinks he's doing."

"Yeah. With any luck, Quill, the poor schmuck'll go broke in three weeks and slink on back to Syracuse."

"I don't think so. He's not a poor schmuck, Meg, he's a rich schmuck, or at least his family is."

"Hedrick Conway's rich? What he'd do, win the lottery?"

"You could say that. If there's a sort of demonic lottery that randomly assigns gold-digging mothers and sisters to people like Hedrick, he's absolutely won that lottery."

"You met his mom and his sister?"

"I met them." Quill picked up another section of grapefruit.

Meg snatched it out of her hand with an exasperated 'tch!' "It takes me a long time to pith these properly, Quill. Get an unpeeled one from the bowl. So, what are they like? Are they something?"

"John thinks they're something. She—Carlyle—thinks Myles is something."

"Hmm." Meg peered at her. "It's a free country."

"That it is."

"And Myles is a free man."

"Yep."

"And you've been worried that John hasn't had a date for several months, so what's the big deal?"

Quill selected a grapefruit, began to peel it, then set it down with a frown. "It's what they know about us. When I met Louisa and Carlyle, they had this little spiel all prepared about how I was this well-known artist and how the flower studies resembled O'Keeffe—"

"You *are* a well-known artist," said Meg loyally.

"They claimed to have seen that show I had last year. You know, the Hemlock Falls studies."

"It wasn't so little."

"Meg. Get real. It was at the rear end of Dan Feinman's shop in SoHo, and barely anyone saw it. Nobody here even knows I held it."

"Myles went," said Meg. "And so did Andy and I. And it was written up in the *Times*, in the Art section. June twenty-third. I remember."

"That's not the point."

"The point is . . . ?"

"The three of them know way too much about John, about me, about God know's what."

"And what are we supposed to do about it?"

"Kick 'em out," said a familiar foghorn voice.

Quill jumped. "Doreen, don't do that!"

"Do what?" The housekeeper stumped into the kitchen, her lower lip at a belligerent angle.

"I swear you listen for exactly the right entrance line."

Doreen exchanged a look with Meg.

"She's not grouchy, actually," said Meg. "At least, she is, but she has a reason, this time. Did you find Dina, Doreen?"

"Yep. This crisis you got—have to do with the plumbing?"

"No," said Quill.

"Then I ain't got time for it. Got a crisis of my own."

"What kind of crisis?" asked Quill.

Doreen folded her hands under her apron and regarded Quill with satisfaction. "You got to kick that Stoker out on his keister."

Meg chuckled, then took a large bag of ice from the Zero King and put it in the Cuisinart, a clear signal that she refused involvement. As it usually did, the Cuisinart noise drove Quill and Doreen into the dining room.

"I told you," said Doreen. "That Stoker's a menace."

"Look, Doreen. I know Mr. Stoker can be a little difficult, but I honestly think he can improve the way we do things around here."

Doreen came to a full stop, placed both hands on her hips, and glared. "He told Dina to do the registration different, right?"

"He didn't tell her any such thing. He sat down with her in a team meeting and brainstormed a solution to the problem of registering guests more efficiently." Quill cocked her head, distracted. "Did you hear anything unusual?"

Doreen ignored this last question, fierce in the pursuit of her point. "We ever overbook before?"

"Well, no. What *is* that bunch of thumps?"

"Bill got out that hadn't ought?"

"If you mean have we over- or underbilled in the past, no, not that I know of. Doreen, you didn't hang Mr. Stoker up by a rope or anything, did you? That sounds like kicking. Like somebody's kicking."

Doreen remained immovable. "And we've always collected from Visa and that, right?"

"Right. What *is* that noise?"

"So what I want to know is how come this Stoker was sticking his nose into somethin' that dint need to be fixed in the first place?"

"Everything that you do can be made better, Doreen. It's a basic principle of Quality Improvement. That kicking's coming from the lobby."

"You're durn tooting it's coming from the lobby."

Quill hurried, Doreen following like a grouchy sheepdog; she'd spent a lot of time selecting the Oriental rug that covered the oak flooring, the two huge urns that flanked the desk, and the creamy leather sofa that stood in front of the cobblestone fireplace. The lobby was an elegant introduction to the Inn. Holes in the wall wouldn't improve it.

A large Slavic-looking gentleman in an orange brocaded waist-coat, dark trousers, and Norfolk jacket was on his knees, rhyth-mically beating the wooden registration box against the floor. A middle-aged couple with a Victorian air stood by with mild looks of concern. The woman wore a filmy, calf-length dress with blue rib-bons at the waist; her husband—or so Quill guessed, since they had that indefinable sameness that usually comes from a long marriage—held a parasol in one hand and a Gladstone bag in the other.

Two women sat on the couch, the first elderly and dressed with neat precision in a beige pleated skirt and light jacket. The other, perhaps in her late fifties, was hugely fat in a bright caftan; she responded to Quill's astonished survey of her lobby with a warm, attractive chuckle.

Axminster Stoker shifted from one foot to the other in the midst of this small invasion. "You *all*," he said with a querulous snap, "were supposed to have read the instructions all the way through."

CHAPTER 3

"Z'ere is it," said the orange waistcoat, with a final thud of the box against the floor. He set the box down and picked up a credit card.

"*Th*ere it is," corrected Mr. Stoker fussily. "And it wouldn't have been there in the first place if you'd read—"

"I've never heard of such a thing," interrupted the blue-ribboned woman with soft indignation. "This is supposed to be a four-star—"

"Three star, sweetheart, three star," said her parasol-carrying husband, in the thickest Texas drawl Quill had ever heard. "There are three degrees of bliss in the Gardens of Paradise, you know."

"Three star, of course, darling . . ."

"And whether this is Paradise remains to be seen," said the old lady tartly. "And the rating's for food, after all, not accommodations, or service. Although I must say the room rates would lead one to anticipate a more courteous welcome."

"Lot more than a shilling a day, hoy, Jerzey?" said the parasol husband to the orange waistcoat.

The large lady in the caftan chuckled again. Then all five of them shouted, "'Shillin' a day, bloomin' good pay—Lucky to touch it, a shilling a day!'"

They applauded themselves.

Quill took advantage of momentary good humor. "You must be the Kipling Society. How do you do. I'm—"

"Not Cecily Cardew!" interrupted the husband, who was apparently inclined to be boisterous.

"And not Wilde," said the old lady, to Quill's momentary confusion. She adjusted the pearls at her neck and regarded Quill with kindness. "You must think we're quite mad, my dear. But it's been a long ride in that miserable rented van, and we are fatigued. I take it you are Ms. Quilliam? I am Aurora Kent, spinster of this parish, as Mr. Kipling might say. May I introduce you to Mr. and Mrs. Lyle Fairbanks?"

Mrs. Fairbanks smoothed the ribbons at her waist with a slim white hand and nodded gracefully. Lyle Fairbanks bounced forward, took Quill's hand, and kissed the air above her wrist with a flourish.

"And the gentleman in the waistcoat (she pronounced it "weskit") is Mr. Jerzey Paulovich, of Poland."

"And I am Georgia Hardwicke," said the large woman in the caftan. Quill decided she really liked her chuckle. "I'm fairly new to the Society, and I'm not sure how the Poet would describe me. Widow of this weald, maybe. Let Ms. Quilliam's hand go, Lyle. Then maybe she can straighten this out."

"I'm sure I can," said Quill. "Has Dina gotten you all checked into your rooms?" She looked at the reception desk. "I see she's not here. I have to apologize. Something must have happened. We were expecting you, of course, and Dina's an excellent receptionist . . ."

"There's a receptionist?" asked Mr. Kent.

Doreen gave a loud meaningful sniff. Mr. Stoker cleared his throat nervously once or twice.

"Of course. Dina Muir. She's a very good one. Except that she doesn't seem to be here."

"Well," said Mrs. Fairbanks, drifting to the tapestry chair by the couch, "I did wonder about the propriety of checking ourselves in."

"Checking yourselves in?" said Quill.

Doreen's freckled hand shot under her nose. It held a card printed in large red letters.

THE RECEPTION TEAM SAYS

DO IT YOURSELF!

**(A Total Quality Project from
the Inn at Hemlock Falls)
(Please refer to instructions
on lobby desk.)**

"Do it yourself?" Quill took the card, studiously avoiding Doreen's gimlet eye.

"If you'd just *read* the instructions," said Axminster Stoker, "this would have gone smoothly—and efficiently. That's the Quality Way."

"What instructions?" Quill asked him. "Dina's supposed to check guests in. Guests aren't supposed to check themselves in. They don't know how."

"The instructions are right here." Lyle Fairbanks took a sheet of paper from the top of the reception desk. "Miss Kent, Mrs. Hardwicke, and I managed all right, but Jerzey's English, although gettin' better, isn't all that great. When he dropped his credit card in the box, he was followin' instruction number seven, as you can see. Then he realized that you don't accept the Discover card here, like it says in instruction number twelve, and he tried to get it back."

"It sucks," said Doreen loudly.

"It does not 'suck,' Mrs. Muxworthy," said Axminster Stoker. "The team did not anticipate non-English-speaking customers. That is all. Significant savings in labor can be demonstrated almost immediately if the receptionist position is eliminated from payroll."

"You fired Dina!" said Quill. "You fired our receptionist?"

"In the spirit of continuous improvement, staff cuts are inevitable," said Mr. Stoker.

"On'y thing that'd improve around here is you get your skinny butt back to Detroit, or wherever it is you come from," said Doreen loudly. "Swiping this poor soul's credit card . . ."

"I get it back," said Jerzey hastily. "No problem."

"And harassing these-here guests. What's next? They warsh their own towels? Make their own beds? Mop the kitchen floor?"

"There's a very good Marriott on Route fifteen," said Mrs. Fairbanks in an undertone to her husband.

"We passed a charming bed-and-breakfast on Route ninety-six," said Aurora Kent to Georgia Hardwicke. "Marvelous roses out front, too. What do you think, my dear? I can assure you that this is not at all what we're used to in our travels. Generally the places we've selected for our little conventions are very attentive. The service is usually quite Japanese."

"Japanese?" said Quill.

"Benchmark," said Axminster Stoker, as if this were supposed to make sense.

Georgia caught Quill's eye. She winked and turned her attention back to her colleagues. "I think we just hit a little hitch here. Why don't we stay one night at least? Give poor Miss Quilliam a chance to straighten things out."

"Please don't even think of leaving," said Quill hastily. "I'm sorry that you were greeted by this . . . this . . . confusion. If you can give me just a few moments, we'll get all this settled." She grabbed Mr. Stoker by the arm and hauled him into the dining room.

Doreen marched after them. "Told ya," she said in simple satisfaction when they were safely out of earshot. "You boob," she said to Mr. Stoker.

"Mrs. Mux—"

"Where's Dina?" Quill asked him.

"Pursuing her graduate studies, I should imagine," said Mr. Stoker. "I'm extremely sorry about—"

"Please find her," said Quill. "Explain that you acted totally without my authority. Ask her to come back and see me immediately."

"Very well," said Mr. Stoker. "I shall explain my error."

"And apologize, you," said Doreen.

"I most certainly will. If I had any idea—"

"John will have my head in a basket if we lose this business," said Quill a little ruefully. "So you might apologize to him, too. And Mr. Stoker . . . I think we need a moratorium on this Quality Training."

"Durn right," said Doreen. "If that means what I think it means. We can shoot this bozo here, too, for all of me."

"Doreen, please go find John and ask him to come help me register the Kipling Society, if they're still in the lobby by the time I get back."

"We're all still here," said Georgia Hardwicke cheerfully.

Quill started.

"Sorry. Didn't mean to sneak up on you. Just wanted you to know that the promise of the perennial gardens have tempted Aurora to stay, and the king-size bed the Provençal suite featured in your brochures was what attracted Lyle and Lila Fairbanks, God bless 'em, and I wouldn't miss your sister's food for all the rice in Tokyo."

"And Mr. Paulovich?" asked Quill with hope.

"Well, he got his credit card back, so he's just as happy as a clam. I have to say, though, that he was muttering something about crime in America when the box wouldn't give it up."

"You," said Quill with relief, "are a peach."

"You looked a little harassed," said Georgia. "Glad to help."

"Doreen. Please find John—he's with Carlyle and Louisa Conway giving them a tour—and ask him to talk to Meg about a high tea for the Kiplings. On the house." She turned to Georgia. "Do you think that everyone would come into the dining room for a cream tea while we get the luggage situated?"

"I'll go ask." Georgia disappeared into the lobby in a swirl of green and gold, to reappear moments later with the remainder of the Kiplings in tow. Quill, having dispatched Mr. Stoker and sent Doreen to find John, greeted them with relief.

"We are delighted to take you up on your offer," said Miss Kent.

"Ze food is free?" asked Jerzey Paulovich.

"Lyle, darling . . . the view!" said Lila Fairbanks, drifting to the window overlooking the Falls.

Quill, pulling chairs away from the large table by the windows, indicated with a smile that they should sit.

"You know," said Lyle Fairbanks, settling into his chair with a benevolent air, "we-all'd be delighted to sing for our supper."

"Oh, yes?" asked Quill.

"The Indian cycle," said Miss Kent. "That always goes over well."

"Too long, too long," said Jerzey. "We condense it, yes? What do you think, Mz. Quilliam?"

"I'm afraid I don't . . . Just what *is* the Kipling Condensation Society?"

"It would not be too ambitious to claim that we are Kipling scholars," said Miss Kent. "Lyle and Lila in particular."

"Absolutely not, Aurora," said Lyle gallantly. "You are far more experienced than we are."

"Be that as it may"—Miss Kent acknowledged the tribute with a gracious nod—"at any rate, I cannot claim credit for the original idea. For that we must pay tribute to G and S."

"You mean Gilbert and Sullivan?" asked Quill.

"Yes!" shouted Jerzey. "Prezisely. We condense the poet's works into an hour performance."

"All of them?" asked Quill.

"We select." Jerzey threw back his head. "This I condense myself. 'Now in Injua's sunny clime, where I used to spend my time, if you can keep your head about you, you're a bloke. By the living God that made you, there's nothing else that will do, when a woman's just a woman, and a good cigar's a smoke.'"

"Needs a little work," said Lyle critically, "but you get the idea."

"Perhaps the beauty of the poems in full might be better," said Lila with an anxious eye in Quill's direction. "He wrote the most touching poem about dogs: 'Master, this is thy servant, he is rising eight weeks old. He is mainly Head and Tummy. His legs are uncontrolled.'" She broke off, tears in her eyes. "And of course, it ends with . . . you know . . . the doggie's . . ."

"Death," said Georgia, patting Lila's hand. "That one always gets to me, too. Doug and I had the most wonderful little cocker spaniel."

"At any rate," said Lyle, "we are always ready to perform, for those who'd appreciate it, of course."

Five pairs of eyes looked anxiously in Quill's direction.

"If it'd be any trouble . . ." said Lila.

"Well," said Quill, floundering.

"At one of our stops last year," said Miss Kent, with a crisp twinkle, "the inn owners staged a garden party . . ."

"Under an August moon," said Jerzey.

"And the other guests kept us there for hours. Simply hours." Lila sighed. "It was wonderful."

"And you in that gauzy dress," said her husband gallantly.

"I suppose," said Quill doubtfully, "we could—"

"Only if it's no trouble . . ."

"We wouldn't want to impose . . ."

"Zis America," said Jerzey, with an expansive gesture, "is *not* filled with crooks, I guess."

"I'd be delighted," said Quill, "to talk to my staff."

In the kitchen Meg was folding puréed grapefruit into the crushed ice, whistling softly to herself. The *sous*-chefs worked quietly. Quill summarized, ending with a suggestion that the Kiplings entertain the other guests at the Inn the next evening at a small cocktail party. The Finn, who was new, dropped a copper kettle with a clang and a muttered "Phut!" at Meg's shriek, "Kipling!! How many poems in an hour?! Are you *crazy*!?"

"Shush!" Quill settled into the rocking chair by the fireplace with a sigh. "I think we can keep them to half an hour if it's handled tactfully. Handled tactfully means no shrieking. And maybe a lot of free food."

"For the whole Inn!" Meg added grenadine to the *sorbet* and scooped the mixture into a large glass bowl.

Quill propped her feet up on the hearth and closed her eyes. "They were threatening to check out!" She took a deep breath. "Just give me a second. I want to settle this stuff about Dina getting fired first, then we'll—"

"Dina? You fired the best receptionist we ever had! What the heck is going on here, Quill? Have you lost your mind!"

"Meg. It's been a bad day. There's only one way it could get worse . . ."

The back door to the kitchen opened with a bang. "Quill? What in the name of God is this business about evacuating the Inn?"

"And that's it," said Quill, opening her eyes at the all-too-familiar baritone. "Hello, Myles."

CHAPTER 4

Myles was always tanned in the summer, which turned his gray eyes silver, and he never seemed to sweat. Quill pushed apologetically at the damp tendrils of her hair, suddenly conscious of her appearance all over again.

"Hey, Myles," said Meg. "Have some *sorbet*."

"I can't stay too long. Just following up a report that the building's unsafe."

Meg shrieked. "Hogwash!"

"Hedrick Conway. That idiot." Quill tugged at her blouse. It'd been weeks since their last, painful conversation. "The plumbing's backed up, that's all. We've already taken care of it. Conway was here when the problem came up and thought it would make a good headline. He called you?" She straightened in alarm. "Did he call the EPA?"

"He wanted to know if the Tompkins County Sheriff's Department had an evacuation procedure."

"Do we?" Quill asked.

"We do."

"Quill threw him out," said Meg with relish. "So it's pretty clear he's got an ax to grind with us. And you couldn't have possibly thought that we would jeopardize the guests, Myles. So how come? Ah. Never mind. Myles. Sit down. Stay a while. What do you know about this guy? Have you seen the *Trumpet!*?"

"Yes."

"It's a load of trash. How could you let him have the police blotter?"

"Didn't have much choice, I'm afraid."

"I'll bet Davy gave it to him," said Meg shrewdly. "You would have sent Conway packing."

"He threatened an injunction. The blotter's public information. The result would have been the same. The public has a right to that information."

"There's no problem, though, Myles. So thanks." Quill bit into her third piece of grapefruit.

"If there's no problem here, I'll be going. Good to see you both."

"No problem here?" shrieked Meg after a shrewd glance at her sister. "How can you say that? If you've seen that miserable rag of a newspaper, you know there's a big problem here. Are you just going to let this bozo run loose?"

"There's not a great deal Myles can do," Quill said. "Conway has First Amendment rights like everyone else. And as long as the stories aren't actionable . . ."

Meg, shaking her head in disgust, filled a small bowl with her grapefruit mixture and determinedly shoved Myles onto a stool. "Here. Quill was just going to make coffee." She raised her voice as Quill took a breath to say she had no intention of making coffee. "Sit down, Quill." She filled the kettle from the jug containing spring water and took the coffee beans from the freezer. "I'll make the coffee. Do you want caffe latte or cappuccino, Myles? Caffe latte, I'll bet. Of course outright lies are actionable. What about this mini-mall exposé he's threatening? That's actionable. Unless there's something in it."

Quill sat at the counter and looked past Myles's left ear. "Do you have any idea what Conway's up to? You probably don't know this, but we've invested quite a bit in the mall project. If there's something funny going on, we should probably know about it."

"I don't think you should worry. Not yet. He showed up at the Courthouse to check the site proposal and the property deeds filed with the county clerk. He made a copy of the engineering drawings for the leach field and of the budget proposal. He also requested the incorporation documents for Hemlock Mall, Inc., which are kept at the county seat in Ithaca. I have no idea whether he picked those up or not."

"So," said Meg. She pursed her lips. "Very interesting. *Very* interesting. Wouldn't you say it's interesting, Quill?"

"What's interesting is that Conway and his family seem to know a lot more about Hemlock Falls than they should after being here less than a month. Myles, he threatened to write about John, dragging up all that old business again."

"Did he?"

"Yes. And his mother and sister pretended to know something about . . . um . . . painting . . ." For a moment, she acknowledged, she'd really thought they might have heard of her, and she was a little miffed.

"Miffed? Why?"

Quill hadn't realized she'd spoken aloud. "Just that . . . Never mind. It'd be good to know where they're getting all this information. It's so specific—as if someone in town were feeding them gossip on a regular basis."

"They could have picked up the talk about John, and you for that matter, at Marge's on Sunday."

"Myles, John's history is old news. And no one gives a hoot about my career." There was an uncomfortable silence, which Quill broke rather hastily, "Who talks to flatland foreigners anyway? You know how insular this town is. If we had a malicious busybody in Hemlock Falls, I could see it. But we seem to have been lucky that way. I can't think of a single person who likes to make trouble just for the heck of it."

"We were at Marge's on Sunday," said Meg. "We didn't see Hedrick there. We didn't see you there, either."

"Carlyle and Louisa dropped in after you'd gone."

So Myles had met the voluptuous Carlyle at the Courthouse and again at Marge's. Quill wondered if the meeting at the diner had been by arrangement. Except that Myles's Sunday morning activities weren't her business any longer.

"I'll tell you what we need," said Meg suddenly. "We need that little red book."

"What little red book?"

"He called it the 'goods' book." Quill pleated her cotton skirt between her fingers. "He referred to it when he met John for the first time. With," she added, looking squarely at him, "a certain amount of glee. Apparently he's spent the last week collecting all kinds of gossip and recording it in the thing."

"Distasteful," said Myles. "But not a felony. Or even a misdemeanor." A slight, very slight, warning note sounded in his voice. "Now, appropriating that book without Hedrick Conway's consent would be a misdemeanor."

"Maybe we could snatch it at the party tomorrow."

"About the party?" asked Meg.

"I could call and invite him. Tell him we wanted coverage in his awful rag. Of course they'd all probably show up. Yuck."

"How big a party?" Meg demanded. "And how much food did you promise?"

"It's a small party. I didn't promise a lot. Just some hors d'oeuvres, and perhaps a couple of cold soups."

"How *many* people, Quill?"

"Well. How would you feel about most of the guests? It's a little hard to leave people out. The Kiplings seem to need a large audience."

"The whole Inn? That's . . ." Meg counted rapidly to herself. "That's roughly fifty people! How much are we charging a head?"

"Um, I hadn't really—"

"We're not getting paid for this! I thought you and John said you would never, ever offer free food and drink without discussing it with me and with him. Fifty people for *free*!"

"It's to make up for a bad start to their visit, Meg."

"Oh, *God*! All right! I suppose I ought to count myself lucky I got twenty-four hours' notice." Meg flung open the door to their oversized refrigerator and stared into it, muttering.

Quill caught Myles's grin, and smiled back.

"So," he said, "about this party."

No, thought Quill, I won't. Besides, the only reason he wants to come is because Carlyle and her halter top might be there—and to keep me from committing a misdemeanor. Myles's gaze shifted to the floor. There was a slight stiffening in his shoulders. Nuts, thought Quill. I do miss him, dammit. "Let's say at seven. That okay with you, Meg?"

"What? The time or the fact that you should have asked Myles before he had to ask you? It depends," she said into the awkward silence, "what you want me to serve. Beluga's a snap. I just have to have a lot of ice. Of course, we'll be broke for the rest of the quarter, since it's on the house, but the preparation time is zero. Zip. Nada. If, on the other hand—"

"That Jap's here," said Doreen, opening the dining room door and sticking her head into the kitchen. "Unless you want him to beat feet like the others almost done, you better get him checked in. 'Course, I could call that-there Axminster."

"For God's sake, don't you ever use that word, Doreen! It's Sakura, Mr. Sakura. The Japanese list their last names first."

"He's a durn snooty little cuss," Doreen grumbled. "Snapped his fingers at me like I was somebody's pet."

"We've talked a lot about guest courtesy, Doreen." Doreen sniffed, unimpressed. "Well, the first Sakura's here, Meg. What about sushi?"

"I'll see what I can do. It depends on the supplier. Yellow-fin tuna shouldn't be too hard to get, but it's got to be fresh. And Quill? There's a little surprise in the lobby, or should be, if Mike's gotten to it."

"What kind of a surprise? Did you find Dina?"

"That Stoker did," grunted Doreen. "She's pret' mad, but she's coming back to work."

"So what other surprise waits for me in the lobby?"

"That picture you did of the two of us a few years back."

"Meg!"

"Hey. The son's an art critic. The father's richer than God. Why not?"

Quill slid off the stool. "I've got to go check in Mr. Sakura, Myles. See you tomorrow, I guess."

"Thanks for the invitation."

"Men," Doreen said with vague disapprobation as she followed Quill through the dining room.

"Who? The sheriff? Or Mr. Sakura?"

"Sher'f." Doreen stopped cold, folded her hands underneath her apron, and said, "That's a good man, there."

"And?" prompted Quill.

"And nothing. This modern way of gettin' together? It sucks."

"Doreen!"

"Thing is, you get the eye, you give it back, you try it out, you get married. That's the way I done it. And that's the way I'll keep on doin' it. Three times. You don't," Doreen added fiercely, "have to go through all this touchy-feely stuff."

"What touchy-feely stuff?"

"You know. I tell you something—guy's decent in the sack and brings home his pay, what more do you want?"

"This conversation is ridiculous."

"On'y if you expect men to be something they ain't."

"And what is it they 'ain't'?" asked Quill in a lofty tone.

"They ain't," said Doreen, resuming her march to the foyer, "wimmin. Mr. Sakra, this here's my boss, Ms. Quilliam. Aloha."

Sakura Toshiro, managing director of Sakura Industries, had booked a suite and a single for a week through a New York City travel agency that dealt chiefly with the wealthy and influential. The small elderly man with the belligerent lower lip standing in front of her didn't look like the head of a multinational, multibillion-dollar conglomerate, but then Marge "the Barge" Schmidt didn't look like the wealthiest person in Tompkins County, either, but she was. Quill, who had diligently reviewed a copy of *Japan: The American Businessperson's Guide to Political Correctness* the week before, folded her hands together and bowed. "*Ohio gozaimaisu, Sakura-san.* I am Sarah Quilliam."

Sakura Toshiro bowed back, a hint of arrogance in his back and neck. "This so-beautiful picture, Miss Qurriam"—he nodded at the painting hanging behind the reception desk—"yours?"

Quill rarely tried portraits; she was too young, she thought, and hadn't lived long enough to really paint what lay behind flesh and bone. But she had painted herself and Meg seated on a red couch last year. Meg was looking off into the distance, a slight smile on her open face. Quill sat beside her, one arm protectively over the back of the couch, her head turned to look at Meg. She'd used a photograph for the charcoal sketch that began the painting, and her internal eye to finish it. She'd packed it away months ago.

"Yes?"

"You?" He made delicate brushstrokes in the air.

"Yes," said Quill, and blushed. He sucked air through his teeth, which, Quill recalled, was a gesture of appreciation.

"My son, Sakura Kenji. Terrs me you are velly famous. Velly." He smiled with an appreciative twinkle. "My Engrish." He shrugged, shook his head in apparent regret. "Kenji-san, nei? He come. Velly good Engrish."

A little appalled to find herself speaking slowly and distinctly, as though to a backward child, Quill said, "The travel agency indicated that Sakura Kenji will check in the day after tomorrow. In the meantime, I'm sure we can manage. We have the room ready now for you and is it Mr. Motoyama?"

"Motoyama. *Hai*." He bowed.

Quill returned the bow. "And is Mr. Motoyama here now, Sakura-san? May we take both of you to your rooms? The suite is ready."

"Motoyama. *Hai*," said Mr. Sakura.

"If this Motoyamer's a little skinny Jap older than God, he's outside with the van they come in," said Doreen. "He's a servant, like."

Mr. Sakura's shrewd black eyes slid over Doreen with the slightest flicker of contempt. Quill's own understanding of French was far better than her ability to speak it, which was apparently true of Mr. Sakura's English. Her face warm, she bowed and said "Mrs. Muxworthy meant no disrespect, Sakura-san. Is Mr. Motoyama also ready to check in?"

"*Motoyama*." Mr. Sakura gestured, driving with his hands.

"Your chauffeur," said Quill.

"*Hai*," said Mr. Sakura. "Prease." He withdrew a sheaf of

papers from his immaculately tailored suit coat and presented them to Quill.

She glanced at it. "You've been communicating with the mayor?" said Quill in surprise. "About the mini-mall?"

Mr. Sakura made driving motions.

"You'd like to see the site," Quill guessed. She handed the letters, which hinted at investment, back to him. "Mike will be happy to drive you both there. You don't need to trouble your chauffeur. When would you like to go?"

"Velly soon."

"This afternoon?"

"Velly soon."

"Them Kiplings are takin' the van for a tour," said Doreen "You want I should tell Mike to take the Ja— I mean these fellas, too?"

"'Gentermen rankers out on a spree damned from here to eternity,'" said Mr. Sakura. "Kipring. Velly good. *Hai.*" He nodded toward her painting again. "Velly beautiful. I may see more?"

"Sure," said Quill, dizzy. "Perhaps later?"

"After Motoyama dlive."

"Yes, but there's no need to have Mr. Motoyama—"

"*Mo*toyama," corrected Mr. Sakura, with a frown.

Quill, whose democratic principles frequently collided with her commitment to courteous service, smiled, ducked the issue of honorifics altogether, and once again offered the services of Mike and the van. "It will be easier for you to find the construction site. And the van is much more comfortable than the rental car."

"A Toyota?"

"Oh, dear. No. I'm afraid it's a Chevy Lumina."

"*Hai.* Yes. Velly good, then."

"Ms. Muxworthy," Quill addressed Doreen, feeling an obscure need to make her democratic principles clear, "would you let Mike know? They can all go together."

"So, you want I should get these bags up to the room first, or what?"

"I'll take the bags up."

"Hell, no. You go back to the kitchen. Tolt the sher'f you'd be right back. I'll take care of Mr. Sakra, then I'll get a holt of Mike."

Mr. Sakura watched this fine example of employer-employee

relations with interest. "Fine," said Quill, reminding herself good managers never minded a bit of affectionate bullying. In front of other people. Who understood more English than one could wish. She bowed to Mr. Sakura, who bowed politely back, and went to the kitchen to find that Myles had left and Meg was giving the last of the dinner instructions to the kitchen help. The *sous*-chefs, she noticed crossly, never bullied Meg. Quill sat in the rocker by the cobblestone fireplace and brooded.

The *sous*-chefs and dishwashers dispersed. Meg stowed her clipboard neatly in the shelves she used as a desk. "So, you asked Myles to the party?"

Quill roused herself from a confused contemplation of Kipling, men, the proper way to address a chauffeur, and a strong desire to show some really marvelous work to Mr. Sakura and his billion-dollar corporation. "Myles asked himself to the party. And, you recall, he asked himself to the party after I said I'd invite the Horrible Hedrick and his relatives, specifically the sister with the overlarge hooters."

"This Carlyle must be a ripsnorter." She narrowed her eyes. "But that sort of thing's never bothered you before. What's really wrong?"

"Mr. Sakura recognized my work."

Meg gave her a self-satisfied grin.

Quill stretched restlessly in the chair. "Of course, he seems to be fond of Rudyard Kipling, which says a lot about his politics, so make of that what you will."

Meg rolled her eyes. "Don't sulk, Quill. Here's what you do. Take some time off this afternoon."

"Time off?"

"It's hot. Go swimming."

"I can't. There's a Chamber meeting this afternoon."

"Sure you can. It's not until four o'clock. It's two now. Nothing like exercise to get those endorphins up and circulating."

"I'll go if you go."

"As soon as I settle the menu for this party you've arranged. What do you think about tapanade?"

Glad to concentrate on something concrete and practical, like a menu, Quill said that she loved tapanade. "But we ought to have something a little more conservative to offer the Kiplings."

"Tapanade and Parmesan-artichoke cheese dip, then."

"Don't get sarcastic."

"You started it."

"Never mind." She pulled at her lip. "About the sushi, I've already made arrangements for the fish. And the usual cheeses and fruits. Okay. Did you decide to go swimming?"

"Yes."

"Good. I'll go with you. You can contemplate your future and get some exercise at the same time."

"How's about if I just swim?" Quill sighed. "Just once I'd like to do one thing at a time. Just once, I'd like to get up in the morning and have no schedule, no meetings, no feelings to soothe, no guests to coddle, no nothing. Just time. Lots of time, stretching ahead of me like a lovely trail with no beginning and no destination."

Meg shook her head. "That's not going to help. You'll just go frantic concentrating on all the meetings you're missing and all the soothing you're not doing. You remember what helped me for quite a while after Colin died."

"Work."

Meg nodded. "Work lets your subconscious take care of itself. That first year after he'd gone, I barely remember parts of it. But I do remember the cooking."

"But I don't have time to paint! That's the whole point!"

"No. Not that kind of work. Cooking isn't like painting. I can cook and have a life outside of cooking. The way you've been tackling painting, you can't. Painting consumes you. There's nothing left over for the outside. That's part of your struggle with Myles and kids, and for a long time, Quill, me. Because you took time out of painting for me, to help me. You wouldn't be here running the Inn if it weren't for the fact that I needed you that year. You'd be back in SoHo, getting paint in your hair."

"You forget why I left and moved here. I had just as compelling reasons as you did. I didn't have anything more to say on canvas. Not then. But now. Now it's coming back. Slowly. And now I do have a decision to make."

Meg's flush subsided. "The question's whether there's room for Myles and the art, then."

"Myles and children and the art. Myles and the art, yes. He surrounds it, Meg, he doesn't share it, but he surrounds it with an odd kind of reassurance that I think I may be lost without. But babies? They take it out of you, all of it. Oh, my God. I don't know what to do. Children are as consuming as art. They take that part of you. I know it. I know it."

She wept, standing in the middle of the kitchen.

Meg put the recipe cards back in the file and made coffee. She ground the beans, then filled the kettle with spring water and set it to heat, then pushed Quill into the rocking chair and stroked her hair, saying nothing, but humming a wordless little tune with the cadence of a lullaby. The water rattled, just on the boil, and she poured it carefully into the filter. She brought the cup to Quill, who sipped it, with the sense that she was recovering from the flu. "Here's what we do, chief. We go swimming. Forget about Myles and art and just let it work itself out in your subconscious. Listen, we'll plan to get back by three, so I can pull the rest of tomorrow's dinner together and you can set up for the Chamber meeting. And"—she smiled sunnily—"what you want is a rational, practical problem to solve, with no feelings swamping up your brain. While we're swimming, we figure out a way to separate the Horrible Hedrick from that bloody little goods book. Whatever we figure out will take enough time to divert you to let the old subconscious do its decision-making stuff. And besides, that damn book's important. We have to find out what's inside. We can't have the Bozo of the Year wrecking our new boutique restaurant, can we?"

Quill wiped each eye with the back of her hand, sniffed, and went to get her bathing suit.

"So seducing the little red book out of Hedrick is totally out of the question?" asked Meg, floating on her back and gently kicking her feet. The pond at the park had been filled with kids, and they'd swum over the submerged sluiceway gate leading to the river. Even the current was lazy in the heat, and they paddled with it like wood ducks bobbing on the surface of the clear green water. The granite cliffs rose on either side of them, hands cupping jade.

"I'm not offering up this fair white body," said Quill. Meg was right. Concentrating on this problem was better than Prozac. It was a neat little puzzle, free of emotion. "And Andy'd take violent exception to donating yours, even in the cause of justice."

"Undoubtedly," said Meg, with a hint of complacence. "The two of us have arrived at the state where exclusivity in dating is a priority. What about good old breaking and entering? They're all living in the apartment over the print shop, right? Piece of cake to sneak in and rifle the place."

Quill dived, considering this. She opened her eyes underwater. A brown trout gave her a startled glance out of one doll-black eye, and curved away like a question mark. She rose to the surface and exhaled. "When it's not on his person, I'll bet he sleeps with it under his pillow. We've got to figure out a way to get it out of the sports coat."

"Not bad. You stand next to him batting your eyes admiringly. I create a diversion. You slip your hand into that ratty sports coat and grab it."

Quill shook her head. "Too risky. And pickpocketing's a misdemeanor or something. We've got to get him to take the jacket off, and drape it over a chair or whatever and while I'm hanging it up, I slip my hand in the coat and get it. If Myles finds out, we can always say it fell out of his pocket and we're returning it to him."

"If we get him to strip, we're back to seduction again."

"Meg! What is this bee in your bonnet about seduction? No. We invite him to the party tomorrow night, and if it's as hot as this, of course he'll take his coat off—"

"What if it's in his pants pocket?"

"You haven't seen it. It's too big to fit into a back pocket. He'd have to curl it up. And even if he does that, it'll be duck soup to get behind him and slip it out. You could create a diversion."

Meg addressed the sunny sky overhead. "The old diversion trick? What a new idea. There must be an echo in here." She contemplated the shoreline. "What do you think's in the book, anyway?"

Quill attempted a shrug and took in a mouthful of water. "Who knows? Myles said he'd asked for the names of the bidders on the mini-mall project. Maybe he's found out something about one of them."

"You want to swim downstream and see how it's going?"

"We'd have to walk back over the rocks. And we wanted to be back by three."

"Somebody will give us a lift."

"In our suits?"

Meg rolled her eyes. "Jeez. Come on. First one there has to spend twenty minutes listening to Axminster Stoker after dinner."

Quill, disinclined to that much activity even in the river-coolness, breast-stroked pleasantly along, her mind empty of everything but the sensation of water and sky and sun. The gorge sloped abruptly to a riverbank a quarter mile ahead, an ideal place for a mini-mall with a view of the river. Ahead of her, Meg reached the small beach which fronted the mall property and treaded water, waiting for Quill to catch up.

"We can ride back with the Kiplings," said Meg. "Didn't you say that they were touring the site with Mike and the van? Isn't that one of them now? That Georgia what's-her-name?"

Quill waved. Georgia waved back, her arms describing a wide semaphore.

"That's odd," said Quill.

"I agree. People dedicated to furthering the works of R. Kipling, the last of the male chauvinist Victorian male poets, are *very* odd."

"No. The rescue truck's there. See the lights?"

"Rescuing the carpenters from another version of *Gunga Din*, I'll bet. But we can go up and look." Meg turned herself around and began to float toward the beach headfirst. She had a peculiar version of the backstroke, rather like an upside-down dog paddle that involved a minimum of breath. "Ooonnn the road to Mandalay," she sang tunelessly, "where the flying fishes play, aaannnd the dawn comes up like thunder out of China across the bay . . . tumpty um . . . tee . . . tumpty um . . . ."

"Elephants are piling teak in the sludgy squidgey creek," Quill joined in. "Where the silence . . . oh, God!" She bolted upright, sank, and her foot struck the thing again.

Hair like seaweed, in the river.

CHAPTER 5

When Quill entered the kitchen the day after she'd discovered the body of Louisa Conway in the river, Meg was contemplating a pile of chicken liver, her slight figure cool in a thin T-shirt, cotton shorts, and a hideous pair of tennis shoes. Like the rest of the Inn, the kitchen hid technological efficiency beneath nineteenth-century charm. The cobblestone fireplace was fitted with the latest open-hearth grill, and birch wainscoting concealed the oversize Zero King refrigerator. A late-model Aga stove, flanked by hardwood and granite counters, dominated the large room. When the sisters had updated the three-century-old Inn, they'd decided the one concession to modern comfort they were unable to make was the flooring. The floor in the kitchen was the original brick, uncomfortable to stand on for long periods of time. Meg—who preferred to cook in ancient sportswear—solved the problem with battered pairs of Nikes designed for heavy-duty basketball players.

"Hey," said Meg, plunging her hand into the pink-brown pile as Quill stamped into the kitchen. She hefted the liver with an absent air. "Equal parts butter and minced liver, with a heavy dash of Cointreau and a bit of tarragon. What do you think?"

"Sounds like a heart attack waiting to happen."

"I'm sick of *cuisine minceur*. It's boring. I want scope." She swept both hands through the air, scattering bits of liver. "My experience tells me that the guests are sick of *cuisine minceur*. The world is turning its back on the rabbit-food menus of the eighties and forging toward cholesterol overdose. And high time, too. *Geeve me butter!*" she roared, with a sudden veer to the Teutonic. "Geeve me *beef!*"

Quill glumly settled into the rocker by the fireplace and contemplated nothing in particular.

"So you found another body," said Doreen, stumping in the

back door, the light of battle in her eye. "Maybe now you got this to think about, we can get rid of that-there Stoker."

"Mr. Stoker just needs a firm hand," said Quill. "And I already told Meg last night, I don't want to talk about the body. How are you this morning?"

"J'a know right away it was Louisa Conway drownded in the river? You din't step on her face did you?"

"Doreen!" Meg complained. "It's bad enough to find a corpse in the river, without you acting like somebody out of Salem's Lot after the vampire shows up. Poor Quill." Meg patted her shoulder sympathetically, then settled comfortably at the counter with her liver pâté. "*Did* you feel her nose or anything? I mean, you knew it was a body right away, right?"

"I knew right away."

"How?"

"Never mind how." Quill flexed her sandaled foot and resisted the temptation to scrub at it again with a soaped sponge. It'd been the teeth, and the sensation was going to be with her a long time. She shuddered.

"Anyone get to that Mr. Conway to say they're sorry his mother fell in the river?" asked Doreen. "And what about the funeral? They gonna bury her here? We could take a ham, I guess. I could go over since he don't know too many people in town, yet."

"His mother knew one of them well enough," muttered Meg.

"What d'ya mean?" Doreen's face was alight with interest. Quill knew that look. It wasn't an avid or an unhealthy interest, since Doreen was far too nice a woman underneath the tough exterior to delight in a grisly death for the excitement. She'd seen The Look before, the time when Doreen converted (briefly) to Christian evangelism. And again when Doreen had signed up to sell life insurance, and yet a third time when the housekeeper began attending Amway sales-training classes. Quill hadn't been around for Doreen's flirtation with Nu-Skin and the Tupperware business, but there was no doubt of Doreen's entrepreneurial bent. "Doreen," said Quill, suddenly suspicious. "We got a copy of *Armchair Detective* in the mail this week. I didn't take out a subscription. Did you, Meg?"

"Huh-uh."

Doreen put her thumbs in her dress belt and hitched her shoulders forward.

"Bogart," said Meg accusingly. "Oh, nuts." The sisters exchanged a meaningful glance.

"Some of them guys," said Doreen, whose intuition was acute, "get twenny bucks an hour."

"You think Hedrick Conway's going to pay you twenty dollars an hour to investigate his mother's murder?" shrieked Meg. "Pooh!"

"So it *was* murder," said Doreen, thoughtfully rubbing her chin.

"No, Doreen," said Quill. "No and no and no. You are *not* going to go into business as Doreen Muxworthy, P.I."

Doreen pointed out that not only had Meg and Quill solved several murders, but they'd done it for free; she, Doreen, was merely turning an eye to the profit possibilities, which, if word-of-mouth were true about Hedrick and Carlyle's millions, would be considerable.

"And what if the kids did it?" Meg demanded. "Who'd pay you then?"

"Huh," Doreen said, considering.

"And let's not forget that we have a perfectly capable sheriff in town with an extensive background in investigations of this sort," Quill added. "I mean, he was Chief of Detectives in Manhattan before he left the N.Y.P.D., and a man like that—"

"My, my, my," murmured Meg. "The post-discovery interview with Myles must have been interesting. He was pretty brief with me. 'Did I see anything floating along the river?' 'Nope.' That was about it."

"Was it murder or wasn't it?" Doreen demanded.

"Was," said Quill briefly. "The classic blunt instrument. Louisa Conway was hit on the left temple with something like a hammer—"

"Something like, indeed," murmured Meg.

"—and fell or was thrown into the gorge, sometime between one-fifteen, when she was last seen at the mini-mall, and two-fifteen, when I step—that is, when we found her in the river."

"There's somethin' not right about that place," Doreen muttered.

"Went out there myself to see how our investment's goin'. Them workers give me the creeps."

"Really?" Quill pulled at her lower lip. "I've never been all that comfortable there myself. Why, do you suppose?"

"Them guys don't talk much. Never see 'em in town. DeMarco brings 'em in on buses and takes 'em out again. There's allus at least two of 'em together. Thing folks in town is astin', was she interfered with?"

"You mean rape? I don't have the least idea." A troubled frown appeared between Meg's eyebrows. "That'd be a heck of a note. A rapist in Hemlock Falls."

"She didn't look interfered with," said Quill cautiously. "I mean, she was fully dressed and all her clothing seemed to be in place. There was just this gash on her head."

Meg shook her head and went, "Brruh! It's going to be a heck of a case to investigate. Quill and I counted; there must have been at least fifty people there. The construction crew, the electrical people, some of the Chamber members checking on the progress of the site, the entire membership of the Rudyard Kipling Condensation society, as well as Mr. Sakura and that weird little driver of his. For my money, Hedrick and his sister Carlyle *could* have done it. They all arrived together; Hedrick and Carlyle decided to leave a little after one-thirty and started to look for her."

"So how'd j'a know about the hammer?"

"Oliver Doyle, with the rescue service. You remember him, Meg. He was here with the volunteer ambulance crew that time you made Keith Baumer so—"

"Yes. Yes. Yes," said Meg testily, who clearly recalled some aspects of their first case years ago with little enthusiasm. "I remember Olly Doyle. He's a carpenter and volunteers on the ambulance. I hardly think he's qualified in forensics."

"If you hadn't been so busy being squeamish over the corpse, you would have heard him, too. One of the Kiplings found a hammer with blood on the claw at the lip of the gorge where they think Louisa went over."

"Oh," said Meg.

"What was Louisa nosin' around the site for?" asked Doreen.

"I don't know. She had a camera with her." Quill shuddered. "It was tied around her neck. Hedrick got everybody at the site—the plumbers, the electricians, the carpenters, and the sewage guy—to start looking for her, and called the rescue truck. The Kiplings volunteered to search the woods at the south end of the development, and that's where they found the hammer."

"So what do you think, Doreen? You still want to take on this case?" Meg asked. "I think you'd be a terrific addition to our detective team. You could go out, poke around the site, figure out who saw Louisa last, and where the hammer came from. Of course, that's on top of scheduling the household staff and seeing that the rooms are clean."

"That-there business about the pay . . ."

"No pay. Strictly in the interest of good citizenship."

"Seems to me a good citizen would do something about that-there Stoker."

"You are not to do a thing about poor Mr. Stoker." Quill was firm.

"Then I guess I'll figger out somethin' else." Doreen brightened. "Think those Kiplings might be inn-erested in Tupperware? They do all this stuff in a group."

"No!" said Meg and Quill in unison.

"Then tell me what's on for today, and I'll get to it."

Quill breathed in relief and looked at her watch. "There's an emergency Chamber meeting this morning, to replace the one that was canceled yesterday. But the Kiplings' party has been rescheduled for tomorrow, so we don't have to worry about that. We don't have any checkouts today, so the staff will have to work around the guests."

Doreen pursed her lips and stumped out the back door to get to work.

"That," said Quill, "was a close one."

"You mean you aren't fascinated by this opportunity to solve yet another crime?"

"I am not," said Quill firmly. "The opening ceremonies for the mini-mall are scheduled for Tuesday. This is Saturday. We'll be lucky to get through the next few days with our nerves intact, without adding amateur detective work to the list."

"You know who might be a good addition to the team?" asked

Meg thoughtfully. "Georgia Hardwicke. I really like Georgia Hardwicke."

"There isn't going to be a team, Meg."

"Right," said Meg absently. "First thing is we can find out more about the scene of the crime. And then we need to find out if she died of the hammer blow or drowned. Maybe Georgia would be interested in a little legwork."

"Meg, we're going to leave this one to Myles. And why would Georgia want to be a detective anyway?"

"She was pretty efficient, yesterday. She was the one who organized the search for Louisa. And she was the one who prevented that engineer Eugene something from picking up the hammer and messing with the evidence. And Doreen told me that she's got a lot of detective stories in her room. Besides, I like her."

"Then maybe the two of you can solve this one. Count me out."

"Quill?" Dina Muir, the receptionist, poked her head through the kitchen door. "The Chamber's been trying to settle down to session for almost an hour. The mayor's looking for you."

"It's good to see you back. I think I told you how sorry I am about the mixup with Mr. Stoker yesterday."

"I told him he'd better check with you," said Dina indignantly. "I knew you wouldn't let him do it. But, I wanted to go shopping for a new dress for the opening ceremonies anyhow, so it worked out all right. Shall I tell the Mayor you're coming soon? He's in pretty much of a fidget."

"This murder's upset everyone. I don't blame him."

"Oh, it's not that. The new edition of the *Trumpet!* is supposed to come out today. They're all just wild about it."

"Oh, Lord. Tell them that I don't think even Hedrick would take the time to publish that rag the day after his mother's death. And let them know I'll be right there."

Dina gave her the high sign and withdrew.

"Good," said Meg. "Pick up as much gossip as you can."

"Gossip?" said Quill with raised eyebrows as she left. "At the Chamber? Gossip? Never in this life!"

" 'Bout time you got here," Elmer Henry groused to Quill. "Now maybe we can get somewhere. You ready to take the minutes?"

"We heard you found the body!" Miriam Doncaster said as Quill sat next to her in the conference room where the Chamber's weekly meetings were held.

"Stepped into it, like," said Marge Schmidt with a fat chuckle.

"Heard it was no accident," said Betty Hall, Marge's partner in the Hemlock Hometown Diner (Fine Food! And Fast!).

Miriam, who was town librarian, blinked her large blue eyes, "Not another murder!" she whispered to Quill. "Are you and Meg going to . . . I mean now that you and Myles . . . that is, if it's true about you and Myles . . ."

Elmer *thwacked* the official gavel on the table and demanded the Chamber's attention. The twenty-four Chamber members settled like geese landing on a pond, their gabbles and squawks smoothed into an expectant quiet.

Quill reached for the meeting notebook and produced a pen. She'd vowed to straighten herself out after her renunciation of Hemlock Falls' sexiest (and only) sheriff, pay strict attention to taking complete, coherent, readable minutes, and not stray from the point of the meeting to make sketches of the members (she'd given up being an artist), or make grocery lists when she should be taking attendance. She hesitated. It probably wouldn't hurt to take note of any suspicious behavior—just in case Meg grilled her about possible Chamber suspects. Meg, when her interest was caught, had the tenacity of the better breeds of pit bulls. Quill flipped to a fresh page, and wrote: INVESTIGATIONS.

Elmer Henry, rotund and red faced, surveyed his troops with a slightly troubled air. "Revrund Shuttleworth? Would you lead us in an openin' prayer?"

The Reverend Mr. Dookie Shuttleworth, of the Hemlock Falls Church of God, unfolded his storklike length, and gazed benignly on his flock. "Let us pray," he said and compressed his lips. Dookie, although amiable in the extreme, and possessed of an unnerving goodness, tended to phrases without nouns or predicates, which severely impaired the quality of his penitents' progression toward enlightenment. He'd completed a three-month-long correspondence course in "Christian mentalism" some weeks before; C-Ment appeared to be based on a sort of religious ESP. C-Ment sermons, Dookie had explained to his bewildered but receptive parishioners, were delivered through mental messages, and not the traditional verbal peroration. He was touchingly pleased when church attendance jumped the Sundays following his announcement. Christian mentalism made post-sermon discussion at Marge's diner (a test rendered by the more severely religious Hemlockians as an edge against laxity) blissfully nonspecific.

The silence in the conference room stretched on. Quill thought about the hammer that had killed Louisa, and Hedrick's little red book. "Amen," Dookie said and sat down.

"*Thank* you, Revrund," said Elmer. "Our first order of new bidness—"

The room erupted into discussion in which Hedrick Conway's name, the manner of Louisa's demise, and the next issue of the *Trumpet!* (due momentarily, according to several indignant voices) figured prominently. Elmer pounded the gavel with increasing irritability. The furor rose, primarily, Quill suspected, so that people could hear themselves over the hammering.

Elmer, whose Southern roots were very much in evidence when under stress, threw the gavel on the carpeted floor and scowled down the length of the table. "I'm orderin' *silence!* We'll get to the Conways when we get to it, and not before. This here's a bidness meeting of bidnessmen and women and not a hog calling. First order of bidness, last week's minutes."

"There ain't gonna *be* any 'bidness' in this town if that damn fool Conway runs lies in the paper about us!" shouted Harland Peterson. "I heard he was up all night after his ma's unfortunate accident in the river, runnin' that damn printing press." Harland, the president of the local Agway Co-op, and cousin to Petey (Septic and Floor Covering), slammed a meaty fist onto his thigh. "I say the first order of business is to run that bum out of town."

"I say the wrong Conway got bumped off," Marge Schmidt added in her assertive baritone. "That Louisa didn't have anything to do with the damn *Trumpet!* 'cept bankroll it. So a good question is, who'd want to kill her?" Marge swiveled a small blue eye at Quill. "What went down at the site today anyway?"

Quill, a little alarmed at the overt hostility being exhibited at the table, said, "Well, well, well," in a deprecating way, which Marge greeted with a snort of contempt. Quill cleared her throat. "I guess there was a bit of a problem."

Marge rolled her eyes at the ceiling in mute appeal. "Somebody got a bit free with a hammer. That right?"

"Apparently," Quill said.

"Think maybe Hedrick done his ma in for the bucks?"

"That'd work out all right," said Harland. "Then we could run the murdering bastard out of town."

Harvey Bozzel rose to his feet, trembling. "You're being a bit hasty here. And it just doesn't do to be hasty. I think we should sit down and discuss the whole problem calmly like the rational people we know ourselves to be."

"Siddown," snarled Marge.

Harvey jutted his jaw and ran a hand just above his moussed blond hair. "The man's got an image problem. I grant you that. And Bozzel Advertising is well situated to deal with image problems, particularly in the publishing and media areas. Crisis management, it's called, and Boz—"

"Just shaddup, Harve," said Marge. "We all know you're angling for a piece of the creep's business!"

Howie Murchison, town attorney and justice of the peace, rapped his knuckles on the table in fair imitation of a judge quieting a rowdy courtroom. "Shall we start by defining the problem here?" he asked with a mild glance over his half-glasses. "A discussion of whether or not Louisa Conway was murdered, and by whom, isn't a suitable topic for our agenda."

"You wanna know the problem?" shrieked Betty Hall. "You saw last week's newspaper! You saw what that lyin' snake wrote: that he's got something on the mini-mall project. And today's the day the next paper's gonna come out, and who the hell knows what-all lies he's gonna print! I got all I saved invested in that mini-mall!"

"And since his ma gets knocked on the head and tossed into the river," added Marge, "it's gonna piss him off something fierce, is my guess." She ruminated a moment, her massive jaw working slowly. "Less, like I said, he did it himself. Since somebody knocked his ma on the head with a hammer, who knows what he's gonna write about us next?"

Elmer said they'd know soon enough, as he'd asked Esther West to pick up a copy of the *Trumpet!* as it came off the press at the Nickerson building.

Marge suggested the meeting adjourn to the Nickerson building so they could stuff Hedrick into his press if the *Trumpet!* offered calumnies of any description. Harland Peterson said it was too hot to walk downtown, even for that scum, reminded Marge of the existence of his Norwegian cousins who farmed west of the village, and were notable for their ability to wield ax handles and had excellent night vision. A surge of approbation met this suggestion for a nighttime raid on the Nickerson building.

Quill, strongly in mind of a lynch mob, made an alarmed face at Howie, who winked at her in a reassuring way before saying, "What precisely has Conway written that's actionable or even alarming, so far? This"—he drew a neatly folded section of the first *Trumpet!* from his sports coat pocket—"merely indicates that revelations are to come. He hasn't specified what those revelations are, and, indeed, if the front-page story is any indication, that's all the story's going to amount to."

"Dog shit," said Marge.

"A direct if inelegant description," said Howie. "Now, as soon as Esther brings the latest copy of the *Trumpet!* we can determine the most appropriate way to pro—"

"Coo-ee!" Esther West posed at the conference room door like Gertrude announcing Ophelia's demise in a particularly bad production of *Hamlet*. Like Gertrude, she took an unconscionable amount of time to get to the point. "I had to stop for gas, because I was almost out, and I couldn't find anybody but Gordy Micheal-son's boy Odie at the newspaper office, and he didn't want me to take a copy without Mr. Conway's approval. *Quelle dommage!* I said to him." (Esther had renamed her dress shop Ouest's Best, after signing up for conversational French at the local junior college.) "This paper is for the public, *n'est-ce pas?* That means 'is it not so,' Marge. Is it not so? I said to Odie."

"J'a bring the copies?" demanded Elmer.

"I guess it is so, I said to him. So here's your five bucks, I said."

"Five bucks!" Marge interrupted in dudgeon. "What the hell. Five bucks!"

"And Odie didn't know how to make change . . ."

"We ain't gonna pay no five bucks for that sleazeball paper!" roared Harland.

"I don't care what it cost!" said Elmer. *"Did you get it!"*

"I got ten copies," said Esther primly. "Fifty cents each. I'd appreciate quarters, please. I can't make change myself." She rummaged in her capacious shoulder bag, withdrew a sheaf of newspapers, and unfolded one: MALL MADNESS!! screamed the front-page banner.

The air stirred with the members' expelled breath.

"Forty-point headline," said Harvey helpfully.

"Lemme see that," demanded the mayor. Esther passed the pile to Howie who scanned it with the grave deliberation appropriate to his position as town attorney and justice of the peace. Norm Pasquale, principal of Hemlock Falls High School, grabbed the pile, took one, and passed the rest to Harland as though it were the pregnancy statistics for the cheerleading squad. Harland passed the rest to Miriam, who passed it on to Harvey, who turned it over to the mayor with a hope-filled smile.

The mayor read for a lengthy moment, his face crumpled like a frustrated baby's. "Gol-dang!" he said. "You hear this? 'Is the sewage system safe? Will toilets be backed up all over Hemlock Falls as a result of the hasty and cheap installation of the leach field at the Hemlock Falls Mini-Mall? Will the citizens of this fair village be soon awash in rivers of unspeakable filth? This reporter will have the answers to this and other tough questions in the next edition of the *Trumpet!* The mayor of this fair city, it seems, has a lot to answer for.'" Elmer's pudgy hands tightened on the newsprint. There was a ripping sound. "He can't do this, Howie. He can't say those things about me—I mean the Chamber—here. Hasty? We done it quick, is what we done, because we promised we'd be done in time for the holiday sales. And cheap? We went and did it cost-effective, which is why we got that DeMarco and that out-of-town work crew doin' it so cheap. There's nothing wrong with that leach field, let me tell you. Why, Harland's cousin has been putting in leach fields all over Tompkins County for twenty years or more, and if he don't know leach fields, I'd like you all to show me somebody who does know leach fields. He's been down there four, five times tryin' to talk to that DeMarco about lettin' him in on it, and he says it's bein' put in proper."

Was Louisa, Quill wrote in her minutes book, getting pictures of the septic system when she was killed?

Howie gazed at the mayor over his wire-rimmed spectacles with a benign and reassuring expression. "Hang on to your pulse rate, Elmer, and let me finish." Halfway down the page he sat up with an exclamation. "Payoffs!" he demanded incredulously. "My fee for handling the anchor store contracts was not only legitimate, it was twenty percent less than my normal billing rate! That big banananosed son of a bitch!"

Dookie cleared his throat in a mild though meaningful way. Howie subsided, cheeks reddened.

"Hold on to your own durn pulse rate," said Elmer with a regrettable degree of satisfaction. "See what I mean?"

Quill, with a vague intention of making everyone a little more comfortable, suggested lunch. Elmer rather sourly intimated that "lynch" was more to his liking. This was seconded by more than one outraged Chamber member; Norm Pasquale went so far as to suggest that Sheriff McHale arrest Hedrick.

"Guys," said Quill, who hadn't managed to get her hands on a copy, "isn't there anything at all about his mother's death?"

"This boy hasn't got a word about his mama?" Elmer paged frantically back and forth through the paper. Quill was surprised and a little disturbed at the intensity of his search,

"Holy crow," said Miriam. "Here it is. It's outrageous!"

There was a rustle of papers. Quill grabbed Miriam's copy and read:

OBITUARIES

Conway, Louisa, aged 54, suddenly at her home in the summer resort of Hemlock Falls. Survived by a daughter, Carlyle, and son, Hedrick. Donations to the Volunteer Ambulance Fund.

And below that, a boxed item, reading:

> DO YOU HAVE INFORMATION LEADING TO THE
> ARREST OF "MINI-MALL" PERPETRATORS? EARN
> A FREE!! YEAR SUBSCRIPTION TO THE TRUMPET!
> CALL TRUMP-27 TOLL FREE!

"That's it?" demanded Elmer. "His ma bites the big one and that's it?"

Marge tossed her copy contemptuously to the floor. "What a pile of crap. That boy's taste is all in his mouth."

Harland Peterson gnawed his lower lip. He picked up the paper, set it down, then shoved it to the center of the table. "So we wait for next week for more bullshit."

Howie folded his paper into neat quarters. "A bit of an incitement, that boxed item underneath the obituary," he observed.

"Incitement to what?" asked Quill.

Howie pursed his lips and said nothing.

"Mr. Mayor," said Miriam primly. "I take exception to the scatological turn of this meeting."

"You what?" Elmer wiped his forehead with a large handkerchief. "You going to air-condition in here, Quill?"

Quill, who had written, "Uh-oh. The mayor?" under the INVESTIGATIONS heading in her meeting's notebook, gazed thoughtfully at Miriam.

"Scatological," said Miriam. "All this reference to bodily functions. I'd appreciate a little more decorum. I mean, the opening ceremonies are in three days . . ." Miriam's hands crumpled a tissue into a ball, smoothed it out, then crumpled, smoothed, crumpled, smoothed, crumpled, smoothed, until she caught Quill's startled eye. Tissue-crumpling was not at all like Miriam. Nor were her objections to Marge and Harland's pungency; she'd known both for years and was prone to an occasional "Oh, shit!" herself. Quill wrote "MD: NO!!??" and sketched a little alarmed face next to it. "Howie," she said suddenly. "Could you give us some possibilities?"

"Possibilities?"

"You know—best case, worse case." Quill looked up and down the table. "The thing is, I'm not sure just what's at risk here. What . . . um . . . crim—I mean, scandalous activity could he discover?"

"You mean what criminal activity is possible in a project like this? Jesus Christ, Quill, the possibilities are endless."

"They can't be," Quill urged. "I mean, Mr. Conway's mentioned payoff twice. Payoffs for what? This is a private investment and most of the town bought into it, and the records and transactions have been reviewed by every regulatory office in the entire state. What could be crooked or devious about that?"

Howie removed his glasses, polished them, then fitted them carefully over his nose and peered at her over the rims. "You don't understand how the state works. Or the county."

Lawyers, thought Quill, had a trick of putting you on the defensive even when all you'd asked was a simple little question.

"This is not a simple little question," said Howie. "Just offhand, although if the Chamber wants me, in my capacity as town attorney, to prepare a summary memorandum for them, I'd be happy to do so. So my present response is by no means complete. By no means."

Caveat Avocat, thought Quill, and was so pleased with this that she wrote it down in the meetings book and sketched a frowning Howie shaking a minatory finger. The figure looked so much like Richard Nixon that she erased it.

"Everyone's aware of the more obvious areas of defalcation, fraudulent behavior, and criminal activity. Bids can be rigged. It's a simple matter, for example, to sneak the lowest bidding figure to a favored contractor, and award the job to him. Or her. Simple, but illegal. It's possible to bribe inspectors, or to use cheaper-grade materials when more expensive items have been specified. The mini-mall is forty thousand square feet. Concrete is sixty dollars a yard. You pull a bag or two of cement from each yard of concrete, and the illegal profit can be considerable."

Quill scanned the assembly for telltale twitches, guilty flushes, or suspect indifference. She thought she was being unobtrusive until she met Marge's affronted glare.

"Our initial proposal for the mini-mall stipulated that no one individual could own a controlling interest. Opportunities for

collusion here, of course, are rife. Rife," Howie repeated complacently. "I suspect, however, that Mr. Conway is after smaller fish.
As a former state employee . . ."

"He was employed by the state?"

"The Department of Motor Vehicles," said Marge. "'Till Louisa
up and married some rich old coot who died."

". . . he is undoubtedly aware of the many, many ways in which
an individual—or even a corporation—can be in violation of a
state code or a municipal regulation."

Quill, who spent a lot more time than she wanted to mediat-
ing disputes between Meg and the DOH, began to get an inkling.
Take the intense opportunism of Hedrick's prose. Add the power
of any media to form public opinion in a country where injustices
were the price to pay for freedom of speech. Mix the sad truth that
Meg refused to pull the Aga away from the wall to clean underneath more than once a year, with the fact that DOH regs required
"frequent" cleanings, the degree of frequency to be determined by
the local inspector. Meg hated inspector Arnie Cunningham with
a passion equal to Jael's for Sisera. The passion was reciprocated.
Result?

INN KITCHEN CLOSED FOR FILTH!!!!

Her mind's eye saw the headline all too clearly. She poked at her
copy of the *Trumpet!* with dismay. "Wow," she said. "I begin to see
what you mean. If the OSHA inspections for a mini-mall are anything like the DOH regs for our kitchen—"

"Oh, it's not just OSHA. It's the DEC. It's NIST. It's state regs,
country regs, village regs, municipal regs." There was, Quill noted,
a pleased satisfaction in Howie's voice. "It's thousands and thousands of pages of government manuals—some with conflicting
requirements."

"J'a know that OSHA's self-funded?" asked Marge. "Fact.
Those guys come out to inspect and don't find nothin', they get
whacked when they get back to the office. They're supposed to
bring in enough money in fines to cover their salaries and overhead. Fact."

"You don't know that they get 'whacked' when they get back to the office," said Howie sternly.

"May not know," said Betty, "but we can guess."

"Well, it's my opinion that that's what Conway's doing. Guessing. But a guess is as good as a bull's-eye in a project like the mini-mall. Something's bound to be out of spec. It always is. Some contractor may have not placed a prepayment in a trust account; that's a lot of trouble for a small operator, and expensive to set up, although it's a strict requirement of New York State's. There are, in short, very fertile fields for Mr. Conway to plow."

"Oh, my," said Quill. "Maybe we should just ignore the whole thing." This was met with varying degrees of scorn, which was, Quill admitted somewhat justified. The meeting wound down several hours later; the sole area of consensus: Hedrick Conway had to be stopped.

Nobody mentioned Louisa.

CHAPTER 6

"It's a shame, this Conway guy slipping a snake into your Eden." Georgia Hardwicke looked over the balcony to the herb gardens; beyond the purple lavender and scented geraniums, the Falls flowed white under a bright moon. She was wearing a purple caftan trimmed with gold threads. The gold glittered cheerfully in the darkness of late evening, a little, thought Quill, like Georgia herself. "This is just gorgeous, Quill." She'd responded to Meg's invitation to dinner in Quill's suite with alacrity, having been Kippled, she'd said, almost to screaming boredom; she'd love an opportunity to discuss the murder, as long as it didn't involve a lot of physical labor. "I'd say that I envied you, but I have a hunch there's a heck of a lot of work involved. After Doug died, I realized that life is too damn short to work hard."

"Most of it falls on Quill," said Meg loyally.

"And John and Meg, and Doreen and Kathleen . . ." Quill sipped her wine and yawned. "God, I'm tired. I usually have more energy."

Georgia shot her a shrewd glance. "It's been a tough couple of days. Exhausting work, discovering a body. Maybe I should make an early night of it and let you guys go to bed."

"Not before we thoroughly hash over who murdered Louisa Conway." Meg sipped at her predinner glass of wine. "I can't believe that this town's ignoring a murder. There must be something rotten in the state of Denmark. Who in town do you suppose is guilty of crimes against the mini-mall? Nobody, of course," Meg answered herself. "Conway's an idiot. A muckraker and a slime. Which means everybody in town who's invested in it has a motive." She took another swallow of the '87 Glenora Chardonnay and stuck her lip out at a belligerent angle. "Including me. If the horrible Hedrick wants to get my kitchen closed, just let him try. I'll make a couple of headlines, all righty. Try 'Cook Kills Creep' on for size. But that still doesn't give us a clue as to who killed his mother."

Georgia shook her head slightly. "From what you tell me, Mr. Conway's brand of journalism might lie behind Louisa's murder, don't you think?"

"His mother didn't have much to do with the *Trumpet!*" Quill offered.

"She bankrolled it, didn't she?" Meg stretched out in her lounge chair. "Maybe whoever killed Louisa thought the source of funds would dry up and then Conway would trumpet himself right out of town."

"It'd be better to knock off Hedrick himself, wouldn't it?" said Georgia. "Seems to me that there's a lot more here than meets the eye."

"You're probably right. But I've never liked to conduct an investigation on an empty stomach." Meg got to her feet. "I vote we wait until after dinner. It'll take me just a minute to get the crab salad out of Quill's fridge and warm up the sourdough. And beans. We have these marvelous marinated green beans. I'm trying a new set of spices. You guys hold the investigation until I come back. Talk about something else." She stepped inside and closed the French doors behind her.

"You two make a habit of amateur investigation?"

Quill chuckled. "In a way. Meg's pretty good at it, actually. When she gets back, ask her about our other—I guess you could call them—cases."

"Ah!" Georgia leaned back with a pleased sigh. "What could be better? Gorgeous view, fabulous place. A bit of amateur detection to keep things interesting. And green beans à la Quilliam to come. Meg's a terrific cook. I suppose you test out all her recipes before she tries them on your lucky guests?"

"Oh, yes. One of the advantages."

"Then how the hell do you stay so slim?" Georgia patted her comfortably sized stomach. "After my husband passed on seven years ago, I thought, well, I can starve myself, get a face-lift, and trip around on stiletto heels trying to entice some sixty-five-year-old geezer into warming the sheets at night. Or I could buy an electric blanket and say the hell with it. I have three. Electric blankets, that is." She wriggled her eyebrows. "And, come to think of it, there's been a couple of geezers, too. But to tell you the truth, honey, at my age, a permanent male around the house can be such a pain in the tail it's kind of a relief to be on my own."

"Did you have children?" Quill asked diffidently.

"Douglas and I?" Georgia's homely face clouded. "No. One of my few regrets. He couldn't . . . that is, he could, he was great at it if you want to know the absolute bottom-line truth, there hasn't been a geezer yet that can even come close, but I never got pregnant, and by the time we realized that there might be something wrong, I was really kind of past it, from a physical standpoint. It was the usual, low-sperm-count kind of thing. And who knows? If we'd had kids, the little bastards might have turned out God knows how. But it would have been nice." She sighed, wistfully. "Sometimes I think, if we'd had kids, I'd still have a little bit of Doug. The curve of a cheek, a way of walking, that would remind me of the kind of man he was. But life didn't give us that. Gave us a lot of other things. But not that. We had a hell of a good time together, except toward the last, and who could have predicted that? I still miss him."

So many cruel things, thought Quill, that age and disease could do. She hoped for Georgia's sake that Douglas's death had been merciful, although from the distress on her face, it didn't look like it.

They sipped the wine in silence. Quill thought about children. Would a child of Myles's inherit his strong hands, or the quiet, attentive way he had of listening? If Myles died, would a son or daughter keep his spirit alive for her?

"I hadn't thought much beyond the first part," she said aloud. "Diapers and whatnot."

"About kids, you mean?" Georgia's smile was reassuring. "I've got nieces and nephews, and let me tell you, honey, the good stuff comes after the diapers part. There's a point where they get faces, you know? I'm here to tell you, as the most involved auntie of years past, present, and future, that all babies look alike. Then they hit three years old or so, and all of a sudden, there's the Nose." She patted her own rather prominent one. "And then the Chin. And they start to talk, and from being sort of soft, little, boring bundles that fit just right into the curve of your arm, they turn into people. Real ones. It's the damnedest thing, watching a kid grow up. You know that bit of life when you think things will always be like this? That part where any change is a big-time threat, because you're perfectly happy the way things are? That's a fantasy and kids are the best antidote I know for keeping things real. They change every day, in the most amazing, fundamental ways. And it keeps you straight, as a person. Makes you understand that life is hard, life is change, life is a battle. And the minute you sit down and try to grab the waves to keep the tide from going out, which is something we all want to do now and then, honey, here comes the kid, a living breathing agent for life assurance. Not insurance. Assurance."

"Jeez," said Meg, stepping through the French doors with a loaded tray. "The green beans à la Quilliam are going to be quite an anticlimax after that."

"Well, you asked us not to start the detective stuff until you got back." Georgia leaned forward. "God! That smells fantastic!"

Meg picked up a bean and handed it over. Georgia ate it, rolled her eyes, and said, "More! More!"

"What do you think, Quill?" Meg set the tray containing the

beans, the crab salad, and a fresh loaf of sourdough bread on the wrought-iron table. Quill sampled the vegetable. "Rosemary. And garlic. I like it a lot."

Meg served with quick deft movements, then poured them all a second glass of the chardonnay. "I'll put the beans on the menu for the party tomorrow night."

Georgia swallowed a mouthful of crab salad. "Wow and more wow. That's it, guys. I'm moving in. I want to be a permanent guest. I'm absolutely serious. Do you have a rate schedule for the year?"

"We have one year-round resident," said Quill. "Mr. Stoker. Well, he paid for three months in advance, and he's talking about staying on after that. And we had to charge him the daily winter rates, which are a bit cheaper than the summer, but not all that much."

"No problem." Georgia stuffed a second forkful of crab salad into her mouth. "Doug left me pretty well fixed, bless his heart. Let's talk about being detectives, and about me becoming a permanent addition to the team." She stopped in midsentence, the remainder of the crab halfway to her mouth. "Unless you think I'd be a pain in the neck. I wouldn't, you know. I've got a lot friends who'd come to visit, and my needlepoint, and I make a religion of inertia."

"That's not it at all. We'd love it. It just seems so expensive, Georgia. There are a few lovely little houses in town you might like to look at."

"Do they have a cook in residence? Maid service? Great company? Not to mention a couple of at-home detectives?"

"Well, no," admitted Quill. "As a matter of fact, we'd love to have you as a permanent guest."

"Then let's talk about it. Not right this second. Later, after my head's a little clearer. Now, before we get to the case, let's talk about this party tomorrow night. Who's coming? Is it just for the Kiplings? Because you don't have to do it, you know. Everyone in the whole society is loaded to the gills, including me, and they need freebies about as much as a picnic needs ants. Food like this ain't cheap, I'll be bound. And that little *contretemps* yesterday afternoon was nothing. No need to apologize."

"We'll end up serving everybody at the Inn and a bunch of the townspeople, too," said Meg. "We always do. Quill invites anybody she thinks is lonely, or isn't getting enough food, or maybe a little depressed, and we'll be serving a hundred if we serve five. I'm not going all out, if that's what you're worried about, Georgia. We grow a lot of our own herbs and practically all the vegetables we serve. We bake our own bread. The only thing that'll cost is the wine, and we'll charge for that, and the sushi, and nobody except the Sakuras will eat that."

"Cherry blossom," said Georgia, her mouth full.

"In the spring," said Meg helpfully.

"No. *Sakura* means 'cherry blossom' in Japanese."

"How do you know that?" asked Quill, fascinated.

"The Japanese are nuts for Kipling. Don't ask me why. Anyway, the society took a trip to Tokyo in April, and Lyle Fairbanks delivered a paper on the influence of Robert W. Service on Kipling's later work to the Rotary Club in Kyoto."

"There's a Rotary Club in Kyoto?" Meg buttered a piece of sourdough.

"The Japanese are nuts for Rotary, too."

"Robert W. Service?" asked Quill. "'A bunch of the guys were whooping it up in the Malamute saloon'? That Robert W. Service?"

"That's the one! Lyle has a theory that he and Kipling knew each other in the late eighteen eighties. Kipling lived in Virginia for quite a while, you know, and Service was on the lecture circuit in the northeast in 1888 or some damn thing. I don't recall for sure. Can I have a little bit more of the potato thingy?"

"Dilled potato mousse," said Meg. "I like potatoes. I like potatoes almost as much as I like onions. When I die, if I come back as a vegetable, I want to come back as an onion."

"I wonder what Louisa Conway will come back as." Georgia helped herself to the mousse, took a sip of wine, and shouted suddenly, "My stomach is so happy! Sorry. Back to business. Well, I never met the lady, alive and breathing, that is, but from what I heard, she'll probably be back as an overripe mango." She looked up from the mousse, and her expression sobered. "I'm sorry. Doug always said I had a flapping lip, especially after a glass and a half of wine. This isn't a joke, is it? The poor lady's dead, and nobody seems to care. Now, how do we start this investigation?"

"John always says to follow the money," said Quill. "And that's been true for two of our cases, at least."

"Sounds like a great idea to me. Does anyone know anything about these people? The name of their lawyers, or even what city they came from? I mean, from what I can gather, they've only been in town a few weeks, and nobody really had much to do with them."

"You have no idea how much we know about the Conways already," said Meg with a smug grin. "This is a small town. And a small town gossip mill is the amateur detective's best friend."

"So what does the town know about them?"

"The nonessential stuff is that Hedrick worked for the Department of Motor Vehicles," said Quill. "Before Louisa married money. And they've traveled quite a bit since Louisa inherited. Carlyle and Louisa were talking about the Côte d'Azur yesterday. The essential stuff is that Hedrick keeps all of his story notes in a little red book he calls his bible. That's what we want to take a look at. Then we need to make a list of everyone who was at the site to find out who had access to the hammer."

"Everyone?" said Georgia. "My God, the place was a zoo."

"It might not be that much of a hassle." Meg picked up a piece of sourdough, regarded it for a long moment, and put it down again. "The very first thing, I think, is to find out where the hammer came from." She shot a sidelong glance at Quill. "We used to have an in at the sheriff's department, and maybe we can revive that contact again."

"That gorgeous hunk?" said Georgia. "The one who's six-foot plus with the terrific tan and the steely gray eyes? This job's starting to sound more interesting by the minute. If I were thirty years younger and forty pounds thinner . . ." She looked at the meringue piled with strawberries and cream that Meg had made for dessert, chuckled, and dug in. "Forget that. Who's got the in?"

"Kathleen Kiddermeister," said Quill promptly. "Our head waitress. Her brother's the deputy."

"A-huh," said Georgia skeptically. She raised an inquiring

eyebrow at Meg, who shook her head and smiled. "But how is it going to help to know where the hammer's from? I mean, don't you suppose it came from the site? Somebody just walked by and picked it up and hauled off and socked Louisa?"

"If we can pin down which of the carpenters missed it, then we can maybe get a better fix on who had the opportunity to pick it up," said Meg. "Carpenters love their hammers—it's like Quill with her paintbrushes or me with my paring knife. And good hand tools are expensive. The guys either have them in their tool belts, in the trucks, or they're using them. I don't think pinning down the disappearance of the hammer is going to be as difficult as it sounds."

"But what if somebody brought it with them?" asked Georgia. "Then we're talking premeditation, if I've got the term right."

"And it doesn't have the feel of a premeditated murder, does it?" asked Meg. "So the first two questions are: Who was there? Who had access to the hammer? Then we can make up a list of suspects and take the next step."

"And that is?" asked Georgia eagerly.

"To link the preliminary list of suspects with Louisa."

"How the heck can we do that? I mean, let's say we interrogate them one by one. The murderer's going to lie isn't he? Or she, as the case may be?"

Meg grinned. "As I said, we have an in with the sheriff's department. Myles will be digging up all kinds of information. He can access computer records, subpoena lawyer's documents—like the will—find out if Hedrick's discovered any mini-scandals for real, or if it's just smoke. If Quill, that is, Kathleen, gets us the facts from the sheriff's department, we don't have to interrogate anyone. We do the legwork and put the facts together."

"And that dishy sheriff is going to give you these facts?"

Meg shrugged. "Most of this is a matter of record somewhere, isn't it? The facts are the facts, and most of them are available to anyone who wants to look for them. And Myles has always cooperated. Especially with Quill."

Quill cleared her throat and folded her napkin carefully. "If we're going to do this—and I'm not at all sure we should get involved, Meg—"

"Me, either," said Georgia frankly. "It's beginning to sound like a lot of work."

"But if we decide to do it, I think we should recruit Kathleen. She and Davy are pretty close. If she can get him over here for one of your meals, Meg, we can ply him with wine and get a data dump. Myles will go into Louisa's background with a fine-tooth comb. *If* there's a link in her past to anyone who was at the site this afternoon, Myles'll find it. Davy is his assistant—and he'll be able to keep us up-to-date."

"Myles doesn't tell Davy everything," said Meg. "It's far far better if you and Myles—"

"Meg! I know exactly what you're trying to do. It's not going to work. If Myles and I . . . I'll get to it, in my own good time. If we decide to get mixed up in Louisa Conway's murder, I want to handle this ourselves. I already have a list of people here in Hemlock Falls who seem worried over Hedrick's behavior. And we have a number of suspicions about the DeMarco Construction company. Why isn't anyone from the Falls working at the site? Why don't we ever see any of the workers in town for lunch, or to do a little drinking at the Croh Bar? We don't need Myles as much as we need to do a little legwork."

"Legwork," said Georgia dubiously. "There's that term again. Easy Rawlins does a lot of legwork. Spenser, too. Not to mention Travis McGee. Those guys all work out. We're not talking about a lot of exercise, are we? Can we just get the suspects here one by one and question them until they confess? Legwork sounds—tiring."

"Pooh!" said Meg airily. "It's a piece of cake."

"Meg's forgetting some of the more strenuous aspects of detective work, Georgia."

Meg grinned. "You mean like climbing into second-story windows and rolling under wire fences at two in the morning and that sort of legwork?"

"Yes," said Quill. "Not to mention being held at gunpoint, swallowing drugged drinks, and being attacked by guard dogs."

Meg patted Quill on the shoulder. "We survived all of that just fine. Not to worry. This one should be a piece of cake. Hedrick has plans to run articles exposing some scandal about the mini-mall, right? And Louisa funded the *Trumpet!* We've got a whole raft of possible motives if we look at this from the most obvious angle. That somebody wanted to stop Hedrick from publishing his lousy rag. It seems pretty likely to me that the murderer is right here in Hemlock Falls and has some connection to the opening of the mini-mall. So let's parcel out some assignments, here. Georgia, what if you volunteered to do something with the mall opening—you know, work on the Jell-O Architecture committee, or something. You're new in town, just sort of passing through, and nobody's going to get suspicious if you chatter away asking obvious questions. Quill's already got a plan to swipe the little red book. And once we get it, it's bound to be loaded with significant clues. Quill can handle the liaison work with the sheriff, starting tomorrow to find out about Louisa's nefarious past, and I—"

"Yes," said Quill. "And just what are you going to be doing while Georgia and I run around collecting clues?"

Meg waved her fork triumphantly in the air. "I will do the deduction! And another miscreant is brought to justice!"

"I," said Quill, quoting the notorious *New Yorker* cartoon of the little boy being enticed to eat his vegetables, "say it's spinach. And I say the hell with it."

Meg patted her sister affectionately on the knee. "Pooh! You're going to love it. The Snoop Sisters plus one ride again."

"Hmm," said Georgia. "It's beginning to sound like spinach to me, too."

"So?" Meg demanded "What's it going to be? I'll be busy tomorrow with the party arrangements. I think you should just sort of drop on by the sheriff's department, just in a casual way, you know, and Georgia and I—"

"No and no and no. No sheriff's department. No visits, casual or otherwise. Excuse me, Georgia, I hear the phone." Quill rose and stepped into her rooms. The air was cool and a little musty after the freshness of the Falls.

"Quill."

There would come a time, Quill thought, when the sound of Myles's voice wouldn't catch her under the heart.

"How's the detective biz?" she asked lightly.

"We've got one of your guests here for questioning, and he doesn't speak English. Is there anyone traveling with him that does?"

"Not my Japanese guest! Myles, the man's the retired head of one of the largest multinational corporations in the world."

"That may be," said Myles dryly. "But he's got a rap sheet as long as your arm."

CHAPTER 7

"Thank God it's the chauffeur and not Mr. Sakura," said Quill in the darkness of her Oldsmobile. She signaled a left-hand turn and drew onto Main Street. They were on their way to the police station to rescue Mr. Motoyama. It was just after nine, and the last bits of daylight trailed on the horizon like the luminous wake of a ship. "If Myles arrested a billionaire industrialist for murder, we'd never hear the end of it. The media'd have a field day."

"It's bad enough that it's the chauffeur. Can't you see the *Trumpet!* headlines?" Meg pulled at her hair. "'Foreign Terrorist Checks In at Murder Inn. Sisters Sign In Killer!' And, in a discreet subheadline: 'Did He Register His Gun?!'"

"Sshush! Mr. Sakura understands more English than you think."

"Pooh!" Meg turned her head and raised her voice, "You okay, Mr. Sakura?"

A crisp, rather frigid voice behind them responded, "*Hai.*"

"We'll straighten this out in no time," Quill assured him. A glance at the rearview mirror made her add hastily, "Mr. Motoyama should be out in time for the party tomorrow night. I hope you both will come."

"*Mo*toyama," said Mr. Sakura, firmly.

Meg settled back into her seat. "I can't believe Myles fell for this racist crap."

Quill was so startled she braked. "What the heck are you talking about?"

"It's pretty clear, isn't it?" asked Meg darkly. "Innocent foreigner in a small town lynched by paranoid citizens. The poor man doesn't even speak English. And there he is—alone, scared, petrified that the *gaijin* will string him up by his—"

Quill stepped on the accelerator with a jerk. "All Myles said is that he's pulled Motoyama ... Mr. Motoyama ... whatever ... for questioning. He may have been a witness to something, Meg."

"Doreen heard through the grapevine that Mr. Motoyama attacked Louisa at the mini-mall project with a broom handle and chased her into the woods. On such evidence are the Billy Budds of this world strung up on the yardarm."

Quill, still stung at the wholly gratuitous insult to Myles, didn't answer.

"Louisa Conway wasn't killed with a broom handle, she was killed with a hammer," Meg continued, apparently unconscious of Quill's irritation. "Myles must have known that, but no, he attacks the most defenseless person around. An elderly citizen of a foreign country, eking out his poverty-stricken existence behind the wheel."

"That bozo O'Doyle, the well-known volunteer fireman and forensics expert, was the one who said it was a hammer. And I'll thank you very much not to impugn the reputation of one of the most honorable men I know."

Meg glanced at her out of the corner of her eye and hummed a fragment of "As Long As He Needs Me," which made Quill crosser than ever.

"It won't work, you know."

"What?" said Meg innocently.

"You know what. Trying to make me defend Myles. We've arrived, Mr. Sakura." Quill pulled into the municipal building parking lot, put the car into park, and turned off the ignition.

"Porice?"

"Yes. This is the police station."

"Sakura Kenji comes soon?"

"Yes. I spoke with him. Cornell University is less than twenty minutes from here. He'll be here very soon."

Mr. Sakura grunted doubtfully.

"So." Meg sighed "The great art critic arrives. Not that you'll want to talk about your work. Your former work, I should say. Now. About our true calling as detectives. Will you ask questions, and me take notes? Or vice versa? This is a great opportunity to pursue inquiries."

"Let's just forget the whole thing." Quill pushed the car door with barely enough force to keep it open. "I'm tired. I want to go home. And you're just thinking of ways to get me alone with Myles. I don't want to be alone with Myles."

"Heck, no. This little trip to the station house is right up your chivalric alley. Here we are, the Sisters, rushing off in the night to save—"

"Cut it out! I hate it when your imagination runs riot. Half the time you're in some twilight movie world."

"And which half would that be!?" demanded Meg with a grin. "Not the cooking half. Admit it's not the cooking half. I'm very realistic about that."

"Not the cooking half. You're very real world about cooking."

"You'd be bored without my imaginative contributions to our daily grind." Meg got out of the car with a Clint Eastwood slouch and whistled the opening bars of the theme from *A Fistful of Dollars*. Quill got out, slammed the driver's door shut, and opened the rear door for Mr. Sakura.

The parking lot was nearly deserted, except for a black-and-white police cruiser and Myles's Jeep Cherokee. Their footsteps echoed on the asphalt as Quill led the way to the station.

Quill, while not intimately familiar with the workings of multinational corporations, was braced for at least a hedge of lawyers, if not a planeloadful, appearing instantaneously like so many crew members beamed down from the starship *Enterprise*, The sheriff's office contained only Myles, his pinkly eager deputy Dave Kiddermeister, and a short, elderly Japanese with a fierce scowl: Mr. Motoyama himself. The latter rose as they entered, prostrated himself on the floor before his employer and groveled. Mr. Sakura responded with a flood of furious, highly guttural Japanese and short, angry chopping motions of both hands.

"Good heavens," murmured Meg. "It's a good thing he doesn't have a sword."

Mr. Sakura finished his tirade. Motoyama rose and bowed. Mr. Sakura bowed back, and with an abrupt change of manner, turned to Quill and asked, "Porice chief?"

"Yes. Mr. Sakura, may I present Myles McHale?"

"*Konnichiwa*," said Mr. Sakura. "My aporogies for this . . ." He hesitated. "This benighted 'eathen."

Myles looked a little startled.

"Kipling," said a voice behind Quill. "My father is very fond of Kipling's poetry, and is, in fact, learning English by memorizing selected poems."

Quill turned to the tall Japanese who had come in unnoticed behind them. "Ken Sakura. I've been an admirer of your paintings for a long time. I'm delighted to meet you, although I'd hoped it'd be under less stressful circumstances."

"Wow," said Meg, under her breath, either in response to Sakura Kenji's eloquence or his looks, or perhaps, thought Quill, both at once. He was one of the most beautiful men she'd ever seen. Like many Northern Japanese, he had a compact, graceful swimmer's body. He dressed as most Cornell University professors did in summertime: blue work shirt rolled past his muscled forearms, chinos, and Docksiders.

"I can assure you, Ms. Quilliam," Sakura Kenji continued, "that my father's taste in the plastic arts is much less idiosyncratic than his taste in poetry. I told him, for example, that he would find your own work had the quality known to us as *shibui*."

Quill, out-of-proportion pleased, recognized the accolade for what it was with a violent blush, then made an effort to maintain her dignity with a skeptical frown.

"Except for the fondness for Kipling, his artistic taste is impeccable. I believe Kipling's chauvinism, his imperialism, his conviction that a selected race of men is destined to rule others, make the poet attractive to those of my father's generation." He smiled affectionately at his father, then took Quill's hand and held it a fraction longer than necessary.

"Well," said Quill helplessly. "Um. I'm delighted you came over to help with the translation effort. I'm sure this will be cleared up immediately. Sheriff McHale is just . . . is just . . ."

"Pursuing inquiries?"

"That's right," Myles interrupted equably. "You may be aware, Professor Sakura, of the events that took place here yesterday."

"So Miss Quilliam informed me when she called."

"Were you also aware of Mr. Motoyama's criminal record?" Myles leaned forward and read: "Three battery convictions, one assault, one vehicular intent to harm? All occurring on the same date?"

Ken Sakura's classic brow creased. He turned to his father. The conversation was rapid: courteous on the son's side; deprecatory on his father's.

"Sheriff McHale, there does appear to have been a prior incident." Ken hesitated. "My father says it was of no consequence,"

"Concerning?"

"Arising from Motoyama's war experiences. He's still somewhat resentful over the outcome."

"The war?" said Quill, bewildered. "Which war?"

"*The* war, Miss Quilliam. For Japanese of my father's generation, there is only one war."

"World War *Two*!" shrieked Meg. "Pooh! That was fifty years ago."

"My father is seventy-eight, Miss Quilliam, and Motoyama some years older. Motoyama associates certain English words with his experiences in an internment camp in the Pacific. The battery charges you refer to on his rap sheet, Sheriff, were brought by an elderly veteran of your Pacific campaign. The assault charges were made by a confederate of his who got in the way of the corncobs when the veteran ducked."

"Certain English words?" demanded Meg. "What kind of words? You mean racial slurs? Mr. Motoyama threw corncobs at somebody because of racial slurs?"

Quill, with misgiving, recalled Hedrick's offensive characterization of John Raintree. Attitudes like that ran in the family. "And there weren't any corncobs handy yesterday," she said aloud, "but there were plenty of hammers."

Meg gave her a glance which somehow seemed to be approving and conspiratorial all at once. "So, Myles, Mr. Motoyama got in a fight with Louisa Conway? Over . . . um . . . certain English words?"

Myles, his attention caught by something beyond the office walls, didn't respond.

Dave Kiddermeister offered, a little diffidently, "It was Jell-O."

Mr. Motoyama stiffened, drew himself erect, and made a noise indicative of extreme displeasure.

Receiving no sign from his boss, Dave continued in a slightly more self-assured way, "And the fight wasn't with the deceased, it was with Mrs. Mayor."

"Adela Henry?" said Quill. "Mr. Motoyama got into a fight with Adela Henry over Jell-O?" The repetition of this (apparently) racially offensive word prompted another growl from Motoyama. Quill felt herself blush and said, "*Gomen na-sai*, Mr. Motoyama," which earned a reproving glare from Mr. Sakura.

Meg was scribbling notes on the back of a recipe card drawn from her pocket. "What was Mrs. Henry doing there?"

"Well, you know she's president of the ladies auxiliary," said Dave. "The auxiliary went to the mini-mall site with Harvey Bozzell to check out the location of the tent for the opening-day festivities. The ladies auxiliary's got this Jell-O architecture contest going—"

"Jell-O architecture?" said Ken Sakura.

"Yes. You know, buildings made out of Jell-O. Model buildings. Best buildings gets a cash money prize that's been put up by the Chamber, and the ladies auxiliary wanted to be sure ol' Harvey put the tent out of the sun, because it's August and bound to be hot and they don't want the exhibits to melt before the judging. They were thinking air-conditioning."

"Buildings out of Jell-O?" said Meg, her professional interest temporarily aroused. "Air-conditioning won't help much. You'd have to add sand to the gelatin, or something."

"Anyhow, this bird Motoyama starts hollering and Mrs. Mayor hollers back and Motoyama grabs a broom handle and starts waving it around in what Mrs. Mayor calls a threatening manner—"

"Broom handle?" asked Quill, bemused. "But what does this have to do with Louisa Conway?"

"Tae kwon do," said Meg, with an annoyingly superior air, "turns broom handles into lethal weapons. No, never mind, that's a Korean martial arts discipline. But I'm sure there's some Japanese equivalent. Why did you arrest Mr. Motoyama, Myles? Did Louisa Conway get into this argument over the Jell-O and start calling him names?"

"He hasn't been arrested for Louisa Conway's murder," said Myles. "Adela Henry swore out a complaint of battery against him." He turned his head suddenly, his attention drawn to the front door.

Ken Sakura leaned against the wall and folded his arms, his gaze direct and warm. Quill wanted to go home. "So this is really none of our business, Meg, now that Ken's here." She looked past Ken Sakura's left ear. "I really think it's time we were going."

"It is *too* our business, Quill. Anything that affects the reputation of the Inn is our business. Myles, please pay attention to me. It is just typical of this town to accuse a non-English-speaking person of a different race of—"

"Quiet," said Myles. Meg stiffened in indignation. Myles rose from behind his desk, his eyes intent. In the silence Quill became aware of a low murmuring outside; the scrape and shuffle of many feet.

Myles was across the floor to the front door in three strides. He opened it to a parking lot suddenly packed with vehicles. The cars and trucks disgorged men, their faces shadowy in the uncertain light cast by sodium lights. The three Japanese became very still. Quill started after Myles and was stopped by Meg's urgent hand on her arm.

"Quill, it's a mob!" Her voice was astounded.

"It's a what?!"

"A mob. M-O-B. As in a large group of pissed-off citizens, mostly male, from the looks of it, ready to lynch somebody. Most likely poor Mr. Motoyama there, and all because he's Japanese. My God! I was just trying to snap you out of your lousy mood before. I couldn't have been right. A racist mob in Hemlock Falls!"

"That's absurd!" Quill protested.

"Sher'f!" came a shout from the parking lot. "Bring that Jap on out!" Myles jerked his head at Dave Kiddermeister, stepped outside, and shut the door behind him.

"My God," said Quill. "It *is* a mob." To her own amazement, she gulped. "You stay here, Meg, out of sight."

"Where the heck do you think you're going?"

"Out to help Myles."

"No, ma'am." Dave Kiddermeister, a little pale around his ears and nose, hooked his thumbs in his regulation leather belt. His attempt at official cool was somewhat undermined by his trembling chin. "Myles said to put you all in the lockup, just for safety."

"He said no such thing!" Meg glared at him. "Put the Sakuras in the lockup, if you want to, but we're going out there."

"No, ma'am, that's not part of riot-control procedure."

"The heck with riot-control procedure."

Quill pulled the door open and stepped outside, Meg at her heels. Myles looked very tall against the crowd of men facing him. He stood easily, balanced on the balls of his feet, hands at rest against his sides.

Meg began a nearly inaudible version of the theme from High Noon. "'Do not forsake me, oh, my darlin . . . '"

"Shut up," Quill hissed.

"'On this our weddin' da-a-ay,'" Meg hummed, several decibels lower.

"Meg!" Quill's whisper was furious.

"You know I always sing when I'm nervous," Meg hissed back. "Besides, it diffuses the tension."

"Try giggling if you want to diffuse tension. What's wrong with a nervous giggle?"

"It makes me more nervous. And right now, I'm scared out of my tree." She resumed her tuneless hum.

"Well, gentlemen?" Myles didn't raise his voice, but it carried in the humid night air.

An ominous shifting of many feet, a low-voiced muttering: "We want that Jap."

Quill's bare arms prickled with gooseflesh.

"Elmer. Harland." Myles picked the men easily out of the crowd. "You men have some questions I can answer? Mayor? You have something to say, step out here in the light. Where I can see you."

There was a short, significant hesitation, followed by a sort of ripple in the thick of the crowd and subdued cries of "G'wan *out* there!"

"Leggo!"

"You chicken?"

"I'm *going*, durn it."

Elmer Henry's tubby figure emerged from the clustered group, the collar of his shirt rucked up around his neck.

"Adela sees that shirt, you'll get what for," Myles observed.

As always, the mention of his formidable wife's name made Elmer jump.

Myles smiled a little. "Now what's this in aid of, this meeting?"

"We demand to see that Jap." The anonymous voice came from somewhere behind a battered blue van.

Elmer directed a tremendous frown in the van's direction, then cleared his throat twice. "Yes, Sheriff. That Mr. Sakra? He as rich as they say?"

Myles nodded.

"Like, a billionaire?"

"So I'm told. You thinking of holding him for ransom?"

"Well, it's like this. We were having a little informal meetin' at the Croh Bar, just the fellas here, and we started talking about that mall project. And the unwanted publicity. Yes, unwanted publicity."

"From Mrs. Conway's death?"

"What? That? Yeah. That and other unwanted publicity. Of any kind. And we thought as how—"

The voice from beyond the blue van came in a belligerent shout: "*We wanna see*—"

"Pete," Myles interrupted. "Come out of there."

The van, Quill now realized, belonged to Peterson's Septic and Floor Covering. Petey Peterson himself, as broad as his cousin Harland, and as indefatigable as a rusty set of box springs, edged reluctantly into view.

"Ms. Quilliam?" Petey touched his billed John Deere hat. "Them terlits working okay?"

"Just fine," said Quill, a little huskily, "thank you."

Meg straightened herself to all five feet two of her inches and shouted suddenly, "So, Petey. You want to see Mr. Sakura? You and forty of your liquored-up buddies? Hah! Well, you can't, see? Before you do, you'll have to go through him"—she jerked her thumb at Myles—"and my sister. Got that?!"

"What about you?" Quill muttered.

"What d'you mean, what about me?"

"They just have to go through the two of us?"

"*Yankee go home!*" Meg shouted.

"Uh, Meg—" said Quill.

"You mean you already got to him?" said Petey a little desperately. "He bought your shares in the mini-mall project already? He don't wanna buy any more?"

Meg, who had swung into the "lookit that big hand move along" chorus of *High Noon* at the threatening level of a mosquito whine, stopped humming abruptly and said in a normal voice, "You want to make a deal with Mr. Sakura to buy out your shares of the mini-mall?"

"Yes, ma'am." Petey touched his hat in what was apparently a nervous reflex. "Rich as Jesus, this guy, right?"

"Croesus," Meg corrected. "This isn't a mob hunting justice?"

"A what, ma'am?"

"No attempts at lynching an innocent foreigner because of the color of his skin?"

"Ma'am?"

"You mean this is just a mob over a merger!?"

"Meg, darn it!" Quill cast an exasperated look at Myles, who jerked his thumb toward her Oldsmobile. "We're going home."

"Tell you what, Petey," said Mayor Henry. "Maybe we can talk to this Mr. Sakra at the party tomorrow night. Is he invited, too, Quill?"

"The party?" repeated Quill a little stupidly.

"Chamber's looking forward to it. Thing is, if he's gonna be there, we wait a bit to discuss bidness. That all right with you, Sher'f?"

"The Chamber's coming to the party?"

Meg started to laugh.

Quill looked at Myles out of the corner of her eye. "Meg. It's time to leave."

"Hoo!" Meg said.

"Meg!" Quill grabbed her sister firmly by the sleeve and pulled her through the crowd to her Oldsmobile. "Say goodbye, Meg."

"Goodbye, Meg!" Her face pink with suppressed giggles, Meg waved farewell, trailing a final "waaaaittt, waaaiit along . . ." as Quill squealed an illegal right turn at the red light.

"They're all going to think you're crazy," said Quill back in the kitchen. "Or drunk." She'd scooped up her phone messages from the front desk as they'd come in, and was separating them into two piles: return immediately and get-to-it-eventually.

"Well, I'm neither. Did you ever think about the total usefulness of country-western music, Quillie? I mean, there's a song for every emotional crisis known to the human heart. This is an *insight*."

"Who cares?" asked Quill callously. "There are three calls here from Hedrick Conway."

"Maybe he wants a date," said Meg flippantly. "Can you believe that Ken Sakura? Wow!"

Quill held Hedrick's messages over the get-to-it eventually file. "Oh, damn, I'd better call. It's probably about his poor mother." She crumpled the paper and went to the phone at Meg's recipe station.

"Ask him to the party tomorrow."

"Oh, right. With the entire Chamber of Commerce there, petrified he's going to expose some pathetic little secret? Not to mention the fact that he'd insult Mr. Sakura, or something. Besides, even Hedrick wouldn't show up at a party just two days after his mother died."

She dialed. He picked up with a careless "Yeah" on the third ring.

"Mr. Conway? This is Sarah Quilliam. I'd like to say how very sorry I am over your mother's . . . um . . . passing."

"She will be missed," he said, breathing through his nose. "Sadly missed."

"The . . . um . . . observances? They're scheduled soon?"

"The funeral, ya mean? You gotta talk to Carlyle. She handles all that."

"Well, if there's anything we can do, please let us know."

"About what?"

"About your mother's, um, passing."

"Oh. No. No. Casket. Grave. Not much to it. Although she will be missed."

There was a prolonged silence. Quill dropped the pink slips into the garbage bin. "I'm sorry to call so late, but I noticed that'd you left a couple of messages for me."

"Yeah. I did. About this party tomorrow night. I didn't get the time."

"The time?"

"Yeah. What time's the party going to be? I gotta arrange coverage. There's no telling what kind of news day it's going to be, so I can't promise I'll be there myself—people gotta get used to that, around here. They think they're gonna get my personal attention, they got another think coming. But Carlyle will be there with Sheriff McHale."

"Indeed," said Quill icily. "How nice."

"So when is it?"

"Seven," said Quill. "Seven o'clock."

"Dress?"

"Oh, is Carlyle planning on wearing clothes?" asked Quill sweetly. "I mean, especially? It's white tie."

"White tie!" shrieked Meg.

Quill covered the receiver with one hand and glared at her.

"Got it," Hedrick said into her ear and hung up with the careless bang of a busy man.

"What!" Meg demanded. "White tie? Are you crazy? That's gloves and floor-length and colored stones."

"Huh," said Quill.

"She'll be so embarrassed, she'll go home," said Meg thoughtfully.

"Maybe."

"Even Hedrick will be embarrassed and go home. And how are we supposed to swipe the goods book if he's not there?"

"We'll create," said Quill, "a diversion."

"Like the diversion we had tonight? Thank God Myles stopped it."

"Stopped what?! A bunch of guys storming the sheriff's station over a business deal? You made a complete and utter bozo of yourself. And if it weren't for me, it would have been even more complete."

"You mean you didn't notice?"

"Notice what?"

"Quill, dammit. Marcos DeMarco was there with three of the guys from the site. In the shadows, behind Petey's van. Myles saw them, too. They had guns."

CHAPTER 8

"Meg said they had guns." Quill, behind the desk in her office, fiddled nervously with her paper cutter. The windows were open to the sweet summer air; lavender mingled with the scent of August lilies and the air was as soft as bathwater. It was just after nine o'clock. She and John were waiting for Doreen and Meg to start the weekly staff meeting.

"But you didn't see them?"

"I was so flipped out by her behavior that I wouldn't have seen Godzilla flattening the Town Hall."

"But as far as you know, the incident's closed. Nobody harmed the Sakuras, and Motoyama's out of jail."

"Mr. Motoyama is, yes. I think they're all back in the suite, including Ken—that is, Mr. Sakura."

"The art critic."

"It does not make a particle of difference to me what he is," said Quill.

John looked at her.

Quill had spent a restless night. She had dreamed her paints had been locked away and that she'd lost the key. She'd dreamed she was lost. She'd wakened to a bed without Myles, and wakened crying. "About the guns."

"I don't know about the guns. It's odd, certainly."

"Guns in the Falls. John. What's going on? Do you think there's something criminal about the mall project? Louisa was out there with a camera. What if she found out that . . ." She trailed off. Her mind was foggy. She was tired. She focused on the job at hand with an effort.

"What?"

"I don't know. I guess I'm worried about the investment. About the employees. We talked them all into subsidizing part of the project with payroll deductions. And Meg's savings, too. And mine, and yours, I guess. We'd been doing so well."

"We'd been doing very well. Which is why we put that three hundred thousand into the mini-mall. And which is why we're cash-short at the moment. We're watching expenses, remember? Now, I'd like to talk about this party tonight."

Quill, who'd forgotten to tell John about the mysterious increase in party attendance, said hastily, "I remember the days when three hundred thousand dollars seemed like a fortune. Six of my friends in SoHo could have lived on that for five years, each." She felt wistful. "And buy paints and canvas with it, too."

"Well, look forward to the time when you and Meg will be retired. That's your pension fund. Three hundred K may seem like a lot of money now, but it won't when you're ready to retire."

She reached across the desk and took his hand. "You're so good to us, John. We're feckless, Meg and I. Feckless. Without you, we'd be up the creek for certain."

"Without me, you might have invested that cash into certificates of deposit. Which is maybe where it should be."

"You're not *really* worried about the mini-mall investment, are you?"

He rose from the couch and went to the window. The buzz of the lawn mower reached them, one of the comforting sounds of summer. "Yeah," he said after a long moment. "I am."

"What makes *you* think that there could be something wrong with our investment? I know why I think that . . . but it's no more than a feeling. An intuition. Well, an intuition based partly on the fact that there's been a murder, and that the out-of-town construction crew was lurking around the sheriff's office with weapons last night. Myles always discounts intuition in an investigation. He says that you have to stick to facts. I have this horrible feeling that the mayor and Howie and Harvey are involved. All I've really got to go on is the reaction of some of the Chamber members to the latest edition of the *Trumpet!* Goodness knows I could be imagining it."

John rubbed the back of his neck. "I have to admit you've got a point. You know what's bothering me most? I don't know anyone from the work crews. The construction company that has the bid for completion is from New Jersey, so I'd expect the foreman and the supervisors to be from out of town—but they brought all the workers with them. Not one's from Hemlock Falls."

"We didn't do a what-d'y-call it—background check on the low bidder, did we?"

"Of course we did. DeMarco seemed to check out. He posted a bond, his bank gave us the go-ahead, and he gave us photos and letters of reference from various jobs he said he'd done before. But we never personally talked to anyone who actually dealt with the company before. Letters and photos can be faked. And his bank's a small, privately owned one, which means he could have a lot of influence over the kind of information released to us."

"But construction's going well. All the deadlines have been met. And the mall itself looks wonderful, John. I didn't look at progress yesterday, of course, because of the tragedy, but I'd been down to see it the week before—everyone who's invested has dropped by. It's terrific. It's beautiful. So, maybe I'm just imagining things."

John shrugged. "There was a murder. You didn't imagine that."

"Yes," said Quill. "Have you talked to Myles about this?"

"Myles talked to *me* about this. He's the one that noticed the work crew. He's been doing some checking on his own."

"And?"

"It's inconclusive."

"Inconclusive? What do you mean, inconclusive?"

"Quill, you know how he feels about you and Meg mixing into these kinds of things. You're both civilians."

"You're a civilian, too!"

"That's true. But I don't spy on Inn guests, which is a misdemeanor, by the way—"

"It was surveillance!" said Quill. "On the Parker case. And we only did it once."

John grinned. "And I haven't hung out my shingle—if only

metaphorically—as one half of a private detective team, and I don't go breaking and entering every chance I get."

"Now, wait just a second, John Raintree. You most certainly have contributed to the sort of mild bending of little laws that Meg and I occasionally—*occasionally*—engage in."

"I helped once. Under extreme provocation."

"I also know precisely what you're trying to do. You're trying to divert my attention from what Myles may or may not have found out about crimes at the mini-mall by laying down red herrings to make me forget it. Between you trying to keep me off this case, and Meg trying to keep me on it, I think I'm just going to go to Detroit."

"Detroit?"

"Detroit," said Quill firmly. "Nobody who knows the least little thing about me would ever dream that I would go to Detroit. Which means I couldn't be found, which would suit me just fine at the moment."

"That little depression hasn't lifted?"

"I am *not* depressed, thank you very much. Now. What's Myles discovered?"

John hesitated. "I really can't say, Quill."

"You 'can't say' to me!? Your partner in crime heretofore? And, dare I say it, your boss! If you don't deliver the goods, Raintree, you're fired."

"You can't fire me, I quit."

"Before you quit, give me at least a *hint* of what Myles has found out about DeMarco."

John shook his head.

"Does it have anything to do with any of the principal investors here in town?"

"Give it a rest, Quill."

"It just can't be anyone we know. Whatever it is. Almost everyone we know has invested in the partnership. And they're either too honest or too smart to get involved in anything crooked. Howie Murchison is an old-fashioned kind of lawyer—honest, professional—and he's very smart. Now, admittedly, Elmer and Harvey aren't the most brilliant guys to come down the pike, but Harland Peterson is one of the shrewdest people in the village. He's made a fortune in farming, and you know how tough that is. And finally, Marge Schmidt, who is nobody's fool. Collectively, those five own more than sixty percent of the mall. And you're not going to tell me that any one of them is going to be involved in something crooked. I just won't believe it. It has to be this DeMarco. He's behaving very suspiciously, don't you think?"

"He's not behaving suspiciously at all, Quill. I've met him. You remember him. He stayed here at the Inn while we were getting the funding together last year."

"I do remember him. He had a secretive sort of face," Quill mused. "I remember thinking about it at the time."

"Well, you never said a word to me, if you did."

"It'd be just like Myles to keep interesting stuff about DeMarco under his hat. And let me hare off investigating some of my best friends, instead of focusing on the real culprit. I'll have to put DeMarco on my suspects list. If I do decide to investigate this, that is."

"Quill! He isn't a culprit if there hasn't been any crime."

"Murder isn't a crime?"

John groaned and put his head in his hands. "Do me a favor, will you? Leave me out of any further discussions about this. And I'd really prefer that you not mention my name when you talk to Myles." He sat up. "If you talk to Myles."

"Maybe I won't and maybe I will," said Quill, struck by this opportunity for a little harmless blackmail. "If I allude very carefully to this conversation and let him know that I know what you know, I might trick him."

"No allusions, please. I gave him my word."

"And you haven't told me a thing. What if I—"

"I mean it, Quill. Let's stick to business, okay? Now. What about this free party this evening, for some of the richest people in America?"

"It's more than that. Meg sees the party tonight as a chance to find out if there's anything behind Hedrick's threats. We're going to create a diversion, and I'm going to get my hands on Hedrick's goods book. Now, about this diversion—"

"We're not going to have any trouble selecting a diversion," said John. "It'll be all our suppliers demanding payment, storming the back patio in a body like the cavalry driving my relatives to Canada."

"That was the Nez Percé."

"All AmerInds are brothers. Can we talk about business for a minute? Just how many people are coming tonight?"

"Well, there's twenty-four members of the Chamber, as nearly as I can tell, and the fifty guests we have staying here, and the sheriff's department, I guess, because Kathleen apparently invited Davy, who invited the rest of the deputies, and Myles is coming, and the Conways, so it's less than one hundred people, John. It can't cost all that much."

"So why has Meg brought in six extra kitchen staff from Cornell?"

"Six! Gosh. I don't have any idea."

"So there's extra labor. From the figures Meg gave me, I've estimated a cost of sixteen dollars a head."

"It's not too bad, is it? At least, not very. And it even includes the yellowfin tuna shipped in for the sushi, which is a million dollars a pound or something. She doesn't think many locals will eat it, so she probably didn't order very much."

"Thank God for that, at least. We're looking at a minimum two thousand out of pocket, Quill. How are we going to recoup a two-thousand-dollar loss this month? An unnecessary two-thousand-dollar loss, I might add. The Kiplings seem to be wealthy enough to afford their own party, and I'm not real sure I understand why we're in the middle of this whole thing. We can recoup some of the losses if we have a cash bar."

Quill sank a little lower in her chair, scratched her left ankle, then pulled at her lower lip. "Well, they are our guests. Don't you think—"

John shook his head. "This is an inn, Quill. A profit-making business, supposedly."

"A cash bar seems so rude! The numbers have been good this quarter, haven't they?"

He smiled a little. "The numbers are never good enough."

"And of course, they are going to provide entertainment with their poetry reading." She added doubtfully, "Which will be good publicity."

"We hope."

"I hope so," said Quill seriously. "It'd be awful if everyone ignored their poetry. I'm so afraid it's going to be ridiculous. Although Doreen says the Kiplings are very demanding, except for Georgia, of course. I expect that comes from being rich. Anyway, they're much too nice a group of people to be publicly embarrassed. Georgia Hardwicke especially. Except that they've done this before, so maybe they don't care about being embarrassed. So I guess I'd have to say I don't want a cash bar."

John shook his head. "I like your logic. They're rich, but nice. If they were rich and rotten, you wouldn't object to a cash bar. But they're rich and basically pleasant. I will never understand your politics, Quill."

"We're here," announced Meg. She and Doreen came into the office and settled on the couch. "What are you two up to?"

"Staff meeting's up." Quill began to search for the agenda in the mass of papers on her desk.

"No, I mean what's up with you and John? John looks subdued. And you look . . ." Meg settled back, crossed her ankles, and regarded her sister though half-closed eyes. "Abashed. Wait. Wait. I'm applying my famous powers of deductive reasoning! It's the party, right?! John's bummed because you invited too many people to the party and it's going to cost too much!"

"I got a way you can save money," said Doreen grimly. "You can leave my salary off the budget. And that-there profit-sharing, too. I quit."

"Oh, dear," said Quill. "Not again."

"You can save mine," said Meg. "*I* quit. I in no way want to be associated with the events this evening. It's not enough to say I'm dreading this party. I have a Foreboding. A Feeling. A Distinct Impression. Something awful's going to happen."

"I know why you want to quit, Meg. You're getting anxious over the food preparation. You always get anxious over the food preparation. And you always pull off something marvelous. What is it with you, Doreen?"

"That Stoker."

"I don't want to hear any more about Axminster Stoker. Not

a word. Not a peep of complaint. What'd he do this time?" she added, reversing herself.

"He's follering me around."

"Following you around? If that's all he's doing, take it as a compliment."

"That ain't all he's doin'. He's stickin' his nose in. Like this-here party for example."

"How the heck did everyone get invited, anyway?" asked Quill plaintively. "We've got the whole town coming, for free. Poor John's in a swivit."

"I'm tellin' you, ain't I? It's that-there Axminster Stoker." Doreen folded her arms across her meager chest. "Said it's part of a customer satisfaction 'thank you' campaign, or some durn thing, and went around blatting to the whole town."

"You're kidding!"

"I don't kid about that boob."

"How many people do you think will show up?"

"We'd be safer figuring who ain't."

Quill looked at Meg. "Okay."

"Okay what?"

"Okay how come you're not swinging from the chandelier?"

"Because he told me about it. I've got extra help coming in from Cornell. And I've tripled the supplies order."

John made a noise like a tire losing air.

"Oh. Well. Good. So we're prepared. Except for the fact that we're going to be broke." She patted John's knee. He winced. She didn't blame him. It was more of a blow than a pat. Somewhere in the back of her mind, she knew she was being unreasonable, but she didn't care. "I'm so glad you guys saw fit to tell John and me, Meg. I mean, I'm only the manager here. And John, too. He's merely in charge of profits. Not to mention losses. John, why don't you quit, too? And me? I'll just go ahead and get that ticket to Detroit." She threw up her hands. "We agreed to control expenses this month. As a matter of fact, we agreed to talk to each other about what's happening, and do we ever? No. I set up these boring weekly meetings just so we can plan ahead, and look what happens. Do you know what I could be doing instead of wasting my time here? Do you?" She smacked her hand flat on the desk. "I could be painting! But I'm not! Because you guys just go ahead and arrange huge parties and order mountains of supplies for a free party for a bunch of people I don't even want to talk to. And I'm tired of it! There! You guys satisfied?"

"Jeez," said Meg. "Sorry."

"PMS," said Doreen.

John cleared his throat diffidently. "No offense, Quill, but you were the one that gave Axminster Stoker *carte blanche*. And he's the one that did all the inviting. And, kiddo, the party was your idea in the first place."

"Just . . . wait." Quill put both hands over her face. Outside, the lawn mower sputtered to a stop and started again. She wanted, suddenly, to be standing in front of her easel, her hair grayed with paint, her jeans smelling of turpentine. She took several long breaths. "Is that Brat of the Month award around anywhere? I'll wear it for a week, I promise."

Nobody said anything. Quill peeked at them, then lowered her hands to her lap. "I have been that bad, really?"

Doreen smoothed her apron. Meg whistled a few bars of "Who's Sorry Now."

John just looked sympathetic and said, "You'll get through this somehow."

"It's just—"

"We know," said John. "Take your time. We're all here. Quill, whatever you decide about what you're going to do. About Myles. About your work."

Quill blinked back a sudden sting of tears. "What I'm going to do is settle down and get to work. So. What's on the agenda this morning?" She found the memo she'd been searching for under the stapler. "Oh, dear. Employee satisfaction. Oh, dear again, I scheduled a lecture from—"

"Good morning," said Axminster Stoker. "I'm sorry I'm a bit late but someone"—he pointedly avoided Doreen—"asked the desk to suspend my wake-up call."

"Wasn't me, if that's what you're thinkin'," said Doreen belligerently. "'Course if I'd bin a ree-ceptionist what temporarily lost her job on account of some meddling fool, I might forget stuff like that myself. Not sayin' I would, but I might."

"Well!" Axminster rubbed his hands together with a dry, papery sound. "Merely a process upset. Shall we get down to business? Sarah? You've passed around the prereading for today's little discussion on team building?"

"Um," said Quill. "I'm truly sorry. I forgot."

"But you do have the results of the Quality Circle problem-solving sessions with the *sous*-chefs."

"My *sous*-chefs?" asked Meg. "What were you doing messing with my *sous*-chefs, Quill? Especially in the mood you've been in lately. They'll all quit, too, I'll bet. Just before the party."

"I haven't done a thing with your *sous*-chefs, truly, Meg. I haven't done anything about the Quality Circles for a week."

"A whole week?!" Axminster's voice rose in what, in a more ebullient man, might have been a wail of despair.

Meg crossed her legs in satisfaction. "I *thought* things were going a little more smoothly than usual these past few days."

"Now, Meg, I'm sure we all appreciate Axminster's efforts on our behalf." Quill sighed. "It just takes so much time, Axminster."

A slight gleam of desperation appeared in Axminster's eye. "You'll recall from our meeting last week that you were all assigned homework, *outside* your major competency areas, to hone your leadership skills. You were to problem-solve with the maintenance people, Margaret. Sarah was to meet—" He broke off. "Who's that in the garden?"

Quill sat up straight. Ken Sakura walked in the rose gardens, the sun striking coally glints from his hair. He stopped by the fish pond and sat on the stone bench, looking down at the koi. "That's Ken Sakura."

"Checked in with his pa last night to the extra bed in the Shaker suite," said Doreen sourly. "After they come back from the sherr'fs."

"Did Mr. Motoyama come with them?" asked Meg in mild interest.

"Yep. That Mr. Sakra senior was some kinda pissed off at him, too."

Quill, who was remembering Ken Sakura's essay on "Energy in Art," said absently, "It's Sakura, Doreen. S-A-K-U-R-A."

"You did say Sakura!" Axminster interrupted, with excitement. "A Japanese gentlemen? He isn't by any chance related to Sakura Toshiro, the multibillionaire?"

"Yes," said Quill.

"Do you know who he is?!"

"Sakura Toshiro," said Quill. She realized she'd risen part way out of her chair. That she was drawn to the garden and the answers that might lie there. "Managing director of Sakura Indus—"

"Pardon me, pardon me, pardon me." Axminster raised a hand shaking with excitement. "He is *only* the inventor of the KOP theory. He is *merely* a byword in the world of key operating processes. That's all."

"Goodness," said Quill feebly.

"My *God!*" Axminster looked into the distance, his khaki-colored eyes alight. "My *God*. The master! Here in Hemlock Falls. I must speak to him."

"Not here," said Doreen laconically. "Drove off with that crazy Jap driver—"

"Doreen, darn it!" Quill frowned at her. "Please don't use that term."

"Well, chauffeur, then. And he ain't crazy, for real, I guess, although he drives like a sum-a-bitch."

"Can you arrange it, Sarah? A proper introduction? My Lord, he'll be fascinated with the improvements I've installed here at the Inn. Perhaps he would consent to observing a team in action— Wait! I have something even better. The results from the Do-It-Yourself reception team. No? I can see you all are not taken with that idea. Well, perhaps that wasn't quite the success we had anticipated. I know! He'll be at the customer celebration tonight, will he not?"

"Axminster, I've been meaning to ask you about that." Quill, conscious of an extreme impatience quite unlike her usual capable response to business problems, made a deliberate attempt to keep her voice from rising. "This party is going to cost us a great deal of money." She felt much better at the expressions of approval on John's, Meg's, and Doreen's faces. She felt effective. "We really *must* put a stop to—"

"Please! All of you. I have a great, very great favor to ask."
Axminster stood in the center of Quill's Karastan carpet, to the
right of the peach medallion, his hand upraised. "To my regret,
I must ask you to please adjourn this meeting. I have factored in
your disappointment. I am accountable. But I must have time to
prepare a cogent, yet eloquent summary of my Hemlock Falls Strategic Plan in time to present to Mr. Sakura this evening. I'm sorry
to disappoint you all. I have taken us off-line. But even the strictest interpretations of process control allow for exceptional events.
This is clearly an exceptional event. Will you forgive me? Will you
let me go?"

Quill thought: *I can go in the garden and ask him. He can help
me paint again.*

"No problem here," said John.

"Hotcha," said Doreen, "I got real work to do."

"You bet," said Meg, rising with unflattering alacrity. She
paused on her way out the door and wriggled her eyebrows at
Quill. "You," she said, "stay away from my *sous*-chefs. Take a little
time off. We've got it all under control."

"Margaret! Hold on! We'll reconvene next week," said Axminster. "Same start time, but we'll have to allow another two hours
for a makeup session."

John, Doreen, and Meg turned to look at Quill as a unit. An
accusing unit. In the garden Ken Sakura got up from the bench and
walked out of sight, down the graveled path. "Axminster . . ." She
stopped. Took a deep breath. Looked at her staff. Blew out with
a sigh. "Let's talk about it later. Would you guys excuse me for
a moment? Customer satisfaction survey, Axminster, very important." She stuck her head back in the door. "By the way. Meeting's
adjourned."

She found him by the waterfall, watching the cascade of water
through the branches of a willow curved over the gorge.

He turned with a welcoming smile.

"Mr. Motoyama's back?"

"The charges were dropped. Your sheriff arranged an apology
between Motoyama and your mayor's wife. My father is impressed
with Sheriff McHale. He finds him capable. For an American." His
smile was infectious. "Motoyama should have been retired years

ago—but it would have killed him, I think, to have no purpose in life."

"And that's important," said Quill. "A purpose."

He glanced at her. "It's all there is, don't you think? A worthy purpose, of course. Such as your work."

"I've been waiting to get a chance to speak to you. I appreciate what you said. The comment about *shibui*, last night, I mean."

"The 'essence of the beautiful,' *shibui*. Beauty itself. There's no real translation possible into English. Plato came close to describing the idea, and, I've always thought, so did your Transcendentalists. But it's a concept that's been submerged by commerce in current times. Not just here, but in my own country as well."

Quill watched the water fall with a sense of perfect understanding that made her very nervous, and completely inarticulate.

"Will your father stay with us long?"

"It depends. He's interested in your mini-mall project. A few of the men from the Chamber talked to him last night. He's asked me to help with translation. I've agreed. I'm leaving tomorrow, since I'm needed back at Cornell, but I'll drop in every few days to see how I can help."

"I'd like to talk with you. About why . . ." She took a deep breath. "About why I haven't been painting." She waited, rubbing one thumb over the other. "It's an imposition, I know, but would you have any free time today?"

"Today? Today I have completely free. Motoyama has taken my father on a drive to the Finger Lakes. And I've admired your work—what I've seen so far. Shall we sit here, by the water? This grass is very appealing."

Quill settled next to him. Her arm brushed his shoulder. Aware that she was being quixotic, nervous about the inevitable, she demurred, "Isn't the mall a rather small project for someone like your father? I mean Sakura Industries is huge, isn't it?"

"He hasn't been active in the business for years, Sarah, since a small *contretemps* forced him to retire. A public brush with a woman, not my mother, which is something of an affront to decency in conservative Japan. The public nature of it, you understand, not the *affaire* itself. The mini-mall project is just a way of keeping his hand in." He seemed to accept, and understand, her

evasiveness, and continued in a comfortable way, "This is a vacation trip for him. He went to see my children, of whom he's very
fond, and then came here to see me. I thought he'd enjoy the Inn.
It's serene. Quite lovely. Quite Japanese. And of course, the fact
that he's staying here gave me a chance to meet you. Perhaps to see
your work. I've seen it in New York, of course, but nothing that
you've done since your last show."

The sound of falling water cradled Quill's silence.

"So, are you an artist that can talk about work in progress? Are
you shy of supposed experts with reputations like mine? May I
intrude on your pleasant life here, Sarah Quilliam?"

Quill caught his glance and held it. The sound of the water
receded. She thought of all the things she had to do today: check on
the preparations for goodness knew how many guests; make sure
that the Kiplings had a stage for their presentation; review the reservations for the next month; not think about Myles.

"There are a few pieces," she mumbled. "I've packed them away.
But we could . . . I'd like your opinion. Even," she added anxiously,
"if you think they're not very good. You must promise to tell me
the truth."

It'd been too many years since she'd talked about the balance
of color and form, the transformation from perception to idea to
canvas, the carrying forward of her voice as an artist. And he was
easy to be with. With the rapid intuition of a passionate expert,
he understood her sentences before they were completed. And her
work, itself, that burden which she carried sometimes like a black
dog on her back, sometimes like a treasured child, he saw what she
was trying to do, when she succeeded and when she failed. And he
talked about it. Not as Myles did, or Meg, with expressions of support ("It's . . . nice."), but with passion. Often with gratitude, once
with astonishment—and twice with disapproval for the abuse of
her gift.

"And that's all you did all day? Looked at your paintings?" Meg
pursed her lips and sliced the yellowfin tuna with quick, delicate
strokes of her sharpest kitchen knife.

"We had lunch in Ithaca. At Renee's. We had the most marvelous wine, Meg."

"So are you ready to work again?"

Quill moved the wooden mallet three inches to the right and back again.

"Or did you spend most of the day in the fetal position? Curled up and defensive—"

"Stop."

Meg rubbed one hand through her hair, leaving a bit of fish stuck over her left eyebrow. "I *should* make this sushi right on the patio, except that I'd die to have Mr. Sakura see me. Why the heck did I decide to do sushi for people who eat it every day of their lives and can tell good from bad, from C-minus?"

"Because you've got guts. No risk, no gain. You're an artist."

Meg shot her a shrewd glance. She deftly rolled a tablespoon of rice into a piece of seaweed. "So. About this investigation. You'll just have to lift that goods book from Hedrick's pants pocket all by yourself. I'm going to be stuck in here for hours."

"I'll manage just fine." Meg's hair was standing up in short dark spikes, her usual response to the stress of preparations for a large party, and Quill added gently, "It's not a big deal, you know. It's not like we're serving a gourmet club, or a New York crowd."

"It's always a big deal. Have you thought about a diversion so Hedrick doesn't catch you committing a grade-one felony or whatever it is?"

"The Kiplings should provide enough. Dina told me that they've been distributing posters about their act all over town. Come to think of it, maybe that's another reason why we're getting all these uninvited guests. But I can't imagine that Georgia would let them do it. Or that the prospect of a thousand lines of Kipling's poetry in sixty minutes would attract anybody but Dookie Shuttleworth. Anyhow, the act is called The Kipling One Thousand! And I didn't totally forget my responsibilities, Meg. I asked Dina to take charge of the staging and the microphone and whatever before I went to lunch with Ken, and I checked with her when I got back when I went up to change for the party. She thinks it's going to be . . ." Quill stopped, searching for a reassuring translation of Dina's expressed opinion that the Kiplings were crazy. "Interesting."

"As in 'oh, what an interesting baby' when it's the ugliest thing you've ever seen in your life? Hah!"

Quill decided to abandon this line of discussion. "And I had an interesting talk with John this morning. About those guns. He's been concerned, too."

"I knew something was up. What is it?"

"Myles has been checking up on the contractor for the mall, DeMarco. There's something suspicious going on."

"Yeah? So maybe we'll find out why from that goods book."

"Maybe."

"I'm glad to see the old detective juices have started to . . . rats! What time is it?"

"Six forty-five."

"Damn!"

"Are you wearing that for the party?"

"This? My shorts? My bandanna? And why not? You expect white tie? You expect me to go up and change *now*! Into a little summer something in gauze and cotton lace like that!" She waved the knife in Quill's direction. *"Now!? When I'm cooking?!"*

"Why don't I go check on the buffet?"

"Why don't you? *Bjorn!*" she shouted suddenly, over her shoulder. "You guys have that tapanade ready yet? Will you *get on the stick!*"

Quill escaped to the patio, where she found John and Nate the bartender supervising the placement of the bar.

"You look great," said John absently. "How's the chef?"

"The usual. Testy, cranky, and bossy."

"Glad to hear it. I've decided on a compromise for the drinks, Quill, if it's all right with you. Nate's selected five dozen cases of the Glenora chardonnays and chablis to circulate among the guests. If they want hard liquor, they'll pay the regular rates."

"Okay," said Quill meekly.

"I don't think we'll have too much of a problem with drunks. Myles and the deputies are guests," Nate said. "But you never know. Couple of the volunteer firemen can swill it down like anything, and they don't give a damn if they get arrested."

"They're coming, too?"

"That Mr. Stoker's been—"

"So I heard." She exchanged a rueful grin with John. "All we can do is our best."

"Halfway through, we run out, I'll bring up some of the Gallo," said Nate. "Kathleen knows who to give it to, so's no one will notice."

"You guys have covered everything," said Quill gratefully. "I didn't exactly mean to take time off today, but . . ."

John and Nate exchanged a look.

"That guy's an art critic?" Nate polished a glass with particular attention to the inside. "Saw him looking at your stuff this morning. Seemed to have an awful lot to say about it." He set the glass on the temporary bar and looked at her earnestly. "Maybe I never told you, Quill, but I really like your paintings. I mean, it's . . . nice. You know what I mean? Some of it, it makes me happy to look at it. Some of the other—I don't know. Makes me kind of sad to look at. That picture that used to be in the lobby and that Mike put back up again? Makes me happy-sad. Just thought I'd let you know I really like it. Not that anyone had to tell me to tell you I really like it."

"Thank you, Nate."

"Thing is, John and I were thinking that we don't tell you how much we like your painting. So I don't know that you need to import some Jap—sorry, Japanese art critic to tell you the things we can tell you here."

"Seemed to like your work," said John. "And he's a fairly big noise in the art world, isn't he, Quill?"

"Myles likes your pictures, too." Nate started in on another glass. "Told me so a couple of times."

"How nice," said Quill through gritted teeth, "to have the love and concern of the staff." Both men avoided looking at her. "I appreciate the commentary, Nate. And John. But I'm standing here to tell you that my affairs are my affairs. I mean, not that I'm having an affair-affair, I mean affairs in the sense of—" She stopped. "Never *mind!*"

"What about a glass of that nice little Montrachet," Nate suggested. "Smooth you right out."

"I don't need smoothing out, thank you very much. What I need to do is take a look at the staging for the Kipling's show. Which I am going to do. Right now. Leaving you guys to gossip about me to your heart's content."

The Kiplings milled around the French doors leading to the patio like lambs in search of a sheepdog. Quill counted backward from ten as she marched to meet them. Just once, she thought, it'd be nice to have a little life crisis all by herself, with people (unspecified) indifferent to her state of mind, and unsolicitous of her well being. Although, she admitted, to be fair, she wouldn't like it for long.

She half turned in her march across the floor to the Kiplings. Nate and John were staring after her with—what had Meg called her expression this morning? Abashed. They had abashed looks on their faces. She stopped Kathleen Kiddermeister on the way to the bar with a tray of wineglasses. "You're going to the bar? Would you do me a favor? Tell the guys I'm sorry I blew up at them. Tell them it's just *agita*. Tell them it's PMS."

"Nate and John? PMS? That's it? Got it." She gave Quill a nudge. "That Mr. Sakura's son? I saw you two today. Wow! You introduced him to Myles?"

"They are the closest of friends. True buddies. Brothers under the skin."

"O-*kay*. Just asking a simple little question. Uh, Quill. I know I told you before, at least, I'm pretty sure I have, but that iris painting that used to hang in the Tavern bar, over the fireplace? It's . . ."

"Nice?" supplied Quill helpfully.

"Yeah! That's it. Nice!" She hitched the tray to one hand and used the other to pat Quill on the shoulder. "John told us we should appreciate you more. Meg, too—told us, I mean."

"Thanks."

"And we do. That Georgia Hardwicke's calling you. See what she's got on? That dress is *really* nice."

"You look gorgeous!" Georgia Hardwicke boomed across the floor. "Nettled, but gorgeous. What's the problem, sweetie?" With the Fairbanks, Miss Kent, and Jerzey Paulovich trailing, she swept toward Quill in a blaze of teal green and gold thread and enveloped her in a hug. Quill hugged her fiercely back. Georgia, with her cheerful, matter-of-fact approach to life crises, was just the person she wanted to see.

Quill said into her ear, "Listen, before we're engulfed here, do you want to come up to my room after the party? I have to talk to somebody, and you're just about perfect."

"As soon as it's over." Georgia released her, gave her a wink, and said loudly, "Well, here we all are. What do you think?"

"You're dressed like Victorians!" Quill was delighted. "You all look terrific!"

"It's authentic evening dress," said Miss Kent proudly. "The Victorians, as you know, had a sense of decorum and order lacking in today's present fashions. Georgia's turban and satins distinguish her as a widow of substance. My lace cap and black taffeta state clearly I am an unmarried lady of certain means and *une age certaine* and Mrs. Fairbanks is quite obviously a married belle. The color of her overskirt was quite popular in the 1880s—it's called *feuille morte.*"

"Dead leaves?" Quill smiled. "It sounds lovely in French."

"Our men, of course, don't have the colorful options open to them that we ladies do. But they are quite correct in crisp black and white. Except for Jerzey's waistcoat. We've never been able to do a thing about Jerzey's waistcoats. He claims that the Polish aristocracy is of a tradition older than the Empire's—and who's to say he is not correct? When one thinks of the Mongols! Well. I shall not bore you with the historical details. Do you think," she asked a little anxiously, "that there will be sufficient numbers in the audience?"

Quill eyed Jerzey's crimson brocade. "I think the brocade's lovely. And we hope for a very good turnout. Is the stage satisfactory?"

"Miked and ready to go!" boomed Lyle Fairbanks. "We'll start in fifteen minutes, run for an hour, with a ten-minute intermission, and then circulate among the guests, in costume of course, to answer any questions they might have about the poet. One wouldn't, by any chance, have notified the—ah—press?"

Carlyle Conway came onto the patio from the lawn, wearing a black slip. Quill squinted. No, it wasn't a slip. You couldn't really call it a dress, either, except that it did cover her stomach and rear end. But that was about it. If the earrings brushing her shoulders were diamonds, she could buy the mini-mall three times over—and the Inn, as well. Hedrick shambled along beside her, carrying a camera. She didn't see Myles.

"One did, sort of," said Quill, in response to Lyle's disingenuous question. "But one isn't sure what the coverage will be like. That's our local newspaperman over there."

"Who's the tart with him?" asked Miss Kent with a delicate air. Quill smiled at her. "His sister."

"Tell them we shall be available for interviews immediately after the show," said Lyle with an expansive gesture. "Friends?" to his cohorts. "Shall we circulate?"

"As soon as I circulate to the ladies', dear." Georgia winked at Quill. "Bit of tummy trouble. I'll see you later, will I? After the show."

Carlyle and Hedrick headed straight for the bar. Quill pushed herself in their direction, stopping to greet people as the patio began to fill up. By the time she reached them, Myles had come in from the dining room entrance. That, and the affable but distancing sort of way he greeted the Conways, made Quill wonder if she'd been jumping to conclusions. Then she wondered why she was bothering to jump to conclusions, since she didn't care.

"Hello, Myles. Ken Sakura said that the business over Mr. Motoyama was settled peacefully."

"I like that dress," he said. "You should wear lace more often."

"It's just the most useful fabric," said Carlyle, wriggling her way past a goggling volunteer fireman, his indignant-looking wife, and two gaping deacons from Dookie Shuttleworth's church to join them. "Lace hides all kinds of flaws, don't you think so, Sarah? That sort of crepeyness at the neck that creeps in after thirty-five. Or so I'm told."

"We were all very sorry to hear about your mother," Quill said a little stiffly. "If there's anything we can do, please let us know."

"Poor Mamma." Carlyle's eyes filled with tears. She took a hefty swig of champagne. "A party animal like her would have loved this." She examined the glass with a critical eye. "Wouldn't have liked the champagne, though. Tastes flat."

"Press room?" demanded Hedrick.

"Excuse me?" Quill eyed his sports jacket. There was a notebook-sized bulge at the breast pocket.

"Place for this reporter to sit, take notes, that kind of thing. Places like this usually have a press room all set up, with special food for the reporters."

"Who in the world are all these people?" Carlyle frowned, then stretched her hand over the bar to Nate for a refill. "You have anything a little less provincial back there?"

Nate raised his eyebrows. Quill shook her head slightly, then caught Myles's eye. He grinned.

"Sorry, ma'am. We're out."

"You might find the hors d'oeuvres less provincial, Carlyle," said Quill. "How do you feel about sushi? Lo-cal, in case you want to take off a few pounds, and really quite delicious. It's not to everyone's taste, of course, but a woman with your experience might find it just the ticket."

Carlyle smoothed her throat with one red-tipped nail. "Myles, what do you think?" She drew her finger down to the top of her cleavage. "Mamma always told me men didn't like a skinny woman. A question of geometry, she always said. 'Curves, Cay'"—she flicked an eye in Quill's direction—"'rather than angles.' You want to escort me over to the sushi tray? I see the two Japanese gentlemen appear to be enjoying it."

"That's the one, Cay." Hedrick scooped a fistful of tapanade from a passing waiter's tray and tossed the toast triangles into his mouth one by one. "The old guy. Worth a bundle."

"As though that mattered, Heddie." Speculation narrowed her eyes. "But the fish looks wonderful."

"Do try it," urged Quill. "And Hedrick, we don't have a press room, but I did set up the possibility of an interview for you. Why don't we see if we can get Mr. Fairbanks aside for a moment? He'd love to tell you about his performance for this interview."

"An exclusive," warned Hedrick. "Stories that show up in the *Trumpet!* don't get covered by other newspapers."

"I haven't said a word to anyone," Quill promised. "We'll find somewhere you can take off your coat and be comfortable. Myles? If you'll excuse us? Why don't you help Miss Conway to some sushi."

The look of alarm in his face, she thought, as she led Hedrick through the crowd, was more than satisfying.

"There's such a great view from the gazebo, Hedrick, and it's well away from the noise of the party. Shall I take you down there to wait while I find Lyle Fairbanks? You can sit and listen to the

Falls, maybe take off your jacket, and perhaps write down a few questions about the Kiplings."

"Sure," said Hedrick unenthusiastically. "You got some food to take with me?"

"Certainly. Shall I get you a plate, or would you like to select it yourself? There's a bit of a buffet, over by Carlyle."

"Raw fish? It's not this reporter's cup of tea. But I'll do it." He sighed, martyred. "Don't go off."

"I'll be right here," Quill promised.

Hedrick slouched his way over to the buffet table, whispered into his sister's ear, grabbed a fistful of food, which he dropped on a plate, and shambled back.

"Carlyle is having a whee of a time," Quill observed. "Although a bit of food seems to have slipped down the front of her dress."

Carlyle, the slip dress having attracted the attention of the mayor, the Sakuras, Petey Peterson, and a short, muscular man Quill recognized as the mysterious contractor Marco DeMarco (whose presence Quill couldn't account for, unless Axminster Stoker had decided to inflict his Total Quality Management theories on the construction business, too), wriggled her shoulders, tossed the jeweled earrings, and retrieved the bit of fish from her décolletage.

"Huh," said Hedrick. "She usually gets someone to help her. This is a pretty dead burg."

"Help her get food out of her dress?" said Quill, too amazed to think of a polite way to phrase the question.

"Yeah." He chuckled. "Old party trick. Ma used to do it, too. Watch what she does now."

Carlyle tossed the bit of fish into the air, swallowed it . . . and died.

CHAPTER 9

Why Andy Bishop, Meg's lover and Hemlock Falls' only physician, wasn't at the party, Quill didn't know. But he told her, later, nothing could have saved Carlyle once she'd ingested the poison. At the time, watching it, Quill was stretched to breaking point, waiting for help, and helpless.

It wasn't a pretty death, or an easy one. The worst was her terrified eyes. Carlyle's eyes were to haunt Quill's dreams for years. The poison was merciless in its attack, trailing agony and awareness in its wake. DeMarco and Myles, the strongest men there, held Carlyle down, until whatever had poisoned her became stronger than all three of them. The convulsions tore her hands and feet from their grip, arcing her body backward until her head touched her heels. At the end, a terrible rictus stretched her mouth wide, exposing the perfect teeth in the grin of a year-old corpse.

And it took forever.

"Twenty-seven minutes," said Quill, on her balcony, after the body had been taken and the guests had gone home.

Georgia sighed. "Who timed it, for goodness' sake?"

"Myles. It's automatic, I guess."

Meg, silent, refilled her brandy glass, and lit a forbidden cigarette.

"I am glad I didn't see it," said Georgia forcefully. "Doesn't sound like this detective stuff is as much fun as I thought. So what do we do now?"

"Forget it," said Quill. "Leave it to the experts."

"Forget it? Do you know who is in my kitchen right now?" Meg demanded huskily. She stubbed the cigarette out and threw it over the balcony. "Right *now*? A forensics team. A real one. Going over that damn tuna. They've closed me down, Quill."

"It's just until they've bagged everything and sent it off to the lab."

"What are we going to do about breakfast? Lunch? About all the people who'll check out? What about Hedrick? What his newspaper doesn't do to the reputation of this Inn, his lawyers will."

"But what could have killed her?" said Georgia. "There's no food poisoning that acts like that, is there? I mean, there's no way that it could be your cooking, Meg. Hell, you can keep on feeding me, and I'll sit outside with a sign around my neck. 'Get well-nourished here.'" She patted her ample stomach and tried a chuckle that died in the silence. Below them the sounds of the evidence team grimly at work in the kitchen floated across the air.

"Andy did say food poisoning doesn't act so quickly," said Quill. "Botulism takes thirty-six to seventy-two hours. Salmonella six to twenty-four."

"Fugu is that fast," said Meg.

"Fugu?" Georgia set her brandy glass on the table with a click. "I know what that is. From the Kipling's trip to Japan. It's a poisonous fish liver."

"And it's a neurotoxin. One of the deadliest." Meg kicked the table leg.

"That doesn't make sense," said Quill. "How in the world could the liver of a Japanese fish get into your sushi?"

"In the tuna," said Meg glumly. "I told you. That's why those idiots underneath us are going through my kitchen."

"You mean to tell me you can't tell fugu liver from tuna filets?"

"Well, of course I can. But it might have gotten mixed up in the shipment, somehow, and been removed, leaving a few drops of fluid. Even a little touch is deadly. It's nasty stuff."

"That seems truly unlikely."

"The alternative doesn't make sense either, does it?" asked Georgia. "That someone carried it with him—or her—and deliberately introduced it into the sushi."

"If it was the sushi," said Quill absently.

"What else could it have been other than the sushi!" Meg's voice was thick with tears. "And I made it." Quill put her hand out and closed it over her sister's wrist. "I suppose we should be celebrating the fact that I didn't kill half the population of Hemlock Falls."

"Maybe somebody wanted to bump off the 'voluptuous slut.'"
Georgia's chuckle sounded again, a little more confidence in it.

"The what?!"

"I told Georgia that's what I was thinking about her," said Quill.
"I felt awful about it."

"Confession's good for the soul," said Georgia comfortably.
"And I told you then and I'll tell you now, the fact that she may
have been murdered doesn't change her character. As a matter of
fact, it's probably why she was murdered: her character."

"Murder!" said Meg with scorn. "It's a pretty damn inefficient
way of murder. There is no guarantee that Carlyle herself was going
to eat that sushi. I prepared it in advance—which you're not supposed to do, but I was too nervous to do it in front of Mr. Sakura
and his son—and it was sitting out on the buffet for at least twenty
minutes before Carlyle popped it into her mouth. And several other
people had tried it before that. I counted. I made three dozen pieces,
and there were twenty-two left on the platter. I found six half-eaten
pieces in the potted rosebushes by the lounge chairs. Some of them
were wrapped in napkins. They all had bites taken out of them."

"People trying it on a dare, I suppose," said Georgia. "Did you
turn those over to the police for testing?"

"Yeah." Meg ran her hands through her hair. "I just don't
understand it."

"Let's do this the logical way," suggested Georgia. "Who served
her the sushi?"

"Somebody said she picked it off the tray herself." Quill shuddered. "That was a long twenty-seven minutes. Half the crowd was
asking questions and the other half . . ."

"The other half, what?" asked Georgia.

"Just watching."

"Oh, God. People."

"Somebody else—one of the men—said that she didn't eat it
right away. She held it for a while, toying with it, then flipped it into
the air. DeMarco said she was trying to catch it with her mouth. It
slipped down the front of her dress. I was watching from across the
room with her brother, and I saw her dig it out and try again. She
caught it the second time."

"She didn't drop it on the floor, and maybe someone picked it up for her?" Georgia suggested.

"Nope. Not that I saw, at least. Maybe someone else would know."

"And nobody handed it to her."

"That's what they said."

"Could she have picked it up from a separate plate? Was it off the platter that everyone else ate from?"

"Georgia, I don't know! I assume so."

"Sorry, sorry. Just trying to get to the bottom of this. I can't believe it's Meg's fault. I mean, it has to be deliberate. With her mother murdered not one day ago? There's a pattern here, ladies."

Quill sensed Meg's muscles relax a little.

"That's true, isn't it?" Meg said. "And nobody's accusing me of smacking Louisa over the head with a hammer and throwing her into the river to drown."

"They most certainly are not." Georgia was empathetic. "Now. I think we should make a list of the people who were both in Louisa's vicinity and near Carlyle at the time she ate that stuff."

"I still don't see how the poison could have gotten on her piece, and not on other pieces," said Meg stubbornly.

"Maybe someone had a squirt gun. Or a teeny-tiny dart in a blowgun. Maybe someone next to her poisoned her at the same time she ate the fish. So it might not have been the sushi at all. Did you see anyone touch her, Quill?"

"I wasn't paying close attention," Quill said. "But there were a lot of guys standing around her. And she was the sort of person who invited touching."

"Now we're cooking with gas." Georgia heaved herself to her feet. "You have a pencil and paper around here?"

"Sure. Near the phone in the living room."

"I'll be right back." She stumped heavily into the living room, closing the French doors behind her.

Meg looked at Quill. "Teeny-tiny blowgun?"

"She's pretty neat, isn't she?"

Meg nodded.

"She's right, you know, Meg. It probably wasn't the sushi."

Meg's face lightened.

"Here we are, ladies. Now." Georgia returned and settled herself with a groan in her chair. "Who was within spitting distance of the late, unlamented deceased?"

"Spitting distance?" said Quill doubtfully. "Wait a second." She closed her eyes, imagining that she was going to paint the scene. Carlyle stood in the center of a group of admiring men, the thin black strap of her dress slipping off one tanned shoulder. Marco DeMarco stood nearest; to his left were Elmer Henry and Pete Peterson. To Carlyle's right was Sakura Toshiro, and behind him, a faithful shadow, Mr. Motoyama, a tray with a hot towel in his hands. The other figures were faceless. Quill opened her eyes. "I can't see everything."

"Draw it," suggested Georgia.

"Draw it?"

"You're an artist. Your fingers will remember what your brain doesn't. Draw it."

"I need my sketch pad."

"I'll get it." Meg darted inside and was back in a few seconds. "I've got the graphite pencil, too."

"Great. Now here's Carlyle, and yes, of course, Jerzey Paulovich." Quill set the scene in a few quick strokes. "And here—good grief. Harvey Bozzel. And Howie. And Marge Schmidt. And Lila Fairbanks."

"And who are Harvey, Marge, and Howie when they're at home?" asked Georgia.

"Howie's town attorney. Harvey's our local advertising guy. Marge is one of the richest women in Hemlock Falls."

Georgia took the drawing pad and cocked her head. "Then she can afford not to wear a bowling jacket to a posh party. Big women like me should pay attention to clothes."

"Marge always wears a bowling jacket."

"Avid bowler, is she?"

"Well, no," Quill admitted. "She just likes bowling jackets."

"I love Hemlock Falls! Go on, Quill. Are these people connected in any way?"

"Oh, yes, all of them are. With the mini-mall project."

"Well, well, well, well, well. Now we're getting somewhere,

ladies. And who among this group was at the mini-mall site two days ago when Louisa died?"

Frowning, Quill flipped to a new page in the sketch pad and wrote the names down. "Everyone except DeMarco. I think Myles told me he was in San Francisco checking on a shipment of leach-line piping."

"Next question, ladies, would seem to be, who'd have access to fugu?"

"The Sakuras," said Meg. "Naturally."

"Why would Mr. Sakura want to dispose of Carlyle? He hadn't even met her before this evening, had he? You might as well suggest that *I* had a motive."

"The mini-mall project?" Meg suggested. "You said he was interested in it, Quill."

"The mini-mall project is too small, unless it turns out to be the site of a proposed government installation or a silver mine, and worth millions. And I really doubt that, don't you?" said Quill. "Ken told me his father was interested in buying it as a sort of hobby. That would give Mr. Sakura a motive if he thought the stories in the *Trumpet!* might wreck the mall's success, but it's a really, really weak one. The motives are much stronger for the people who want to sell it to him."

"Your mayor?"

"And Harvey. And Marge. They're all big investors," said Meg. "But then, we are, too, which puts us right back to suspecting me and my kitchen."

"It doesn't!" said Georgia forcefully. "Put that right out of your head. Neither you nor Quill was near the lady when she bought the farm."

"Bought the farm?" said Quill, bemused. "You know something . . ." She trailed off. She sketched a tall, shambling blond male in a badly fitting sports coat. "Hedrick went over to the buffet to get a plate of food while I waited to take him down to the gazebo."

"The gazebo?" Meg smiled. "So you *did* decide on seduction to get his jacket off."

"I did not! I was hunting for Lyle Fairbanks. I thought that he and the Kiplings would be pleased to have a newspaper article about the group, and I was setting up an interview. I figured it was a safe topic, since even Hedrick couldn't write a nasty article about a fan group for a poet."

"Hedrick," mused Georgia. "Look at all the money he'd inherit with his mother and sister gone."

"Great minds think alike. It's remotely possible that he could have carried the poison in his jacket—it was bulging with all sorts of stuff, by the way."

"Did you get the goods book?" asked Meg.

"No, Meg, with a woman dying at my feet, I did not have time to rifle her brother's pockets for the goods book. Anyway, he could have carried the poison over, dropped it on her sushi while no one was looking, and skittered back to me with no one the wiser. There was an awful crowd around her."

"So we add Horrible Hedrick to the suspect list." Meg's color was returning, and the animation was back in her face. "Okay. I like this." She turned to Georgia. "What do we do next?"

"We're getting closer to who—but we're just guessing as to the means. Fugu seems very unlikely to me. It could have been something else entirely. Cyanide."

"No bitter almond smell, though," said Quill. "I always thought that cyanide poisoning was accompanied by a smell of bitter almonds."

"The 'how' is important," Georgia said decisively, "because it has an impact on the 'who.'"

The phone rang inside Quill's rooms. She got up, took the call, and came back. Meg looked at her face. "What?!"

"That was Andy. He's sending in a preliminary cause of death. By a naturally occurring neurotoxin ingested through the fish."

Meg closed her eyes. "Did he ask to speak to me?"

"His preliminary guess is that it was on the sushi. He's sent all of it off to be tested. It'll take a few weeks. So we're back to square one. And Meggie, we're going to have to keep the kitchen closed for a few days. Just until a sweep for the poison is made."

"He didn't ask to speak to me."

"I think he's afraid you'd be upset with him, Meg."

"Of course I'm upset with him! I'm thoroughly pissed off. I know he's just doing his job. Any of us here would have done the same thing. *But he could have told me himself.*"

"You know men and how they hate fuss," said Georgia. "They just refuse to understand that if you *do* understand you still need to be able to whack them around a little bit."

"Makes sense to me," said Meg.

"Try telling any of 'em that. Doug was the same way. Rather leave town for a few days than talk it out."

"Myles, too," said Quill, suddenly aware that this was a small part of her whole anxiety about their possible future together. "There's too much that men refuse to discuss."

"It's genetic." Georgia was firm. "Probably accompanies testosterone in the endocrine system."

"Or Andy could just be putting his job first, and me second," said Meg, with a touch of bitterness.

"I don't believe it," said Georgia. "It's just a preliminary, right? He's being careful. All those medical guys are too careful. It was not your cooking, Meg. Andy, bless his heart, and not that I've ever met him, loves you too much to be personally present when he causes you pain. Everything is going to be all right. I feel it in my bones. And believe me, at my size, the feeling has to be pretty strong to get all the way to my bones."

"Maybe, maybe not," said Meg. "Earlier today you mentioned something about quitting?" She hummed a few bars of "Detroit City" in an angry way and tossed off her brandy. Her lips were tight. "That's it for me. I'm going to bed."

"There's one good thing about the big kitchen being closed," said Georgia. "It's going to give us lots of time to conduct a proper investigation. We'll get this cleared up, Meg, see if we won't." She heaved herself to her feet. "I'll see you two in the morning? At breakfast? They aren't going to stop you cooking for an old friend, are they?"

"Nope," said Meg. "Both Quill and I have kitchenettes in our rooms. Why don't we meet in mine, about eight o'clock tomorrow morning? What would you like for breakfast? You can have anything you want."

Georgia grinned. "Just as long as it's not tuna. Pancakes. Casserole. Soufflé. Whatever. Solidarity forever!"

"So here's the plan," said Quill after she and Meg had escorted Georgia to the door. "We quit. We buy a little house on the beach.

You, Georgia, and I retire. And there will be *no men* allowed except twice a week for, you know—"

"Sex," said Meg with a small grin.

"That. And conversation. There is something about the masculine point of view that adds to life, when you keep it on impersonal topics, like the lack of a national healthcare plan. It's just when emotion gets in the way that you have to watch the backs of their heads receding into the distance. I mean, can you imagine Myles, or Andy, offering Georgia's kind of support?"

"Andy's just doing his job," said Meg. "Did he think I'd be angry with him? Did he say anything at all?"

"Call him when you get to your room and ask him yourself."

"Why shouldn't he call me?"

"Because he's a man."

"Aristotle wouldn't like this train of logic."

"It is somewhat circular," Quill agreed. "I'm going to call Myles."

"You're kidding."

"I just learned something."

"What?"

"I'm not sure. Something about women having hearts, and men having souls, with no voice to express them. I haven't worked it out yet."

"When you do?"

"Yes?"

"Don't tell me. I know I'm not going to understand a word of it." She stopped on her way out the door, her gray eyes direct and clear. "Tell Myles hello for me, when you see him."

"I'll do that."

Quill went out on the balcony to clear the wrought-iron table of glasses and retrieve the brandy bottle. The moon was a silver thumbnail in a quiet sky. A small animal rustled in the herb garden. The scent of crushed thyme curled though the breeze from the river nearby. She lit the citronella candles, left the French doors open, then rinsed the glasses in the sink and put them in the dishwasher. She went back outside and leaned over the railing. The kitchen was dark. A car door slammed in the parking lot. The car motor started up and drove away. Footsteps sounded in the gravel path near the kitchen. Quill leaned out and called, "Hello?"

"I saw your light." Myles's voice was tentative. "You're still up?"

"It's hard to sleep," Quill admitted. "Will you come up?"

Myles was quiet, his body a large shadow in the thin moonlight. "Are you sure?" The uncertainty in his voice warmed her (although a part of her admitted it could have been the brandy).

"Yes. Very sure."

"Any other man," said Quill drowsily, several hours later, "would have thrown a rock at my window and said something inspired." She adjusted her head against his chest; she could hear his heart beating.

"I can't remember all of it."

"All of what?"

"'What light through yonder window breaks? 'Tis the east and Juliet is the sun. Arise, fair sun and kill the envious moon . . . ' and that's it."

"But it occurred to you. Love and homicide, even in Shakespeare."

"Particularly in Shakespeare. The man was a great psychologist."

Quill was silent a moment, working this out. "I'm not sure what you mean."

"I'm never sure what *you* mean, Quill." He grasped her by the shoulders and pulled her upright. He was very dark against the unbleached muslin of her headboard.

"Can't you say it?" she asked gently.

"Can't I say it? Can't *you* say it?"

"This conversation is ridiculous. If it is a conversation." She pulled away and got out of bed.

He rubbed both hands over his face. "All right. Here goes. I love you."

"I love you too, Myles." And she did.

"And this is where we were three months ago." There was an unfamiliar note of impatience in his voice. He swung his legs over the side of the bed and looked at the floor. "Isn't it?"

"Yes."

"Until I asked you to get married and start a family."

"Yes."

"And you said, as nearly as I can understand it, that you already had a family."

"I did?" said Quill, startled. "I guess I did."

His face was dark. A vein pulsed in his forehead. "I still don't understand what you meant. Have you changed your mind?"

He knows, thought Quill. He knows I haven't changed my mind. She cleared her throat. "No. I haven't changed my mind."

"Then what is this? What is this?"

"I haven't seen you like this before, Myles, what—"

"What was the last hour about, Sarah?" He was impassive, except for the vein in his forehead.

Quill watched it, fascinated. "I just missed you."

He picked up the lamp sitting on the night stand and threw it at the wall. It hit base first, and shattered. "Then what the *hell* are you doing?"

"What I was going to say"—Quill's voice was tight with anger—"was that, yes, I have a family, and my work, Myles, my work. I'm a painter, Myles, or I was, and no, I don't know if there's room in it for you. I don't know where you would fit, Myles. And now you've started smashing my furniture. And now I don't know a damn thing. And we're back where we started. Or where we ended. So just leave, please, but before you do"—she marched toward the bathroom, the only place in her small suite where she didn't have to look at him—"pick up that lamp."

She sat in the bathtub and cried a little, into a towel, and when he didn't knock at the door, and she heard him leave, she went back to bed and cried into the pillowcase that still smelled like the back of his head.

"So that was the crash I heard last night." Meg swirled the hollandaise in her copper sauté pan and plied the whisk with energy.

"He picked it up, though. Did you talk to Andy?"

"He called, yeah. Last night."

"Everything okay there?"

"Seems to be. We're going to Syracuse for a couple of days, as soon as this is over."

"What did he say about the case?"

"Not a lot. We agreed not to talk about it."

"Everyone else in town is going to be talking about it." Quill moved restlessly around the room. The essential differences between the two of them were nowhere more in evidence than in their rooms. From childhood, Meg had been a collector, and she liked chaos. Cookbooks, magazines, and kitchen equipment catalogs spilled out her bookcases and lay stacked on her windowsills. She'd chosen bright, sunny colors for her drapes and furniture: pinks and oranges with touches of a vivid spring green. Quill could never imagine Meg in anything but sunlight.

"You heard about the emergency Chamber meeting this morning?" Meg pulled the crumpets from the toaster oven and set them on three plates, slipped the poached eggs on top, and poured out hollandaise in a thin stream.

"Yes. This town has more emergency meetings. Did *you* hear that it's going to be held in Marge's diner?"

"No! Nobody wants to eat here?! That does it! Let's sell the damn place. Maybe Mr. Sakura will buy it."

"As a matter of fact, the mayor was very disappointed it couldn't be held here. But Myles thought that the less activity around the area where the death occurred the better. But I don't think we have to worry about people checking out, or refusing to come to the Inn to eat. You remember our first murder? And how we thought it would empty the Inn? And instead, everybody stayed out of some perverse interest?"

"That's a lot different from people thinking I'm poisoning them in my kitchen."

"Nobody thinks that."

"Did you ask Myles how the investigation's going? How soon we can reopen? Whether or not he thinks it was murder by persons unknown—or murder by *me*!"

"I didn't have an opportunity to bring it up."

"Hmm." Meg glanced her sidelong. "Could you drain that spinach for me, please?"

Quill ran the spinach through the colander.

"So, what was the argument about?"

"What are you going to do with the spinach? I thought you were making eggs Hollandaise."

"It's eggs Florentine. There's no ham. And stop ducking the issue, Quill."

"It wasn't about anything." Frustrated, Quill slammed the spinach on the counter, leaving a green trail of water on the floor. Meg bent and wiped it up without comment. "I caught him just as he was leaving the kitchen last night. And he came up, as I told you . . ."

"And you had a lovely reunion, and then what?"

"He wanted to know if I'd changed my mind."

"And you said what?"

"I started to explain that I hadn't really, and then he threw the lamp against the wall!"

"Quill. Let's get this straight. Three months ago you tell the poor man you don't want to marry him, or bear his children, or have anything to do with him as a human being, but he's fine as a sex partner."

"Now, wait just a minute!"

"No. You wait. And last night you'd had a glass of brandy to settle your nerves after that awful business and it was a warm summer's night, and we had some good female bonding going and there's Myles crunching his way powerfully across the gravel and *you* holler the equivalent of 'hey, sailor' and after you've had your wicked way with him, you say, sorry, I didn't really mean what you thought I meant, and you're surprised when he throws a mere lamp against the wall?"

"When you put it like that, it sounds sort of mean."

"Sounds mean? It stinks! If a guy had done that to you, you would have thrown him against the wall."

"A sailor, maybe," Quill said between giggles. "Not the sheriff."

"Well, I think you owe the poor man an apology. Honestly, Quill. You kicked him right in the ego."

"Coo-ee!" said Georgia, knocking as she opened the front door and came in. "Looks like you've recovered from the little setback last night, ladies. Sorry I'm late, but!" She paused dramatically. She was wearing yet another bright caftan, this one red, white, and blue with silver stars embroidered at the *V*. "I have discovered a Vital Clue!"

"Before eight-thirty in the morning?" said Meg. "Good work. What is it?"

"You'd both better sit down. This is big. This is really big. This is bigger than I am."

"Well, let's sit at the breakfast table," Meg suggested. "We can eat while you tell us." She pulled out one of the bentwood chairs at her kitchen table and waved Georgia to sit. "So, what have you got?"

Georgia settled herself, her expression sober. "This." With a curiously restrained gesture after her exuberant entrance, she withdrew a small notebook from her sleeve.

"The goods book!" Quill picked it up. "My goodness! Where did you get it?"

"This morning. I got up early. That brandy hadn't set too well on my stomach. As a matter of fact, I'd been a little queasy all day yesterday, nothing to do with your cooking, Meg, just a spastic colon that hits now and then. Anyway, I couldn't sleep, so I got up this morning at a simply ungodly hour—six, for Pete's sake—and went down to sit in the gazebo. By the way, you'll be delighted to know that I called Adela Henry, the mayor's wife, and offered to help carry Jell-O buildings to the tent tomorrow, so that's set. I figured I could catch any town gossip that they might not let you in on, Quill. Anyhow, back to the gazebo—that guest—the skinny one that looks like he's been ironed?"

"Axminster Stoker," said Quill, paging through the book.

"He was out jogging. Well, he jogged right past me and yelled over his shoulder that I'd dropped something over the edge of the railing. So I found it in the sweet peas."

"Myles and his men didn't search down there, did they?" said Meg. "Here. Let me see."

Quill handed it over and asked Georgia, "Did you read it?"

"Are you kidding? Of course I read it. Hedrick Conway's that slobby blond man, isn't he? I saw him last night talking to you. Well, he may be a sloppy dresser, but he's a very organized note taker. There's a lot of garbage in there, Quill. Your manager, John Raintree? I didn't know he'd been involved in a murder case a few years back. . . ."

"Yes," said Quill, tight-lipped.

"And did you know that somebody named Miriam Doncaster . . ."

"Our town librarian," Quill said.

". . . is having an affair with a fellow named Howie M.?"

"Howie Murchison?!" shrieked Meg. "No!"

"He's town attorney," said Quill. "What else did you find?"

"Well, there's a lot of background stuff on you, Quill. I had no idea you were so famous. And Meg . . . there was a little about your husband's accident. My dear, I'm so sorry—but none of that's important—at least, not to our investigation. Look here." She took the book out of Meg's hands and flipped to the back. The three of them bent their heads over the table.

"It's a lot of stuff about a chemical called neurobenzine," said Meg after a moment.

"Used in printing . . . guess what?" said Georgia.

"Newspapers?" hazarded Quill.

"And guess what it is?"

Meg and Quill looked at her.

"A neurotoxin. A deadly neurotoxin."

"No!" they chorused.

"See? There's a lot of stuff here about the EPA regulations on disposing of it. And see this here?"

Quill read aloud: "'Hi. Haz.' That must mean highly hazardous. 'Contact with skin, soft tissues. Symp: anoxia.' That's oxygen deprivation, right? 'Convulsions. Death within minutes. Anecdotes.' Anecdotes? He must mean antidotes. 'None.'"

"Oh, my God," said Meg. "He killed his own mother and sister. Oh, good grief. How awful. I'd better give Andy a call. And Quill, Myles should know about this. No, you won't want to call him. I will."

"Wait a minute." Quill, paging through the 'goods' book, found a few sentences which cast her relationship with Myles in a highly unflattering light. The reference was listed under 'Poss. Stories.'

and a putative headline noted: 'Innkeep Trades Sex For Freedom! Sheriff's Girlfriend Avoids Plumbing Prosecution!'"

"Those damn toilets," Quill muttered.

"You found that, huh?" said Georgia.

"Yes."

"There's more, of course. The guy's a creep. With a mind like a sewer. But that's not the only thing. There's a list of New Jersey phone numbers written under DeMarco's name, and in several pages following that—look for yourselves."

"You're kidding!" Meg ran her hands excitedly through her hair. Georgia paged through the book and displayed the page triumphantly.

"That settles it. We have to turn this over to Myles."

"No," Meg said. "If Hedrick knows the book's been turned over to the police, he's going to take steps to destroy evidence."

"We can't suppress this, Meg," Quill protested. "What if he kills somebody else?"

"I want my kitchen open, Quill. Soon. We can solve these murders ourselves. And we don't have to go through official channels like Myles and Andy do. We can be a lot quicker."

"And a lot more illegal," Quill muttered. "It'd be quicker if we gave the police this book, wouldn't it? I'm just afraid Hedrick will kill someone else."

"What if we suppress it just for a little while? And as for more murders, it looks to me like Hedrick's run out of relatives."

Georgia shouted with laughter. "Sorry. I don't know why I think that's so funny. Let's work backward from what we know." She held up one finger. "First, it's pretty clear that Hedrick's none-too-subtle threats to disclose something nefarious about the mini-mall operation have everyone in town upset. So upset that they're looking to Mr. Sakura to buy them out. Yes?"

"That's right," said Quill. "But there's a slight discrepancy in what we know, here. When Sakura Toshiro checked in, he showed me a letter from Elmer Henry, inviting him to tour the mini-mall site when he arrived here in Hemlock Falls, with an eye toward purchase. Ken Sakura claims that his father discovered the investment opportunity the day before yesterday, when the group of men arrived at the sheriff's office to talk to him directly about it. So which is it? Second, if Elmer had been in contact with an investor, why didn't any of the other investors know about it? And if it was supposed to be a secret, why did Mr. Sakura show me the letter?"

"So we need an explanation of what that's all about," said Georgia. "Let's make a list, and we can assign activities to the best investigator." She dug a spiral notebook out of her capacious purse. "Okay, that's question number one. What's next?"

"Who is Marco DeMarco, and why is Myles investigating him? John claims that it's very odd that there are no local people employed at the construction site. Hedrick"—she tapped the goods book—"clearly has been following the same trail. So someone needs to call these numbers in New Jersey and do a little digging. Is DeMarco involved in something crooked? What kind of reputation does his construction company have? He's got to be a prime suspect in the murders. Maybe he's knocking off the Conways one by one to keep a story from being written."

"Investigate DeMarco," Georgia wrote, speaking aloud. "Let me tackle that one, will you? Sitting and making phone calls is my idea of how to do legwork. And while I'm at it, I can do a little background digging on Hedrick, as well."

"Our restaurant's nearly ready, but DeMarco would expect me to want to take a look myself," said Quill. "It'd be really easy for me to drift on down to the mall site and ask him a few questions myself."

"If it's DeMarco behind the murders, Hedrick's next in line to be killed, isn't he?" said Meg. "Which, I admit it, gives us the more reason to turn this book over to Myles, Quill." She paged through it. "Sheesh! How did he *get* all this stuff?! Here's something about poor Marge's affair with Gil Gilmeister. Now, that was a sad thing. I'll tell you what I'm curious about. Who's nasty enough to dump all this ancient dirt into the lap of a newspaperman?"

"Beats me." Georgia, eyeing the cooling eggs Florentine with a wistful look, said in an abstracted tone, "Meg." She rolled her eyes pathetically. "Those lovely, lovely eggs are getting cold!"

"Oh, rats. There's grapefruit, too. Hang on." She bounced to the counter, served the eggs, and began peeling grapefruit. Georgia tucked her napkin into the V of her caftan and began to eat.

Quill picked up the red notebook and said thoughtfully, "The final suspect is, of course, Hedrick himself. And the notes about the neurobenzine are very suggestive. Very."

Georgia swallowed and nodded. "Hedrick gets my vote as the murderer. He's got the best motive of all. All that cash."

"We don't know that for sure, do we?" asked Meg. "There's been talk . . . but there's always talk. Have you ever noticed how people want to believe that other people are rich? They nod at you in this significant way and say something like, 'Oh, yes, *she's* doing all right,' based on no evidence whatsoever."

"Men especially," said Georgia. "No, thanks, honey, no grapefruit. I don't want to ruin my record for highest amount of healthy food *not* consumed in a day. As a matter of fact, those crumpets are wonderful. Could I have one plain, with just a bit of jam? Well. I can maybe help there, too. As you know, I'm loaded. I've got a couple of banker friends who can maybe help us out. It'll take a few days to get the info back."

"Do we have a few days?" asked Meg. "There's a much shorter way. There's an emergency Chamber meeting this morning, and Howie Murchison will be there. He handled the Conway closing on the Nickerson building. Quill can pin him to the wall about Hedrick's finances. Believe me, those baby hazel eyes and curly red hair of hers conceal a steely mind. Howie'll talk, and not even know he's talking. And there's the local OSHA office."

"The local OSHA office?" Georgia stopped with a crumpet halfway to her mouth.

"They can tell us where Hedrick is likely to buy neurobenzine, what it's used for, how much is on hand. They'll have copies of the MSHS."

"And what's that when it's at home?"

"Materials safety handling sheet," said Meg offhandedly,

"She's showing off," said Quill. "We had a case last year . . . anyway, Meg, I don't know what the local OSHA office could tell us that Andy couldn't. Why don't you put him, in your own inimitable way, onto neurobenzene as a possible murder weapon. Without letting him know how we know, of course."

"I can't do that unless I know what the heck it is, can I? I mean, how do I introduce it casually into a conversation? 'Andrew.

Speaking of neurobenzine . . . or Andrew, I was wondering a lot about the properties of neurobenzine.'"

"Meg, you can do it more subtly than that."

"Okay, okay! I'll try my wiles on Andrew. Are you going to try your wiles on Howie to see if Hedrick really does have any cash?"

"Sure. But I'll bet that Gee will have better luck with the bankers. Howie takes confidentiality stuff seriously."

"And what do we do about this?" Georgia tapped the red notebook.

"We copy it," said Meg smugly, "on the office copier. And we put it back where you found it, Georgia. Myles's men had the chance to discover it last night. They'll have a chance again today, if Hedrick doesn't come looking for it first. So we are not interfering with an investigation at all."

Quill frowned. "And if Myles doesn't find it before Hedrick?"

"We'll give the copy to him. This is Monday, right? How much time do we need to pursue our leads and solve the murder?"

Quill threw up her hands. "How the heck should I know? A couple of days to answer the question we've raised. You know Myles's resources—he'll probably solve this before we do anyway."

"Hah!" said Meg. "But we are going to give him a run for his money. If we don't turn up anything significant by Friday, I vote we give the goods book copy to him then."

"Agreed. Georgia?"

"Fine with me!" She spread a third crumpet with blueberry jam. "Just as long as I continue to get to play the Nero Wolfe part, and not the Archie Goodwin part. Wolfe never left his house, he ate terrific food, and somebody else did all the running around. Archie?" She wiggled her eyebrows at Quill. "When you get back from the Chamber meeting, report. And Fritz, this crumpet?" She burped. "Satisfactory."

Quill picked up the red notebook. "Shall we reconvene after the Chamber meeting at Marge's diner? It's for lunch, so why don't we meet in my office about three o'clock and compare notes. In the meantime, I'll copy this off, then put it back where you found it, Georgia. Are you going to make those phone calls?"

"Wrote 'em down and will do."

"I've got to go down to the sheriff's office and give Deputy Dave a statement about how I prepared last night's dinner," said Meg. "I'll bring some of that sour cream pastry with me. If Myles isn't there, maybe I can drop tidbits into Dave's mouth like Bathsheba with the grapes and charm him into letting me know what's going on at the official end. Quill? You'll put that copy in the safe?"

Quill, reading, answered her absently. "Sure. If you think we need to take precautions."

"Georgia? Did anyone see you pick the book up this morning?"

"Just that little fellow, Stoker."

"Well, act ignorant if he asks you anything. And Quill? Quill!"

Quill, her hands icy, had come to the end of the goods book.

Meg nudged her. "Make sure no one sees you slip the book back into the sweet peas. I think we should be careful."

Quill looked up. Her voice was distant to her own ears. "You didn't get all the way through this, Gee, did you?"

"No. Wanted to bring it up to you guys. Why?"

"Hedrick's been trying to find evidence that the mall's been built over a toxic waste dump. There's a note here: 'Check DeMarco Toxic Waste Disposal, Inc. Relative?' And another set of notes from an OSHA Materials Safety Handling Sheet. About mercury poisoning."

"Oh, my God," said Meg. "Oh, no! If it's true, this is even worse than the murders!"

"Then you've lost all your money," said Georgia soberly. "And so has half the town."

"It's worse than that. Don't you see," said Meg, perfectly white. "If it's true, that mall will be killing people. Lots of people. Just like the Love Canal in Niagara Falls. It took years for them to stop the dumping. And in all that time people died, and died and died."

CHAPTER 10

"Let me see that." Georgia grabbed the notebook and frowned. "This is ridiculous, Quill. DeMarco with a brother in toxic waste disposal? I don't think so." She threw it onto the breakfast table. "More muckraking."

"It doesn't say brother. The note says 'relative.' It might be a father or an uncle or a sister."

"Didn't you say DeMarco was from New Jersey? I've been to New Jersey. It's filled with Italians. And DeMarco's a common enough Italian name."

"Do you think it's true?" Georgia shook her head in disgust. "I've seen and heard what this little newspaper of Hedrick's is doing to the Falls. It's my guess that the little bugger is thinking of going big-time. Creating more of those stories in which the adjective *alleged* is in little tiny type and the noun *coverup* in huge letters on the front page."

"It would explain a lot," said Quill soberly. "Except that I haven't had a chance to tell you about the guns, Gee."

"The *guns!*"

When Quill explained the near riot that Meg had quelled with off-key renditions of movie theme songs, she threw back her head and laughed so hard her whole body shook. "Oh, my." She wiped her eyes. "I'm sorry. It isn't funny. From what you've said, it could have a real disaster. But, oh, I wish I'd seen it!"

"I've changed my mind," Meg said. "We've got to turn this over to Myles."

"He'll take it public," Quill warned. "You know him, Meg. He'll call in the DEC and the EPA, and if Gee's right, Hedrick will have exactly what he wants."

"Quill's right, Meg. It seems to me that you have a very

delicate situation here. If there's any truth at all to these allegations Hedrick's alluded to in this notebook, your little town's in trouble."

"It'd explain the mayor's nervousness," said Quill. "It makes no sense at all that he'd contacted Mr. Sakura to buy out the mall unless he'd discovered . . . this." She set the notebook on the table. "Everyone's excited about this project. Why sell out? Unless there's a rumor about toxic waste disposal that's making the rounds, and frightening people. It frightens me, that's for sure."

"We would have heard about it. And if not us, then John," Meg said. "We're investors, too."

"Would you?" Georgia asked shrewdly. "Quill said herself that you two wouldn't participate in a coverup for one minute. And neither would John. If most of your investors have their life savings tied up in this, it'd make a great deal of sense to sell what they could and get out, and let Mr. Sakura handle the hassle with the EPA and the DEC. What you two should think about, or rather the three of us, is whether or not there's anything in this. I still think it's just another sleazy idea of Hedrick's to sell newspapers."

"Louisa was killed at the excavation site for the septic tank," said Quill. "And she had a camera around her neck. The film had been removed. What if she found cylinders containing mercury under the tank? And DeMarco saw her, hit her with the hammer, and dumped her body in the river? It would explain the boldness of the crime, too. I mean, the woman was killed in broad daylight, in an area where fifty or more people were potential witnesses."

"You're going to go down there, aren't you?" said Meg.

"I think one of us should. It'd be unusual for you to take the time from the kitchen to go visit the site, but it's totally logical for me to be there to check on the progress of the boutique restaurant. And we have to find out what we can, Meg, before we turn this over to Myles. I agree with you. It wouldn't be right to sit on it for long. But what if Georgia's right, and there's nothing to this but Hedrick's vivid imagination?"

"Even if it isn't true, it doesn't mean that DeMarco didn't find it easier to knock Louisa and Carlyle off than deal with a fraudulent claim that the place is a toxic dump," Meg warned. "It could be dangerous to be alone with him. Why don't you take John with you?"

"He's in Syracuse, checking on the delivery of the kitchen unit. He's due back at the Chamber meeting at noon. I don't think we should hang around waiting to see if everyone in town begins to develop central nervous system disorders. I think I should go look right now. Besides, the fewer people who know about this, the better."

"Hey, I'll go with you," Georgia said.

"No." Quill grinned at her. "You hate legwork. You said so yourself. And running like heck from DeMarco and his revolver-wielding minions could be real legwork. I'll just go down there, poke around in an innocent way, and see if I can pick up enough sinister vibrations to justify blowing the whistle on the whole project."

"Quill, I don't like this." Meg ran both her hands through her hair.

"I promise you, Meg. I'm not going to do anything silly. I'll admire the progress on the mall, bat my eyelashes, and see if I can discover whether the septic tank was set before or after Louisa visited the site. If it was after, the probability that she found something suspicious in the hole is higher. I'll also ask DeMarco directly if he knows of anyone to handle our toxic waste. If he gives me the name of his uncle Frankie, we've got another reason to turn the goods book over to Myles."

"And I'll include a background check on DeMarco Disposal in my phone calls this morning," said Georgia.

"I might as well leave right now, then." Quill got up.

"Sounds reasonable," Meg admitted. "Just as long as you remember not to go in the basement."

"The basement?" said Georgia.

"All those gothic novels we read when we were kids," Quill explained. "The dumb heroine *always* went into the basement. Alone. At two in the morning. With the homicidal first wife lurking near the freezer with an ax. Meg, I'll be very careful to run like heck at the first sign of suspicious behavior."

"I'll just bet. Quill? If you don't call here by eleven-thirty, I'm going to get Myles and those Norwegian cousins of Harland Peterson's and come out to get you."

"Deal," said Quill, and went to change her clothes into something more appropriate to sleuthing than shorts and a cotton T-shirt.

Quill drove through the summer morning. She'd copied the goods book, tucked the copy in the office safe, then dropped the original unobtrusively among the sweet peas by the gazebo. There had been no sign of Hedrick. She let her mind drift for the few miles it took to get to the mini-mall site. The less she concentrated on the possibilities ahead (kidnapping? being whacked in the head with a hammer? maybe it wasn't mercury but plutonium packed in Baggies, and she'd fry like a potato in hot fat?), the cooler she could be. As fond as she was of fictional detectives who welcomed the rough stuff, she much preferred a more civilized approach to bringing miscreants to justice, like policemen and courtrooms.

The countryside was drenched in green, and the air sweet with the smell of cut grass and ripe corn. She and Meg had chosen this spot at a time when Meg had been recently widowed and Quill dried up as an artist. The decision had been made in haste, but neither had truly regretted it. The town and its surrounding countryside were too beautiful for regrets.

Hemlock Falls was located in the middle of the path of glaciers which had moved through the region tens of thousands of years before. Farther south, toward New York itself, the countryside recalled the English Cotswolds in spring and summer, with gentle hills, meadow-covered, and stands of ash and birch. Central New York was harder country. Granite poked its rocky knuckles through the soil, leaving land too thin for intensive farming. The glacier's chief legacy here was water, for which Quill felt a passionate affinity. It fell in clear ribbons from the lips of gorges; wound in streams through grasses thick with clover, timothy, and red fescue; and formed an occasional ribbon wide enough to be called a river.

It was on such a river—the Taughannock—that the Hemlock Falls Investment Group (Ltd.) had selected the site for its mini-mall. Harvey Bozzell (Bozzell: The Agency That ADS Value!) had named it The Mall At The Falls, even though the nearest real waterfall was three miles upstream near Trumansburg, in a rare burst of professional reticence.

In far too short a time the familiar and soothing landscape gave way to construction and Quill approached the mall with increasing trepidation. The sounds of Carlyle's death, the memory of her face, were a rising accompaniment to the distant hum of tractors cutting hay and the occasional birdsong.

Quill parked the Olds on the newly asphalted parking lot, turned off the ignition, and thought hard for a moment. How would she know what she was looking for when she saw it? She really doubted that if DeMarco was dumping, it was in canisters labeled ILLEGAL DISPOSAL. On the other hand, neither Carlyle nor Louisa Conway appeared to be the sort of women who would know more than Quill would about building sites, much less toxic waste disposal. If the late Mr. Conway had made his fortune in construction, then it was remotely possible that Louisa had been a forewoman on a job site, but somehow, recalling the creamy skin, the lazy, sensual bodies of both women, Quill didn't think so. Louisa'd probably picked him up in line at a bank. She made a mental note—"Find out how Conway made his fortune"—and decided that if either Louisa or Carlyle had come across something at the mall that was suspicious—and been killed for it—Quill could figure it out, too.

Except if that were true, wouldn't one or more of the other investors in the project have noticed it? The thought of a vast village-wide conspiracy flashed through her head, and she shivered in the heat. Louisa had been killed near the site of the leach fields, a spot which didn't particularly interest anyone, unless they'd been tipped off to a problem, as Louisa may have been. No one else would have been especially interested, except Petey Peterson, out of professional curiosity, and he'd have been the first to cry an alarm, since he'd been vociferous about his failure to get the contract to install the leach field.

She got out of the car and surveyed the new mall.

Like the village itself, the mall had an American Colonial air, with white clapboard storefronts, cobblestone paving in the open-air atrium, and flower-filled planters painted black. At forty thousand square feet the mini-mall had been designed to accommodate six small retail stores, the Inn's boutique restaurant, and a McDonald's. The six stores and the two restaurants formed a horseshoe around a small paved court. The mall entrance had four thick pine doors, ten feet high, with a span of sixteen feet. They were painted in a cross between robin's egg and teal blue with Paramount Exterior Latex Paint, obtained at cost from the local Paramount Paint factory.

The large doors were open to the warm summer air. Quill passed a hand-lettered sign that read: GRAND OPENING !!! with a date two days away in bright red paint. Beneath it, someone had taped an old *New Yorker* cartoon that read "Watch this space" and featured a hill with three empty crosses on it. Quill stopped and looked at the cartoon with a frown.

"Can I help you?"

"Mr. DeMarco."

"It's Sarah Quilliam, isn't it?" Marco DeMarco was unmistakably a construction boss. His skin was deeply weathered. His eyes were a bright blue in a nest of wrinkles. His hair was graying, but showed traces of brown. Quill liked the way he looked; a thick-set, barrel-chested body that spoke of years of hard, manual labor. His face was expressive, his eyes were watchful. He reminded her a little of someone; she couldn't recall who.

"Ignore that cartoon. It's just a little employee humor. Some of the boys think I'm driving them a little hard. I'm not sure how to thank you for the party last night."

"Oh, it was nothing, really."

"No. I mean I'm genuinely not sure how to thank you. I've never been to a celebration that ended quite like that before." His tone was wry, and slightly apologetic. "It must have been quite a shock for you and your sister. I understand they've closed the kitchen temporarily."

"It should be open soon."

"I sure hope you didn't lose much business. My guess is that everyone pretty much sticks around to see what happens next. People." He shook his head. "You can always count on the bastards to do the wrong thing. Well, have you come to check on the progress of the restaurant? We're ahead of schedule, thank God. Your plumbing's not hooked up, but almost all the wiring's done, and the fixtures are in place. Your kitchen's scheduled to arrive any time now. I've got a crew ready to install it as soon as the truck delivers it."

"I wish Meg and I'd had your crew on the Inn remodeling." Quill crossed the courtyard at his side. "I've never heard of a construction project that was *ahead* of schedule."

"You acted as GC on your remodeling yourself? General contractor," he added, with a hint of impatience.

"Oh. Yes. It was a mess," said Quill. Establish rapport with the suspect—it was a maxim she recalled from somewhere. Or was that hostage-taking? "I mean, everybody was wonderful, but it seemed impossible to keep to a schedule. I used," she added casually, "local firms, of course. But then I was going to do business here, so I thought it'd be better to keep the business in the village. The locals tend to talk too much, if you know what I mean."

"Smart."

They stopped in front of the new restaurant. Quill sighed.

"Got a problem?"

"Oh, no. Not all all. It's beautiful. It's overwhelming, as a matter of fact. This is a new venture for us, you know. Every time I see it, I get cold feet. I tend not to think about it much when I'm not in front of it. My business manager takes care of all the details and he's just terrific. But I'm standing here thinking—"

"What have I done? Buyer's remorse? Don't worry. It's going to work out just fine. People will come here to eat just because of the design. And once they taste your sister's food? No problem."

"Do you like the design?" asked Quill wistfully. "I wanted to sustain the associations to the Inn—which is quite historic, you know—and I think it's lovely, but then, I did the sketch myself. I wanted to suggest pre-Colonial without being too . . ."

"Kitschy?"

"Exactly. You don't think it's too kitschy, do you?"

"I think it's great. The brickwork on the open hearth is a real nice design. Real nice. And I like bricks for flooring, although the mason cussed a bit laying it."

"So did the mason with the Inn remodeling. Of course, that was mainly a restoration job, with all that cobblestone, and that was a trick, getting the old to blend with the new. I had to go out of town for that job. I used a Guy Jones, out of Syracuse? He's a Welshman.

We have some excellent masons here in town, though. Where did your worker come from? I'd like to meet him and thank him for doing such a wonderful job."

"He's been done for a few days. Sent him on back."

"To where?"

The bright blue eyes narrowed. "To another job."

"I see," said Quill, looking at the hammering, nailing, and sawing going on frantically around her with what she hoped was an air of convincing surprise, "that *you* decided not to use any local workers. Smart," she echoed his comment.

"As you've discovered," he said in a rather dry way, "part-timers and jobbers can lead to a lot of disruption. And when you've got a penalty for not making deadline, as I do, you use the guys you can count on."

"You've got a penalty if you run over the opening date?"

"Yeah. The lawyer you've got on the contract end of things?"

"Howie Murchison."

"Right. Like most lawyers, a real bastard. Pardon the expression. Nailed my back to the wall on this one. If I don't make the deadline, I pay a penalty of six hundred bucks a day."

"You're kidding!"

"Not about money I don't kid. I'll tell you something, though, there's a guy I want on my side in a fight."

"Howie?" Quill, who usually didn't think much about Howie at all, began to see the balding, bespectacled town justice in a different light. "We're a small town," she added proudly, "but that doesn't mean we're small town, if you know what I mean."

"You sure got some big-time murders."

"Yes." Carlyle Conway's dead face rose before her mind's eye. "The sheriff hasn't said anything official, has he?"

"McHale? If he had, fat chance the bastard'd tell me. There's another one for you, Miss Quilliam. Like Murchison. Not much gets past that one." He shook his head. "Changed my mind about small towns, I'll tell you that."

"Sheriff McHale is retired from the New York City police department," said Quill. "He had quite a career there, I understand."

"That a fact?" DeMarco rubbed his hand thoughtfully along his lower jaw. "Wish I'd known."

"Excuse me?"

"Nothing. Look. We're having a few problems with the septic, and I want to get on over there to take a look. You look around all you want. Anything I can do for you, just let me know."

"I wouldn't mind seeing the septic tank."

"The septic tank?"

"You may have heard. We're having some problems with the plumbing at the Inn. There was an article about it in yesterday's *Trumpet!*"

"Come again?"

"Our local newspaper. Anyway. I'd be really grateful for any plumbing advice you could give me. And . . . um . . . we have another small problem I thought you might help us with?"

"Yeah?" He looked at his watch. "My engineer might have some time. I really don't."

"If you don't mind, it's something a little private."

His glance flickered over her. She'd decided that jeans and a tank top would be the best uniform for detecting toxic waste in a hostile environment. She'd lost a little weight in the past few months, and she was suddenly aware that her stomach was exposed. She pulled self-consciously at the tank top. "You know my sister and I run the Inn at Hemlock Falls."

"Yep."

"And we, um, well, we run into problems with the DEC, the EPA—you must know how difficult it can be dealing with the government on issues of, um, disposal of certain substances."

"What kind of substances?" His glance was unfriendly. Quill, who'd thought this question out beforehand, was ready. "Gasoline."

"Oh, shit. Don't tell me you have buried tanks?"

"We think so. The Inn's quite old, and it's had a great many owners. We're pretty sure at one time in the thirties and forties they had pumps put back."

"And you think you've got contaminated soil? Shit," he said again. "That's a tough one. You're looking at a quarter million, maybe three hundred thousand in removal expense."

"I am?" said Quill, genuinely astonished, and extremely glad there were no gasoline tanks buried at the Inn.

"Oh, yeah." He placed a hand on her shoulder. Quill jumped. "I'm really sorry. The EPA regs will kill you."

"You don't know of any way we could dispose of it for less than that? The EPA doesn't know anything, and I'd surely hate for them to find out."

"Best advice I can give you is ignore it. What they don't know won't hurt them."

"Couldn't we just dig up the tanks and put them somewhere else?"

"Ms. Quilliam, you seem like a nice little lady to me. I have to tell you, if you did decide to get some fly-by-nighter to take those tanks up for you, I sure don't want to know about it." There was a faint, very faint, look of contempt on his face. "I can tell you this, if you won't take offense where none is meant. There's too many people with the kind of attitude you've got. Let it be someone else's problem. The earth, Ms. Quilliam, is everyone's problem. You've heard of the Sierra Club? I'm a charter member. It's a fine organization, and I can give you some literature on . . ."

Quill (who contributed faithfully to the Audubon Society every year) thought it was just her luck to hit the only green construction company in Central New York.

She apologized, which stemmed the flow, then, in dogged pursuit of the requirement to at least take a look at the place where Louisa died, asked DeMarco if his engineer could give her advice on septic systems. With DeMarco's admonitions in her ears, they left the mall by way of the service entrance and walked over a field gouged and rutted by the passage of heavy equipment. A bulldozer and a backhoe were running at full speed. The noise, which had been mere background inside the mall, was astonishing, and DeMarco's lecture petered out.

"We're getting sod in tomorrow!" DeMarco shouted at her. "All this'll be green by Wednesday. Eugene! Hi!" He waved energetically at the backhoe driver, a scrawny, hollow-chested man in his late thirties. "Pray for rain!"

"What?!"

"Pray for"—Eugene flipped a lever, and the dozer and backhoe cut off simultaneously—"*rain*!"

"Not for a few days yet, Marco. I want to wait to get this covered up, and rain, it'll slosh it up." He climbed down from the back-hoe and nodded abruptly at Quill, his eyes sly and a little curious. "We've got a hairline crack at the other end. Happened when it was sunk, I think."

"Shit," said DeMarco. "Sorry, Miss Quilliam."

"A hairline crack?" said Quill. "That's not good, I take it."

"Show ya, if you like. It's this big pit over here." Eugene flicked his eyes over her jeans and tank top with genuine appreciation. Quill followed them to the lip of a huge pit. The hole was three-quarters filled with half of a giant concrete tank. The top lay upside down in the dirt on the far side of the hole. "Can't put the top on right yet, Marco. We're testing the tank with water. If it goes all the way through, the tanks got to be patched. It's going to take a couple of days to dry, and we're not going to have the plumbing up and run-ning in time for the opening-day ceremonies, Marco. If it doesn't, no sweat. Either way, we have to keep the top off so the cement patch will dry, so no rain, please."

"Going to run into some regulatory problem if we don't put the top on, quick. Some kid could fall in."

"What is this thing, exactly?" asked Quill.

"Five-thousand-gallon sewage tank, ma'am." Eugene grinned. His teeth were in terrible shape. "You interested in sewage?"

Quill considered several responses to this. Whatever was going on here, and it was getting increasingly unlikely that it was illegal dumping of toxic waste, she still had to find out. "Passionately," she said and batted her eyelashes.

Eugene the engineer had clearly been marked from birth as a man dedicated to sewers. "First thing," he explained, his rather muddy brown eyes alight, "is the location. You got to have gravel and sand, not clay. Clay does things to drainage you don't want to think about. You don't have gravel and sand, you got to bring in."

"And did you draw in sand and gravel here?" asked Quill.

"Here? In this kind of glaciated soil? Heck, no. Beautiful gravel. Fantastic sand. No sweat at all. Perc test was beautiful, just beautiful."

"Perc test?" asked Quill, thinking of coffee.

"The percolation test," DeMarco supplied. "You dig test holes, pour in a couple of gallons of water, and time the absorption rate."

"Six minute holes," said Eugene with pride. "Now the field itself, out here,"—he swept an arm in an expansive wave—"is where your PVC pipes go. The sewage comes from along the gray line from the building, into the holes along the top of the cover of the holding tank, and through a four-inch pipe into the tank itself. The concrete tank's in two pieces, like you see."

"The tank's awfully large," ventured Quill.

"Tricky to place. But the bottom half went into the hole just as nice. Can't understand why the darn thing cracked. Marco's real picky about his suppliers. Can't afford any trouble. Well, concrete's a mystery."

"When did you set it?"

"Three days ago, just before that woman was murdered. And they sequestered the site temporarily. The crack and that business with that woman drowning set us back a couple of days while the police were here."

"You were there that day?" Quill asked, her eyes opened to their widest extent.

"Day the tank was set? Wouldn't have been anywhere else. Dang, I wish I knew why we got that crack."

"Did you see it, Mr. DeMarco?"

"Me? Nope. I was in San Francisco, sizing up another job. Came back here soon as I heard what happened."

"The guys were as careful as a mother with a baby," said Eugene, a slight flush along his cheekbones.

"Aw, I know that, Eugene. You boys do good work. I came back because of the accident. God knows what the family's going to do. We're insured and all, but you just never know what the hell kind of bug the survivors are going to get up their ass . . . begging your pardon, Miss Quilliam. I've talked to our lawyers, and it doesn't look as though anyone could hold us liable, but Jesus, these days with juries you never know. Woman gets cracked on the head around a construction site, all kinds of crap jumps out of the bushes."

"Well, she sure as hell didn't come near the tank when it was set. Not that her head could have caused that crack anyhow," Eugene added generously. "Not enough weight." He stared doubtfully into the pit.

Quill, mindful of Howie's list of the spread of criminal activities engaged in by contractors, impulsively decided to try another tack. "Perhaps there wasn't enough concrete in the concrete? You know, maybe the numbers of bags per square inch was short, or whatever?"

The silence was deadly.

"You can't possibly mean what I think you mean," said DeMarco, his eyes icy.

"In paint, you know," said Quill feebly.

"Paint? What the hell's an accusation of my shorting the concrete got to do with paint?" DeMarco's tan darkened to an ugly red. "I've been in business—good, honest, straightforward business—for twenty years, Miss Quilliam."

"You mean it is a bad thing not to have enough concrete?" Quill, perjuring her feminist principles without a qualm, tried to look guileless. "I'm an artist, you know. I paint pictures. And if my paints aren't mixed just right, they crack when they dry. I'm truly sorry. I seem to have offended you both."

DeMarco clipped his words as though he was biting the heads off cigars, or chickens. "I defy anyone, at any time, to find a damn thing wrong with my concrete. You bring any inspector in here that you want. You bring the Feds, the state, the town, and test this concrete."

"I'm sure it's excellent concrete."

"Damn straight."

There was an ugly silence.

"My, um, septic system?" said Quill eventually.

"Right." DeMarco shot a fulminating glance at his watch. "Gotta go, Eugene. Fill her in, will you? Unless she's trying to find out if we're cheating on that, too."

"C'mon, now, Marco. The little lady was just asking. Probably got as tough a boss as I do." Eugene winked at her.

"Uh-huh. Catch you later, Eugene. Ms. Quilliam." He tugged at his billed cap and stalked off, his ears still red.

"How come the guys at the Inn put someone as pretty as you in charge of the drains, anyhow?"

"You were telling me, Eugene," said Quill, "about how the sewage comes from the gray line and then through these holes?"

"Yeah. Drains on down. Sits for a bit. Bacterial action breaks down the sewage. When the level gets high enough, the overflow goes into the outlet pipes and out into the field, where capillary action diffuses it into the air."

"This has been very helpful," said Quill. "We've got some problems at the Inn, as you know. But everything's perfectly clear to me now."

"What kind of problems?" asked Eugene.

"The toilets back up."

"How long's it been since you had her pumped out?"

"Oh. I don't know that we have had it pumped out," said Quill vaguely. "I just didn't realize how important it was unless it didn't work."

"Well, that's it, you see." Eugene was confiding. "People just ignore sewers. One of the most important things in life, isn't it? Making sure the toilets work good? People take it for granted, neglect it, until it's too late and then bam!" He flicked his fingers upward. "You got trouble. And then what they do? They blame you because they didn't get routine maintenance on a perfectly good system." He shook his head once in disgust. "I could tell you stories. Anyway, you get your tank pumped out. If the toilets still don't work, you look for a plug in the pipe."

"A plug in the pipe."

"Yessir—uh, ma'am that is, a plug in the pipe. One time I got a troubleshooting call on a system. A fox was trapped in the input valve. Couldn't get nothing into that tank from the gray line. Little sucker's head was jammed right up against the end."

"How did the poor thing get in there?"

"Sucker must have been pretty determined. Vet thought maybe it was rabid. Squeezed itself right down into that hole. Fact. Toilets didn't work for three days while we got that cover off of her and pulled that fox out. Look, you want some coffee? Tell me about your plumbing problem? I got a little time, while we test for the leak, maybe I can come on up and take a look."

"That would be very, very kind of you, Eugene. But you're a professional, and I couldn't possibly impose on you. We seemed to have solved the problem. Temporarily at least. But I'd love a cup of coffee. Maybe you could give me some suggestions on preventive maintenance."

"Sure thing."

Quill received what she was sure was excellent, although irrelevant, advice on the frequency of pumping the tank (yearly, given her usage), the cost of a replacement system, the virtues of sewers (None. He was a leach field man all the way), and desirability of plastic pipe over iron. The coffee, from a much battered Mr. Coffee located in the trailer the men used as construction headquarters, was strong, sweet, and curiously comforting.

"My goodness," said Quill, after Eugene had exhausted his opinions on artificial bacteria for rapid decomposition. "Eugene? I couldn't help but overhear that you were around the day Mrs. Conway was killed."

"Oh, yeah. Jeez. Quite something, wasn't it." He moved a little closer.

"Terrible," Quill agreed. "And then her daughter, last evening."

"Yeah! I heard that! Man!" He put a tentative hand on her knee. He smelled of damp earth. Quill was perched precariously on an orange plastic chair; she edged back as unobtrusively as possible. His eyes were eager. "You saw it?"

"No. No, I didn't. I was in the kitchen seeing to an order."

"I thought you worked up at the Inn. A waitress, are you?"

"That, and in charge of the plumbing system," said Quill amiably. "Anyway, by the time I got there, the ambulance had come to take the body away. I'm sorry," she lied, "to have missed it. I don't suppose you were, um, in on it, here. That day her mother was killed?"

"Well." He drew a deep breath. "Not really. No, I can't say as I saw anything. Although I did see her, of course, before she went into the woods. And I saw the argument with that Japanese fella. Crazy around here, Wednesday. Crazy vibrations." He grinned. "Maybe that's what cracked my tank."

"But you noticed Mrs. Conway."

"Hell, who wouldn't of, looking like that."

"Was she around here very long?"

"Mmm. Sheriff asked me the same thing. She was taking pictures, I remember that. Quite a lot of them."

"Of anything in particular?" asked Quill. Her heart went a little faster and she set the coffee mug on the metal drafting table.

"People more than things, really. She took a picture of that Japanese guy, which he didn't like by a long shot, and that big shot who's his boss. He was here looking for Marco, and was some kind of teed off when he wasn't here."

"Mr. Sakura was looking for Mr. DeMarco?"

"Yeah. Marc said he's some kind of big shot—or was—he's retired now. So instead of being worth maybe a billion dollars, he's worth half a billion."

"And she took other pictures?"

"Of the hole, here, for the tank. And some of the guys on the big wheels."

"Pardon?"

"The backhoes and the dozers. And then a bunch of other people came up in a van, and she was taking pictures of them and that one guy, yeah, I remember that one guy. Jeez!"

"She got into an argument with him?"

"Heck no, I did. Little short son of a bitch looked like he had a ramrod up his ass. Oh. Sorry. Anyway, I complained to Marc. 'That's just Stoke,' he said. Doesn't mean any harm."

"You must have run into Mr. Stoker."

"Wanted to know if I had some kind paperwork for how often I finished my work on time. What is he, from the government?" Eugene snorted. "I'm telling you, those sons of guns from the inspection offices, they'll drive a good man to drink in no time. I . . . hey!" He gave a patently artificial start of surprise. "Speaking of drink. You wouldn't want to stop by a little place I found in town for a drink, say, after quitting time here?"

"Gene. Thanks. But I have to work this evening."

"You do, hah? Tough boss?"

"Really tough. You know how it is."

"I do. It's why I went into business as a consulting engineer. You ought to think about, miss . . . I didn't get your name. Marc out there gets kind of forgetful about those things."

"My name's Sarah." She stood up carefully in the confined space and extended her hand. "I really enjoyed our talk. It's been tremendously helpful. I'll definitely know what to do when my toilets back up again."

"We could pace off the leach field if you wanted to get an idea of how much space your boss would need for a good new system. You'd be amazed at how those new bacteria save on line space."

"I would love to." Quill looked at her watch. "But it's lunchtime, and I have to get to the Hemlock Hometown Diner by twelve o'clock."

He held her hand warmly. "You're not carrying two jobs, are you? Being a waitress at that Inn's got to be tough enough."

Quill disengaged herself and stood up. The trailer was very small, and she brushed against him inadvertently.

"Boy, Eugene, doesn't everyone have more than one job?"

"Guess that's the brush-off," he said. "Can't say as I blame you folks. 'Course, you might have the wrong idea about me. I never served hard time, myself."

"Hard time?"

"Just a little fiddling with some checks. Some of the guys on the big wheels, you want to stay away from them. Couple of assaults, one or two rapes."

"You mean the work crew's made up of ex-cons?"

"You didn't know?" His muddy brown eyes were sly. "Sure thing. That's why Marco there can get us so cheap." He opened the door to the outside with an elaborate regard for the space between them.

"It's not that, Eugene." Quill, flustered, eased herself down the rickety metal steps. "I'd be glad to go out for a drink with you. It's just that I'm already involved . . ."

Eugene slammed the door shut. Quill, thoughtful over this new piece of evidence, drove slowly down the hill to the emergency Chamber of Commerce meeting.

CHAPTER 11

"You see any sign of Hedrick Conway yet?" Elmer Henry directed a depressed whisper fragrant with meat loaf into Quill's left ear. They were crowded into Marge Schmidt's and Betty Hall's Hemlock Hometown Diner! (Fine Food and Fast) with twenty of the thirty-six members of the Chamber of Commerce. Elmer glanced from side to side and added with an attempt at his usual ebullience, "I told'm one o'clock. Said all we was going to have was lunch, and he said he didn't have time to eat but wanted to address the Chamber, that's what he said, address the Chamber at this emergency meeting, so I said fine, after lunch then, one o'clock. But we got a couple of things I want to talk about before he gets here."

Quill, wondering if Hedrick had discovered that the work crew at the mall site was composed of—what should she call them, the formerly incarcerated?—nodded in an abstracted way.

"Mr. Big Bucks couldn't be here in time for lunch?" demanded Marge Schmidt. "I ordered the Blue Plate for 'im, and he'd better fork over the three ninety-eight like the rest of you done. What is he, cash-short paying for all them funerals?"

"Cash-short?" said Mayor Henry with a short, scornful laugh. "Oh, he can afford to pay for lunches he don't eat, I guess. No skin off the Conway nose, no sir. Got money to burn, Hedrick does. That's what he said to me, anyways, last night. By the way, Quill, good party, except for the murder of course."

There was a murmur of agreement and a general atmosphere of "thanks." John Raintree, on Quill's left, gave her a nudge and a wink.

"Anyways," the mayor resumed with gloomy relish, "he goes and tells me the family motto. 'Just send me the bill, Al,' he says to me. 'That's the Conway motto, just send me the bill.'"

"Bill for what?" asked Marge with a disapproving air. She

repeated, "All them funerals?" Marge, whose build rivaled that of one of the smaller sumo wrestlers, and whose jaw was remarkable for its resemblance to the rockier promontories of Hemlock Gorge, was impressive in disapproval. And as senior partner in her diner and one of the wealthier citizens in town, there was nothing like fiscal improvidence to incur her contempt. "And why'd he call you 'Al?' Your name's Elmer."

"Not 'Al'—'El.' Calls Harvey Bozzel 'Har,' Esther West 'Es.' Probably call you 'Mar.'"

"I'd like to see him try," said Marge with a notable air of belligerence. Then back to the issue, "Bill for what?"

"I suppose the sheriff'll be 'Sher' or 'Sherry,'" said Elmer, not looking at Quill. "Cain't see Myles puttin' up with that."

"Quill don't give a hang what Hedrick Conway calls Sheriff McHale," said Marge with all the subtlety of the Sherman tank she resembled. "Least not anymore." Quill, who had wrongly assumed for months that public interest in her love life would cease to be a topic of interest after a suitable period, cut a piece of lemon pie carefully apart with her fork and said nothing. " 'Course maybe Miriam Doncaster was right and she did see you two over to the Hilton in Syracuse last week." Marge stopped in midsentence, her little eyes narrowed to thoughtful slits. "On the other hand, what I shoulda asked is what Miriam was doing in the Hilton Bar and Lounge at one o'clock in the morning on a Saturday, anyways." She leveled her gaze at Quill. "She with Howie Murchison over there, or what?"

Howie, absorbed in a sheaf of papers, looked nearsightedly around at the sound of his name.

"No," said Quill. Both Elmer and Marge looked at her with smug grins. "I mean 'no,' I have no idea who Miriam was with because I wasn't there."

"Oh," said Elmer, somewhat crestfallen. "I wonder who it was, then. Miriam was sure it was Myles. And a redhead like you, Quill. Or maybe she didn't say it was Myles. Maybe she said it was somebody else. Who were you with at the Hilton, Quill?"

"I wasn't at the Hilton with anybody," said Quill between her teeth. Quill, her feelings a little hurt that she'd put her life in jeopardy (well, it *could* have been in jeopardy) wasn't in much of a mood for the mayor's heavy-handed jocularity. She took two deep slow breaths, then said as amiably as she could, "Shouldn't we get the meeting started, Mayor? If you want to discuss the murders with the Chamber of Commerce members before Hedrick gets here, there isn't much time. It's twelve-thirty."

"Murders?" Elmer blinked rapidly. "Oh. That. Myles is takin' care of that, isn't he? No, we got something a little more urgent."

Quill, not sure that anything was more important than solving the murders, said, "If you could tell everyone why Hedrick wants to address the meeting, it might be helpful. Then we can all be prepared."

"Right, right." Elmer lumbered to his feet and whacked the mahogany gavel against its rest. There was none of the usual settling down; the silence was instant and complete. "We got a problem here, folks."

"I'll say." Harvey Bozzel leaned back in his chair, his hands behind his head. "You realize the opening-day ceremonies for the mall are the day after tomorrow. The plans are going well, very well, I want to assure you folks about that, but I'm calling for action, folks, action!" He got to his feet, ready to pace impressively up and down, considered the crowded dimensions of Marge and Betty's dining area, and sat down again. "We've got to put our eyes to the ground and our shoulders to the wheel—"

"Not now, Harve." The mayor mopped the back of his neck with a large checked handkerchief. Quill listened intently, and with some distress, to the ferocity of their conversation.

"Yes, now!" Harvey said in an urgent undertone. "This other can wait! Until afterward. This mall opening is one of my biggest projects." He broke off, a little teary-eyed, and raised his voice. "We've got to put our noses to the grindstone!"

Quill, whose minutes pad was sticking slightly to the Formica top of Marge's table, sketched a hunched-over Harvey with his eye on the ground, his shoulder to the wheel, and his nose to the grindstone.

"Siddown!" the mayor hissed in a violent whisper. "We talked about this alread— I mean, I'm gonna talk to them, okay? So just shut up."

Harvey sank back into his seat, his face red.

The mayor rose, and with uncharacteristic hesitancy said, "Now, folks, I got some good news for you. Harvey and Howie here know all about it already, and I know I got their support. We got a chance to get out of—that is, to sell the shares in the mini-mall to a very good buyer. A very good buyer. One of the top men in his field. But he's put a time limit on the offer which is five o'clock tomorrow. I think we ought to discuss it before that Conway fella gets here."

The room erupted into loud noise, overrode by Esther West, whose correspondence course in Projecting for the Stage had clearly paid off. "Sell our shares in the mall? Why should we do that?"

"I got my reasons," said Elmer. "Now, we don't aim to make a lot on this sale—"

"When you and Howie and Harvey put this deal together, you told us we'd make eight to twelve percent on our investment," Esther said firmly. "Now why in heck should we give it all up?"

Howie Murchison drummed his fingers quietly on the table. Harvey ran his finger around the collar of his neatly pressed striped shirt. Elmer swallowed hard. "I don't know that I care to say, at this point. What I got to say is that we have a tentative offer from Mr. Sakra."

"Now, Howie here and I have looked this tentative offer over good. And it seems pretty decent to me."

Elmer named a figure. The room erupted again. Quill began to sketch a volcano with Chamber members tumbling out of the top and the mayor writhing at the bottom in hot lava.

"That's barely what we put into it!" shouted Norm Pasquale, the high school principal. "We'd make less than four percent on our investment. I could have made more money at Mark Anthony's bank!"

"Three and a half percent more, to be precise," said Mark Anthony Jefferson, vice president of the Hemlock Savings and Loan. "Our savings rates have always been competitive. I hate to say I told you so, but—"

"You're still miffed because we didn't go local for the financing," said Marge. "Go on, Mayor."

"Howie here's horsed up a short summary of what Mr. Sakra's offering," said Elmer. "And I think you want to take a look at it. He's gonna pass this prospectus around." He raised his voice over the tumult. "And you all *put this stuff away* the minute that newspaper fella shows up, you got it? Because that muckraking son of a gun is gonna be here any minute, and if he gets ahold of this, we'll all be in the soup. Now, quiet! Howie? You want to take over here?"

Quill turned to John. "Do you have any idea what's going on?"

John scanned the short paragraph handed to him and waited a moment before replying. "I'm not sure, but if what I think has happened has in fact happened, we'd better sell out."

"But our restaurant!"

"This offer provides for the leasing of retail space. We can keep the restaurant. What's interesting is that the lease is for a very short period of time. Put it together, Quill."

"Put what together?!" Quill demanded. "I don't have the least idea what's going on."

"Shh!" said Marge fiercely. "We got company."

The diner (a former launderette) had two large glass windows and a glass door fronting Main Street. Everyone watched as Hedrick Conway pulled his Cadillac under the PARK HERE AND DIE! sign Marge had installed to keep access to the front door clear. He unfolded himself from behind the wheel, stood on the sidewalk and tugged at his sports coat, then looked up to see the entire Chamber staring at him through the glass. Quill, out of some obscure impulse toward courtesy, felt compelled to wave. He looked behind him, then up and down the street, and raised one pale hand in a half-hearted response. He shambled through the front door and into the diner.

"Have a seat, Conway." Marge extended her foot and hooked an empty chair. Hedrick sat down and hunched forward, his large hands dangling between his knees.

"Sorry about your ma," said Elmer, rather diffidently, "and my condolences on your sister."

"Has the sheriff found out anything yet?" asked Esther.

Hedrick opened his mouth and closed it with a mutter.

"Nice car," offered Harvey. "You get it locally?"

Marge rolled her eyes.

"Is there something we can do for you, Mr. Conway?" said Quill. "Do you need any assistance with the, um, observances?"

"You're kind of stuck on funerals, aren't you?" Except for purplish smudges under his eyes, Hedrick looked much the same as he had the day before, and the day before that. Quill began to consider seriously the possibility that Hedrick had killed his own mother and sister, if only because he seemed so unaffected. "I came to cover the Chamber meeting, of course. Wanted to get some comments on this new mall coming into town."

"Opening ceremonies are scheduled for three o'clock, tomorrow," said Harvey briskly. "And I'll be happy to give you a quote on that, Hed."

"*Hed*," thought Quill, bemused. *"Hed?!"*

Harvey spoke with the gravity suitable to the occasion. "Some of the stuff we want to keep off the record until the big day, of course, but I can tell you, in strictest confidence, that we've extended an invitation to Helena Houndswood, the star of stage, screen, and TV—"

"That bitch?" Marge threw her head back and hooted like a diesel truck on a downward slope. "Harve, you got about as much chance of that ol' girl showing her face in this town again as a snowball in hell."

"We've extended an invitation," repeated Harvey stubbornly.

"That's not the mall I was talking about." Hedrick, a light in his eye Quill didn't like at all, flipped slowly through his book. "Acting on information received, this reporter discovered that plans for a new outlet mall on Route fifteen have been finalized this morning."

Marge sat forward with a sudden thump. Her gimlet eyes narrowed.

"Bingo," said John under his breath. "I thought so."

"A new *outlet* mall? Our mall isn't an outlet mall," said Esther. "Our mall's a mini-mall. A collection of small but select shopping opportunities for discriminating shoppers. You said so yourself, Harvey. You mean there's another mall going up? If there's another mall going up . . . There can't be another mall going up. There's no way our little mall could compete with another mall!"

"That's right." Hedrick's loose, rather wet lips stretched in a grin. "Got the list of investors right here."

"So!" the mayor interrupted heartily. "We appreciate this

information, Mr. Conway. I expect that we'll be able to read all about it in that fine paper of yours. Harvey, maybe you want to take Mr. Conway outside and give him a few—"

"Wait just a goddamned minute." Marge folded her arms underneath her substantial bosom. "Who's on that investment list, Conway?"

"You'll read all about it in the next issue of the *Trumpet!* This reporter can't divulge his sources. You're not going to catch me giving away a scoop, like some." His eye drifted toward Elmer and away again. "So what's your comment on this new mall, Mayor?"

"I'd absolutely have to study this situation to see how it affects the people of this good town before I could commit myself," said the mayor. "But I can tell you this. Any new enterprise that brings new faces and taxes to our fine village is to be welcomed. Unless, of course, it adversely affects jobs and raises taxes in the area. Which it won't. I don't think. But if it does, I'm against it."

"'Mayor Sees New Mall as Threat,'" Hedrick spoke as he wrote. "Murchison? What about you? You lawyers always have something to say."

"No comment," said Howie tightly.

"'Town Justice Invokes the Fifth.'"

"Now, wait just a goddamned minute, Conway!"

"Bozzel? You've anything to say?"

"I think we'd do better to take a meeting over at your place, Hed. Folks, if you'll just excuse us, we'll go off-line with this." Harvey placed a hand on Hedrick's shoulder and propelled him to the front door. Hedrick turned to face them once before they left. Quill's pen, busy with her cartoon drawings, stilled. She'd never seen such malevolence on a human face before.

"Jeez," said Meg. She, Quill, and Georgia were eating a late supper in the dining room. The room was dominated by floor-to-ceiling mullioned windows looking out over the Falls, and a huge cherry sideboard along the long wall facing the foyer entrance. Quill had taken a chance with the color scheme; the wallpaper border was cherry maroon mixed with sunshine yellow and celadon green; the carpet was a soft, light mauve; the tablecloths a deep pink. It shouldn't have worked, but it did. Meg sighed and swallowed a bite of lemon chicken. "So it's not a toxic waste dump, but it's a waste. There's no way our poor little mall can survive the competition."

"Mr. Sakura's offer isn't generous, but it's fair," said Quill. "At least that's what John says. And Meg, no one can compete with your cooking. You've made the Inn a success, and the boutique will be a success, too, no matter where it is."

They'd turned more than forty walk-ins away for dinner; curiosity seekers, Quill suspected, since there was a discreet sign, plainly lettered, on the front door that read, KITCHEN UNDERGOING REMODELING—PLEASE COME AGAIN, a feat of tactful prose by Georgia. "So the mayor let the cat out of the bag. Then what happened?"

"Elmer called a breakfast meeting of the investors for tomorrow morning, to give everyone a chance to go over the prospectus. Then he and Howie hustled out of there."

"Did you get a chance to talk this over with John?"

"Meg, the poor guy's going crazy getting the boutique restaurant ready to open. We've all been too busy to even think about this, this afternoon."

"There must be something I can do to help," said Georgia. "I mean, this is a big deal for you guys, a new venture."

"Quill is actually very well organized." Meg smiled at her sister. "Sorry, that sounded as though people don't expect you to be organized, but if you weren't, how would you do all that has to be done to run the Inn? Actually, all the up-front stuff was planned months ago, Georgia. We issued invitations to the opening in early June, got a good acceptance rate, ordered flowers, china, equipment, prepared the staff, all that stuff well in advance. Making sure that everything is delivered on time and put in place is something John does—which is why he's busy now and we're not. At least, not more than usual, when my poor kitchen's closed because of your boyfriend."

"Myles is not my boyfriend. People don't have boyfriends anymore."

"Then what do they have?"

"An insignificant other?" Georgia flung both her hands out.

"Sorry. Sorry. Give me another glass of that super white wine, and I won't be rude, I swear."

"Because your good friend and buddy, then, closed my *kitchen*! Anyhow, all we can do now about the opening is worry, and there's absolutely no use in doing that. What we can worry about are these murders. Quill, do you think Eugene was serious? That the work crew at the mall is made up of . . . of . . ."

"The recently incarcerated?" Quill suggested, rather pleased with the political correctness of this phrase. "It sounded like the truth to me."

"New evidence, then." Meg put her elbows on the table with a smug air. "And Georgia, you've been grinning like a cat in cream since we started dinner. You've got something, too, don't you?"

"You don't think it could be the chicken marinated in plum sauce?"

Meg smiled. "Could be."

"Or the second bottle of wine?"

Meg burped. "Nope."

"Well, you're right. I've got something. Something big. But I want to save it. Let's see what you guys have, first, then we'll see how my stuff fits in."

"Okay by me." Meg took a healthy swig of her wine and began to tick off each point on a finger. "We have two murders, linked by the victims' familial and professional relationship."

"Gawd," Georgia interrupted, "you're pretty good at this. That was so . . ."

"Succinct?" said Quill. "Direct? Unambiguous? You ought to see her cook." She drained her glass.

"The murders occurred a month after the Conways moved into town and announced their intention of taking over the *Gazette*. Louisa's murder occurred on the third day of the publication of the first issue of the *Trumpet!*, Carlyle's on the very day of the second issue of the *Trumpet!*"

"Maybe the murderer hadn't seen it until Thursday?" Georgia suggested.

"Wait," said Meg. "We're simply listing facts, here. We'll extrapolate later."

"Then I definitely need another helping of this fantastic dessert. And another glass of wine."

"It's new," said Meg, momentarily diverted. "Strawberries, rhubarb, and raspberry tart. You're the first to try it."

"It's fantastic." She helped herself to a third tart from the dish in front of them. "Okay, the engine's stoked. What's second?"

"Louisa was killed from a blow to the head with the classic blunt instrument."

"How blunt is a hammer, anyway?" Quill mused, aware that four glasses of the Italian white she'd drunk were making her extremely mellow. "Some hammers aren't blunt at all. A tack hammer, for example."

"Never mind. Anyway, her body was dumped in the river, presumably—and I'll allow myself a little extrapolation here—by someone *not* familiar with Hemlock Falls."

"Not familiar?" echoed Georgia. "Why do you say that?"

"Because anyone from around here knows the current in the river. We all swim in it, or if we don't swim in it, we at least understand how it flows. Anyone from Hemlock Falls . . ."

"You're repeating yourself," reproved Quill, and hiccuped.

". . . would know if you tossed a corpse in the river, it wouldn't be carried away by the water's flow. It'd stick around. We've got a lazy river in these parts."

"Hmm," said Quill, "I hadn't thought of it, but you could be right."

"Could be? I am," said Meg with innocent satisfaction, "rarely wrong. When was the last time I was wrong, Quillie?"

"September first, 1993," Quill replied promptly.

"September . . . oh! Ha-Ha."

"What?" Georgia demanded.

"An ill-fated foray into blintzes. On September second, I repented."

"But, Meg, what if the murderer didn't care if the body was discovered?" asked Georgia.

"All murderers care if the corpse is discovered."

Quill offered the fact that Carlyle Conway's death rather negated that.

"In this instance," said Meg, "the murderer clearly wanted to plant the murder on me." She brooded for a moment. "And it may come to that."

"Meg, for heaven's sake. You haven't heard from Andy yet. We don't even know—"

"Wait. I haven't finished my succinct, direct, and unambiguous summary of the facts." Meg swallowed her third glass of Pinot Grigio with a flourish and poured a fourth. Quill peered at her rather dubiously. "When I, with all that time on my hands this afternoon because Evil Forces have closed my kitchen . . . evil forces . . ." Quill took the glass from Meg's hand, got up, and placed it on the sideboard, then poured her a cup of coffee. Meg gave her a sunny smile, got up, retrieved her wine, and sipped it. "I wrote down who was at the mini-mall site. Then I wrote down who was near Carlyle at the party, and I compared the two." She hiccuped, and articulated carefully, "I excepted, of course, ourselves and the citizens of Hemlock Falls. And here it is." She produced the list with a flourish from her shorts pocket and spread it on the table.

"Sakura Toshiro, Mr. Motoyama, Marcos DeMarco, Hedrick Conway, Axminster Stoker, Jerzey Paulovich," Quill read.

Georgia frowned. "The suspect list is wider than that. Even buying the theory that no one from the Falls would throw a body in the river, which I guess I do, there's the rest of the Kiplings, including me, not to mention the criminal construction crew. All of us were around when the murders occurred."

"The recently incarcerated have paid their debt to society," said Meg mournfully. "And besides, the only one from the site in both places was Marco DeMarco."

"He wasn't at the site," said Quill. "I told you that. He was in San Francisco. I think you've had a little too much wine." She considered this. "I think I've had a little too much wine."

"Deee-Marco in San Francisco? Oh, dang." Meg frowned, then brightened. "He could have had an agent?"

"True. But then, so could have any number of the guests at the party. And that includes the forty-eight or so current residents of the Inn."

"But none of them were near Carlyle on the fatal night, except DeMarco," said Meg. "And Andy told me that whatever it was that she ate, symptoms would have appeared within seconds. Seconds.

Which means that it had to be someone in that circle of guys around her."

"Motive," said Georgia. "Since we're being succinct, direct, and unambiguous, let's talk about motive. Why would any of these six want to kill Louisa and Carlyle?"

"DeMarco might want to keep everyone from knowing that there were ex-cons at the site," said Quill. "But I doubt it. I mean, who would care?"

"Lots of people, I should think," said Meg, on whom the wine appeared to be having a sentimental effect. "You're such a nice liberal, Quill, but it obscures your mind."

"Obscures my *mind*?"

"Think about it. How would Mrs. Elmer Henry feel if she knew that the 'formerly incarcerated' were loose and running around Hemlock Falls? What about Esther West, bless her heart? Or any of the ladies in the Society for the Advancement of Jell-O Architecture, for that matter?"

"Or even us, if you want to be fair about it," said Quill wryly. "Wouldn't be all that good for the reputation of the Inn, would it?"

"Probably not," Georgia agreed. "It would certainly distress Miss Kent."

"So we should add ourselves to the suspect list, Meg."

"Except that *we* know that a body thrown in the . . ."

"Okay, okay. Drink your coffee."

"Motive," said Georgia, again, with firmness.

"Obviously we are clueless as to motive, at this point"—Meg scowled—"which brings me to the second reason we should discount the murderer being from Hemlock Falls. If Elmer, Harvey, and Howie knew about the discount mall going up on Route fifteen—"

"We don't know that for certain, do we?" Quill protested. "I mean, not only do I have a hard time believing any one of those three would actually kill somebody, I can't think that they'd knowingly—"

"Screw their friends?" interrupted Georgia cynically. "C'mon, honey. You know what people are like where money's involved."

"No, I don't," said Quill, with unaccustomed firmness. "I know what some people are like over money, but not the mayor. And not

Howie. DeMarco told me today that Howie's a fine lawyer, and there's a man that should know. Howie could have gone to a big city practice any time these past years, but he didn't. He chose to stay here."

"Here," echoed Meg.

"Sentimentality," said Georgia, attempting the word twice, "is a surefire way to torpedo an investigation, in my view." She laid her fork on her plate. "What about this Harvey Bee. No. Bossy. No. Bozzel?"

"Harvey . . ." began Quill.

"Harvey," said Meg.

They looked at each other.

"Harvey," said Meg, again, "could very easily be tempted by cash. But he has such a loose lip that everyone would know about it within days. I mean, he's in advertising, for goodness' sake."

"That's true of Elmer, too," said Quill. "He's a small-town politician. Neither one of them could keep a secret to save their little souls."

"Aha," said Georgia. "Now we're getting somewhere." She hitched herself forward. "I've listened to you talk about the people in the Falls for a couple of days now. And I've seen how you all relate to each other. I like it, by the way, which is one reason why I very well may decide to settle here, but that's another story. Anyway, let's look at motive like this. The discount mall project must have been in the works for how long—several months?"

"It took almost a year to get the mini-mall project up and rolling," said Quill.

"What was the period of time from project approval to the pros-pec-tus? The offer to invest?"

"Eight months or so?"

"And from the pros-what's-it to the raising of the actual money?"

"Not very long at all," said Meg. "Howie had a lot of people he wanted to approach. I'd say it took a couple of weeks."

"So it's likely that the offer for investment in the discount mall has been out—what—two weeks? Three?"

"About the same time that the Conways took over the *Gazette* and turned it into the *Trumpet!*" said Quill slowly.

"But—" Meg stopped herself. "Nothing. Never mind. I think I've had too much wine. Go on, Georgia."

"I can't. I was just using deductive reasoning."

All three of them found this incredibly funny. Bent over with laughter, Meg shoved her chair back, went to the coffee stand, and brought back the second bottle of wine. Quill split it between the three glasses.

"Oh, dear." Meg wiped her eye with her sleeve. "So. Are you ready to spill the beans?"

"You mean the grape?"

"I mean the sushi! Oh! God! That was awful, wasn't it?" Meg covered her mouth and rolled her eyes.

Quill coughed and tried to sober up. "What Meg wants to know is . . . what did your bankers tell you about the Conways?"

"A-hum!" Georgia's laughter shook the small table, rattling the glasses. "Ladies. Sit back. Listen up. Get this." She leaned forward and said in the loudest whisper Quill had ever heard, "Now that his ma and his sister have bought the farm—"

"Kicked the bucket," improvised Meg.

"Fell off the roof!" said Quill.

"Fell off the roof?" Meg swayed in her chair. "Quill, what kind of metaphor is that?"

"Listen, ladies!" Georgia stamped her foot. It made an impressive thump. "Mr. Conway is the sole inheritor of—"

"Half a billion?" Meg sat up straight.

"The sole inheritor of . . . nothing! He's broke!"

"That sorry piece of liver pâté?!" shouted Meg.

"That sausage!" cried Quill.

"That pork *roast* . . . !"

"I like pork roast!" Georgia said. "Don't make him a pork roast!"

". . . is broke?! He has no motive? Aagh! I can't stand it!"

"Oh, dear." Quill balled her napkin and wiped each eye in turn. "This isn't funny. This just isn't funny. What about Louisa's supposedly rich husband, Georgia? I thought he died and left her tons."

"If Louisa had it, it's gone now." Georgia looked smug. "I found out something else, too. Hedrick and Carlyle are the offspring of a first marriage, the origins of which, my attorney tells me, are lost in the mists of time. Louisa herself has a bit of checkered past. One of those women that turns up in the pages of *Town & Country* magazine in the background at parties which are definitely on the fringe, or shows up in the racing news at the Saratoga sales in August, hanging on the arm of an ersatz Italian prince. Mr. Conway senior—after a marriage of some three years to our Louisa— died under very suspicious circumstances at his home in Boca Raton."

"What sort of suspicious circumstances?"

Georgia looked smug. "Food poisoning. From an unidentified neurotoxin. In the *hors d'oeuvres*."

Quill opened her mouth and closed it. The wine suddenly seemed an encumbrance.

Meg ran both hands through her hair. "So. Hedrick's a real suspect, Georgia. What do you think we should do next?"

"With a little bit of luck, I think we can nail him the day after tomorrow. At the opening-day ceremonies for the mini-mall."

"How?" Meg's breath was soft and whiny. Quill pushed her gently back into her seat.

"Ssst! Sit back and look innocent." Georgia rearranged her draperies around her ample shoulders and waved to someone behind Quill. "Whooee! Here we are!"

"Innocent? I'm not guilty," muttered Meg. "Who said I was guilty?"

Quill turned in her seat. "Myles!" She flushed, painfully, the warmth rising from her neck to her hairline. Andy Bishop, Hemlock Falls's best (and only) internist, was right behind him. Myles crossed the soft carpet noiselessly, his eyes casual; Quill knew that twenty-four hours from now, he would be able to give a complete description of what he saw, down to the number of wine bottles and the color of Georgia's hair bow.

"We've got some information on what killed Carlyle Conway," he said. "May I join you?"

CHAPTER 12

"Did I do it?" asked Meg.

Andy pulled a chair next to her and sat down. He was just above medium height, with a sinewy jogger's body. He'd recently taken to wearing glasses; the light from the chandelier reflected off the lenses, and Quill was unable to read his expression. He put his arm around Meg's shoulder. "I told you from the beginning you didn't do it."

Myles's glance flickered over the wineglass. "No. You didn't. It wasn't the sushi."

"Neurobenzine," said Quill. "I knew it!" She exchanged significant looks with Georgia.

"Neurobenzine?" Andy turned in surprise. "Where'd the heck did you get that idea?"

"Just a thought," said Quill airily. "I was reading up on neurotoxins the other day"—she ignored Georgia's stifled snort of laughter—"and thought perhaps that could have been it. You know—it's used in printing. Like newspapers."

"Forty years ago it may have been," said Andy. He pushed his glasses into place with a forefinger. "But Carlyle Conway didn't die of it, that's for sure. It's highly corrosive. If she'd gotten that on her breasts, I would have seen it right away. That would have been an even more unpleasant death than the one she suffered."

"Not neurobenzine?" Two thoughts flashed through Quill's mind: the first, disappointment that a perfectly good number one suspect seemed to have been moved down the list to number two or three; the second, that she didn't feel quite as guilty about not turning the goods book over to Myles right away. "What was it then?"

Myles didn't say anything for a moment.

"You don't mind?" asked Andy, with raised brows. "It was the neurotoxin derived from fugu, Meg, but—"

"Shit!" Meg turned pale.

Andy covered her hands with his. "But it wasn't in the sushi, Meg. It was between her breasts."

"Between her breasts?!"

Andy nodded. "It'd been wiped on."

"Wiped on! Are you serious?"

"That's what it looks like."

"But how?" The taut, unhappy look had vanished from Meg's face.

"Someone wearing surgical gloves is my guess. I'm not sure. It's ingenious, I have to admit."

"Good grief," said Quill. "It must have been Hedrick!"

"Oh?" Myles drew a chair up beside Quill and sank easily into it.

"He's the only one who knew her. He told me she had this party trick, he called it. She'd flip an hors d'ouevre in the air and let it fall between her breasts, then take it out and flip it into her mouth." She looked at Myles. "Is that a sexy sort of thing to do?"

"Under the right circumstances." A grin flickered behind his eyes. "But the killer didn't necessarily have to count on the party trick. Andy's checking with a toxicologist in San Francisco to determine the interval for the absorption rate. We don't have a good idea of when the first symptoms appeared. We were hoping you could help. I take it you were in the kitchen, Meg. So Quill—do you remember precisely when you saw her arrive?"

"Yes. I do. It was just before seven o'clock. I was standing with you, Georgia, and the Kiplings. She came in with Hedrick."

"Did you notice any unsteadiness in her gait?" asked Andy. "Did she seem unstable?"

Georgia and Quill looked at each other at precisely the same moment. Georgia went *ahum!* to conceal a laugh. "Look, sweetie," she said to Myles. "The woman was wearing stiletto heels and swinging that pair of hooters like the ladies my youngest nephew used to call street sweepers. Of *course* she had an unsteady gait."

"You went over to greet her, then?"

"I went to the little girl's room. By the time I'd gotten out of there, the trouble'd started. I have to say, it was one of the worst sights I've ever had in front of me. And there wasn't a damn thing I

could do to help the poor woman." Quill squeezed her hand sympathetically. "But you, Quill, went over to the bar to say hi, right?"

"Yes. But she seemed perfectly fine to me. Normal. I'd only met
her once before."

"Do you recall anything unusual at all?" asked Andy.

"What was unusual was that either Hedrick or his sister was
there at all," said Meg. "I mean, good grief, their mother had been
brutally murdered the day before, and the two of them invite themselves to our party and show up ready to have a whee of a good
time. That's what I think is unusual. Did you talk to the Horrible
Hedrick? What did he say, Myles?"

"I didn't ask him why he had the gracelessness to attend a
party within a day of their mother's death. They're living in the
apartment over the newspaper offices, and they left there at about
six-fifty. It took them a few minutes to come up the drive. Hedrick
let Carlyle off at the entrance while he parked the car around back.
She didn't go through the foyer, apparently, but walked around the
side of the Inn and entered the patio through the gardens. Which is
odd. It's a longer route. We're checking to see if she met anyone on
her way in. And when she got to the bar, she said the champagne
was flat."

"It wasn't," said Quill indignantly.

"Which may have been the first indication that she was in
trouble."

"The symptoms of fugu poisoning are a diminution in the sense
of taste, numb lips, convulsions, paralysis, followed by death," said
Andy. "Eyewitness accounts, including yours, Quill, and Myles
himself, indicate that she may have been wiped with the poison on
her way into the Inn. It's possible that she was exposed to it earlier,
but Hedrick claims the two of them spent an hour getting ready
for the party—and I know that the interval between exposure and
symptoms would have been less than that, even with the poison
absorbed through the skin of the breast initially."

"Who could have access to such a thing?" asked Georgia. "I
mean, the obvious choice is the Sakuras. It's a Japanese poison that
comes from Japan."

Myles grunted.

"But then the question is why? They hadn't met her before, had they?"

"I don't know that geography is as important as knowledge of the drug itself," said Myles. "Although it's certainly relevant. The fish is available in certain stores in San Francisco, Los Angeles, and, of course, overseas."

"So you're looking for a sophisticated world traveler," said Georgia. "All of the Kiplings are well-traveled. Including me."

"Marco DeMarco had just come back from San Francisco," said Quill. "He told me so himself."

"And poor old Axminster Stoker toured the country a lot before he settled down with us," said Meg. "I know 'Frisco and L.A. were on his itinerary."

"So we're no closer to a solution," said Quill, frustrated. "I still vote for Hedrick. Georgia, did your lawyers find out what happened to all that money Louisa was supposed to have? I mean, he's the likeliest suspect here."

"Your lawyers?" asked Myles politely. "I take it you all have been pursuing inquiries on your own?"

"Sort of," said Meg.

"In a way," said Georgia.

"Nothing major," said Quill.

Myles looked stern.

"Jeez." Meg ran her hands through her hair and left it sticking up in spikes over her ears. "Let me get you guys some fugu-free coffee."

"Decaf for you, kiddo," Andy ordered. Meg nodded meekly.

Quill met Georgia's large brown eyes. "Yes, *sir*, doctor sir!" Georgia muttered.

"What?" said Meg.

"Nothing," said Quill. "We're just amazed to see you in love . . ."

". . . in thrall," Georgia contributed.

". . . to the doc, that's all."

"Shut up," said Meg amiably, bringing down two fresh cups from the sideboard, and hesitating over the dessert plates. "You guys want tarts? There's more than enough for everyone. I'm going to have another."

Andy raised his eyebrows and patted his flat stomach. Meg

looked dubiously at her own slim middle, then left the dessert plates on the shelf.

"*Oof! Hah!*" trumpeted Georgia, suddenly, striking the wine-glass with a fork. "*Oog Hah! (clink)*"

"What the heck, Gee?" Meg, caught between a scowl and a laugh, sat next to Andy and grabbed his hand.

"Thaaat's the sound of the meeen, working on the ch-a-a-ain, gay-ang-ang!" sang Georgia, in a surprisingly lovely (and loud) alto. "That's the so-oo-u-nd of the me-en working on the chain. Gang."

"Jeez! Is that supposed to be some sort of political comment?"

"Not *some* sort. A *direct* sort, honey. You want to eat, eat."

Meg grabbed a fork and speared a tart from the plate. "There. Solidarity forever."

"Yes!" Georgia shot her fist in the air.

"About those lawyers, Mrs. Hardwicke," said Myles, a hint of impatience in his voice.

"My Gawd, look at the time! It's bed for me." Georgia winked at Quill. "Coward that I am, I don't want to stick around and be interrogated by your sheriff. You tell him. That's the way Nero Wolfe works, isn't it? He had Archie cooperate with Lieutenant Cramer. She'll cooperate." She pinched Myles's cheek and trundled out of the dining room, swaying like a two-wheeled cart with a heavy load.

"Me, too," said Meg. Andy got up and held her chair. She looked up at him with a smile that sent a pang through Quill. "See you at breakfast, sis."

After they left, the silence in the dining room was profound.

"Andy and Meg seem to be getting along."

"Yes." Quill folded her napkin into a neat triangle. "What do you think of Georgia?"

He smiled.

"Myles, I want to apologize for last night."

"I owe you an apology for losing my temper."

"You had reason, I suppose." Quill's throat was full. Cautiously, as if she were very careful about it, he wouldn't see, she unfolded the napkin and pressed it under each eye in turn.

"I've been thinking. What would you say if we gave us another

year or so. Let things go on the way they were before I became"—
he stopped, searching for the right word—"insistent."

"Do you mean it?"

"I mean it."

"The, um, business of children? That's important to you."

"You're important to me."

Quill bit her lips hard and concentrated on the pile of crumbs
Georgia had left beside her plate, pushing them into a pyramid
with her finger. "Okay," she said finally.

"Okay."

Neither of them spoke for a moment.

"I had to go to Ithaca today to pick up the results on the autopsy.
I stopped at the art store. Here. I brought you this." He reached
into the breast pocket of his sports coat and brought out a camel's
hair artist brush with an ebony handle. It was an elegant one that
Quill had longed for, and never had the heart to purchase. "You
told me it'd be a waste, not to use a brush like that."

"Oh, yes. It would." She took it. The curve in the center fit between
her thumb and forefinger with a feeling of much-loved music.

"I talked to Ken Sakura today." Quill stared at him. Myles,
who'd never, in all the time she'd known him, failed to meet her
look directly, lowered his eyes. "He teaches at Cornell. He agreed
to see if he could bypass some paperwork and let me audit a couple
of classes."

"Art appreciation?" she said, astounded. "But, Myles, you need
to take all kinds of courses before you get to art appreciation."

"Art history, first. I told him I wanted to understand how you fit
in the mainstream of current painters. He started to tell me . . ."

"He did? What'd he say?"

". . . and I stopped him. I wanted to discover that myself. And
I want to understand. So that the next time you use this"—he
touched the ebony-handled brush gently—"I could say 'yes' or 'no'
instead of—what was the jargon term I used before? You know,
that specialized, in-the-know artists and critics-only language that
you artists use?"

"Nice?"

"Nice. That was it. Nice. I swear to you, Quill, I will never again
tell you that a piece of work you've done is nice."

"Oh, Myles." Quill shook her head. "That's so nice of you, Myles. It's so *nice!*"

"Idiot," said Myles. "Let's go to bed."

Quill woke to the sunlight crossing her muslin sheets, and the sound of Myles whistling in the shower. She stretched. The bedside clock said eight-thirty. The paintbrush lay on the nightstand, sunlight catching the swell of the ebony handle. She sat up and took it in her hand. She swung out of bed and walked barefoot to the French doors overlooking the herb garden.

Could she do all three? Art? The Inn? Myles and a family?

She closed her eyes, and the Inn rose before her mind's eye in all its sprawling, untidy, hodgepodge glory. Quill had a set of photographs taken in the days when the Inn had been a way station on the Underground Railroad. Even in faded brown and white, the copper roof, dark shingles, and fieldstone patios were impressive among the rich gardens. They would be that way for another three hundred years. And the guests would continue to come, like Georgia Hardwicke, who'd cheerfully abandoned the Kiplings, for weeks at a time, and even, Quill thought, like Axminster Stoker, who like English gentlemen of the past century, had taken rooms and lived in hotels for the rest of their lives.

The Inn had healed Meg, at a time when Quill thought her sister would never recover from the grief. And Quill had found a refuge, too, at a time when her art, quick to bloom, had become repetitive and stale.

She felt, rather than heard, Myles come across the carpet.

"Are you contemplating the greatness of your work?" His voice was teasing.

"More like Ozymandias," said Quill ruefully. "It's all changing, Myles, isn't it? Meg's recovered from Colin's death, and in love again. That's part of what you're willing to wait for, isn't it? She'll marry Andy, and things will change for me."

"I'm sure there's an appropriate quote about how the more things change the more they remain the same, but I can't think of it."

"You've never thought about giving up police work and maybe becoming an Innkeeper?" Even as she said it, she knew it was wrong. She turned to face him. "Wash that from your mind. Erase it. We're equal."

"But separate." He stood several feet away and made no move to touch her. "Would you want me to paint?"

"Of course I would!"

"Think about it, Quill. Would you want me to paint? Can any relationship stand the world judging the two of us on exactly the same ground?"

"It's not a competition, Myles."

"*Competition* is the wrong word. It's a matter of the part of your gut that's you. Not me. Not someone else. You."

A breeze stirred the muslin drapes at the window. She heard the familiar slide-stump that meant Doreen was hauling the paper cans out to the burn shed. A scent of crushed thyme came to her.

"I faithfully promise to shoot you, if you ever decide to paint. Now, Myles, about this investigation. Oh, my lord." She clapped her hand over her mouth. "That's why! All these years! You haven't wanted me to help! I never realized."

"Jesus Christ, Quill. The reason I don't want you involved is because it's usually dangerous, and I don't want my attention diverted from solving a problem. The other reason I don't want you involved is because you might inadvertently withhold evidence . . ."

Quill, with a guilty start, recalled the copy of the goods book in the office safe.

". . . or worse yet, destroy it. No, dear heart, I am not worried about you supplanting me as sheriff."

He meant it. "Why?" asked Quill. "Is it because I'm a lousy detective?"

"Nope. Actually, between the two of you, you and your sister aren't bad. Dave's a good deputy, but he doesn't have anywhere near your intuition about people, or your intelligence, for that matter. All good investigation relies on teamwork. I don't want you involved, Quill, because you don't have any training, and I don't want you hurt."

"I can take care of myself. And I could learn. Will you teach me, then?"

"Within the limits allowed by law, I might. And if you promise to stay away from the rough stuff, absolutely."

"Myles, you're a fogey. You're forty-six years old and the sexiest man I've ever met, but you're a fogey."

"Right. Now." He sat down on the bed and began to pull on his socks. His chest was tanned, and the muscles rippled under the dark skin. "First rule is turn it over."

"Turn what over?"

"Whatever it is that you've got. Georgia found out something, didn't she? I want to hear it. And if there's anything else, I want that, too."

Quill went to her bureau drawer and pulled out the goods book.

"We found it yesterday morning."

He thumbed through it and set it aside.

"You aren't angry?"

"Next."

"Myles, there are all kinds of clues in there—"

"Hedrick Conway didn't do it. What else have you got?"

"Hedrick is the best suspect we've got!" Quill summarized the results of Georgia's inquiries, ending with Georgia's discovery of the death of Hedrick's stepfather.

"The Conway case? Can't say as it rings any sort of bell at all." Myles stood up to put his trousers on. Quill watched him with what she recognized as doting admiration. "I can check with a few of the guys I know in Florida. She's sure there was an indictment? A trial? Does Hedrick have a record? Damn. I'm slipping. I should have checked it myself."

"She didn't say there was a trial, no. Myles, do you think it's Hedrick? It has to be Hedrick. He's positively inhuman about the deaths of his family. I mean, he hasn't said a word!"

"There could be a very good reason for that. And you may have given it to me just now. No, I don't think Hedrick killed his mother and his sister. But the business about his stepfather is a loose end. And I'll tie it up today."

"But Hedrick must be the only one with a motive. And what happened to all that money! Maybe there wasn't any money. Nothing else makes any sense, does it? I mean, the scandal behind the mini-mall turns out to be that a significant competitor is going up a few miles away. Although I don't know for sure, it's pretty obvious that Elmer, Howie, and Harvey Bozzel have all invested money in it . . . although where Harvey gets that kind of money is anybody's guess."

"Say that again?"

"The fact that a new mall is going up isn't a motive for murder. It's maybe a motive for Elmer not getting reelected if people find out he—"

"No. About Harvey."

"Well, where would Harvey get the money to invest in the new mall? He didn't have enough to buy shares in our mall, remember?"

"Damn. I'm losing my grip." He buckled his belt thoughtfully, then grinned. "It's your fault, Quill. I should have picked that up, too."

"Were you very depressed after we broke up?" she asked shyly.

"Guess so."

"Meg said I was horrible. Doreen said I was horrible. Oh, Myles. I've been such a jerk! Look at me! I never cry! And here I am, a leaky faucet."

"Ssh. Quiet." He came over. Held her. Kissed the top of her head. "It's over. The tough part. We'll just have to be careful from now on. Now, is there anything else?"

Quill, who was beginning to think she should decide to carry a handkerchief as a permanent accessory, rubbed her face on the sheet. "Just a few more things. You know that the reason Marco DeMarco has been so secretive is that his work crews are all ex-convicts."

"Yep. Next."

"You knew that?"

"I've known it for a while. Had a talk with DeMarco soon after he started the project."

"And you never told me!"

"I would have, except for a couple of things. First, you would have been down at the site feeding them soup and making sure that nobody was discriminating against their rights."

"Myles!"

"Second, I didn't want anyone in town deciding that the usual crimes and misdemeanors in a place like the Falls were the fault of

DeMarco's work crew. I've got the records of all the men he's had working for him, and I've kept an eye out."

"I wouldn't have said a word."

"Your behavior would have said a lot. And finally, dear heart, for the past four months we haven't exactly been communicating."

"Oh. That's true." She bit her finger. "So if it isn't Hedrick, and it isn't anyone in town because all the secrets about the mini-mall seem to be secrets that no one would murder for, then who is it? I'm still betting on Hedrick. Unless, Myles, is it someone on the construction crew? With a grudge against the Conways?"

"It's possible."

"Who *is* your chief suspect, then!?"

"There are five people I want to keep my eye on in particular. Paulovich, Fairbanks, Motoyama, and DeMarco. I'd like you to talk to your employees and see if any one of those men was seen walking with Carlyle Conway the night of the murder. Be discreet. Be quiet. But be complete."

"That's four names you gave me. Who's the fifth?"

"Axminster Stoker."

"Axminster Stoker?! The man couldn't hurt a fly. If anything, he's in danger of being knocked off himself, by Doreen. I can't believe he killed two people he's never even met!"

"How do you know he's never met them? And why do you think he's incapable of murder? Where does your opinion come from? It's based on what evidence? That you like him? That you find him inoffensive? Do I need to tell you that some of our worst murderers have been quiet, inoffensive people who the neighbors say could never have hurt a fly?"

"No. No. You're right. I'm sorry. Just the facts, ma'am, all right? So I'll include Mr. Stoker. You want me to question them?"

"No, dammit. I don't want you confronting a potential killer. I want you to talk to the staff. See who could have bumped into Carlyle, literally, since Andy's sure that someone put on a surgical glove and wiped the poison between her breasts a few minutes before she tried the trick with the sushi."

"Why do you suspect these five?"

"Stoker worked for the pharmaceutical company that Conway's fortune came from."

"He didn't!"

"It's how he found out about the Inn. You're attached to the Golden Pillars Travel Company, right? And they offer packaged tours to corporations; yours is one of them. When Stoker decided to retire, he very efficiently went through the list of vacation spots the company offered its employees. He's an efficient man."

"He never indicated in any way that he'd met any of the Conways before!"

"I doubt that he knew the Conway women, or Hedrick himself. The company's huge, and people like Stoker never met the principal stockholders. But it's a lead, and we've got damn few leads at this point."

"And DeMarco?"

Myles wandered into her kitchen and began to make coffee. "Now, there's a guy who might knock a couple of people off as a warning to Hedrick not to print something about the mall. That's a strong possibility. And I don't want you going near him, understand?"

"I'm far readier to believe that DeMarco is involved than Axminster."

Myles flipped the coffeemaker on. "I can't argue with that. But the second rule about an investigation, Quill, is to follow every lead. Sometimes the trail starts with the tip of a fingernail. As a matter of fact, there was a murder solved years ago that began with the tip of a finger, literally."

"Ugh! So DeMarco's a strong contender."

"The strongest to date."

"And Mr. Paulovich?"

"Mr. Paulovich knows something he's not telling me. It's no more than that. There could be a number of reasons for it. But I don't like it. He's lying about it, whatever it is, and until I find out, he's on the list."

"What about Lyle Fairbanks?"

Myles removed the coffeepot from the hot plate, and stuck his cup under the filter before the pot was full. "Do you want some of this?"

"I'll wait a bit, thanks. Lyle Fairbanks?"

"He's not a suspect as much as he is a potential source. And unlike those others you can talk to him directly. Just be discreet and unobvious. I want a list of where the Kiplings have been in the last three years, and the dates when each of the members joined. We'll cross-match that with similar information from Hedrick, and from DeMarco. See if I can come up with some idea of when their paths crossed." He gulped the coffee. "That's it."

"Mr. Motoyama?"

"I'll handle him."

"But I could talk to Ken."

"Exactly." He smiled. "Even my tolerance has its limits. Quill. I want you to call me as soon as you get anything. And listen, you're to keep this to yourself, understand? It's important. Do you promise?"

"I promise. But, Myles—"

"I've got to go." He kissed her. "Dinner tonight?"

"Yes. Wait. Myles. Will the kitchen be open?"

"Up to Andy. He's in charge of forensics. I'm through with it."

"If it's open, I'll meet you at the usual time. I'll be busy."

"Ten-thirty, then, unless I hear from you." The door closed behind him.

Quill went downstairs to find that the kitchen was open and the dining room empty, and Meg crossly banging her copper pots with a wooden ladle.

"What's wrong?"

"They moved all my *stuff*! Poking around in here!" She slammed the Cuisinart to one side of the butcher block counter and glowered. "And we're open tonight and two of the *sous*-chefs called in with bogus excuses, and nobody who's supposed to be here for the morning shift has shown up, so I'm going to be short-staffed on top of everything else! *Go away!*"

"Don't you want to hear about Myles?"

"Any fool could have predicted that last night," said Meg loftily.

"Myles doesn't think Hedrick did it."

"So?"

"So he's not upset about the goods book. As a matter of fact"— Quill pulled at her lower lip—"he didn't seem to think much of my investigative efforts at all. He assigned me to the sort of thing he'd assign a junior investigator."

"Go investigate where my underchefs are, will you? I can't cook tonight without them."

"I'm sure they'll turn up."

"If you're so sure, then *find them!*"

"You got it, sis," said Quill with a fair imitation of Humphrey Bogart. She went through the swinging doors into the dining room, and from there to the foyer. It was going to be a good day. She could feel it. Meg in that kind of mood always cooked superbly. People were starting to arrive for the opening of the mini-mall. They'd eat at the Inn. Meg's legendary fame would spread. She had some really interesting detective work to do. And Myles . . . Quill smiled to herself. There was Myles. Who was going to be very surprised at the quality of her investigation. She crossed into the foyer and saw that the Chinese vases either side of the mahogany desk were filled with giant dahlias. Quill felt the impulse to dance across the floor. Dina was sitting behind the reception desk, winding up a phone conversation. Quill waited until she'd hung up the receiver.

"Finally, Quill! Things are getting back to normal! We've got a third of the dining room filled already for lunch, and six reservations for dinner! And it's not even nine-thirty." Dina's face was flushed, and she picked nervously at the phone cord.

"Any messages?"

"Lots. John called in from the site. The kitchen came. He's going to be there all day making sure it gets in right. He took his PC with him, so I think he said to tell you he'll have the quarterly numbers by this afternoon. And he wants to know about Mr. Sakura."

"What about Mr. Sakura?"

"He said, 'Offer?'" Dina wound the phone cord around her wrist, pulled the phone off the receiver, and said, "Gosh! Sorry!"

Quill paged through the pink slips. "What's this next message?"

"It's from Mr. Stoker."

"I see that. It says 'will deliver results from A.M. employee meeting, one o'clock.' What's that all about?"

Dina shrugged and began erasing an entry into the bookings ledger with careful strokes. Then she rewrote it.

"Dina? What's going on?"

"Maybe you should find Mr. Stoker and ask him."

"Well, I needed to see him anyway. I'll just get my notepad and go find him. Where is he?"

Dina had emptied the contents of her purse on the desk and was intent on sorting through the various gum wrappers, blushers, lipsticks, and Cornell Student Parking stubs that littered the top. "Huh?"

"I said, do you know where he is?"

"Yeah."

"Well?"

"Oh. You want me to tell you where he is? He's in the gazebo. With . . ." she trailed off in a mutter.

"With whom?"

Dina opened her checkbook, looked at it, and sighed.

"Dina!"

"Yes'm? Gee, I'm not sure who he's with. Anything else?"

"Meg said that some of the staff haven't shown up for work. Would you check the roster and make a few calls?"

"Some of them may be at the gazebo," Dina said with an air of sudden enlightenment.

"They're where?"

"They're at the gazebo. With Mr. Stoker. Everybody but me. I told them," said Dina, "that I would never betray you. Never. Besides. I didn't invest in the mall anyhow."

A suspicion of trouble sped across Quill's mind. "Oh, my goodness." She swallowed, then said again, "Oh, my goodness."

"Actually, I think you'd better get out there," Dina said pointedly, now that the secret was out.

Of course. The news of the discount mall would have spread like wildfire. And everybody in the Inn had cheerfully signed for weekly payroll deductions to make up the amount that she and John had invested in the mini-mall on their behalf. Quill had a cowardly desire to hide in her office.

"Are they, um, expecting me at this meeting? Dina?"

"They didn't say."

"I'm not expected at any other meetings right now, am I?" said Quill with hope.

Dina shook her head. "Nope."

"You think I should go out there."

"Yep."

"And John's where?"

Dina picked up the pink message slip Quill's nervous fingers had let drop on the desktop. "'At the site. Kitchen came. Here all day. Took PC.'"

"The rat," muttered Quill. "The big rat. I would have been happy to go out to the site and supervise the kitchen install. I'm good at that."

"He didn't know about. . . . that before he left." Dina waved vaguely in the direction of the gazebo. A distant sound of applause— and a few belligerent "Right ons!"—drifted through the open door.

"Well, okay," said Quill.

She walked through the lounge and stopped at the doors leading to the patio. She had a very good view of the gazebo from here. To the left lay the rose garden, the fountain in the middle of the koi pond sending glittering drops into the sunny air. To the right was the curve of the Inn itself, and beyond that, the path over the bridge to the village. In the center, of course, were what looked like the Inn's entire staff (dressed, Quill noted with burgeoning hope, in dining room and kitchen kit). Doreen stood conspicuously apart. She was carrying a sign that read THROW THE BUM OUT! which Quill surmised referred to Mr. Stoker, although given Doreen's attitude toward Quill the past few weeks, she wasn't entirely sure.

Axminster Stoker stood in the middle of the gazebo, which gave him a two-foot advantage over the heads of the crowd. Quill stretched on tiptoe. Seated behind Axminster in the latticed recesses were Mr. Sakura and his faithful shadow, Motoyama.

Quill cracked the glass doors open and peeked around the corner.

"Empowerment saves jobs!" Axminster's voice had astonishing carrying power. "It is your right to be in on decisions which affect your future!"

Doreen raised her sign, blew a gigantic raspberry, and shouted, *"Three cheers for the boss!"*

Quill breathed a small sigh of relief.

"What's going on?" Georgia's voice was amused.

"Are you all right?" asked Meg. "We heard all this hoo-ha through the open window. What is it?"

"An employee meeting."

"I can see that, stupid. They look mad."

"They do."

"About what?"

"The discount mall, I should imagine. Their investment." "They care about money? Now!? With the kitchen just reopened? How long is this meeting going to take?"

"Well, you know what Axminster told us about empowering the employees, Meg, these things take time. Problem resolution can take weeks. Months."

"Bullshit. They want a solution? I'll give them a solution."

"Remember our values statement, Meg. Concern. Caring. Commitment."

"Try Cooking, Cleaning, and Doing Your Damn Job!"

"Well, heck," Quill said to Georgia and crossed the flagstone patio behind Meg, with (she hoped) firm and unfaltering steps.

"It's just Stoke," Georgia said comfortingly. "Doing his thing."

"Hey!" Meg marched up to the edge of the crowd and elbowed her way purposefully through. "Bjorn. Frank. What the heck are you guys doing here? You called in sick!"

"We're not sick, exactly," Frank said. "We just got notice of this meeting, and thought maybe we should be here."

"It is the employee's right to strike!" said Axminster excitedly. "When deceived and burdened by the unfair practices of management, it is the employee's right—no, I should say the employee's *duty* to establish direct and unambiguous lines of communication."

"*Boo sucks to you?!*" yelled Doreen.

"Boo what to whom?" Meg said. "Is everybody crazy? *Hey!*" she shouted suddenly. "Stoker!"

"And here is management now!" Axminster beamed. "Come, I would wager, ready to sit down and discuss this issue with the goodwill and trust that characterize the finest Quality leadership in the finest companies. Remember, team. Concern! Caring! Commitment!"

Meg, taking care to avoid the sweet peas, marched into the gazebo, elbowed Axminster out of the way, and leaned out to address the troops.

"You! Bjorn. Frank. We've got dinners to cook tonight. Get back in the kitchen."

"But, Meg," said Kathleen, her hands twisting nervously in her apron. "About the mini-mall investment—"

"Who wants out?"

Several of the employees raised their hands.

"See Quill. She'll give you your money back. Anything else?"

"Margaret! We are trying to establish a dialogue here. This is simply not demonstrating proper concern for the integrity of the employees."

"Anybody else want out?"

Doreen, scowling ferociously, waved her sign (to the imminent danger of two waiters nearby) and hollered, "I'm keepin' mine in it. I tolt you bozos not to listen to this sorry sack of horse poop!"

"Well?" Meg demanded of the crowd.

Most of the employees shook their heads.

"Anytime anybody wants out, see Quill. Or John. Anybody else want to say anything?"

There was a general murmur which indicted a negative.

"Good." Meg turned to Axminster. "Solution presented. Meeting's over. That's it, guys, back to work." She gave Axminster a shove which was not quite a blow. "You can go give Doreen a hand with the rooms, since you've thrown the cleaning schedule totally out of whack with this stuff. Doreen? You have an extra vacuum cleaner?"

"I got scrub brushes and filthy terlits."

"My goodness," said Axminster in great distress. "Of course, I am ready to put my hand to any task in the pursuit of productivity, but. . . . Sakura-san, I appeal to you. Please. Tell her what she has done."

Mr. Sakura rose solemnly from his bench, put his hands together, and bowed to Meg. "Vely good work. Vely. Quick!" He snapped his fingers. He turned to Axminster. "You watch. She is good. Vely good. *Arigatoo gozaimashita*, Stoker-san. It has been vely interesting. Vely. Mis Quiriam is vely good to suggest crean *obenjo, nei*? You help that one." He chuckled genially, but the way he jerked his head toward Doreen was not genial at all. "Teamwerrrk! *Hai!*"

Axminster clicked his heels together and stood at parade rest. Quill resisted the impulse to pat him sympathetically.

Mr. Sakura clapped Meg on the back. "Many. Times. I. Have. Fert the same." He bowed. Meg bowed back. "As you Amerr-icans say, *Sayonara* for now. Motoyama!" He snapped his fingers, and the two followed the dispersing crowd of employees into the Inn.

Doreen poked Axminster in the back with the sign. "Take this, you, and follow me."

Axminster turned just before he and Doreen disappeared around the corner on their way to the utility shed. "May we discuss this further on?"

"Of course," Quill called. "Any time."

"More meetings?" said Meg.

Georgia's laugh rolled across the lawn.

"Actually, it should work out well. I have a little job from Myles, which I swore I wouldn't tell either of you about, or I would, and more meetings will give me a great excuse to talk to each of the employees individually."

"To find out if anyone saw who gave Carlyle the poisoned finger?"

"Well, yes. But please don't tell anyone else, Meg, or you either, Gee. I'm sort of on assignment."

"I've got an assignment. I'd take it on myself if I weren't going to be so busy with the new restaurant." Meg looked at Quill, her brow furrowed. "Why was Axminster so quick to do what Mr. Sakura told him to do?"

"I don't know. Does it matter? He worships the ground the man walks on obviously, because of his Key Operating thingy, I suppose."

"That doesn't make sense. Would you go clean toilets if Picasso told you to?"

"Never mind that he's dead, why in the world would Picasso ask me to clean toilets?"

"That's it exactly, isn't it? Come on, Georgia, I'll get you some breakfast."

CHAPTER 13

Quill had several hours before she was due to visit the construction site with Georgia and sit in on the Society for the Advancement of Jell-O Architecture committee meeting. She used them to interview employees one at a time in her office. She kept scrupulous notes (guiltily aware that she really ought to pay as much attention to her note-taking responsibilities for the Chamber) and, a short time before Georgia was to pick her up, leaned back and looked at the result of her efforts in bewilderment.

Every suspect had passed that corner of the Inn at or around seven o'clock.

The *sous*-chefs had been in the kitchen and hadn't noticed a thing, although several of them volunteered—strictly in the spirit of empowerment and team efforts to improve productivity—that if Meg could be persuaded to let them take coffee breaks outside at suitable intervals, they would be able to watch the corner of the Inn with a great deal of attention. Quill, doubtful that Meg's Simon Legree style in the kitchen could be modified enough to accommodate these modest demands, said that she'd see what she could do. Meg was prone to utter a maxim about art and sweat which—although she stoutly maintained it was a favorite saying of the French composer Claude Marie de Courcy's—Quill knew very well she'd made up.

The waiters and waitresses, whose schedules fell under John's purview, were much more helpful. Peter Hairston, strolling in the front garden for a ten-minute break just after six-thirty, had seen Mr. Sakura and the faithful Motoyama come from around the back of the Inn to the front, presumably to reenter the Inn through the front door, although he wasn't sure. Marco DeMarco, in desultory conversation with Axminster Stoker, had been smoking a cigarette in the drive. Kathleen, whose break followed on the heels of Peter's, had seen the Kiplings in full Victorian dress, sweeping through the rose garden in the direction of the corner of the Inn where Carlyle and Hedrick were to follow some moments later. It was, Kathleen thought, about five minutes to seven, and all of the Kiplings were together: Mr. and Mrs. Fairbanks, Jerzey Paulovich, Miss Kent, and Mrs. Hardwicke.

The times were wrong. Quill stuck her pencil in her hair. The Kiplings were at the party by seven; she'd confirmed that by her own watch. But Hedrick and Carlyle had arrived some five minutes later, again confirmed by her own watch. She looked at her watch and checked the accuracy against the clock on her office wall. They were within a minute of each other. Mr. Sakura and Motoyama had come through the lounge and out into the patio at about the same time Carlyle and Hedrick arrived on the the lawn side. And Axminster and DeMarco had come in separately, DeMarco from the lounge, Axminster from the other side of the gazebo, which meant he must have walked through the perennial gardens and past the kitchen, the long way round.

Why would he take the long way round?

Where had Hedrick and Carlyle been for that extra five minutes? None of the staff could account for the missing time. No one had actually seen Carlyle encounter any one of the other guests, except in the patio itself.

"You ready?"

Quill jerked upright with a start. "Georgia! Is it time already?"

"Just about. It's about ten minutes to the site, isn't it? It was roughly that in the van, at least, when we went down on the day Mrs. Conway was thrown in the river, poor soul."

Quill gathered her car keys, purse, hairbrush, and notepad. She ducked and peered into the small mirror hanging on the wall near her office door. "Do I look okay? My hair frizzes up like thistles in this heat."

"That's not a perm? Gawd! What I wouldn't do to have naturally curly hair. So, other than employee revolutions, how's the morning going? I saw Myles leave rather early this morning."

Quill smiled.

"Oh, Quill," said Georgia.

"What?"

"Just. That look. I'm glad for you, sweetie."

"Well, hang on to the feeling. You're about to meet Adela Henry, first lady of Hemlock Falls." On their way out to the parking lot, Quill gave an animated description of Mrs. Henry's social career, which bore a close resemblance to Sherman's.

"As in General Sherman, the fella that marched from Atlanta to the sea?" Georgia's round face was red with laughter. "I can't wait."

"At least the Jell-O mania isn't as tacky as the Little Miss Hemlock Falls Beauty Contest, Gee. Remind me to tell you about that some time."

They walked to Quill's Olds in a companionable silence, Quill accommodating her steps to Georgia's slower ones. She waited until Georgia had eased herself into the passenger side of the car, then, as she pulled out onto the road that led to Route 15, asked her if she'd run into Carlyle and Hedrick the night of the murder.

"We all did. Not literally, of course, but we saw them come in. Lila Fairbanks likes us all to arrive at the same time whenever we give a performance. Makes a more impressive effect, although she'd never in this world admit it. So, wherever we go, we're accustomed to being ready a little before we actually need too. We wait until the crowd's panting with anticipation and come in together."

"You did have a splendid entrance at the party," said Quill. "I'm so sorry we didn't get to hear the performance."

"You just might yet, if you don't manage to avoid Lyle for the next couple of days. He didn't think it was suitable to request a second chance until a day or two had passed, but I met them this morning at breakfast, and some wistful little hints were dropped."

"Gosh," said Quill vaguely. "Anytime. Although we're going to be pretty busy with the opening-day ceremonies tomorrow, and the Society's just due to stay until the end of the week. Maybe next time?"

Georgia, who was wearing flamboyant rhinestone sunglasses, dropped them lower on her nose and rolled her eyes sternly over the tops. "Confess. You don't want to hear the Master's poetry condensed into an hour-long performance?"

"Georgia, I . . . well. No. No, I don't. Anyone who can write something as smarmy and sententious as *If*."

"'If you can keep your head when all about you are losing theirs,'" Georgia intoned.

"Then you haven't seen the fire, and everybody else has already found the exit," Quill said somewhat tartly. "Has everyone been together a long time? The Kipling Society, I mean?"

Georgia shot her a shrewd glance. "Still detecting? You can apply the rubber hose yourself, if you want to. They're visiting the site today, with Mr. Sakura, who, it appears, is eager to join our little band. If I do decide to move to Hemlock Falls, he'll take my place in the group. Anyway, they talked Meg into making them a picnic lunch to take to the site today. They love that little woods next to the mall. It's a rehearsal, technically, and I should be there, but," she added complacently, "I have this Ladies meeting instead. Which suits me just fine. At least it'll be out of the sun."

"Is there a limit to the number of members?"

"Oh, no. But a certain degree of consanguinity is required to make a happy little team. The common denominator is probably money. To get to your question—you are a tenacious woman, in your own way, Quill—I've known Lyle and Lila for years. Lyle was a great friend of Doug's and mine. And Kipling's been a favorite of Lyle's forever. So, after Doug died. . . ." She fell silent. The round, cheerful face flushed. Her voice was sad. "It was so hard. I still miss him. Every day. Every day. Anyway, Lyle'd retired and pulled this crazy bunch of people together and I just decided to join them, for the travel and the companionship, mostly. It's been fun."

"So Lyle's the founding member. What about Miss Kent?"

"Aurora? Golly, let's see. She's Worthington Mill money, you know, out of Vermont. I think she met Lyle and Lila on a cruise to St. Thomas three or four years ago. That must have been around the time that Jerzey joined, or maybe it was a little later. He's a heck of a bridge player, by the way."

"Jerzey has money, too?"

"I expect so. I told you we were all loaded."

"Where'd the Fairbanks money come from?"

Georgia burst out laughing. "With that accent? You have to ask? Oil, honey, oil."

"Was Doug in oil, too? Is that how the four of you were friends?"

Quill got the look over the sunglasses again. "I've been meaning to ask you. That dishy sheriff?"

"Myles?"

"You come to an understanding, as they say?"

"Sort of."

"Well, I'm glad. But you tell him from me that Doug and Lyle met over a yearling filly at Saratoga Race Week some years back, bid against each other on the horse. I don't remember who actually ended up buying her—it might have been us—but one of 'em lost I don't know how many thousands on the damn thing, and they went out together on a three-day toot and were fast friends ever since. Men." Georgia shook her head. "Can't live with 'em, can't live without them."

"When did the trip to Tokyo happen?" Quill, chafing under Myles's stricture not to tell anyone that she was investigating, was finding it difficult to keep up the appearance of aimless chatter. Georgia's eyes were too shrewd.

"Japan was actually a business trip for Lyle. I hadn't joined them yet. Isn't that your turn here? Quill, that's a darn pretty mall, if I do say so myself."

"Well, why wouldn't you?" asked Quill affectionately. "It is nice, isn't it? Although, if we accept Mr. Sakura's offer to buy it, I won't feel quite the same about it as I do now."

"If the parking lot's empty for months on end because of that new mall down the road, you're not going to feel the same about it, either."

"The parking lot's not empty enough, now. Look. There's the Horrible Hedrick's Cadillac. And the Inn van, too. The Kiplings must be here already. It looks like the work crew's gone, though."

"Oh, my, look at the tent! I love this!"

They got out of the car. A huge gaily striped awning tent had been set up in the meadow south of the mall itself. The sod had been delivered that morning, and the scent of freshly turned dirt filled the air. The backhoe was parked near the septic tank, and the bull-dozers were gone.

The tent was red and white. A large banner draped across the front entrance shouted HEMLOCK FALLS VERY OWN! The Mall at the Falls!

"Why didn't the Ladies Society just use the atrium in the building for the exhibits?" asked Georgia.

"That was a battle," said Quill. "This is a small town, remember, and all our investors are from around here. The wives didn't want anyone messing up the stores with the food exhibits."

"Did you say food?"

"Oh, yes. We don't have a county fair in the Falls, although Esther West has been talking about starting one up, so the opening is being treated as sort of a dry run. We've got a baking competition, and jams and jellies, and, of course, the Jell-O Architecture Contest."

"Is there any food to eat?" asked Georgia. "I'm feeling a bit peckish, as a true Kiplingite might say."

"The restaurants will be serving tomorrow. Ours and of course the McDonald's. And I think the Agway will have a beer booth and hot dogs."

"But I'm hungry now!"

Quill chuckled. "I think there's a diner wagon for the work crew. Maybe it's still here. Shall we walk over and see if they're still open?"

"Are you hungry?"

"Well, no," Quill admitted.

"Then I'll go. You go in and tell the ladies I'll be with them shortly. You want anything?"

"Some iced tea, if they have it. I'll see you in a few minutes."

Quill walked to the tent, and into the meeting. The Falls's *cognoscenti* (Marge Schmidt and Betty Hall, mainly) were of the opinion that the Ladies Society for the Advancement of Jell-O Architecture was the saving of Mayor Henry's marriage, not to mention the Hemlock Falls political structure. Up until the creation of that body, Adela Henry, the mayor's wife of some thirty years and a masterful woman, had been known to meddle with varying degrees of success in village affairs. While no one would deny that Adela's

Vigilante Group (an organization dedicated to sweeping the lockers of the local high school for illicit substances, which had resulted in the confiscation of several dozen packets of No-Doz at exam time) or the Hemlock Anti-Alcohol League (which had circulated an unsuccessful temperance petition for the whole of Tompkins County) had roots in worthy enough values, everyone took mild exception to the high-handedness with which Adela enforced her views. She was a tall woman, with prematurely white hair tinted blue at the Hemlock Hall of Beauty once a month, and a piercing voice. Meg thought she would have made a great prime minister of some unsuspecting republic.

Quill waved to Adela as she entered the tent. Adela, dressed in a cotton print dress and a large straw hat, motioned her to the long table set in the center.

"What do you think?" she demanded without preamble. "You have an Eye, Quill. No one"—she swept the assembled members of the Society with a commanding glance—"no one would deny your Eye."

A long table was set squarely in the middle of the tent. Each of the displays was tastefully arranged on felt-covered pieces of cardboard.

"They're just the most *interesting* buildings I've ever seen." Quill walked around the table with her hands clasped behind her back. The buildings quivered as she walked. She stopped in front of a particularly teetery one. "Is this Eiffel Tower yours, Esther?"

"*Mais oui*," said Esther anxiously. "I had a bit of trouble with the top, as you see."

The edifice, made of either strawberry or cherry Jell-O, Quill wasn't sure which, had a peculiarly thick look to it.

"How did you get it to . . . to . . . tower?"

Esther darted a hesitant look at Adela. "Concrete," she said defiantly.

"You are supposed to be able to eat it," said Adela coldly. "We agreed."

"I'm going to," said Esther. "Concrete won't hurt you. I asked Dr. Bishop. Not quite what it should be for the digestion, but no harm will come to me, he said."

The sun, coming into the tent through plastic skylights in the tent top, struck blueberry, grape, orange, and lemon highlights from the tiny buildings.

"Now this is . . . is . . . most interesting," said Quill "It's obviously, um . . ."

"Mount Fujiyama," said Adela. "The coconut is the snow, of course."

"And the, um, fixative?"

"If you mean by that, what did I use to achieve the height, in a food that is essentially, well, essentially Jell-O, the answer is Rice Krispies. Which are highly edible."

Esther, with a great show of unconcern, took a teaspoon from the coffee tray and nibbled at the Eiffel Tower.

"We thought that perhaps you might consider the position of judge," said Adela, a hint of warmth creeping into the frostiness of her demeanor. "You are, I understand from that extremely attractive young Japanese man at the Inn, an Artist of the First Rank."

Quill who'd always been fascinated by Adela's ability to speak in capitals, murmured something deprecating. The thought of judging the contest struck her bones to, well, she thought, Jell-O.

"We have Artistic Standards," said Adela, correctly interpreting Quill's muttered demurral. "I had them printed up. By that excessively rude young man who took over Our Newspaper from Pete Rosen."

"He took some pictures," volunteered a young, timid matron whom Quill didn't know, but thought perhaps was a Peterson. "We'll be in the paper."

"We shall see," said Adela. "Monica. Perhaps you would provide Ms. Quilliam with the Rules and Regulations."

Quill accepted the sheet with the meekness that Adela seemed to engender in anyone who swept into her orbit.

"I see you've established one-hundred-point ratings, Adela. Twenty points for creativity in color. Twenty points for edibility. Twenty points for suitability. And the remainder for Aesthetic Appropriateness." Quill coughed. It didn't help. She coughed again.

"The judging will take place tomorrow, at the conclusion of the opening day ceremonies. The mayor"—Adela hadn't used Elmer's given name since the day he was elected—"will announce the winner after the speeches and the talent show. The other foods"—she indicated the jars of jellies, the baked goods exhibits, and the flower arrangements lined up on various tables around the tent—"will be announced first. Are you all right, my dear?"

"Just. Something. Caught. In my throat. 'Scuse me. Friend's bringing me some tea." Quill ducked out of the tent and into Georgia, who spilled the tea she was carrying onto her bare ankles.

"What!?" Georgia demanded.

Quill, who was laughing so hard she couldn't stand up straight, grabbed her arm. "Georgia. Georgia, as you love me. Judge that contest!"

"Who, me? I don't know a thing about Jell-O!"

"Who does? Take a look in there! Don't let them see you!"

Georgia peered cautiously around the opening.

"What do you see?"

"A bunch of nice middle-class ladies around a table full of Jell-O. What do you expect me to see?"

"My Fate!" said Quill dramatically. "Every woman in town who has anything to say about anything has entered that darn contest."

"So? Shut your eyes and give one of 'em a blue ribbon, one a red—"

"You don't understand! Do I give the blue ribbon to Esther? Who should at least get it for having the balls to eat concrete so that she can win . . ."

"Concrete!"

". . . and have Mrs. Mayor mad at me for the rest of my life? Do I give it to Miriam Doncaster, who's a dear dear friend and appears to have attempted a train wreck—unless it's L.A. after the quake. I'll be damned if I know which—and have Esther cut me dead in the street for the next three years? Help!"

"Oh, Gawd. I see what you mean. Here, drink what's left of your tea. You know what we should do?"

"No. What?" Quill drained the tea, which was warm.

"Run like hell."

"We can't run like hell."

"Sure we can."

"I have to check with John, to see how the boutique's coming."

"Then we'll run like hell in there."

"You know what?" said Quill. "I think that's the best idea I've heard all day."

John, with his usual air of unruffled calm, was installing the faucet in the kitchen sink when Quill and Georgia arrived breathless at the restaurant.

"Wow!" said Quill. "When I was in here yesterday the kitchen was bare walls and pipes."

"Took a couple of hours," said John. "No more than that. Everything dropped into place. DeMarco had the plumber here and ready to go, and the whole thing—wait a second . . ." He pulled the faucet handle up. There was a burp, a stutter in the pipes, and a gush of water. "Everything works."

"How come you had to install the faucet?"

"The crew was scheduled to quit at twelve noon, and twelve noon it was. The only worker left here is DeMarco himself, and he's setting the top of the septic system on right now. It was the penalties for overtime that did it. But they finished on time."

"Good old sympathetic you." Quill sighed happily. The kitchen was a stainless-steel, self-contained model that fitted tightly together like an elegant little puzzle. Meg would love it. "It's just beautiful. Is her cookware coming in soon?"

"Mike's going to bring it back in the van when he takes the Kiplings and Mr. Sakura home."

"Have you seen him? Have you thought more about the offer? Shall we take it?"

John's glance at Georgia was casual. He paused but said readily enough, "Yes. I do think so. It's a fair offer. It means that everyone will get his or her money back, with a very slight premium attached."

"How much?" asked Georgia. "Sorry, I don't mean to butt in, but I might be interested in doing something about all this myself, you know."

"In that case, let me show the numbers to you." John drew them to the table where his PC sat glowing. "Mr. Sakura has a lot of information about the costs involved. It makes me a little curious as to where he got the information, but that's neither here nor there for the moment. Besides, I can make a good guess."

"I've been wondering who gave Hedrick all that dirt for the goods book," said Quill. "Do you think it's the same person?"

John shook his head. "I don't know. Myles's guess is that the source for the gossip and the source for the information about the investment package are two different people, but he wouldn't tell me why. Now that I think I know who, I'm not certain Myles is right. Anyway, here's a list of the amounts listed by the name of each of the principals in Mall, Inc." He tapped the keyboard and a list of names and figures appeared on the screen. "Quill, Meg, and I put in three hundred thousand from savings, Georgia; we added fifty thousand as a pledge from employees, for which the Inn took out a banknote. Bottom line to get in was a quarter million.

"I input Mr. Sakura's offer this morning while the kitchen was getting set. It breaks down like this." He tapped. A second column of figures appeared to the right of the names. "And when you match the investor's original contribution against the Sakura offer, the payout's like this." His finger moved rapidly, the screen split, and the list of investors and their cash pledges was matched by a payout figure. "You notice anything?"

Georgia cast a practiced eye at the screen. "Howie Murchison's payout is twenty percent over his investment. Everybody else averages about the same. One percent."

"Right."

"Howie! Howie's been going behind everyone's back to talk to Mr. Sakura! I don't believe it!" Quill remembered, suddenly, Miriam's nervous shredding of the tissue at the Chamber meeting three days ago. "Howie!" she said again, the disbelief replaced by anger.

"Don't jump the gun here, Quill. That could be in lieu of a broker's fee—it's a tax issue I won't bore you with. And if, as I suspect, Howie knew about the competing mall a few months after we'd all committed to this, you have to hand it to him. I'll bet he looked for an investor to save not only himself, but the rest of the town."

"That answers another question," said Quill. "I wondered why Mr. Sakura knew about this before he showed up here." She sighed. "So you think we'd better take the offer."

"I do. If Mr. Sakura understands the situation here, he could've taken advantage by waiting a year until the other mall was completed, and then offering us all twenty cents on the dollar. He didn't. Bad business practice, I have to say."

"Bad business to give us our money back!"

"Oh, he's a good man. That's different." John grinned slightly. "The short form of the offer which Howie passed out yesterday provides for a sell-out of the equipment each of us put into the stores, and a one-year lease, which can be terminated after twelve months, with fifteen days' notice. That's a little rough."

"Maybe he won't want us to move," said Quill. "Maybe the mall will work despite the discount place down the road."

"Maybe. And maybe Mr. Sakura is thinking of building a golf course."

"A golf course? A *golf* course?!"

"Or a resort. Japanese investment in American real estate isn't just for big cities, Quill. This is an ideal spot for a resort. And to the Japanese, who are used to land prices ten to twenty times what we pay here, this looks like a pretty good deal. Mr. Sakura's grandchildren are here. His son's here. What better place for a former director of Sakura Industries to retire part-time?"

"Well. None, I suppose. But a golf course?"

"Could be a very good thing for the town. And for the Inn."

"Did I hear a new project?" Marco DeMarco appeared at the open door and walked in. He nodded to Georgia. "How do you do?"

Quill smiled at him. "This is Georgia Hardwicke, Mr. DeMarco."

"We met at the party the other night. You were wearing quite a dress."

Georgia laughed. Quill, remembering Georgia's geezer speech, had a sudden, happy inspiration. They were roughly the same age, and they even looked a little bit alike. Although Georgia's hair color owed more to a bottle than to nature, their coloring was close.

She darted a swift glance at DeMarco's ring finger. Bare. "Mr. DeMarco, everything looks just wonderful. And you finished on time!"

"In the nick of," he agreed. "Just stopped in to tell you I'll be locking up, and to take a last look around. I just buried the septic tank, and I want to flush a few toilets, see if they work. Otherwise, I'm finished for the day. I'll be back for the ceremonies, of course."

"When you've finished here"—Quill glanced at Georgia with a mischievous look—"why don't you stop by the Inn for dinner? We can celebrate the opening of the mall. And the fact that we seem to be going to sell it."

"Heard about that. Kind of sorry. It's a great little project. If I could take a raincheck on the dinner, I'd appreciate it. I'd like to get back to Syracuse tonight. I've got a bid to get in."

"Anything we should know about?" asked John.

DeMarco winked. "Big mall going up down the road, I hear. Ms. Quilliam? Mrs. Hardwicke? Be seeing you."

The sun was setting over the treetops when Quill and Georgia walked to the Olds to go home. The site was quiet, the awning tent empty. The grounds held an air of expectancy. The parking lot was empty except for Quill's Olds and Hedrick's Cadillac. Quill frowned at it. "Maybe we should tell Mr. DeMarco that Hedrick is still around. Skulking in the bushes with his little goods book, I should think."

"I'm sure DeMarco will flush him out. You look happy," Georgia commented abruptly.

"Tomorrow should be fun," Quill said. "And yes, I'm happy. Now, tell me the truth, Georgia, about DeMarco. Kinda cute, huh?"

"Not bad for a geezer."

"And he'll be around for a while if he gets the bid on the discount mall project. Are you still thinking of sticking around Hemlock Falls after the Kiplings wend on their way?"

"I wouldn't," said Georgia, "think of settling anywhere else."

CHAPTER 14

The morning of Hemlock Falls Mall at the Falls Opening Day Ceremonies dawned to all the auguries necessary for success. The sun shone. The sky was blue. The Inn was host to Harvey Bozzel's dignitaries: two State Assembly persons, and the second secretarial assistant to the Congressman from New York. (Helena Houndswood, star of stage, screen, and television, had sent an uncharitably worded note of regret.) Meg threw two major snits before breakfast and a spectacular temper tantrum at nine o'clock, which meant she would cook superbly.

Quill came from the kitchen to join Myles, Andy, and John in the dining room with a huge smile and an exquisite sense of well-being.

"The menu for the opening of the boutique," she said as she settled into the chair next to Myles, "is going to be terrific."

"Gazpacho?' asked John, with hope.

"And vichyssoise. A hot ratatouille, and stuffed mushrooms. Dilled cucumber dressing for the salads. Creme brûlée, mousse, and caramel flan." Quill reached for a small brioche and buttered it. "It's all transportable, so actual cooking should be at a minimum." A shriek and a crash from behind the swinging doors to the kitchen broadened her smile. "It's the crab clouds, I think. They delivered the crab here, instead of the mall, and there's not enough ice. And she doesn't think she has enough cornmeal."

"Crab clouds?" Myles asked.

"You missed out on those, didn't you?" said Andy. "Meg created them last month while you two were still on the outs. My guess is they'll help get her that fourth star. They're fantastic. And she's got some ideas for the Christmas season that really sound incredible. You're not going to have to wait long for that final rating, Quill. Next year at the latest."

"So she's not . . ." Quill stopped.

"Thinking of leaving the Inn when we get married? Not on your life. The woman's a genius in the kitchen."

"Married? You're talking marriage?" Quill's feelings were mixed. Glad for Meg. Unhappy that she hadn't told her.

"Not directly, no. But now that you and Myles . . ." Myles's foot moved sharply under the table. Andy winced and changed the subject with no subtlety at all. "Is there anything I can do for you today, Quill? I'm covered at the hospital, so I'm completely at your disposal."

"Do you mean, Andy, that Meg put off discussions of your future because of me?"

Andy looked at John, then Myles, with a hint of what Quill had always characterized as male panic in the face of the Female Unknown. "Not exactly. But you two have been a team for so long . . . like this detective business, for example. How's the investigation coming?"

Quill, struggling with a sudden understanding that should have come to her long before, rather absently took a crêpe from Myles's plate and began to eat it.

"Hey," said Myles. "That's mine."

"I'll accept your diversionary tactic, Andy," Quill said sternly, "for the moment. But at some point in the very near future, my sister and I are going to have a talk. And to answer your question, our investigation, *my* investigation at least, is going nowhere."

"I wouldn't say that." Myles, in lieu of his second crêpe, picked up a muffin. "You and John cleared up a lot of ancillary issues yesterday."

"You mean you know who did it?"

"I've got a better sense of how the murders were committed. And a strong hunch as to who carried them out. I have no motive. And I have no proof." He rubbed the back of his neck with a weary gesture. "And time's running out."

"It's Hedrick," said Quill. "It has to be. Did you get any information about his stepfather's death? Does he have a record?"

"Hedrick was never indicted. I talked to Jerry Matthews last night, who's with the force in Palm Beach; there was a lot of suspicion when Hedrick's stepfather died, and a lot of gossip. The autopsy reports indicate botulism as the cause of death, from a gift set of jellies given to him by a friend at Christmas. The woman—unrelated to Louisa or Carlyle—was cleared of any culpability. It went down as an accidental death through the carelessness of an amateur cook. Jerry's take on it was that Conway was a rich man, and every time a rich man dies without an easily discernible cause, suspicions flourish, as he put it, like kudzu in a vacant lot."

"Hedrick told me he never eats anything canned," Quill recalled suddenly. "I thought it was just another part of his charm."

"Jerry did tell me something interesting, though. I asked for a list of people who were at the party where Conway finally keeled over. Botulism takes what, Andy, twenty-four to thirty-six hours to kill?"

Andy nodded. "Lot depends on the usual: age, weight, gender, prior physical condition."

"Conway died late Sunday evening. There'd been a house party at his mansion on the beach which began Thursday night. Conway ate the jellies sometime that evening and developed flulike symptoms the next morning. He drank quite a bit—Jerry said that the entire crowd was notable for the amount of alcohol consumed at these parties—and drank heavily the next day. By Sunday he was semiconscious. Louisa, for whom Jerry has little or no affection, kept insisting he was drunk and to leave him alone. By Sunday evening Conway'd passed into a coma. He died early Monday morning."

"Which of the Conways were at the party?" asked Quill.

"Hedrick, Louisa, and Carlyle, who was there with the heir to a Mexican cattle fortune, and who was suspected of dealing drugs." Myles took a swallow of coffee, then set the cup down deliberately. "And Lyle and Lila Fairbanks."

"The Fairbanks!" Quill took a deep breath. "They never mentioned it! Hedrick never mentioned it!"

"No. They didn't, did they? Hedrick never went near them at the party where Carlyle was killed. And when I interrogated him afterward, he didn't say a word about having known them before."

"Who," asked John, "made the jelly?"

"Lila."

* * *

The mall parking lot was jammed with vehicles. The Monster Truck Rally (SEE! THE MIGHTIEST MACHINES! IN COMBAT!) had attracted six entrants, and the huge vehicles occupied, Quill thought with irritation, far more parking space than they should have. Mr. Motoyama stood lost in admiration before them, his hands clasped behind his back, looking smaller than ever against the eight-foot tires.

Hedrick had had the foresight to reserve the same spot he'd had yesterday. Quill toyed with the idea of parking her Olds behind him, so that when he came looking for her, she'd have an opportunity to engage in a little artless questioning. "Did you switch Lila Fairbanks's jelly jar for one of your own in Palm Beach six years ago?" might be a good conversation opener.

Quill watched Lila Fairbanks wind her way through the clustered vehicles across the parking lot to the awning tent. She was wearing one of an apparently endless supply of white gauze dresses, this one trimmed with rose-colored ribbons. Lyle, as usual, hovered beside her, carrying a matching parasol to shield her from the bright August sun. She couldn't believe that this small, feminine woman with the sweet face could have made killer jelly on purpose. She said as much to Georgia.

"Myles wouldn't like it, if he knew you told me." Today's caftan was bright pink, with blue and green embroidered trim at the neckline. Georgia looked tired and strained despite the cheerful colors. "It must have been an accident," she said stubbornly. "I remember that Lila went through a real Martha Stewart period, canning, drying flowers, baking bread from scratch. It drove her housekeeper wild. She's vague and a little silly, Quill, but she's no more a murderer than I am."

"And she never said a word about knowing the Conways from before?"

"The rich travel in small, tight circles, Quill. I went into a real moult after Doug died—I wasn't much of a partygoer in the first place. You know me, give me a good book, a plate of Meg's food, and a nice lounge chair, and I'm set for life. But it doesn't surprise me that the Fairbanks drifted in and out of café society. There's a handful of the really rich who all know each other—and Lyle's one of them."

"I guess I won't." Quill maneuvered the Olds onto the grass verge and turned the ignition off.

"Won't what?"

"Park behind Hedrick. I'm going to find him and ask a lot of seemingly artless questions about his stepfather's death."

"Do you think that's a good idea?" Georgia's forehead creased with worry. "It might be dangerous."

"Pooh! as Meg would say. How dangerous can he get in this crowd?"

"Well, I'm going to stick with you like glue. I don't want your body found in the river with a neat little bash in the temple."

"In that outfit I think you should stick to Marco DeMarco," said Quill with a grin. "You're sure that on the day Louisa was murdered, neither Lyle nor Lila wandered off in the direction of the septic system?"

"Positive. Jerzey can confirm it. As a matter of fact, so can Axminster Stoker and Mr. Sakura. We wandered around in a group the whole time, gawking at the construction and getting in the way of the work crew."

"And DeMarco wasn't even there. He was in San Francisco. You know what I think?"

"What?" They began to stroll toward the awning tent. Outside, the Hemlock Falls High School Marching Band swung into a spirited, if flawed, version of "The Stars and Stripes Forever."

"We should just enjoy the afternoon. Forget all this."

"Georgia, we're close to a solution here. Suppose the Fairbanks are killing off Conways as revenge for Mr. Conway's murder? If I can find Hedrick and get him to explain a few things, we might nail them."

"Like what?"

"Well, for one thing, who knew of Carlyle's little party trick?"

"The Fairbanks, probably."

"And why did he refuse to let anyone here know he'd known the Fairbanks before? It's very suspicious, don't you think? If I'd been a fragile little person like Lila Fairbanks, you can bet your bottom dollar I wouldn't acknowledge the man who had substituted poisoned jelly for the good stuff and tried to get me implicated in a murder, either. And if Hedrick is guilty of that first murder, it makes sense that he wouldn't want to acknowledge them, either. So, when I find 'this reporter,' I'm going to ask him the sixty-four-thousand dollar question: Since he murdered Mr. Conway, why the heck doesn't he admit it?"

Georgia threw back her head and laughed, then looked at Quill with great affection. "Just don't," she warned, "see the little blighter alone. What does Myles think of all this?"

"He said to stay out of it. To stay away from the Fairbanks and from Hedrick and let him wrap up the case. There's something," Quill said in frustration, "that I've missed. He told me Hedrick was dangerous. But if Hedrick did it—where's the motive? He doesn't have any money. There's something I've missed. Some vital clue."

"Whatever it is, it'll have to wait until the Jell-O contest is over." The Sousa march came to a crashing conclusion. "And what the devil is that noise?"

"'The Stars and Stripes.' Sousa. The piccolo's got the flu." Quill heard Elmer's amplified voice testing the sound system from inside the tent. "It's just on two o'clock. Hedrick's probably in there getting pictures for the loathsome rag. Will you help me find him?"

Georgia gave a gusty sigh. "Okay. But 'don't go into the basement.' Promise?"

"Promise."

Despite the fact that the tent was open on four sides to the afternoon breeze, the crush of people made the interior stifling. Georgia took the lead, and the crowds parted before her pink caftan like tuna before a trawler. Quill scanned the crowd, waved to Marge Schmidt and Betty Hall, smiled at Chris Croh, and smiled again at Monica Peterson, architect of a Jell-O building Quill had been unable to identify the day before. Monica semaphored urgently. Quill smiled vaguely and tried the Dodge, a trick she'd observed Helena Houndswood use when greeting the legions of fans (six, including Esther West's poodle) that had greeted her on Main Street the week of her ill-fated visit to Hemlock Falls the year before. Basically, the Dodge consisted of a broad grin, eye-contact just above the petitioner's forehead, and a graceful turn-and-wave maneuver Quill had much admired.

"Didn't you see me?" Monica demanded, planting herself directly under Quill's chin.

"Monica! Isn't this wonderful!"

"Mrs. Henry wants you," said Monica despairingly. "She's been wondering where you are. She's a little upset that you haven't judged anything yet."

"Um," said Quill. Georgia, who'd successfully made her way to the small stage set up at the front of the tent, was looking over the heads of the crowd for Quill. Quill raised herself on tiptoe and waved energetically. Georgia caught her eye and mouthed "no Hedrick."

"Quill?"

"I didn't exactly agree to judge the Jell-O Architecture Contest, Monica. I mean, I'm sure there are a lot of people more qualified than I to decide who built the best building." She had an inspiration. "What about Mr. DeMarco? He's in construction."

"Mrs. Henry says the buildings are art. And you're an artist. Could you come over pretty quick, please?" She craned her neck up and whispered in Quill's ear. "Esther's not speaking to her. Miriam's so mad she's sitting on a chair reading a book, because Adela disqualified her entry—it was an homage to Agatha Christie, with the cutest little train out of Knox Blox—because her fixative is Super Glue and you can't eat Super Glue. And even Mrs. Shuttleworth is getting a little cranky. She said, 'Oh, God! Adela,' in this cross way, twice. It's terrible!!"

Quill resisted the temptation to pat Monica on the head and say "there-there." Instead she said confidingly "I'll tell you what the trouble is, Monica. It's that I can't be objective about this contest, knowing everybody that I do. And a judge has to be objective. What about Howie Murchison? He's town justice. And Doreen told me this morning that everyone's mad at him anyway because of . . . never mind. Forget I said that."

"Mr. Murchison said he'd rather shave a bear's behind with a buzzsaw than judge." Monica's eyes sparkled with tears. "Mrs. Henry is just going to be so mad! It'll wreck everything."

"What we need," muttered Quill, "is an objective *panel* of judges. Wait here."

She found Elmer frowning over a sheaf of much-folded paper.

"Quill, d'ya'll think I should greet the second secretary to our Congressman before I present the Assemblymen? Or should I present the Assemblywoman before the second secretary? This-here protocol's tough."

"The Assemblyman and -woman first," said Quill. "They're the elected officials. Elmer, may I make an announcement?"

"What kind of an announcement?" A look of what Quill could only call terror crossed his face. "Not the results of the Jell-O Architecture Contest? You didn't give the blue ribbon to Esther or anything, did you? I'm telling you, Quill, it's a terrible bidness to have the wife involved in something as important as this."

"No," soothed Quill, "and I'm not going to. Judge, I mean. I want to ask the Kipling Condensation Society and Mr. Sakura to judge the contest."

"Hah? You mean outsiders?"

"Elmer! What better way to handle it? They'll all be gone in a week!"

"I get your drift, Quill, I get your drift. It's an excellent plan!" He looked a little wistful. "You think maybe I could announce it? Lot of the folks around here are kinda mad on account of what happened with the mini-mall. But Howie said—"

"Later, Elmer. I think it'd be terrific if you got up, welcomed everybody, in a general sort of way you understand, not"—she eyed the dozen or so handwritten sheets in his hands—"the whole speech, but just that you'd like to ask our out-of-towners, the Kipling Condensation Society, and Mr. Sakura Toshiro, the famous former managing director of Sakura Industries, to contribute to the day's festivities by judging the contest. Oh! And be sure to read a copy of Adela's Rules and Regulations, so they know what they're judging for."

"Got it." He squeezed her arm in fervent gratitude. "I owe you one, Quill. You're a true pal."

In subsequent years, when the Jell-O Battles had passed into town history, and the pros and cons were discussed with the cooler attitudes that the mere passage of time brings, the citizens of Hemlock Falls were unanimous in one thing: Elmer Henry started it. This was unfortunate, and may have had something to do with the closeness of the race for mayor fought the following year (Henry versus Henry) because, as no one but Quill and the mayor knew, it was really all her fault.

"Terlits," said Doreen in Quill's ear, while she watched Elmer ascend to the podium.

"Doreen! I'm glad you finally got here. Did you come by yourself?"

"I tolt you that there Stoker was follering me," said Doreen obscurely. "But the terlits is backed up."

"At the Inn? Again? Darn it! Is Petey Peterson here? I know he was scheduled to drive in the Monster Truck Ralley. Maybe you can persuade him to go back and pump the septic out."

"Ladies and gentlemen!" Elmer's voice boomed, faded, and then came back at a tolerable volume. "I have an announcement to make. Please do not use, I repeat, do not use, the toilets. We have a tempr'y backup in the system . . . what?" He turned and bent down to Marco DeMarco, who was, Quill was pleased to see, standing next to Georgia. They already looked like a long-married couple. "Mr. DeMarco here, is having PortaPotties come in, but it'll take about a half hour. In the meantime please, ah, use the woods. Thank you. Thank you."

"Terlits," said Doreen again. "What I want to know is, how come? All of a sudden we're having all this trouble with terlits, when we never did before."

"Probably something stuck in the system," said Quill, knowledgeable after her septic system lecture from Eugene. She rubbed her forehead. There was something Eugene had told her about the system . . .

"Quiet, please!" said the mayor. "I would like to welcome you all to the Opening Day Ceremonies of this fine mini-mall . . . what? Oh, Howie says it's more like a *de minimus* mall, 'cause it looks like we've agreed to accept Mr. Sakra's offer. Anyhow, I'd like to ask some of our out-of-town guests to he'p us here, with an effort the ladies of this town have made to memorialize some of our greatest memorials."

The Kiplings, Quill discovered, were more bewildered than flattered, but in the true Victorian spirit, up to the challenge. Mr. Sakura (followed by the inevitable Motoyama) with many bows and nods, joined them as they solemnly marched up and down the display table to judge the Jell-O contest. Each of the ladies stood more or less proudly beside her creation, except for Miriam Doncaster, who rather elaborately ignored the whole thing and continued the charade of reading her book. Somebody had upended a bucket over her train.

Mr. Motoyama, trailing his boss, growled, "Jer-ro."

"I beg your pardon?" said Mrs. Henry.

"*Jer*-o. *Jer*-o! *Jer-roooohh!*" howled Mr. Motoyama, with sudden ferocious intent. He snarled. Shook his fist. Dashed out of the tent. In the stunned silence Quill heard a shriek, and clatter, and the ominous sound of a Monster truck being gunned to ear-splitting pitch.

Fortunately, most of the crowd dashed outside, the men, bored, in the hopes that the Monster Truck Rally had started without them, the women, Quill later believed, out of an atavistic survival impulse present in the most obdurate feminist whenever an enraged male is around a large truck.

Motoyama barreled the shiny red truck through the south opening and headed straight for the display table, knocking over the jellies, the baked goods, the soft drink stand, and the flower display on its way. Women screamed. Elmer bellowed. Outside, the several deputies who'd been directing traffic jumped in the black-and-white and turned on the siren. Motoyama, with sporadic cries of "*Jer-roooh!*" threw the truck in reverse (flattening a tuba that had been left carelessly near the Coke machine) and rammed the display table again. The gears clashed. The motor revved. The truck jumped forward like a bull out of the chute and slammed into the tent pole.

The awning collapsed in billows around the truck. The engine died. Shouts, curses, and imprecations issued from various spots under the fallen tent.

"Jerroooh!" snarled Mr. Motoyama, muffled, but undefeated.

"It was Mrs. Henry's replica of Mount Fuji," said Andy, applying a small Band-Aid to a cut above Quill's brow. "Nearly as we can figure out, he thought it was a sacrilege."

"Well, it *was* sacrilegious," said Meg tartly. "What do you think poor Dookie would have thought of a Jell-O crucifix? It was in lousy taste. I'm just glad nobody was seriously hurt."

"Has everybody gone home?" Quill got up and wandered around their restaurant. The staff had decorated it with balloons and crepe paper. The glassware on the café tables shone sparkling clear. The menu on the blackboard displayed the opening day specials. A scent of tarragon and crab made the area pleasantly reminiscent of the kitchen at the Inn.

"Almost." Andy tried, but couldn't suppress a grin. "Between the toilets malfunctioning and the tent collapse, Myles decided it was better to reschedule the event for next week. I co-opted the Inn van, Quill, to run some of the elderly back to the village. So the Kiplings and Mr. Sakura are outside, waiting to get picked up. Myles sent Mr. Motoyama to the lockup with Deputy Dave."

The drone-shove of the backhoe in operation in the distance attracted Quill's attention. "Is the plumbing really messed up? Are we going to be able to open next week?"

"John and Myles are down at the septic tank now." Andy packed up his black bag and snapped it shut. "Whatever the obstruction was, it didn't seem to be in the pipes leading to the system. Myles asked DeMarco to take off the top of the tank."

"Wow!" Meg shook her head. "When I think of what the Horrible Hedrick is going to do with the headlines! You know, if we'd been thinking, we'd have created a plan to get him out of the way today."

"Somebody already did," said Myles. He walked through the open door. His uniform was streaked with dirt. "Andy? I'm going to need you down at the septic tank. Looks like he's been in there at least overnight."

"Christ." Andy picked up his back. "What's your best guess?"

"Hammer blow to the head. Same MO as the first one. Rigor's set in and gone, but there's no bloating. I'd say twenty-four hours or less, but you're the expert. Whoever put him in there must have been in a hurry. The body's shoved up against the outlet valve and blocked the waste line from the building. Quill? Unless you want to come down to the pit with us, I'd appreciate it if you'd go back to the Inn."

Quill watched his eyes. "Myles. It's not your fault."

"Dammit, Quill." He looked at the ground at his feet, then back up at her. She started toward him, then stopped. "I don't have an excuse. Don't you understand? After I talked with Matthews in Palm Beach last night, I knew. Instead, I . . ."

He'd come to her.

"Lila Fairbanks," said Meg softly. "Golly. And her husband, too, I bet."

"It fits," said Quill in an undertone. "They were here yesterday, with the others."

"Do you have proof, Myles?" asked Andy.

"No. No proof. It's been a series of clever crimes. But, goddammit, I could have stopped this."

"How?" asked Quill gently. "You said he'd been in there more than twenty-four hours. When did you talk to Matthews?"

"After dinner. Around eight."

"Then he was already dead," said Meg bluntly. "Quill, are you coming?"

"I'll stay here. I'll make coffee."

Myles looked at her. "Has everyone gone? Quill? I don't want you here alone."

"I'll be fine, Myles."

He made a movement, impatient to be gone.

"Go on, all of you. I'll be here when you get back. Meg? Can you wait just a second?"

"Sure. I'll be with you in a minute, Andy."

"The Kiplings are in the parking lot. I'd better get them and bring them in here until Mike gets back with the van."

"But the Fairbanks! Quill! You're not going to feed a murderer!"

"Did you see Myles's face? He thinks Hedrick died because I distracted him. It's my fault, Meg. He blames me. If he'd been concentrating on his job instead of what was happening to me, I know he thinks this never would have happened. The Fairbanks don't know that he's on to them, but there's a chance, just a chance, that they'll try and slip away now that Hedrick's been found. I'll just keep them altogether and give them a meal and make sure that Lyle and his wife get back to the Inn with the others."

"I'd better tell Myles they're here," said Meg.

"Okay. Just wait for the right moment. Not in front of anyone else. I can't stand to see him like that."

Meg reached out and hugged her. "Okay. Serve 'em a meal and keep 'em happy and oblivious."

"Just tell me what to serve."

"Cold soups and salads are in the frige. Don't try the crab clouds. You can heat the ratatouille in the microwave. Three minutes and stir, three minutes and stir again."

"Got it. Georgia can help me."

"Okay, I'll send them all in."

Quill went to the refrigerator and began to set out the gazpacho and the vichyssoise, then put two portions of the ratatouille in the microwave. Meg had a large supply of sourdough bread stocked in a cupboard, and she removed a loaf and began to slice it into chunks.

There was a whisper of movement across the flagstone patio outside.

"Gawd," said Georgia.

The Fairbanks, Miss Kent, and Mr. Sakura filed in behind her. Marco DeMarco arrived with Georgia, the two of them looking reassuringly solid. "Not much more I can do down there," DeMarco said in response to her inquiring glance. He shrugged. "And Meg said you were serving food. Sorry to bust in like this, but I was hungry. The poor guy."

Quill looked at Lila. The delicate face was flushed, the eyes a little wild. She drew the ribbons at her waist through her fingers, back and forth, back and forth. She never left her husband's side. Lyle cupped her elbow protectively with one hand.

"You all are getting quite an impression of Hemlock Falls," said Georgia lightly, to break the uncomfortable silence.

"We will not talk about it," said Miss Kent firmly.

"Sit anywhere, please," said Quill. "I thought I'd get you a little early supper while we're waiting for Mike and the van."

They settled into the chairs like large birds.

"Did anyone figure out why poor Motoyama went berserk?" asked Georgia with determined cheerfulness.

Quill shot her a grateful look. "Well!" she said, lightly. "It was typically Hemlock Falls, Gee. I hope it adds to your already fervent desire to come and live among us. It was the Jell-O exhibits." Quill arranged the arugula on plates and removed the vinaigrette cruet from the shelf. "You'll have noticed, I'm sure, the *verve* and personal attention which each of the ladies gave to their exhibits. Miriam, for example, is town librarian and a mystery fan, so she did a replica of the train in *Murder on the Orient Express* . . ." The quality of the silence shifted, like a great weight.

She stopped in midsentence.

The bread knife fell from her fingers.

Quill turned. Stared at them. They stared back. All of them, with the unwinking eyes of predators.

Georgia's hand jerked up. Lyle Fairbank's eyes were steady. Miss Kent coughed a little and shifted in her seat.

Georgia rose from her chair.

Quill backed up and hit the counter. She could go no farther. The end of a terrible story she had read once, long ago, came to her, like jaws snapping shut in a trap. She thought.

> *"No!" Tess cried. "It isn't fair!"*
> *And then they came for her.*

"Georgia! You!" Quill pushed back a sudden spurt of tears. "He's your brother," she said, pointing suddenly at DeMarco. "The resemblance. It's not the coloring. It's the shape of the skull. The ears . . ."

"The painter's eye," said Georgia.

"It's you," said Quill huskily. She cleared her throat. "It's all of you."

The Kiplings watched her, with that alien stillness.

"It couldn't have happened any other way. You were all together when Louisa died. You were all at the party when Carlyle died. And yesterday . . ." She took a deep breath. "Yesterday you went into the woods. Together. And Hedrick followed you there."

"Yes," said Georgia. Her face was patched with high, bright color.

"Gee," DeMarco ordered. "Shut up."

"No. I want to explain." She stood, hands crossed over her chest, fists clenched, the pink caftan an incongruous flare of color. "And it's my call. You know it's my call. Can you stop me? Can you?"

No one spoke.

"Explain?" Quill, her heart beating so hard she could feel it in her throat. "Explain three murders?"

"There were more deaths than that," said Georgia. "Far many more than that. We just stopped them, the Conways, from killing again."

"But *why*?!"

Georgia's face closed shut, like a fist. "I was Douglas Conway's first wife. The one he divorced. To marry that rapacious little bitch Louisa North, with her slut of a daughter, and her murdering bastard of a son." Her voice, shaking so badly that Quill could barely understand her, faltered and died away.

"You lied to me!" cried Quill. "You said he died!"

"And so he did, for me, seven years ago."

"I," said Lyle Fairbanks, "was Doug Conway's best friend. And my wife, Lila, was the woman the Conways tried to pin Doug's murder on."

"I was Doug's sister," said Miss Kent. "And Louisa Conway stole the only man I ever loved."

"And you. Mr. Sakura." Quills voice was just above a whisper.

"Hedrick Conway and his women." His black eyes glittered at her with a wise and angry intelligence. "A scandal, brought on by my . . . association . . . with the rapacious Miss Carlyle."

"All of them deserved to die," said Georgia, a terrible satisfaction in her voice. "When they'd drained Doug, and finally killed him—because, Quill, it was murder, no matter what your lover tells you, what those investigators in Palm Beach tell you—they poisoned him. I contacted each one of my friends that that miserable little crew had injured, one by one. And we decided that at the right place, at the right time, they would help me. They would help me get justice.

"I was fifty-two when Louisa North and her poisonous little slut of a daughter crossed Douglas's path. We'd been married almost thirty years. I was Douglas's first and only love. He was a genius, and his partner—my father, Stephen Hardwicke—knew how to parlay Douglas's genius into the empire that they both built. We were rich. We were happy. Douglas had never even been with another woman. Not until that bitch and her brood showed up."

There were no tears, Quill noted. Just a bright, hard blaze behind Georgia's eyes.

"We came across them at one of those parties I'd told you about. We were traveling quite a lot, that year, trying things we hadn't needed to try before. Douglas was dried up. Out of ideas. Spent. He loved his work and there was no more that he could do, so we traveled. We had everything material we could ever want. Except youth. Except change.

"I told you about the circuit for the very rich. And that's what we were, what I still am, the very rich. We accepted an invitation to a party on a yacht in Greece. For a week. I knew, once we got there, that I had to get him home. I knew, once I walked that deck and saw the human garbage tanning in the sun, that this was no place for us, no place at all. But I didn't act on what I knew. And when I found them together—Louisa, Carlyle, and my Douglas, naked in a stateroom—my Douglas, with that thinning hair, those ridiculous glasses . . ." Georgia closed her eyes.

Miss Kent smoothed her linen skirt over her knees and took a sip of water.

"I never should have divorced him. I know that now. Carlyle was into all kinds of drugs. She and her harpy mother battened on him, and then they sucked him dry.

"He was generous in the divorce settlement. He could afford to be. What I told you was true. He died for me that day, seven years ago, he died for himself that day, seven years ago, although his physical death didn't happen until a year later. At that party. In Palm Beach."

"Doug and Gee were talking about getting back together. It's what precipitated his murder, you see," said Lyle. "He was talking on the phone every day to Gee, here, trying to shake the drugs those three had gotten him on to, and there would have been hell to pay for that little tribe, you can bet, if Gee'd come back into the picture. Those of us that loved Doug—and I'm not ashamed to say that I loved him, as nuts as he went for that year—well, were doing our best to get him and Gee back together."

Lila Fairbanks touched her husband's hand. "We think what

happened then is that Louisa, Hedrick, and Carlyle decided to kill him that weekend and arrived prepared. Botulism is easy enough to manufacture. You can do it in your own kitchen. When our own children were grown, and out of the house, I took up, oh, all kinds of things to feel as though I were still . . . womanly . . . I guess is the word, and it may sound silly to someone like you, Quill, coming from me, who has so much in the way of material things, but I just wanted . . . to be ordinary. So I brought Doug some of my canned jellies . . ."

"She'd made a habit of it, the past year." Lyle rubbed his wife's shoulder. "It was kind of a joke around that group—well, not a joke exactly."

"Bored, brittle, sophisticated, and, as Georgia said, human garbage." Miss Kent's voice was crisp. "It was a joke, dear Lila, only to people who hadn't had normal feelings for years, if ever. I, myself, always loved your jellies."

Quill didn't know whether to laugh or cry.

"So they tried to make you responsible for the murder, Mrs. Fairbanks?"

Lila nodded.

"Set her back quite a bit," said Lyle gruffly. "Ended up in the hospital for a while."

"It was a mental institution," said Lila, trembling. "A house for crazy people."

"And as for the rest of us," said DeMarco, "you don't need a detailed drawing, do you? Louisa and Carlyle had a spat soon after they'd snared Doug, and Louisa turned her out without a penny. Mr. Sakura, here"—he coughed—"well, Carlyle tried a bit of blackmail on him."

"And it worked," said Mr. Sakura. "My position, gone. The honor of my house was shamed."

"At least the bastards didn't end up with much," said Miss Kent cheerfully. "Sakura-san didn't pay her a plugged nickel, and Gee's managed to tie up the fortune in litigation for a long while."

"But Louisa and Cay?" said Quill.

"Oh, yes," said Miss Kent serenely. "Cay wormed her way back into the fold. My guess is that Cay tried a bit of blackmail on her own mother. Louisa's appetites were notorious, and after she threw

Cay out, let's just say that Douglas, as besotted as he was, would have divorced her if he'd known what Cay did about her mother."

"And you, Miss Kent?" asked Quill. "Why did you hate him so?"

"I would prefer, my dear, not to go into that. But I can tell you . . ." She raised her finely boned face to Quill's. Her lips drew back from her teeth. "I can tell you. *I had a hell of a reason!*"

"Mr. Paulovich?" asked Quill.

"Cover," Georgia said, her grin white.

"But the law. Couldn't you have gone to the police?"

"Don't be naive!" Miss Kent snapped. "What possible recourse could we have had? Douglas was of age. He was mentally competent. In my own case—" She bit her lip. "There was no proof, you see. Absolutely no proof. There is no law to deal with the ruination of a man. Only laws for his physical demise. So we took, in the classic manner, matters into our own hands."

"You can't," said Quill. "You can't."

"We can," said Lyle, "and we did."

"But you've told me," said Quill recklessly.

"We have, Quill," said Georgia a little sadly. "But no one will believe you, without proof, without another witness. These's no jury in the country that would convict us on your word alone. And your sheriff's a good man, Quill, but we were very, very careful And we will back each other up. There's too much at stake for us, you see."

She took a deep breath. "When you remember me, when you remember our friendship, you'll see that I never lied to you. Never. Not once. I didn't betray that trust, Quill, and as strange as this may seem to you now, it's important that you know it." She looked at the others, and without a word exchanged, they got to their feet. "Do you think Mike's here with the van?"

Quill spread her hands.

"Then we'll see ourselves out, my dear. Thank you." Miss Kent patted her cheek. Her fingers were scented like violets.

Quill watched them leave, heard their footsteps whisper-slide over the cobblestone court.

She waited, as the darkness gathered in the little restaurant, and the sounds of a summer evening filled the quiet. She waited, and Myles came in exhausted, with lines around his mouth where there had been none before, and she said, as he walked in, a question in his eyes at finding her alone in the darkness:

"The thing is, they forgot Mr. Stoker."

CHAPTER 15

There were days in August which carried a melancholy hint of fall. Quill sat in the waiting room of the tiny hospital that served the Falls and the surrounding small communities and thought about the quality of the light: it was gold, round, autumnal. The warm air had lost the round fullness of humidity. An occasional current carried the coolness of September.

Next to her, Meg was restless, fidgeting in the uncomfortable chair, picking at her shoelace. She relaxed. "There they are."

Quill turned and looked over her shoulder. Andy, remote in his hospital whites, came down the hall. His face was somber. Myles walked beside him.

"Let's go into my office." Andy preceded them. It was small, the bookshelves crowded with medical texts, the desk overflowing with journals, magazines, and patient folders. There was a faint smell of antiseptic. Quill settled next to Myles. Meg stood at the window, looking out at the football field. The high school team had started practice. The shouted exuberance of the young was monitored by the coach's whistle, a shrill imperative.

"How long has she got?" asked Myles.

Andy flipped through Georgia Hardwicke's chart. "It's hard to say. Six weeks. Maybe two months."

"So that's why she signed a confession." Quill rubbed her forehead. "She must have known about this. Last year. When she began to hunt the Conways."

Andy raised one eyebrow. "She says not."

Quill was brusque, fighting tears. "Of course she knew. Why

else did she wait six years to take revenge? It's pituitary cancer, you said? Metastasized to the liver? Of course she knew. I don't think the rest of them did. If they had, if they knew that she planned to confess all along, do you think they would have helped her? She convinced them, I know she convinced them, that they'd be safe. That they'd be able to plan to kill and get away with it." She looked at Myles. "Will the others go to trial?"

"I doubt it. Lila Fairbanks might be ready to talk, but her lawyers have her sequestered. The others . . ." He shrugged. "Silence. The evidence rests on Georgia's confession—which denies the complicity of the others—and on Stoker's affidavit that they'd paid him to follow Hedrick Conway and his family and report back on their activities. We've got Stoker's expense acounts, which show that he followed them everywhere for the past year, and copies of his reports on the Conways' activities, but nothing to support a charge of murder, or even conspiracy to murder. Everything can be explained by the civil action the Kiplings have brought against Douglas Conway's estate. Sakura's attempting to recover the income he lost from Carlyle Conway's blackmail scheme. Georgia's suing to have the will contested because of Louisa's and Carlyle's undue influence. Her brother, who's heir to Georgia's fortune, has a legitimate interest in her fiscal status. The Fairbanks claim they were conducting a private investigation to pin Douglas Conway's murder on the Conways so that Lila's name could be cleared. Everyone except Miss Kent had logical—not fair—but logical reasons for having Conway followed by Axminster Stoker. Nothing actionable there. And, as I said, impossible to prove conspiracy."

"Do you suppose we'll ever know about Miss Kent?" asked Meg. Myles shrugged.

"It's the ruthlessness of it," said Meg. "Poor Stoke. The poor man had no idea he was being used as a stalking horse for murder."

"I was blind to it," said Quill, rousing herself from a fixed concentration on a replica of a human skull on Andy's desk. "They all referred to him as 'Stoke.' The family resemblance between Georgia and DeMarco. The connections between HC Pharmaceuticals and the Conways. The fact that all of them were nearby when each of the murders occurred. The lies they told! The lies!"

"The rich," said Andy, "are different from you and me. Quill? Georgia would like to see you."

"Now, Andy?" asked Quill.

"I'm going to transfer her to the prison hospital at Attica this afternoon. She's in three-eleven."

The halls had the hushed silence peculiar to hospitals, blanketing the constancy of its purpose, distancing visitors from the world of life from the reality of death.

Georgia was pale, her face drawn, but the smile was there, and the booming, generous laugh. One of the nurses turned away from her bedside with a grin and a shake of her head as Quill pushed open the door and entered the room.

"Could you excuse us for a second?" asked Quill.

The nurse left on noiseless feet.

Georgia's smile died. "Well, Miss Sarah. This has shaken you up, hasn't it?"

"That's an understatement."

"An inadequate understatement. Not my style at all." She nodded to the visitor's chair. "Sit down."

Quill sat carefully and clasped her hands in her lap.

"You feel betrayed."

"I do."

"And what else? Disgusted? Revolted? Furious?"

"All those."

"I don't expect you to understand. I don't expect you to forgive me. But I want to tell you something. Gawd. I hope I get this right." She reached to the table beside the bed and drank from the tumbler of water. "Yes, I used some people who trusted me. I traded on love, affection, loyalty, friendship. With you. And Stoke. I used poor old Stoke, who thought that he was cooperating in an effort to embarrass Hedrick and those harpy women. Stoke wanted to right a wrong that'd been done to a man he'd revered for twenty years. But that doesn't mean I'm a liar. It means that I made a choice. I know exactly what I've sacrificed, Quill. I know what's been taken from me, as a person, because I did what I did. But I knew what I was doing. The Conways would, *did* get away with it. This"— she swept her hand down, across her chest and belly—"this cancer condemned me, and freed me all at once. I was sentenced before my crimes were committed. And once I decided to kill them—and I killed all three of them, Quill—I had no choice but to use the people I loved. Didn't someone once call them little murders, the crimes we commit against the healthy living?"

"A comedian," said Quill dryly.

"So you see."

Quill shook her head. "Why involve the Kiplings? Why not"— she stopped—"just do it yourself?"

"Because that bitch had to know it wasn't just me." Georgia's eyes narrowed, and that flat glittering stare would remain with Quill a long, long time. "Louisa. In the woods. We followed her. I can move quietly, you know, for all my size. She turned. We stood there. Silent. All of us. And I swung the hammer. And Carlyle, on the floor, with all of us around her. We were the last thing she saw, and she *knew*. For a long time. She *knew*. And the brother. He screamed. Like a rabbit. Like a rabbit."

"It isn't fair!" cried Tess.
And then they were on her.

"You've lost something," said Meg when Quill told her what had happened. "I hope to God you get it back."

"What?" said Quill. "What have I lost?"

They were in the kitchen. The copper pots hung from the wrought-iron hooks like billy clubs. The herbs had a stale grave-yard smell. The afternoon light had died, and night crouched behind the falls.

Meg pulled a comic face. "Your sunny faith in the essential goodness of human beings?"

"I'm tired," said Quill. "I'm not up to light chat."

"Sorry. Sorry. I guess neither of us is especially good at looking into the pit. Now, dancing around the edge of the pit, jester bells in hand, *that* we're good at."

"It was all of them. All of them. Smiling, genial, good humored . . ."

". . . and lethal."

"I always thought there were things normal people wouldn't do."

"Myles knows better. One can smile and smile and be a villain."

"But Georgia was good. I loved her."

"Things fall apart," said Meg, "the center fails to hold."

"Shut up," said Quill fiercely.

"All right. I'll quit the oblique and we'll tackle this head-on. If there's a fixed and eternal good, Quill, you won't find it in people. You'll find it in yourself. And your self needs your painting. Take a month. Go back to New York. Paint. And come home."

"And Myles?"

"And me? And John and the Inn and Doreen and all those things you think you're serving because we're good? Pooh. You'll know what to do when you come home. Do it. Leave us. And come back."

CHAPTER 16

Quill signaled a right turn and pulled into the long driveway that led to the Inn. Bronze and pink chrysanthemums bloomed on either side of the door, and trees were a fireworks of scarlet, bronze, and yellow. There'd been a heavy frost the night before, and the last of the autumn lilies shivered in the October air.

Doreen, her apron filled with late potatoes, stumped around the corner of the old building. She grinned and dumped the potatoes in a tidy pile by the ivy trellis. "You're earlier than you said."

"The thruway was clear. And everybody's driving seventy anyway these days, Doreen."

"Ayuh? You get another ticket?"

"No, I did not get another ticket."

"You got that suitcase?"

"It's in the back. Along with"—Quill paused, a little shy—"a few sketches."

"Huh." Doreen opened the back door and slid the portfolio

out. She flipped it open and stood considering. "Like the way you handled the water. Foreground perspective's off some."

Quill gaped at her.

"Sher'f talks about his art classes some at dinner. That Stoke's thinking about takin' a few." She sniffed.

"How's he doing?"

"Ast *him*. Once he stopped fooling around with that Quality stuff, he started talking like a sensible person, I guess." She hoisted Quill's suitcase.

"Meg wrote that he's found a little house to buy in town."

"Pension'll go to that, I guess, now that he's not pretending to be a rich guy."

"I'm glad he decided to take over the newspaper."

Doreen sucked her teeth, whether in disapprobation or indifference, Quill couldn't tell. "Wait'll you see it. It's somethin'. Go on, they're waiting on you in there. Sheriff'll be along soon."

Quill walked into the foyer. The vases were filled with autumn leaves. A fire burned steadily in the cobblestone fireplace. The small sign they used to welcome guests read WELCOME! ARTIST SARAH QUILLIAM! with two lines underneath: CHAMBER OF COMMERCE WELCOME HOME DINNER 7:00 P.M., and then, QUILLIAM EXHIBIT, THE SAKURA MALL AT THE FALLS EXHIBITED DAILY underneath.

"We wasn't sure you wanted your pitchers hung here, so Meg and the Sher'f hung up 'em down to the mall."

Quill cleared her throat and smiled.

"And the terlits are workin', which is a mercy."

"I take it that's not a comment on the quality of Sarah's work," said Axminster crisply as he came down the stairs from the upper floor. He'd shaved his mustache. He was wearing an Aloha shirt.

Doreen muttered what Quill took to be an imprecation and abjured Axminster to shake a leg and get the luggage.

"Please don't bother," said Quill. "I'll take care of it."

"We're glad to see you back, Sarah." He kissed her cheek. "I'd be delighted to assist you with the luggage. Andy, Meg, and John are in the kitchen. I'll be along in a moment."

"You hustle," said Doreen. "We got to get ready for that Chamber dinner."

Axminster snapped a salute and carried Quill's case back upstairs.

"Doreen, just because poor Mr. Stoker isn't as rich as we thought, there's no need to make a . . . a . . . *slave* out of him."

"Gotta learn, don't he? One gol-durned thing I won't put up with is a lazy husband."

Quill stared at her. "A what!?"

"Well, I married him, din't I? Somebody had to give the bozo a hand with that-there newspaper business. Durn fool can't keep accounts to save his life."

Quill burst into the kitchen. The thymey smell of *boeuf bourguignon* curled through the mixed scents of the wood fire, fresh bread, and spicy chrysanthemums. Meg shrieked and kissed her. Andy grabbed her in a bear hug. John nodded, smiled, and smiled again.

The back door banged open.

"Well, Myles, my dear," she said. "I'm home."

CRAB CLOUDS

from the Inn at Hemlock Falls

one cup fresh Dungeness crab, shredded
2 tsps. cilantro, chopped
1 tsp. fresh parsley, chopped
2 tsps. sweet red pepper, chopped fine
1 tsp. green pepper, chopped fine
2 tsps. Vidalia onion, chopped fine
2 cups cornmeal and flour, mixed in equal parts
½ cup whole milk
one medium-sized egg
one-half cup unsalted butter
several teaspoons each of unsalted butter and olive oil, for sautéing

Steam Dungeness crab for six minutes. Crack claws and body. Set
  crabmeat aside.
Chop spices and peppers and mix together. Add to crab. Sauté
  onion for five minutes in butter, until onion is clear and transparent. Add to crab. Mix crab mixture well.
Measure cornmeal-flour mixture into glass bowl. Place milk in
  separate bowl. Separate egg. Beat yolk to thick froth. Beat egg
  white to soft peaks. Carefully fold egg into milk until smooth
  and very thick. Melt butter in pan, slowly, until it has separated
  into milky/clear liquid. Let butter cool slightly and whisk it into
  the cornmeal mixture, being careful not to curdle the egg, and to
  keep mixture thick.
Put a few teaspoons combined sweet butter and very pure olive oil
  into crepe pan and heat until it sizzles around the edges. Add three
  or four tablespoons of cornmeal to the pan and flatten with back
  of spoon. Cook as you would a pancake, until the edges of the crab

cloud dry and curl sightly. Place a few tablespoons of crab mixture in the center of the crab cloud, leaving an eighth-of-an-inch edge all around. Flip the crab cloud over and sauté until cornmeal-flour mixture is cooked through.

Serve with condiments such as tomato or mustard chutney.

MURDER
WELL-DONE

THE CAST OF CHARACTERS

THE INN AT HEMLOCK FALLS

Sarah Quilliam	owner-manager
Margaret Quilliam	her sister, gourmet chef
John Raintree	their business manager and partner
Doreen Muxworthy	head housekeeper
Dina Muir	receptionist
Kathleen Kiddermeister	head waitress
Mike	the groundskeeper
Bjarne	a Finnish *sous*-chef
Claire McIntosh	the bride, a guest
Elaine McIntosh	Claire's mother, a guest
Vittorio McIntosh	Claire's father, a guest
Alphonse Santini	the bridegroom, former senator
Tutti McIntosh	Vittorio's mother, a guest
Evan Blight	world-famous author, a guest
Nora Cahill	TV anchor, a guest
. . . various bridesmaids, groomsmen, and aides to Senator Santini	

MEMBERS OF S.O.A.P.

Elmer Henry	mayor of Hemlock Falls
Dookie Shuttleworth	minister, the Hemlock Falls Church of the Word of God
Harland Peterson	a farmer
. . . among others	

MEMBERS OF H.O.W.

Adela Henry	the mayor's wife
Marge Schmidt	owner, the Hemlock Hometown Diner
Betty Hall	Marge's partner
Esther West	owner, West's Best dress shop
Miriam Doncaster	a librarian

THE VILLAGE OFFICIALS, AND OTHERS

Frank Dorset	the sheriff
Davy Kiddermeister	Kathleen's brother, a deputy
Dwight Riorden	the bailiff
Bernie Bristol	the town justice
Myles McHale	a citizen
Howie Murchison	a lawyer

The opinions expressed by some of
the characters in this book are peculiar.
The author disavows all of them.

CHAPTER 1

"You've sure got one heck of a lifestyle," Nora Cahill said enviously. "Your Inn is gorgeous, your sister's food is terrific, and your business manager is the best-looking guy I've seen since I nailed an exclusive interview with Kevin Costner after his divorce. I've heard that little boutique restaurant you've invested in got a franchise offer. Even the show of your paintings last month got great reviews." Resentment crept into her voice, souring its carefully cultivated modulations. Pensively, she shoved her sour cream crepe with her fork. "No offense, but if you tell me you've got your love life socked, too, I'm going to hit you with a stick. I haven't had a date for eight months."

Sarah Quilliam set her cup into her saucer in awkward silence. Nora had checked into the Inn the night before and asked if she could speak to the owner. Quill, with a jammed schedule, had suggested an early breakfast. She was curious about Nora, one of Syracuse's most popular television anchors. They'd met at seven in the Tavern Lounge of the twenty-seven-room Inn Quill owned with her sister Meg and their partner, John Raintree. Nora was smaller-boned than she appeared on television, and her hair was darker. She was tall for a woman, about Quill's height. She had the well-buffed perfection characteristic of the very wealthy or the fairly famous: short, precision-cut hair; skin like the outside of a choice fruit; clothes that were so expensively made they never wrinkled. She was probably in her early thirties—about Quill's own age—and the six o'clock anchor for a Syracuse network television affiliate.

Quill, not sure how to respond to Nora's slightly rancorous catalog, said vaguely that she hoped she liked the Inn.

"Perfect," said Nora. Then, "I hope nothing happens to spoil it for you. You did all the decorating in here yourself, too?"

The Lounge was a pleasant room, although during those times when Quill's work as a painter wasn't going well, she tended to avoid it. At her sister's insistence, the deep teal walls were hung with Quill's own acrylics from her award-winning Flower series. Sometimes, Quill would look at her work with deep—if slightly guilty—pleasure. More often she despaired of ever achieving that height of line and intense color again. This morning, if the staff hadn't been setting up a fund-raiser brunch for the Inn's most prominent guest, Senator Alphonse Santini (R., New York), she would have taken Nora Cahill to the dining room; her painting hadn't been going well at all. Not for the last few weeks. Not since the trouble with Myles. Which was going to be resolved once and for all at lunch in Syracuse today.

"Was the breakfast okay?" asked Quill. She looked dubiously at Nora's half-eaten crepe Quilliam. It was a specialty of Meg's, cheese soufflé with sour cream and caviar wrapped in a thin Cointreau-flavored pancake.

"Fine," Nora said absently. "Too fine. I've got a lot to accomplish while I'm here. I don't know now if I want to do it. The whole place is so seductive I just want to sit and stuff myself."

A fire snapped warmly in the stone fireplace. The air was filled with the fresh scent of the pine wreaths over the mantel. The long mahogany bar gleamed with lemon-scented polish, and Nate the bartender whistled under his breath as he restocked the shelves. To Nora, here for a week's stay while she covered the Santini wedding, it must have seemed like a refuge. To Quill, who was facing the emotional equivalent of a train wreck—in the middle of the busiest holiday season the Inn had ever had—it felt like jail. She resisted the impulse to run shouting into the snow, and asked again how she could help make Nora's stay at the Inn more comfortable.

"I don't see how you could make it more comfortable." Nora tucked one long leg under the other.

Quill watched Nora's show on the rare occasion when she had free time in the early evenings. Nora had brains and style underneath the glamour. The stories the station permitted her to cover on her own were pungent and well-balanced. "I liked that story you did on teen mothers," Quill offered. "Every time the station lets you do investigative reporting, the show is wonderful. Are you working on anything in particular now?"

Instead of answering Quill's question, Nora admired her teacup. "Even the china's terrific. I've never seen anything like it. It's like that Wedgwood pattern Kutani Crane, only the birds are more vibrant."

"It's a rose-breasted grosbeak," said Quill. "The design was created right here in Hemlock Falls by some friends of ours. They made the Inn a present of a service for twenty-four. I use it a lot."

"Heaven," said Nora, waving a well-groomed hand. "This place is absolute heaven. From the plates to the location. And so peaceful. All this snow and the gorge and the waterfall—it's like something out of a fantasy."

"There are drawbacks," Quill said.

Nora's eyes, which were black and uncomfortably sharp, flicked over her, but she said merely, "Oh, right. Your sister's a three-star chef, the rooms are stuffed with some of the most gorgeous antiques I've seen outside of a museum, and in case you get bored, you can chat up the famous people who stay here." The corners of her mouth turned up. "Of course, I've heard about the ones who come to stay and leave in body bags. You've had more than your fair share of murders in your swell little village, haven't you?"

Quill rubbed her nose. "I suppose that's true."

"Well, it all sounds like fun. Frankly, a nice little domestic murder'd be a welcome change from the stuff I've got to deal with. Ten-car pileups on Interstate 81, teenage hookers, kids who've been beaten to death."

Quill made a noise in protest. Nora shrugged dismissively. "Life of a small-town anchor."

Quill, who'd been reacting to the listing of society's horrors rather than the impediments to Nora's career, glanced at her in surprise.

"So I'm egocentric," Nora said in shrewd response to Quill's expression. "It doesn't take long to knock compassion out of you—not in my business. Too few plum assignments and too many hotshot kids waiting to take your place if you screw up. Nice guys finish last. If they even get in the race at all."

Quill, despite the press of her schedule for the day, was genuinely curious about a life so different from her own. "Why did you
choose it as a career?"

"I could say: You don't know how many journalism students get
inspired by the Woodward and Bernstein affair. I could tell you: I
got suspended from school for staying home to watch the Watergate hearings when I was sixteen. But the truth of the matter is, I
like to bug people. I like to get in their faces."

"Watergate?" said Quill. "Surely not."

"Oh, yeah, I'm a lot older than I look, Quill. A large part of
my salary goes to what's euphemistically known as aging face pro-
cedures. I had my first lift at thirty-seven. Which was two years
later than Mrs. Kennedy had hers." She grinned abruptly. "You
know, kiddo, come to think of it, I can see where you might have
big-time problems as an innkeeper. Anybody could read your face
like a book. How do you keep your guests from finding out how
you really feel about stuff like face-lifts?"

Quill blushed so hard she felt warm. "I don't . . . I mean, if a
face-lift's what you want—" She abandoned this defense, which
sounded lame even to herself, and stood up. "Would you like a few
more of these pastry bows? I'd be happy to send Kathleen for some.
Unfortunately I've got a full morning and I have to get to Syracuse
this afternoon, so unless there's something specific we can do for
you, I'm going to have to excuse myself."

"Sit down and don't mind me, Quill. I'm in the business of nee-
dling people. What I'd like is a tour of the Inn. Officially, I've got
two days vacation before I go back on duty to report on the senator's wedding—"

"Ex-senator," Quill said automatically.

"And thank God for that, right?" said Nora. "I mean the dirt
I've got on that guy. I wish I could broadcast the half of it, but I
can't. Not for a while yet. It'll curl your toes when I do, cookie, let
me tell you." She examined Quill thoughtfully, and a catlike grin
crossed her face. "You might find out yourself, soon enough. Anyhow, as one of the few members of the media brotherhood to be
allowed to cover the Santini wedding, I'm practically guaranteed
a network feed, but I might as well see what other programming
I can scrape up while I'm here. The Inn'd be just right for a little

Christmas Eve spot—you know, as background for the station's Christmas message. Maybe a ten-second spot on holiday food or child carolers. Too much to hope you've got a local bunch of photogenic carolers, I suppose."

"Carolers we've got. The Reverend Mr. Shuttleworth's children's choir from the Church of the Word of God, the Women's chorus from H.O.W., and I'm pretty sure the volunteer firemen are—"

"Wait, wait, wait, wait, wait. H.O.W.? H.O.W. what?"

"The Hemlock Organization for Women," said Quill. "Most of them are here at the Inn right now. Mr. Santini's organized a series of fund-raisers involving some of the local groups. H.O.W. was the first to accept."

"A feminist organization? In a country village the size of what—three thousand and something? And here I thought the happy villagers were farmer's wives and quilters. Well, I'll be dipped. How long has this been going on?"

"Just a few weeks," Quill said uncomfortably. "And it's not anything really radical. At least, they aren't violently radical."

"There's that readable face again." Nora almost purred. "Come on, cookie, there's a story here. Give."

"There's nothing to give." Quill stood up again. (*And this time*, she thought, *I really mean it.*) "I love the idea of the Inn as background for the station's Christmas message. John's always after us to be more public-relations oriented. We used to use a small advertising agency here in town for P.R., but the guy moved on to New York a few weeks ago. So I've sort of assumed the responsibility. What about collecting the staff around the Christmas tree in the foyer? Or the dining room. We put pine garlands around the windows overlooking Hemlock Gorge every year. That'd make a great backdrop, especially if it snows. *When* it snows, I should say, since it always snows up here in December."

Nora closed a cool hand firmly around Quill's wrist. "Just call me Bird Dog. What about H.O.W.?"

Quill sat down at the tea table again. The table was a drop leaf, made of cherry. She'd found a set of four fan-backed chairs in the back room at a farmhouse auction and refinished them to go with the table. She looked at the empty chair opposite Nora with critical attention. The cotton damask upholstery wasn't wearing well.

"Quill?"

"Hmm?"

"The investigative reporter thing is in my blood. If you don't tell me, I'll just ask somebody else. Like that Mrs. Muxworthy, your housekeeper?"

"Doreen," said Quill. She bit her finger nervously, then folded both hands firmly in her lap.

"That's the one. She looks just like somebody who'd know everything about everybody in a town this size. Kind of like a nosy rooster."

Quill was conscious of exasperation. "Doreen's a friend of mine," she said stiffly, and then immediately regretted it. The most irritating thing about Nora was her gift for backing people—okay, her, Quill—into defensive positions. And for demanding and getting sententious responses. "There's nothing special or unusual about H.O.W."

Nora picked up a pastry bow, inspected it, took a large bite, and set it back on the plate. Quill tugged at her hair in irritation. Who was going to eat a half-bitten pastry bow? The recipe was one of Meg's best. And it was expensive to make. And it wasn't just the one mangled pastry bow, there were three half-eaten ones abandoned on Nora's plate as well as the half-gutted crepe. This was significant of Nora's attitude in general. Mentally she counted backward from five, then said, "H.O.W.'s not a story, really. Just an incident in the life of a small town. We had village elections this year in November and in the general upset—"

"All of New York's Democrats lost their seats. I wouldn't call it a general upset. The whole thing was a rout."

"Well, we both know a lot of incumbents lost their seats. And not just the governor and Alphonse Santini. The Village of Hemlock Falls town government toppled, too. Our justice of the peace has been replaced." Quill hoped her smile wasn't too stiff. "And so was our sheriff, and a couple of other officials."

"The sheriff, yeah," said Nora, clearly bored, "so what kind of job does a small-town sheriff get after he's been dumped?"

"A pretty remunerative one. Myles, that is, Sheriff McHale had been one of the top detectives with the N.Y.P.D. before he retired here. After the—um—upset, he took a job with one of those global investigative bureaus. They made him quite an offer. They're send-ing him overseas for a year." Quill carefully pulled the mint out of her grapefruit juice and set it on the rim of her saucer. Her hands were steady.

Nora lifted a sarcastic eyebrow. "Wow. So what was the reason behind this political cataclysm?"

Quill breathed a little easier. Evidently her readable face was in a foreign language, for once. "Our party lines were gender-based this year. No special reason, really," she added hastily, "I mean, none at all. It started with a marital spat between our mayor and his wife and kind of escalated from there. The women lost, the women voters, that is, and the male voters won, and so the Cham-ber of Commerce split up."

"What does the Chamber of Commerce have to do with the price of bananas in Brazil?" There was an impatient edge to Nora's voice.

Quill offered her the last intact pastry bow, grateful that she'd escaped interrogation about the gender wars, and even more grateful that she didn't have to attempt indifference about Myles McHale. "I'll get to that. You'd be amazed how labyrinthian small-town politics can be."

"If you think that life in Syracuse is any different, think again. It's just a bigger small town, that's all." She dug into her purse for a cigarette, lit it, and blew the smoke upward. "I'm not going to be around that hick town for long if I can help it, or this one either, for that matter. So what about the relationship of the Chamber of Commerce to H.O.W.?"

"The Chamber of Commerce had always been the focal point of social and political village life. Not anymore. The men have formed their own organization and the women have formed theirs, and they meet separately instead of together. It's kind of stalled civic events. So I don't know how successful you'd be in finding a newsworthy story to add to your coverage of the Santini wedding. We have almost no crime here. Just a little shoplifting and that's mainly kids. And, as I said, village activity is at a temporary stand-still. So," finished Quill, getting up from her chair with a decisive movement, "that's about it. I've got to get going, Nora. Between the wedding and Santini's entourage and their fund-raiser and

Christmas, I don't know which end is up today. I can ask one of the staff to take you around the Inn if you want to scout locations for a possible background tape. Or I can call Reverend Shuttleworth and you can listen to the children's choir rehearse this afternoon. Or . . ." Inspiration hit. "You can go listen to Alphonse Santini in the dining room, talking to H.O.W. Maybe there's a story there."

"The camera crew won't be up until tomorrow. And I've listened to that fathead more times than I can count."

"I'd have to agree with you about the fathead part," Quill said incautiously. "Well, you'll let us know if there's anything we can do to make your stay more pleasant."

Nora grinned and brushed crumbs from her wool trousers. They were white wool, beautifully tailored. Quill was immediately conscious of her own calf-length wool skirt (which had never really recovered from an encounter with a damp paint palette) and the small hole in the elbow of her sweater.

"There's one thing you can do to make my stay more worthwhile." Nora cocked her head. With her long nose and high cheekbones she looked like an elegant heron. "I need the guest list for the Santini wedding."

Quill, with six years innkeeping experience behind her, had long accustomed herself to the necessity for small social lies. She shook her head regretfully. "We don't have it, Nora. I'm sorry. But I'm sure the senator does. Why don't you ask him?"

"Quill!"

Quill turned. Dina Muir, full-time Cornell graduate student and part-time receptionist at the Inn, stood at the Lounge entrance waving a sheaf of papers.

"Mrs. McIntosh just called. There's a new guest list for the wedding, she said. What do you want me to do with this one?"

"Um," said Quill.

"I think the new one is much longer than the old one." Dina hesitated. "But before you take a look, I think you should know that there's some kind of problem in the dining room. With the fund-raiser buffet. Maybe you better take a look."

Nora swept past Quill like the bird she resembled and dived for the list in Dina's hand. "I'll throw this out for you, kid."

"Nora," said Quill. "I don't think—"

"Phooey," said Nora, "I can get it from Al anytime. I just want to see what good old *paesanos* the father of the bride's invited before I actually cover the damn thing."

"*Paesanos?*" said Quill.

Nora hummed a few bars of the theme from *The Godfather*.

"McIntosh," Quill said faintly. "The bride's family's name is McIntosh. That's Scot."

"You've met Vittorio McIntosh?"

"Claire's father? Well, no, I—"

"Surely you've *heard* about Vittorio McIntosh."

"Quill!" Dina said. "Honestly, I really, really think you should check out this breakfast thing."

Quill, who'd been aware of a rising hum from the direction of the dining room, rather like the distant sound of a very large wave offshore, resisted the impulse to clutch her head with both hands. "What's the prob—never mind. Nora, it was . . . it was . . . inappropriate," Quill concluded lamely, "that's the word, inappropriate, to grab that list. Even though you have been invited to the wedding. Could you please give it back to me?"

"Wow!" said Dina. "Hear that?"

"Shouts!" said Nora, with a pleased air. "Damn. And I don't have a camera with me. Excuse me, guys."

Quill took a deep breath and followed Nora through the lounge, past the foyer, and into the dining room at what she hoped was a casually unobvious pace: rapid but unworried.

The dining room was one of Quill's favorite spots at the Inn. In the mornings, sunshine streamed in the floor-to-ceiling windows overlooking Hemlock Gorge, flooding the room with light. In summer, the light was freshly gold; in winter, the snow and icebound Falls were a crystal prism, refracting white sunlight across the deep mauve carpet and the round tables. Quill especially liked the room just before they opened for meals with the deep wine carpet glowing and the glasses and cutlery sparkling. Even now, as a fork caught a shard of sunlight as it flew threw the air and landed in front of (ex) Senator Alphonse Santini, Quill found time to appreciate the beauty of the room.

He flung his hand in front of his face and ducked. An ominous grumbling filled the ranks of women seated before him. H.O.W.'s membership numbered around forty; forty annoyed women, Quill realized, made quite a formidable audience. She was the one who'd suggested that eight tables of five women each be arranged in a circle around Santini, his two blue-suited factotums, and his fiancée Claire McIntosh. Claire, blond hair stiffly teased in a sunburst around her angular face, sat pugnaciously silent.

"If I've offended any of you ladies, you certainly misunderstood my little joke." Santini raised his hands to either side of his ears in an eerily Nixonian gesture. Like Nixon, he had jowls that were rapidly moving from the incipient to the pendulous. Unlike Nixon, he was short, with a basketball-sized belly.

"Put a sock in it, Al!" yelled one of the supervisors from Paramount Paints.

"So we can boot your behind!" shrieked somebody else. Betty Hall, Quill thought, although she wasn't sure. She hoped not. Betty was the best pitcher in the Hemlock Women's Softball League. If Betty threw forks, they'd hit the target.

"You gonna take one percent outta *my paycheck* to fee-nance your next campaign?" roared a familiar foghorn voice. "Outta that paycheck you just tole us should go to some outta work man?!"

"Doreen!" said Quill.

"Finance," Claire McIntosh said in a nasal Long Island accent. "It's FI-nance. Not fee-nance. Huh!"

Doreen rose furiously from her seat, bristling, skinny neck thrust out. "I got just as much right to work as anyone else."

"Hoo!" said Nora, clearly delighted. "Quill! You don't think he pulled that conservative bullshit about women staying home to take care of their men with this group, do you? Santini Screws Up Again!" She dug a notebook out of her purse and began to scribble.

"Or maybe you could send me somma that there federal housing money that built your fancy home in Westchester!" Doreen, gray hair frizzed to a righteous height, pitched a spoon after the fork. This piece of silverware struck Santini's right arm and bounced into Claire McIntosh's lap.

"Eeew," she said.

Quill turned to Dina, eyebrows raised. "How did this start, anyhow?"

"He asked for questions from the floor, or something. Doreen asked about that business of his appearing as a character witness for the Mafia—sorry—alleged Mafia guy," Dina said in an undertone. "Then she went on about how he let his own brother use his name in that deal with the Pentagon, and that Santini should be ashamed of himself, and then Claire McIntosh said Doreen should stay home and take care of her family instead of taking up a paycheck that should go to one of the unemployed male heads of households inflicted on us by our Democratic president, then Senator Santini sort of smirked and said, 'Power to the little woman,' or something like that, then Doreen said her political movement—Doreen's, I mean—"

"Doreen's into politics?" said Quill. She swallowed twice. Doreen's transient fancies had always involved the entrepreneurial before this. "She's into politics when we've got a senator's wedding here in four days?"

"Ex-senator," Dina said. "And it's not just Doreen; basically he's insulted all the ladies in H.O.W. WINDBAG!" she roared suddenly.

"Dina, for heaven's sake!"

"Greedy guts, Al!" shrieked Miriam Doncaster, Hemlock Falls' blue-eyed blond librarian.

"Get yer snout outta the public trough, Al!" shouted Marge Schmidt. (Hemlock Hometown Diner. Fine Food! and Fast!)

"Yaaaahhh, Al!" chorused various members of the Hemlock Organization of Women.

"Ladies, ladies, ladies." (ex) Senator Santini's rather watery blue eyes gleamed angrily behind thick-lensed spectacles. Quill had met him several times over the course of his stay at the Inn. It was a curious fact that although he sent his shirts out to be laundered every day (valet service courtesy of the Inn at Hemlock Falls) his shirts always looked as though they had been slept in. "If you'll bear with me just a moment, I'd like to point out that not once, I tell you not once, have I been convicted of any of these alleged crimes."

"They aren't alleged crimes," Dina shouted indignantly. "They ARE crimes."

"Dina!" Quill whispered. "Hush! Let's give everyone a chance to quiet down."

"Not once have I even been indicted for a crime . . ."

"It's a fine state of affairs," Miriam Doncaster said tartly, "when the best that can be said of a politician is that he hasn't been indicted."

A chorus of rumbles from the assembled women suggested a fresh outbreak of cutlery casting was imminent.

"What are you going to do?" Dina hissed. "He'll be pitching stuff back at 'em in a minute. The way he did at that press conference in Queens when he conceded the Senate race."

"Is John in yet?" Quill asked in a cowardly way.

"Not till eleven or so. He drove Mrs. McIntosh to the florists in Ithaca to check on the roses for the reception. LOBBYIST!" she screamed suddenly.

"Senators can't be lobbyists," Quill said, exasperated. "It's illegal."

"There you are," Dina said mysteriously.

Quill cleared her throat and, holding her hands up, wound her way through the tables to the mahogany sideboard where Senator Santini had fled, rather like Robert De Niro at bay in *Frankenstein*. He was gesturing forcefully at Nora Cahill, his voice an angry mutter.

"Marge. Adela." She nodded to Marge Schmidt and Adela Henry, president and vice president of the Hemlock Organization for Women. "How are you guys this morning?"

"Just fine, till this bozo started in on disintegration of the American family," snorted Marge. Her keen little eyes, buried in an impressive amount of muscular fat, bored in on Santini. "Seemed to think it was wimmin's fault."

"I'm certain you misunderstood, Mrs. . . . ah"—Santini ducked forward to glimpse at Marge's name tag—"Schmidt. If any of you ladies took any offense at what was simply meant to be a joke—"

"It's Miss," Marge said shortly, "and I take offense where offense was meant." She rose to her feet, a truculent bulldozer, and gave Quill a friendly punch in the arm. "Good food, as usual. Tell Meg I like the idea of saffron in the scrambled eggs. Ladies, let's beat it."

There was a general scraping of chairs. Adela Henry (who up until the disastrous elections of November 8 had been more widely known as Mrs. Mayor) nodded graciously to Quill. "Have you made a decision about joining our organization, Quill?"

"Innkeepers," Quill said firmly, "should be apolitical."

"It is not possible to be apolitical in these times," Adela said darkly. "A woman has to stand for something."

"Right on," said Doreen, veering in their direction. "Power to the oppressed."

"Amen," said Mrs. Dookie Shuttleworth, the minister's wife.

Adela elevated her chin to a DeGaullean height. "Those who are not with us, must be against us. We will expect you, Quill, at the next meeting."

"Can't we just have the Chamber of Commerce back?" Quill said plaintively. "I enjoyed the Chamber meetings. I *liked* the Chamber meetings. The Chamber meetings accomplished a lot of good. Things like Clean It Up! week, and Hemlock History Days, and the boutique mall where our restaurant . . ." She trailed off. Each of these events, in one way or another, had ended in some degree of disaster. "Um," said Quill. She thought a moment. "Did I tell you I checked the Innkeeper's Code of Laws?"

"You did not. I was not aware there was any such institutionalization of innkeeping behaviors."

There would be by nightfall if she had a few minutes with her computer and printer. Quill gestured vaguely. "The code bars me from any political affiliation. Sort of like judges, you know." She gave Doreen a meaningful stare. "It bars housekeepers, too."

Doreen made a noise like "T'uh!"

"I see." Adela regarded Al Santini, who was shaking hands with as many departing H.O.W. members as would allow it, with disapproval. "We've determined, as you may know, that the fourth Thursday of every month shall be the official H.O.W. meeting date. That's the day after tomorrow, assuming that the conference room here will be free at that time. The Innkeeper's Code cannot possibly bar political meetings of ordinary citizens."

Quill tried to concentrate. There was something about that date . . . She shook her head. "I'll have to check the calendar. I think it will be okay, but I'm not altogether certain."

"I will take that as a yes. Come, Marge, Doreen. We'll retire to Marge's diner. I have a few ideas about the protest that I'd like you to hear."

"Protest?" asked Quill. "Wait a minute. What protest?"

"Never you mind," said Doreen. "I'll see ya later."

"Doreen!" Quill yelled in frustration at their retreating backs. "Are you planning to come into work today, or what?!"

"Labor troubles?" asked Al Santini in passing. "You should vote Republican."

"It's not going to affect the wedding, is it?" Claire, tagging behind her betrothed like a dingy caboose, clutched Quill's arm. She demanded in her nasal twang, "Daddy'd be *reee*ly upset if anything affected the wedding."

Quill opened her mouth to assure Claire of the absolute integrity and quality of the Inn's level of service, but Claire rolled on, "You go ahead, Al. Quill? We need to talk. Where can we talk?"

Quill surveyed the dining room. It had emptied with dismaying rapidity. Even the nosy Nora had gone—before, Quill hoped, she'd heard any intimations of a political protest to be staged by H.O.W. "Of course, Claire. Let's sit down here."

"The tables haven't been cleared," Claire said. "I hate it when the tables haven't been cleared. You're sure that your staff is up to this? I mean, I've had my doubts about this little backwater even though Mummy said your sister is absolutely famous. But, I mean, my *Go*-od, there's nothing here. It's all very well for you. Mummy said everybody who's anybody knows about your painting, although I never heard of you in my art appreciation classes, and I guess you can paint on the moon or anyplace like that if you want to."

"Claire," said Quill. "Follow me over here. To the window."

Claire trailed Quill like a quarrelsome duckling. Quill pushed her gently into a chair at table seven, sat down opposite her, and fixed her with a firm—yet friendly—glare. "Now. How can I help you?"

Somebody, Kathleen the head waitress, most likely, who had been taking evening courses at the nearby Cornell Hotel school, had folded the crisp white napkins into elaborate tulip shapes. Claire picked one up, unfolded it, tried to refold it, and blew her nose in it. "Sorry. Allergies. Look. You've got to think of some way to keep my grandmother out of this wedding."

"Excuse me?"

Claire frowned. She was a natural blonde, in her late twenties, with the dry papery skin that affects thin women who spend too much time in the sun. In a few years, she was going to need the services of Nora Cahill's plastic surgeon. "Tutti," she said impatiently, "Daddy's mother. My *grand*mother."

Quill tugged at her hair, examined a curl, then said, "You don't want your grandmother at the wedding?"

"Of course not. She'll spoil everything!"

"This is just a little case of nerves, Claire. You'll be fine. I can't imagine how your grandmother could spoil your wedding. Is she ill? Are you afraid it might be too much for her? We have an excellent internist here, and a very fine small clinic. If she needs medical help, we'll be happy to make arrangements for a nurse."

"She doesn't need a nurse. She's crazy," Claire said resentfully.

"Oh, dear. Is it Alzheimer's? I'm so sorry, Claire."

"Good grief, no. She's not certifiable. At least a judge wouldn't think so. Stupid jerk."

Quill wasn't sure if this last referred to her, to the unknown judge, or to Tutti, and she wasn't about to inquire. Her own grandmother had been an elegant, forceful lady whom she had loved very much. "Gosh, Claire. I don't think I can do too much about your guest list. That's really the province of, um . . . the family. What does your mother say?"

"You know Mummy. She doesn't *inhale* without Daddy's okay."

"And this is your father's mother."

"My *grand*—"

"Yes," said Quill. Her temper—not at its equable best in the past few weeks—suddenly snapped. "I can't imagine how in the world I would prevent her from coming. Even if I wanted to. Which I don't."

"You could tell her the Inn is full. You could give her room to somebody."

"No," Quill said flatly. "As I said, we can suggest a good nursing service, if you really find it necessary . . ."

Claire sniffed scornfully. "A nurse for Tutti? Tutti can flatten a nurse in two seconds. Maybe less." She blew her nose once more in the napkin and dropped it disdainfully on the table. "All I have to say, if this wedding's wrecked . . ." She stood up, leaned over Quill, and hissed, "It'll be all your fault!"

CHAPTER 2

Margaret Quilliam tucked a sprig of holly under the pig's ear and stepped back to regard her work.

"Guy I knew in the old neighborhood looked a lot like that after he welshed on a bet," said Alphonse Santini. He flung both hands up and cowered behind them in mock self-defense. Quill, who'd fled into the kitchen in search of respite, hadn't been pleased to find him there. "Hands out" was a gesture she was becoming all too familiar with, since Al had spent a large portion of the last three days harassing Quill and her sister Meg, when he wasn't aggravating the citizens of Hemlock Falls. The gesture always accompanied his notions of what was funny. Al considered himself quite a humorist.

"I'm sorry," she said, "about the fund-raiser. You've arrived at Hemlock Falls at sort of a peculiar time in the town's political history."

"That bitch Cahill," he said without rancor. "The press. Go figure."

"I don't think . . ." Quill paused. For all she knew, Nora may have prompted the H.O.W. revolt at breakfast, although to be fair, she couldn't see how.

"So. This roast pig's for a special occasion? Or what? Kinda early for Christmas."

The pig contemplated the ceiling. Meg contemplated the pig. Quill, whose testiness was increasing as the time for her lunch with Myles drew nearer, drummed her fingers on the butcher block counter. She stopped, not wanting to be rude. Ex-Senator Santini hacked into a well-used handkerchief, wiped his nose, and repeated his question about the roast pig. One of Meg's sneaker-shod feet began to beat an irritable tattoo on the flagstone kitchen floor. Quill held on to her own temper firmly and said in as diplomatic a tone as she could manage, "It's a special order for a men's organization in the village. Now, to get back to your wedding reception, Mr. Santini."

His eyes slid sideways at Quill. "I keep the title Senator, you get my drift? Even though I lost this time around. Most of my compadres call me Senator Al."

Quill, who'd been refusing Mr. Santini the honorific out of nothing more than perversity, decided to relent. For one thing, Senator Santini did have a miserable sloppy cold—or allergies—and he wasn't complaining about it. In Quill's opinion, far too many people with colds made their misery yours. For another, he was short for a man, about her own height, which made his frequent demands for attention more understandable, at least to Quill.

Quill had never gotten used to the fact that celebrities in person looked smaller than they did on television. This shrinkage made her sympathetic. Or maybe, she thought, they weren't smaller than they appeared. Maybe she'd only met celebrities who were smaller than the average person. The alternative was that her subconscious enlarged public figures based on the size of their reputations, which still didn't explain why she'd expected Senator Al to be bigger than he actually was, since his politics were so awful.

He certainly wasn't conventionally good-looking. He was balding, with lank brown hair that flopped over his ears. He had small, rather watery blue eyes and a potbelly. None of this explained his undoubted appeal. Despite his height and rather flabby appearance, ex-Senator Al Santini definitely had charisma. The charisma might have been due to his voice, which was deep and resonant. Since he had a heavy Long Island accent, Quill didn't think so. It'd be a challenge to paint his portrait. She'd have to capture the charm and still get across the greed, vulgarity, and boys-in-the-back-room politics that had—finally, after three terms—lost him the race for the Senate.

"Quill?" Santini rapped his knuckles on the butcher block counter. "I got snot on my face or what?"

"Sorry, Senator," Quill said. "You were saying?"

"We got a few more people coming than we'd planned on."

Meg clutched her forehead, groaned, and said mildly, "Your mother-in-law—prospective mother-in-law, I should say—has been taking care of everything just fine, Senator. Did you check this new number with her?"

Senator Al waved largely. "She's busy with the other stuff. My guys've been on the horn. I'm telling you, we've gotta be prepared for a crush."

Meg and Quill carefully avoided looking at one another. Senator Al had been unseated in a rash of very bad publicity six weeks ago; *Newsweek*'s editorial on the demise of his career had been scathingly final. Earlier in the week, they'd wondered if anyone would show up at all.

Meg said patiently, "Your fiancée Claire booked our Inn in April for a December wedding. In May you gave us the count for the reception—small, you said, since you didn't want a media circus. Forty, you said. Twenty of the immediate family, and twenty of your nearest and dearest friends. In the last few days you've gone from twenty to forty to seventy. Now, four days before the wedding, you want to bounce it to two hundred!?" Meg's face got pink, which made her gray eyes almost blue. Her voice, however, remained soft, although emphatic. "Our dining room won't *take* two hundred. I can't *cook* for two hundred. Not in four days."

Al Santini waved expansively. "Hire all the help you need. Money's no object."

This blithe disregard for the fiscal gave Quill a clue as to a possible reason why the senator's campaign finances had occasioned such investigative furor from the national media.

Meg stared at him expressionlessly. "If I could hire somebody else to do what I do, do you think *I'd* be doing it?"

"Say what?"

Quill, grateful for Meg's unusual equanimity, and not too sure how long it would last, interrupted, "My sister's a great chef, Mr. Santini. A three-star chef. There aren't a lot of people who can cook with her style. I know that's one of the reasons your fiancée and her family wanted to have the wedding here. And, honestly, this last-minute change just isn't possible. You can't expect Meg to do a five-course dinner for two hundred. Not with this kind of notice. And not in our dining room. We don't have the space." Especially, she added to herself, for a guest list that was unlikely to materialize.

Senator Al put a large hand on Meg's shoulder and bent down to look her earnestly in the eye. "Five-course dinner? Am I asking you for a five-course dinner? Absolutely not. No question. But I got a problem here, you understand that? I got a hundred, maybe two hundred people that are going to be coming to my wedding."

"Which is it?" Meg asked patiently.

Santini shrugged. "Who knows? All I'm saying is we gotta prepare for the contingency."

"Contingency," Meg said. "Right."

"I got a couple of Supreme Court justices, a couple a guys from the Senate, ambassadors, and what all coming to this shindig. Important people, you know?"

Meg rubbed her forehead and squeezed her eyes shut.

"Which is how come I can't give you an exact count. If there's a war, or something, or like Bosnia heats up again? You gonna tell General Schwarzkopf he can't hightail it to the action on account of he's supposed to be at my reception?"

"General Schwarzkopf's coming?" said Quill.

Senator Al shrugged. "He got an invitation. I expect him. Look, I don't want to say too much, okay? But there's something of national significance coming down pretty soon. And the eye of the nation is gonna be on Hemlock Falls."

Meg rolled her eyes at Quill.

The double swinging doors to the dining room banged open. One of the blue-suited men from the Santini entourage stuck his head inside the kitchen, a portable phone in one hand. Quill couldn't remember which of the men it was; they all looked and sounded alike. "Senator? We finally got Nora Cahill to agree to the interview. We have her in the conference room."

"Yeah, yeah, yeah, I'll be right there. You see? It's starting already. Now we got the media. So we bag the five-course dinner for seventy. We do heavy hors d'oeuvres. Stand-up. A buffet, like. The dining room can handle that if you take out the tables. So, Meg, dolly. No dinner."

"Dolly?" Meg said blankly. *"Dolly?"*

"We're looking at serving two hundred, right? If we can't seat 'em, let 'em stand. That pig, there?" He flicked his finger at the holly under its ear. "You roast a couple of those, we're all set."

"Heavy hors d'oeuvres for two hundred," Meg said stonily, "means a steamship round, pasta and shells, and baked BEANS!" She planted both hands on either side of the pig and drew breath. If one didn't know her very well, the expression on her face might pass for a smile. It put Quill herself, who knew her sister better than anybody, in mind of the wrong side of an outraged baboon. To Quill's amazement, Meg swallowed twice, and said merely, "Why don't we take the change in the menu up with Mrs. McIntosh?"

Santini, clearly unaware he'd escaped a verbal tsunami, continued, "So, no roast pig. I can live with it. If the food's a little less fancy than we planned—don't sweat it." His pat on Meg's shoulder was dismissive. "I gotta take this interview. So, look. You got more questions about the menu? Talk to the ball and chain."

"The what?" Meg demanded.

"Claire. My fiancée. Or her ma. Either one. Same-same." He waved at Quill, gave Meg the high sign, pointed a pistol-like forefinger at them, and went *pow*! "Catch you all later."

The double doors swung shut behind him.

"I don't believe it," said Meg. "Ball and chain? Dolly? Oh, *God.* I can't *stand* it!" She ran her hands through her short dark hair.

"Steamship round?" said Quill. "And pasta and shells?"

Meg grinned. "It's tempting, isn't it? That idiot."

"That's all you've got to say? That idiot?"

Meg shrugged. "Why should I waste my breath? It's kind of pathetic, thinking that all these people are showing up for this party. Mrs. McIntosh told me herself that one of the reasons they picked our Inn is because it's so hard to get to in the winter. He's got a guaranteed excuse for nobody accepting the invitations. I have no idea where all this last-minute *agita* is coming from."

"Maybe he's nervous about getting married," said Quill.

"Whatever. Anyway, Claire and her mother have had seventy acceptances. Almost all relatives. Five-course dinner with no expenses spared. That's what the McIntoshes are paying for and that's what they'll get. General Schwarzkopf, my eye."

Quill twisted a strand of hair around one finger and tugged at it. "You don't think . . ."

"That two hundred politicians, ambassadors, and the President's cabinet are going to show up for this wedding? On Christmas Eve? In central New York?" Meg gestured toward the window. The kitchen faced the vegetable gardens at the back of the Inn. Quill could barely see the tops of the brussels sprouts for the snow. "They're predicting four inches more by this afternoon. If the rest of the wedding party doesn't get here by tomorrow, we'll have to cancel the reception and eat each other like the Donner party since we'll undoubtedly get snowed in. Which reminds me. I thought you were going to have lunch with Myles in Syracuse. You better give yourself plenty of time to get there."

"I'll be fine," Quill said. "I told him two o'clock."

"You're sure about it," Meg said, after a pause. "I mean, this business about it being the last lunch."

Quill nodded. "This relationship is just—not going anywhere."

"You want to talk about it?"

"No."

"You're sure?"

"I'm sure."

"Well, at least it should end all this angst."

"What angst?" Quill demanded.

"The angst that's kept you functioning at half speed for the past couple of months. Good grief, Quill, you haven't even gone through the mail this past week."

Quill, who absolutely did not want to talk about her farewell to Myles until it was all over, changed the subject abruptly. "What's with the pig? It's down on the schedule as a delivery before noon. It's half past eleven now. Would you like me to take it somewhere before I leave for Syracuse?"

"One of the *sous*-chefs should be here soon. Unless the snow gets worse." She pulled the clipboard that held the day's rota from the wall by the small TV and studied it. "Bjarne's on today. He's a Finn and they're used to the snow. I'll get him to do it." Meg moved the roast pig into one of the aluminum pans they used to transport food and looked at it with a frown. "Do *you* think the holly's too Christmassy?"

Quill vaguely recollected Santini's offhand comment. "On the pig? Maybe a little."

"The holly's not in celebration of Christmas. It's a subtle reminder of the Druid influence on the S.O.A.P. rituals. Not that those idiots would know a Druid from a downspout."

Quill looked doubtful. "Suckling pig only serves twelve to fourteen, doesn't it? Last count, actual S.O.A.P. membership was thirty-two."

"The meeting this afternoon isn't the whole membership. It's just the executive committee. Elmer Henry, Dookie Shuttleworth, Harland Peterson, and those guys."

Quill sat in the rocker by the cobblestone fireplace, propped her feet on the hearth, and rocked back and forth. Menu planning had been a lot simpler before the Chamber of Commerce had split into two rival factions. S.O.A.P. wanted earthy, primitive fare with a gourmet touch, and H.O.W. was seriously considering vegetarian. She had a vague recollection that holly had something to do with Druid rites, but she wasn't sure what. "I don't think that S.O.A.P. is based on Celtic mythology. I think it's AmerInd."

"Do American Indians strip to the waist, paint themselves blue, and stick stones in their hair?"

"Is that what they do at those meetings?"

Meg grinned. "So I've heard. But it's just gossip. The men won't talk about it, and the women don't know anything because the men aren't talking." She began to pack the pig in aluminum foil. "It's all Miriam Doncaster's fault, anyway. She never should have let the mayor have a copy of *The Branch of the Root*. It's a stupid book."

Quill's mood wasn't improving, and wouldn't, she knew, until the final lunch with Myles was over. She said crossly, "How do you know it's a stupid book? Have you read it?"

Meg raised her eyebrows. "See this look on my face?"

Quill shoved the rocker into motion and muttered, "Never mind."

"Cheerful sarcasm," Meg said, "that's the look on my face. We're still recuperating from the Thanksgiving rush. We're headed into even worse chaos between Christmas and the most boring wedding of the decade, and you want to know if I've found time to read a seven-hundred-page book that's supposed to get white guys in touch with their maleness, for Pete's sake?"

"Good point."

"You betcha." She glanced at her watch. "You go on to your lunch in Syracuse."

"I've got lots of time." Quill wriggled her toes in the warmth of the fire. The kitchen was redolent with cinnamon, sage, and garlic. Meg had left the Thermo glass doors to her grill open when she'd removed the roast. Every now and then a bit of cracking fell from the rotisserie spit onto the flames with a hiss. The smell of seared pork and the warmth of the fire contrasted pleasantly with the wind-whipped snow outside.

The back door banged and Bjarne the Finnish *sous*-chef burst into the room.

"I am late," he announced. He was very tall—as most of the Finnish students seemed to be—and had a ruddy, hearty sort of face with bright blue eyes.

"So you are," said Meg. "Don't take off your coat. I want you to deliver this pig."

"It is a beautiful pig," said Bjarne. "A prince of a pig."

"It is, isn't it?" said Meg, pleased. "It's for the S.O.A.P. meeting."

"Ah," said Bjarne, with an air of enlightenment.

"You've heard about them, too?" asked Meg.

"Oh, yes."

"Have you been to a meeting, Bjarne?"

He shook his head.

"Well, take this pig and see if you can crash it. Then report back to us. Quill and I want you to be a spy."

"*I* don't," said Quill. "Who cares what goes on at those meetings?"

"I do. Ever since the Chamber of Commerce split into these two factions, the village hasn't been the same. It's depressing. It's depressing me and everyone else. Although, to be fair, it's not what's depressing you. This business with Myles is what's depressing you."

"Stop," said Quill.

"It's not that the women aren't incredibly curious about S.O.A.P. Marge Schmidt thinks they hold sacrificial rites under the statue of General Hemlock in the park. Betty Hall thinks they toss the bodies into the gorge because Esther West told her she's heard weird noises at night near the waterfall."

"Esther thinks *The X-Files* is based on factual information from the FBI," Quill pointed out. "She's not what I'd call a reliable source."

"*The X-Files* is what's going to happen now that the Republicans have been reelected," Meg said darkly.

"I know what happens at the men's group," Bjarne offered, to Meg's surprise. "There are drums. Drums are an important part of the ritual. *The Branch of the Root* connects the hand and the heart and the"—his pale blue eyes looked wistfully down at Meg—"male root. Through the drum. The root of the primitive puts us in touch with ourselves. They chant. They eat. And beat drums."

Meg, who was short, bent her head back to look Bjarne in the eye. "How do *you* know? Nobody's even sure what the acronym means."

Bjarne shrugged. "I hear. From the other students. At the hotel school. This S.O.A.P. is the Search for Our Authentic Primitive. It is perhaps based in a true Norse heritage. The heritage of the dominant, all-conquering male. There is a warrior code, involving this pig. Pigs are well-known hunter-gatherers of the animal kingdom. They are a forest animal, living off of roots and berries. There is a spiritual link to the earth when you eat a pig. This is not merely a pig. This is an emblem for the wild boar. Wild boar is warrior food. The strong, the heroic, the conqueror warrior male is very Finnish. This S.O.A.P. search is a familiar one to us Finns."

"*We* Finns," Meg said, a little testily. "Norse. Indian. Druid. Whatever. It's hooey. If I catch you joining these bozos, Bjarne, I'll turn you blue myself. With a rolling pin."

Bjarne grinned. Meg's temper was a matter of legend among the Cornell students who apprenticed in her kitchen.

"Besides, in this weather you'll catch cold and sneeze all over the sauces."

Bjarne frowned. "This cold, it is nothing. You should be in Helsinki in November. Besides, Finns don't catch cold. We are quite tough."

Meg planted her wooden spoon firmly in the middle of Bjarne's chest. "Wrap the pig. Then deliver it to the park. To the statue of General Hemlock. And forget spying and get back here fast. We've got a lot to do today."

Quill looked past Meg, Bjarne, and the pig to the mullioned windows. One of the big advantages of the location of the twenty-seven-room Inn she owned with Meg and their partner John Raintree was the sprawling grounds and the room for a good-sized vegetable garden. Quill could see most of this garden from her seat by the fire. The snow was falling faster than ever and the parsnips weren't visible at all. She said aloud, "It's going to be cold and miserable in those woods. Maybe we should add hot coffee to the delivery. Those S.O.A.P. guys will freeze their blue-painted chests off. Or what about some mulled cider?"

"Nothing but what the woods provide," said Bjarne. "They cannot eat or drink food from unauthentic civilizations."

"Unauthentic?" asked Quill.

"Any culture that's been afflicted by technology."

Meg snorted. "Well, this pig's the product of some of the best farm technology around." She leered like Jack Nicholson after his wife in *The Shining*. "It was a happy pig. A clean pig. A pig with buddies. A pig that never even knew the end was coming."

"Cut it out," Quill said testily.

"Anyhow, this pig came straight from the Heavenly Hoggs farm yesterday morning. They're not only the best pork producers in central New York, they're the most up-to-date. This pig's never even seen a tree, much less rooted in the mud for grubs. Half the guys in S.O.A.P. know this. So, phooey on this authentic wild man stuff, and phooey on thinking it's a stand-in for a wild boar."

Bjarne frowned again, then gazed at the pig with a fond expression. "Perhaps I am wrong about this being a boar. Perhaps it is a representation of a poem," he said to Meg, his pale blue eyes alight with passion. "Yes! This pig is an epic poem. An *Edda*."

"It's not a poem, it's a pig. Headed for a party in the woods. 'The woods.'" Meg added, with inspiration if little accuracy, "'are lovely dark and deep/ and we have promises to keep.'"

Quill smiled. "What part of the cold and snowy woods does this get delivered to, Meg?"

"Just to the park. Mayor Henry will be there at noon to pick it up." Meg looked at Bjarne in an abstracted way, as if calculating his market weight. "I'd almost sell my Aga stove for a chance to see what those guys really do in the woods. Myles has got to know where they meet. He was the sheriff, for goodness sake. I don't suppose you'd want to ask him about it at—never mind. I'll join the women's group and bring it up at the next H.O.W. meeting. We'll find out. Nothing can stop a bunch of women with their minds made up."

Quill set her feet on the hearth with a thump. "Why don't you just leave the poor guys alone? If they want to meet in the woods, let them. And let's stay out of this whole village contretemps. We've talked about that before."

Meg gestured grandly with the wooden spoon. "Because the village is falling apart. We don't have a Chamber of Commerce anymore. We've got the Search for Our Authentic Primitive instead and their archrivals the Hemlock Organization for Women and goodness knows what else. Now, I don't care that Elmer and those guys bounce bare-naked around the statue of General Hemlock in twenty-degree weather. But I do care that what passes for town government and plain old social intercourse has come to a screeching halt. Not to mention other kinds of intercourse. Most of the members of the rival groups are married to each other, and nobody's speaking to anyone else. Ever since Elmer started S.O.A.P. and Adela Henry started H.O.W. it's been chaos. Total chaos. Look at what happened with the town elections. Howie and Myles are right out on their kiesters. And we've got some weird new guy in charge of the sheriff's office that gives me and anyone who gets a traffic ticket the creeps. It's not just that S.O.A.P. is ridiculous. It's that something is going on in those meetings that's a threat to comfortable community living."

"I am going now," Bjarne announced. He picked up the foil-wrapped pig. "You will come with me, Meg?"

"No," Meg said. "Don't go out without your hat and gloves. It's freezing out there!"

"I am not so cold," Bjarne said stubbornly.

"You just think it's not so manly to protect yourself against the snow. Wear a hat. And if you drop that pig or join that men's group, don't bother coming back!" She scolded him out the back door, then returned, accompanied by a swirl of cold air. "Now, where was I?"

"You were giving a Margaret Quilliam lecture, 'The Decline and Fall of Hemlock Falls.' We'd be better off planning the Santini wedding."

"Let me tell you something about the Santini wedding. I've decided we can't plan it until after it's over."

"You might have something there," Quill said.

"So, since we can't plan the Santini wedding, we can plan your love life." Meg settled on a stool behind the butcher block countertop and tugged at her short dark hair. She was wearing a fleecy green sweatshirt with the emblem of the Cornell medical school, a red bandanna around her forehead, and her favorite fleece-lined jeans. She looked about sixteen. "How come you've decided to whack Myles around? I thought things were going relatively well. A couple of months ago, you two were talking marriage. Does he even know you're planning on dumping him this afternoon?"

"I'm not planning on dumping him," Quill said indignantly. "I'm terminating the relationship with tact and affection. And does he expect it? Probably not. This new job keeps him on the road. I don't have a chance to see him."

"I can't believe we lost the election," Meg said, momentarily diverted. The results of the town elections in early November had been the topic of exhaustive, repetitive discussion for weeks. Myles had been replaced as sheriff by newcomer Frank Dorset. Howie Murchison was no longer town justice. Bernie Bristol, a retired Xerox engineer from nearby Rochester, had campaigned successfully for Howie's job. The only member of the Old Guard left was Elmer Henry who was the founding father of S.O.A.P. The mayor had retained his job by the merest margin, since H.O.W. sympathizers represented slightly less than fifty percent of the voting population. While most townspeople put the election upset down to what Howie Murchison called the gender wars, Quill herself wasn't so sure. Meg was right. Something very peculiar was going on in the village.

Meg dropped the perennially promising discussion about town politics and bored back in on Quill. "So what are you going to tell him?"

"I haven't thought about it."

Meg went "Phut!" and sprayed Quill.

"Don't go 'phut'!" said Quill.

Meg appeared to be honestly startled. "I went 'phut'?"

"Yes. Do you go 'phut' all over Andy?"

"I don't go 'phut' over anybody."

"You just went 'phut' all over me."

"I give up. Sit there, be a jerk, and just forget it." Meg began to hum through her nose with an elaborate air of indifference.

"And while you're at it, don't make kazoo noises, either."

"All right," Meg said with a deceptive assumption of amiability. "Why don't I just wrap my emotions in Ace bandages like a certain red-haired, straightjacketed, uptight, rule-abiding lady manageress—"

"Lady manageress?"

"Victorian enough for you? Yes! *Lady manageress* who can't stand it when the seas aren't calm." Meg set her hands on her hips, leaned forward, went "Phuut! Phut! PHUT!" and started to hum a Sousa march through her nose so unmelodiously Quill couldn't tell what it was.

"'Stars and Stripes Forever'?" asked John Raintree, coming through the doors that led into the dining room. Doreen stumped in after him.

Meg grinned and increased her volume.

"Has Meg got a new idiosyncrasy?" John guessed. "I liked the socks."

"This one sounds like two cats fightin' over a back fence," Doreen grumbled. "Whyn't you go back to them colored socks? At least they was quiet."

"Doreen," said Quill. "About this protest you mentioned at breakfast . . ."

Doreen glared at the grill sizzling in the fireplace, grabbed a pot holder, pulled the spit free with a sniff of disapproval, then disappeared out the back door, holding the spit. Quill gave it up. She'd find out only when Doreen was ready to spill it, and not before.

John frowned. He had an attractive frown. He was three-quarters Onondaga Indian, and his coal-black hair and coppery skin made him attractive altogether. He was a big success with a substantial portion of the Inn's female guests.

"What's wrong?" Quill asked. "There's no problem with the florist, is there?"

"No. We've got three thousand sweetheart roses arriving early Friday morning and a whole crew of Cornell students to drape them all over the Inn. The flowers are fine. But on the way back from Ithaca, Lane mentioned that she's made a few changes in the reception." John swung his long legs over a stool at the kitchen counter and drew his notebook from the breast pocket of his sports coat.

"We've got a final count?"

"One hundred and fifty. And she's changed to black-tie."

Meg shrieked. "It's for real!?"

Quill sat bolt upright. "One hundred and fifty?! You mean the senator was right?"

"This was supposed to be a small informal ceremony!" Meg yelled. "What are we going to do with one hundred and fifty guests? In evening dress, yet. That means champagne, salmon, the whole high-ticket lot."

"The ceremony's still small. It's the reception that's gotten bigger. So, no dinner, just heavy hors d'oeuvres."

Meg clutched her hair, muttered, and began scribbling frantically on her memo pad.

Quill took a deep breath. "Where the heck are we going to put them all, John?"

"The dining room will hold a hundred and fifty."

"The fire code's for one hundred and twenty. And I hate crowding guests."

A cold eddy of air from the back room announced Doreen's return, minus the spit. "Snowbank," she said in response to Quill's raised eyebrow. "Freeze that grease right offen it. And it's snowing a treat out there. You going to Syracuse, you better get a move on."

"You knew Lane McIntosh in school, didn't you, Doreen?" asked Meg.

"Wasn't Lane, then. She was Ee-laine. Elaine Herkemeyer. Daddy owns that there dairy farm up on Route 96. Marge Schmidt knew her, too. Marge says she's done pretty well for herself, marrying that Vittorio."

Marge, owner and senior partner in the Hemlock Hometown Diner (Fine Food! and Fast!), was probably the wealthiest (and certainly the nosiest) citizen in Hemlock Falls. Lane McIntosh was a former Hemlockian; Marge would know the McIntoshes' balance sheet to the penny because Marge knew every past and current Hemlockian's net worth to the penny.

"I like her," said Meg, although nobody'd said anything derogatory about Lane.

"I like her, too," said John. "But she is . . . ummm . . ."

"Nervous," Quill supplied.

"A little dithery," Meg offered. "Now, that Claire . . ."

"Ugh," Quill agreed.

"That Elaine's gone crazier than an outhouse rat," said Doreen. "Didn't used to be. Always full of piss and vinegar, that one. And now look at her. Worrit about keeping holt of all that money, I shouldn't wonder."

"Well, I think it's very nice that she wants her daughter to be married in Dookie Shuttleworth's church," said Quill. "She told me that's where she married Vittorio, twenty-five years ago. Did you go to her wedding, Doreen?"

Doreen snorted. "Me? Not likely. Marge didn't go neither. On'y ones ast to that weddin' were Vittorio's fancy friends from New York City." Her beady eyes narrowed in recollection. "Elaine tolt you twenty-five? That was thirty years ago, or I'm a Chinaman. Elaine shaving a few years off herself?" She eyed Quill from beneath her graying frizz. "There's plenty of us remember how long ago it was. So. I don't expect to get invited to this one, neither. This Alphonse Santini's some hotshot senator, ain't he?"

"Was," said Quill. Santini's defeat in the recent elections had revived her somewhat shaky faith in the electorate. "He lost. By the way, who gave you all that information about him?"

"Hah?"

"Don't 'hah' me. All that stuff about Mafia hearings and kickbacks you were hollering about at breakfast. Did you read it somewhere?"

Doreen gave her an innocent blink. "I'm a citizen, ain't I? I can subscribe to *Newsweek* like anybody else. Thing is, Santini never shoulda bin elected in the first place. Stuffing the payroll with his sisters and his cousins and his aunts. Bein' bought off by fat-cat political interests."

"Allegedly," said John. "Nothing was ever proven. The official line is that Santini was defeated in this year's general ousting of incumbents, Democratic *and* Republican."

Doreen's snort, honed by years of use against those guests she felt to be both intemperate and obstreperous (Quill surmised this was approximately ninety percent of the Inn's registry at any given moment) had the force of conviction behind it. "Ha!" she said. "And ha! I bin readin' about conspiracy ever since Sheriff McHale and Mr. Murchison got their asses booted out of office six weeks ago. Conspiracy's behind this whole crapola about S.O.A.P., too."

"Conspiracy?" asked Quill. "What conspiracy?"

"On account of Al Santini."

"Doreen, Al Santini lost the election," said Meg. "This is a good thing. He was a bad senator. I voted against him, and I assure you, I am not part of any conspiracy. The election for the Senate has nothing to do with the town elections. Although the town elections may have a lot to do with S.O.A.P. That's a possible conspiracy, I admit it."

"There's a pile that goes on that us citizens don't know nuthin' about. I ast Stoke to look into it on account of it's time he did an editorial."

Doreen's husband, her fourth, was Axminster Stoker, editor and publisher of the *Hemlock Falls Gazette*. The *Gazette* specialized in weddings, funerals, lost dog reports, and, in February in central New York State, a "Notes From Florida" column, which consisted of chatty notes from those residents of Hemlock Falls fortunate enough to afford to escape the brutal winters.

Quill, conscious of foreboding, asked anxiously, "About this protest, Doreen? And this political group? Did you mean H.O.W.? I didn't know H.O.W. considered itself a political group as such."

"Depends on what you mean, 'groups.'"

This was ominous. "Citizen committees. Or anti-federalist

committees. Or, you know," Quill floundered for a moment, "activists."

Doreen was a joiner. Her joining proclivities could be relatively innocent—like Amway—or on more than one occasion, riot-inducing, like the Church of the Rolling Moses. Up until now, her intentions had been good—even worthwhile, but with Doreen, one never knew for sure.

Meg, her attention drawn from her menu planning, looked up. "You signed up for the NRA, Doreen? Or maybe with those guys who dress up in camouflage on weekends and mutter about the FBI planting transmitters in their rear ends?"

Doreen's expression brightened at the mention of gluteal implants.

"Never mind," Quill said hastily. "Just *please*, Doreen. No more throwing stuff at the guests. No forks. No spoons. Got it?"

Doreen grunted. Quill couldn't tell if this signaled agreement or indigestion.

Meg scowled. "We've got a final count for the Santini reception, Doreen. It's a lot larger than we'd thought, so we may be looking at more overnight guests. That's going to affect your maid staffing. What about registration, John? How many people will actually be staying? And for how long?"

John scratched his ear. "Slight overbooking problem."

"That's terrific," Quill said warmly. "I mean, usually we're scrabbling for guests in the winter months. And we've got too many? We can just send the overflow to the Marriott. I've already discussed that with Lane McIntosh, anyhow. She won't mind."

"It isn't overnight guests. It's the conference room. Mrs. McIntosh would like Santini's bachelor party to be held the night before the rehearsal dinner in the conference room. They—er—would prefer not to have to drive after the event."

Doreen sniffed.

"Well, that's okay, isn't it? I mean, ever since the Chamber of Commerce breakup over S.O.A.P., we haven't had any meetings scheduled there at all. I mean, the only thing all December is . . ." She faltered. "Damn and blast. The S.O.A.P. meeting. On the twenty-second. The day before the rehearsal dinner. *That's* what I was trying to remember this morning."

"Right. So?"

"So Adela wants that date for a H.O.W. meeting. And if I tell Mayor Henry and the guys we need them to cancel the S.O.A.P. meeting, they'll be totally bummed, and if I cancel H.O.W., Adela Henry's going to have my guts for garters. She's mad at us already for allowing the men to meet here last month. I can't break my commitment to either one. Now if I ask them to reschedule, she'll think this is a direct shot at H.O.W."

"Right again," John said.

"Ugh." Quill slid down in the rocker. "Ugh, ugh, ugh." Meg was right. The dissolution of the Chamber of Commerce and the formation of the rival rights groups had done a lot more than affect the election for sheriff and town justice.

"Nuts," said Quill. "Any suggestions?"

"Let's lay out the options," John suggested. "We can cancel both and have Adela Henry *and* the S.O.A.P. membership really annoyed at us. This is not a good idea. Village meetings account for a large portion of revenues in our off-season. We can tell Mrs. McIntosh that we can't handle the stag party and risk having her move the whole wedding party to the Marriott."

"There's a good idea," Meg muttered. "Seventy extra people. Three days to prepare. Phuut!"

"Or?" said Quill.

"Or what?"

"There's got to be another option!"

John grinned. "The only other thing I can think of is to disband S.O.A.P."

"There's another good idea." Meg tossed her pencil onto the butcher block countertop. "You're just full of good news, John. I don't suppose there's anything else to gladden our hearts and minds?"

"Not," John said, "unless you count the warrant out for Quill's arrest."

CHAPTER 3

"Jeez," Doreen said into the silence.

"Good grief," said Meg.

"A what?" said Quill. "A warrant?"

John smiled. "Follow me."

Quill got to her feet and followed John through the double doors to the dining room. Winter pressed in on them from the floor-to-ceiling windows overlooking Hemlock Gorge, dulling the mauve and cream of the walls. The wind had risen; swirls of snow the width of a hand slapped against the glass with a sound like shifting sand. Quill glanced at the familiar view, so welcoming in spring, and was oppressed.

"A warrant?" she said feebly to John's back.

Kathleen Kiddermeister, dressed in the fitted mauve jacket and slim black skirt of the dining room staff, sat at the table Quill permanently reserved for Inn personnel. She was sipping coffee. Otherwise, the dining room was empty. John, maddeningly, slowed to talk to her. "Any lunch reservations, Kathleen?"

"Not yet. The weather's too punky. We might get a few drop-ins, though. There's an RV convention at the Marriott, and those guys are nuts for snowmobiles. Big tippers, too."

"If no one's here by one-fifteen or so, why don't you take the rest of the afternoon off. I can handle any late lunches."

"You sure?"

Quill fidgeted.

John smiled, and continued, "Absolutely, Kath. You know what things are like this time of year."

"Uh, John," said Quill.

"Why don't you go ahead to the office, Quill. I want to talk with Kathleen about scheduling for the wedding reception."

"John!"

He feigned surprise. "And while you're at it, why don't you go through the mail."

"The mail?"

"Yeah, you know. Little envelopes with stamps on them? Letters. Bills. Communications from the Justice Department?"

Quill blushed. "You mean the mail that's been stacked up on my desk for the past week? That mail?"

"That mail."

"There was," said Quill, "a parking ticket. Last week. I sort of forgot about it."

"Parking ticket?" John looked politely skeptical.

"Well, that's all Davy said it was. Actually what he said was that it was the *equivalent* of a parking ticket."

John's teeth flashed white in his brown face. "Take a look."

The foyer seemed less welcoming than usual. The fireplace was cold and the four-foot Oriental vases flanking the registration desk were empty. Quill, never too enthusiastic about mail to begin with, paused to consider the vases. She was never entirely certain how soon the bronze spider chrysanthemums she used at Thanksgiving should be replaced by pine boughs. She usually waited until the 'mums began to droop. The shipment this year hadn't lasted long, and the first week in December was too early, she'd thought, for pine, so she'd waited, and now it was practically Christmas. She kicked disconsolately at the vase.

Dina Muir, their receptionist, was yawning her way through a textbook at the front desk. She looked up.

"Whoa," said Dina. "You're still here? I thought you were going to lunch with the sheriff. Anything wrong?"

"Not really."

"That's just what John said when he stomped out of the office a few minutes ago. I asked him, 'Anything wrong, John?' 'Not really, Dina,' he said back, when it was perfectly clear that something was really, really bugging him just like it's perfectly clear something's really, really bugging you. Is it the lunch with the sheriff?"

"Did he say anything to you?"

"John? Yep. I just told you. He said not really."

Quill, putting off the inevitable, was glad, for once, that Dina was inclined to chatter. "How are things?"

"Fine," Dina said brightly.

"School going okay?"

"Yep."

"Dissertation coming along? Are you reading a text for it?"

Dina lifted the book in her lap. "You mean this? No. I figured I'd better take a look before he got here, is all."

"Before who got here?"

"Evan Blight. He wrote this book that's made everyone so mad."

"You're actually reading it? *The Branch of the Root?*"

"Well, sure."

Quill took the book. The cover was a painting—a bad one—of a dark tree with the kind of roots found on a banyan. The leaves were vaguely oaklike. The branches were widely spaced and symmetrical, like a Norfolk pine. The title, *The Branch of the Root* by Evan Blight, was metallic, in Gothic type. Inside, the typeface was small, the paragraphs dense. The chapters had subtitles like "The Father-Spirit" and "The Soul of the Tree." Quill flipped to the back leaf. Evan Blight looked like Robertson Davies. Quill was conscious of a spurt of annoyance. She liked Robertson Davies a lot. She didn't want somebody who wrote a book that had caused as much trouble as *The Branch of the Root* to look like one of the better writers of the twentieth century. "Can I borrow this after you've finished?"

"Sure. But I'm only halfway through and it's due back at the Cornell library next week. Mrs. Doncaster at the library here said the waiting list is two weeks for the Hemlock Falls copy. You could buy your own copy. The Wal-Mart's carrying it. It's been deep-discounted to twenty bucks."

"Twenty dollars? I'll get on the waiting list at the library."

"That won't give you enough time. You want to read it before he gets here, don't you?"

"Before who gets here?"

"Evan Blight."

"Evan Blight? Evan Blight's coming to Hemlock Falls?"

"Well, sure."

"Wow."

John, walking into the foyer, shook his head, gave Dina a pat on the back, and opened the office door, gesturing Quill inside. "After you, you felon, you," he said, and shut the door in Dina's interested face.

Quill walked over to her desk and regarded the pile of mail stacked in her in-box. John settled into the leather chair behind the desk. She tugged at her hair and attempted unconcern.

"Quill. Some of this mail has been sitting here for two weeks."

"Hmm," Quill said. "Anything urgent?"

"If you mean are we going to get the phones cut off, like the last time you let the mail sit, no. But there's this." He waved a scarlet envelope at her.

Quill sank meekly into the chair in front of the desk. "What?"

"It looks like a bench warrant."

"A what?"

"A warrant for your arrest. For a speeding ticket."

"Me? I didn't get a speeding ticket." Quill took the envelope with a strong sense of indignation. "I would have remembered getting a speeding ticket. Now the equivalent of a parking ticket, yeah. I remember that. Last week."

"You didn't remember the phone bill last year," John said mildly. "And the phones were shut off for three hours."

"Yeah, but." She opened the envelope and took out a piece of cardboard marked BUREAU OF TRAFFIC VIOLATIONS, VILLAGE OF HEMLOCK FALLS, NOTICE OF VIOLATION AND IMPENDING DEFAULT JUDGMENT. THIS IS YOUR FINAL NOTICE.

"I never got a first notice," Quill said indignantly.

John waved a second, unopened envelope at her.

Quill ignored it and stared at the warrant. "We don't have a Bureau of Traffic Violations in Hemlock Falls."

"We do now. Sheriff Dorset and Bernie Bristol arranged for it last week. Don't you read the *Gazette*? It was part of their campaign platform."

Quill turned the cardboard over. "It says here I can plead not guilty by requesting a hearing Wednesday morning at nine a.m. Which Wednesday?"

"Any Wednesday."

"But I didn't get a speeding ticket!" She read it again. "This says I got a speeding ticket last Friday. Davy Kiddermeister stopped me near the school. He gave me a warning and the equivalent of a parking ticket. But he didn't give me a speeding ticket."

"You'd better give Howie a call and get on down to the courthouse tomorrow to get it straightened out."

"I won't. This is ridiculous!"

"Then they'll come after you."

"Who's going to come after me?"

"Deputy Dave, most likely. Maybe Dorset himself."

"I'll just call Myles. Oh. I can't call Myles, can I? He's not sheriff anymore. And besides . . ." She trailed off. John's eyes were uncomfortably shrewd.

John held one hand up and took the phone with the other. He dialed, waited a moment, got Howie Murchison on the line, described the situation briefly, then said, "I can't, Howie. I've got a meeting with some suppliers. Meg will have to do it. You want to talk to Quill? She's right here."

He held the phone out.

"Do what?" asked Quill, hesitating to take the receiver. "What will Meg have to do instead?"

"Just talk to him, Quill. He's agreed to represent you in traffic court tomorrow, but he wants more details."

Quill put the receiver to her ear. "Howie?"

Howie, who was one of the most patient, equably tempered men Quill knew, was admirably calm and agreed to meet her at the courthouse the following morning. He asked her questions about the ticket. Quill expostulated, Howie demurred; Meg, he said, would be needed as a character witness. He'd heard odd things about this sheriff. Quill thanked him, hung up, and looked at John. "Are you still upset?"

"About the mail? No, Quill. I know about you and mail. About the traffic ticket, yeah. It's dumb. Meg's told me often enough about you and traffic tickets. When you offered to take care of the mail last week when I was finishing the year-end accounting, I should have followed up. But this ticket stuff isn't anything to mess with. I've heard funny things about this new sheriff."

"What kind of funny things?"

John shrugged. "Nothing specific. But the town's changing."

Quill made a face. "Everything's changing." She brooded a

moment, shook herself, then said, "About the mail. I'm sorry, John. I booted it."

He reached over and squeezed her hand. "It seems to be taken care of. And you've had a lot on your mind lately. I thought you were going to Syracuse today."

"Yep."

"You'll feel more like yourself after you've settled things. Weather's getting bad. You want to give yourself enough time. Just let me run over a few of the arrangements for the rest of December, then I think you should get on the road early. You know this is the first year we're totally booked through the holidays."

Quill nodded. "Dina told me. I hadn't heard about Evan Whosis. When is he coming to Hemlock Falls?"

"Day after tomorrow."

"Two days before the wedding? He's not staying here, is he?"

"Yes, he's staying here."

"I thought we were booked up for the Santini wedding."

"I moved one of the bridesmaids to the Marriott instead." He leaned forward and flipped through the registry. "A Meredith Phelan. I called to ask about the change. She was charming about it."

Quill put her head in her hands. "Why here!?"

"Elmer Henry wrote to him. He's a guest of S.O.A.P."

"Are they paying for him?"

John nodded again. "We received a deposit check from Harland Peterson in yesterday's mail. He's the treasurer. I thought it'd be better to have Blight here—it's good for business."

Quill exhaled. A long, long sigh. She'd always thought John's pragmatic approach to celebrity guests rude. It wasn't right to exile poor Ms. Phelan to the Marriott in favor of a more prominent guest. If she protested, John would merely point out that the Inn was making money.

But the implied insult to a prospective guest paled beside the public relations problem she was going to have. When word got out that they were the hosts for Evan Blight, proponent of manly men, Adela Henry would blow a gasket. The H.O.W. membership was furious with S.O.A.P. and all it stood for. Quill's imagination rioted. The foyer would be yet another scene of confrontation between agitated people of varying age, sex, and gender. Elmer, Harland, Dookie, and the other earnest disciples of primitive man (or whatever the heck Blight called it) would show up half-naked and painted blue right in the middle of the Santini wedding. Alphonse, his prospective in-laws, and Claire, the bride-to-be, would be furious. They'd all be furious.

She'd spend Christmas like a gerbil on an exercise wheel.

Her face got warm. She realized *she* was furious. She had a sudden, overwhelming urge to throw something. "You know this is going to create more hassle for us. Why didn't you just tell the stupid jerk to STAY HOME!"

John looked sympathetic, but firm.

Quill took several deep breaths, tried to calm down, then said gloomily after a long pause, "Everybody's paying for my bad mood."

"Not everybody." He laughed a little. "Me, maybe. And Meg. And Myles, of course."

She stretched her legs out, folded her hands over her middle, and leaned her head against the back of the sofa. The office had a tin ceiling which she'd never really liked. The stamped ivy design marched from molding to molding in regular patterns. She'd always found this regularity, this dependability that one square looked exactly like the next, a little depressing. "You know what?"

"What?"

"It's people I want to be dependable. Not art."

John blinked.

Quill sat up. "I've been thinking about this a lot, John. I mean, I'm thirty-four years old and I just realized I don't like people to be . . . to be . . . well, people. Normal, rowdy, un-self-controlled. That artist's retreat I went to? Just before Thanksgiving? For a bit after I came home, I was painting really well. Then I stopped. When Myles asked me to change my whole way of life and marry him. He wants children, John, companionship every day, someone to be there when he comes home at night. I can't do it. It freezes me. I want all the randomness, all the ambiguity, all the uncertainty of life in my paintings. And yet, not in people. And I don't know if I'm right or I'm wrong. Meg just told me I've got my emotions all wrapped up in Ace bandages. People like Meg may be right. If

I don't allow that . . . that . . . *direct* sort of messiness of emotion into my life, it can't get back to my work."

Quill fiddled with a sofa cushion. It was a wild iris in needle-point, the gift of one of their regular guests. "I don't want to talk about it anymore. I'm sick of thinking about it. I'm so tired, John."

"You can, you know. Talk about it. I'm always here."

Quill took a breath. "You are. And I'm taking advantage of it. I swear as soon as—I mean after I get back from Syracuse you are going to see a new reformed Quill. I'll go through the mail. Remember to pay all my parking tickets. Be diplomatic to all the guests." She groaned suddenly. "Nuts. What am I supposed to do about this stupid bachelor party for Santini? Tell me you really don't want me to kick S.O.A.P. out and cancel H.O.W. and get everyone mad at me."

"Why don't we put the Santini bachelor party in the dining room, H.O.W. in the conference room, and S.O.A.P. on the terrace?"

"In winter?"

"Sure. We'll get some smut pots from Richardson's apple farm and line the terrace with nice primitive light and a modicum of warmth. They'll love it."

"A modicum," muttered Quill. "The warmth will certainly be less than a modicum. What's less than a modicum?"

John shrugged. "I don't think they'll complain. From what I can gather, the rites of passage involve exposure to extremes. They're spending all day in the woods barbecuing a steer the day of the meeting, and Elmer said they'll be bringing it with them. They don't want service or food—just the space. I'll get Mike to bring up the barbecue spit from the shed. And we'll put the bridal shower in the lounge. So all you have to do is let everyone know the schedule."

Quill sighed and looked at her watch. "I could catch Elmer in the park if I hurry. They're meeting there today. Meg roasted them a pig. And I'll tell Doreen about H.O.W. And I'm meeting with Senator Santini and Claire at five o'clock to get the particulars about the bachelor party and the shower and the rehearsal dinner. I wonder if he has any idea of the number of men that are going to show up."

"You'll meet the Santini party after Syracuse?"

She nodded, feeling that internal shift that meant her hesitation was over. She said goodbye, left the office, and went into the foyer to get her coat and boots. She'd been meaning to replace the coat, which was a tattered red down, and her hat, which was ugly but warm, but had been too depressed to do it.

"You're seeing Sheriff McHale?" Dina asked as she crossed the foyer to the coat closet.

"Just lunch," Quill said with an airy wave of her hand.

Dina's large brown eyes were moist. Quill, to her alarm, detected sympathy. Nothing, absolutely nothing was private in this place. "Well, be careful. And, Quill?"

Quill paused, her coat slung over one arm. "What!"

Dina quailed. Twenty-four-year-old graduate students spent a lot of time waiting for opportunities to quail and made the best of it when the least little chance happened by. "Nothing. Just. Ah. Watch for icy spots."

Quill carried her boots through the dining room. Kathleen had gone, so Quill couldn't ask her why her crazy brother thought he'd given her a speeding ticket when he hadn't. A faint sound of singing came from the back of the kitchen. Meg, with a particularly tuneless version of "The Boar's Head Carol." The sound was too muffled to be coming from the kitchen itself. If Meg were in the storeroom, Quill could sneak out without a lot of last-minute questions.

Quill edged the swinging doors open a few inches. She could see part of the birch shelving, a few bundles of dried red peppers hanging from the beams, and a copper saucepan bubbling on the Aga. Quill pushed the doors open. Meg was nowhere in sight.

"'The bo-o-a-ar's head in hand bear I/Bedecked with bay and rosemareee . . .'"

Quill winced. Meg's music suffered more in minor keys for some reason. But it tended to deafen her awareness of the outside world. Quill made it to the back door and stopped to pull on her boots.

Meg popped her head out of the storeroom. "Off to Syracuse?"

Quill jumped.

"You're wearing that ratty down coat? And that fur hat?"

"What's wrong with this coat?" Quill asked defensively.

"It's ugly," Meg said frankly. "It's so ugly you can tell it a mile off. And that fur hat with the flaps? And to think some poor rabbit died for that hat. Yuck."

"It's warm," Quill said stubbornly.

"Leaving without saying anything?"

"Um," Quill said. "You were right. John is right. The weather looks a little stormy and I thought I'd get an early start."

"'Don't know why'" Meg sang, "'There's no sun up in the sky/ Stormy weather . . . since my man and I . . .'"

Meg dropped the egg whisk she'd been using as a microphone. "Oh, Quillie, don't. I didn't mean it about the coat and the hat. Well, I did, but who cares? Don't cry. It's not . . . it's not like he's dumping you. You're dumping him." She set the box of onions she was carrying on the butcher block and approached Quill rather warily. "I'm sorry. But you're right to push off the dock like this. The relationship just isn't going to work."

"There's no reason why it shouldn't," Quill sobbed, amazed at her own tears. "He's a great guy . . ."

"A terrific guy."

"And he's been absolutely wonderful, and patient, and so . . . so . . . calm. And steady."

"I know." Meg patted her on the back. "Do you want a glass of sherry or anything?"

"And this is going to hurt him so much."

"I know. What about a cup of—"

"You know!? And you're just going to let me go off like this and do it? Tell him I want to break it off? That I've really, really tried, but I just can't. I just can't. It's just . . ." Quill, convinced she was looking too piteous for words, scrubbed at her face with her scarf and made a conscious effort at coherence. "I don't like tin ceilings."

"Of course you don't."

"I need more than a tin ceiling. Not that tin ceilings aren't good for some people. Just not me."

"You're absolutely right."

"Do you think he'll do something?"

"Like what?"

"I don't know. Yell. Or cry." Quill began to take off her coat. "I can't do it. I can't do it to him now. Not so soon after he's lost the election. It's like kicking him when he's down. I'll call the restaurant and tell him I have the flu."

"Quill, this detective agency he's joined is one of the best. They're sending him all over the world. Do you know how much he's making? If you're going to tell him, tell him now, while he's up about this job. He's off to the U.K. this afternoon, isn't he? You don't want to wait until he gets back. That'll be weeks. And," she added frankly, "no one around here is going to be able to stand it if you don't get this over with. Soon."

"I know. And I know about the European assignment." She put her coat back on. "But I didn't know about the money. Of course, I know it has to be a lot better than that ridiculous amount he was paid as sheriff. How much is he making?"

"Seventy-five dollars an hour. After the agency cut."

Quill felt better. "Wow. Who told you that?"

"Marge Schmidt, of course. To tell you the truth, Quill, I don't think Myles would have stuck around Hemlock Falls as long as he has if it weren't for you. I mean, this isn't exactly a hotbed of crime. Although," she added reflectively, "we do seem to have an unusual number of murders per capita. But honestly, Quill, do you think a guy like Myles should waste himself on being a county sheriff?"

"He wasn't wasting himself." Quill, not sure if she was indignant on behalf of Hemlock Falls or Myles, or herself, kicked off her shoes and pulled on her boots. "So. It's my fault he's been stuck in this backwater, huh? I'm going to be doing him a favor by dumping him, as you so charmingly phrased it?" She straightened up. "Okay. I'm going. But don't you dare hum one note of 'Release Me.'"

"It's going to be fine. Well, not fine. But you'll get through it."

"I thought I'd tell him how much I admire him."

"That's good."

"And that somewhere there's a wonderful woman who's not as tied up in knots as I am about commitment."

"That's okay, but I wouldn't dwell on it."

"And that I'm not worth it."

"Self-abasement, in these situations is usually not effective." Professional curiosity entered her voice. "Where are you meeting him?"

"That Italian restaurant just off Exit 56." Quill tugged at her hair. "It's called Ciao."

"Oh, God." Meg swallowed a chuckle. "It's a New-Ager. Sort of self-consciously healthy while slipping you all the fats and carbohydrates a bottled salad dressing is heir to. Not too bad if you stay away from the pasta. They precook. Try the wood-smoked pizza. Don't stay too long, okay? This weather's turning nasty."

"I'll be back around four-thirty. I've go to talk to Santini and Claire about the pre-wedding parties." Quill made a face.

Meg made a face back.

Quill, driving south on Route 15, was actually grateful for the storm. The plows had been through earlier in the morning, and at least three inches had fallen since then. The roads were slushy with packed drifts concealing stubborn patches of ice. Her Olds was a heavy car, with front-wheel drive, but it was slippery. She concentrated on driving until she hit the Interstate.

I-81 to Syracuse was clear and fairly dry, and Exit 56 came up too fast. She glanced at the little battery-run clock John had stuck on the dash when the car clock had died several years ago. One-thirty. She'd be early. She was never early. One of Myles's few complaints about her had been about her lateness. Myles was always spot on time. Maybe she'd order a glass of sherry while she waited.

She looked at the sky, pregnant with heavy clouds. No sherry. She'd order hot tea, to keep her head clear for the drive back and her emotions under control. She parked. The lot was crowded, but she noticed Myles's Jeep Cherokee right away.

She sat in the car. Her toes got chilly as soon as she turned off the heater.

Myles would be civilized. He was always civilized. But anxious. If he was here early, it meant he was anxious. But civilized, Quill reminded herself.

The very first thing, she'd order a glass of wine, not tea. For both of them. He rarely drank during the day; a glass of wine might help both of them through this. And the order for wine would be a subtle signal, a flag that bad news was coming. Maybe without even having to say it.

Halfway across the parking lot, Quill paused in mid-slush. She knew, all too well (at least from watching Gerard Depardieu movies) the leap in the heart when a lover caught sight of his beloved across a crowded room. She could spare Myles that leap by going in the back way, scanning the crowded room for him, and quietly walking up behind him. A discreet touch on the shoulder, a welcoming but suitably depressed "hello," and then a few well-chosen sentences of farewell.

Quill resumed her march across the parking lot and went in the door marked exit. She'd find Myles. Walk up unnoticed. She'd sit. Raise her hand to forestall his kiss of greeting. Hope that the waitress would be quick, and not too perky, and not named Shirelle. Or call her honey. Then she'd order, quickly, two glasses of merlot. No. Not merlot. Not from a restaurant that had a sign in the back room—"We Value Your Patronage—Thank You for Not Smoking." Any restaurant that valued your patronage before they got it probably bought merlot in plastic bar bags. And Meg avoided smoke-free restaurants on principle, a consequence of a year's study in Paris, where tobacco was considered a civilized finale to a meal. She'd ask for an Avalon cabernet sauvignon. It was great stuff. Not spectacular enough to make up for devastation, but it'd go a long way to assuaging what they both had to know was an intolerable situation.

The restaurant wasn't crowded at all. Of the maybe sixty tables scattered across the bleached oak floor, ten were filled. Myles saw her as soon as she walked down the hall leading to the restrooms and into the Euro-Tech ambiance of Ciao.

The blonde that was with him saw her, too.

And not just a blonde, Quill thought, suddenly conscious of her own hair, her snow-splattered boots, the muddy hem of her skirt, and, worst of all, the coat, conspicuous for its ugliness. A sophisticated blonde. With large breasts, tastefully presented behind a scoop-neck silk tee. A slouchy Armani jacket. And, as she rose from the table, one of those boyishly hipped figures that made even jeans look elegant. Much less the bottom half of the Armani suit. She wasn't pretty, Quill thought. She was distinctive, with a decided aquiline nose, well-defined lips, and direct gray eyes.

Myles rose and waved. Quill crossed the floor. He introduced the blonde with a slightly apologetic air.

"Quill, I'd like you to meet Mariel Cross, my partner on the U.K. assignment. Mariel, this is Sarah Quilliam."

Her handshake was firm, decisive. "I won't interfere with your lunch. The Bureau got a fax Myles had to see. That's the only reason I'm here. The Brits need an answer by seven o'clock tonight. And with the time change, that's two o'clock here in Syracuse." She smiled. "I'm glad I've met you, though. I've heard a lot about you. I've seen your work. I like it very much."

Quill, who knew herself to be graceless whenever discussion of her painting came up, blushed and looked at her feet. Her boots were leaving muddy puddles on the polished floor.

"Well." Mariel hesitated, a behavior Quill instinctively knew was uncharacteristic. The woman oozed self-confidence. "I'll fax this back to the client, Myles."

"Fine. I'll meet you at the airport around six."

Quill sat down in Mariel's place. Myles covered her hand with his.

"I don't need to say anything, do I, Myles?"

"It's awkward," he said.

"She's really attractive. She has . . ." Quill paused, searching for the right word. "Presence. A lot of presence."

"You're beautiful," Myles said. His hand tightened on hers. "But yes, she has presence."

She was back at the Inn by four.

"There you are," John said as she walked in the back door. Meg raised her eyebrows. Quill gave her a halfhearted wave. "Santini wants to push the meeting up. Can you see them now? I've got to check the wine shipment."

"Sure," Quill said listlessly.

"Are you all right?"

"Fine. Where are they?"

"Having tea. At the regular table."

Quill removed the coat, swearing to purchase another as soon as the damned Christmas rush and the stupid wedding and the barbaric rites of Santini's bachelor party were over. She grabbed the planning clipboard from its hook on the wall and pushed through the swinging doors into the dining room. There were six people at the table, Claire and a pretty girl whom Quill hadn't met, and the senator and three of his aides.

The youngest aide got up as she approached and pulled a chair out for her.

"You know Frank, Marlon, and Ed," Santini said breezily. Quill nodded. "And the ball and chain, of course."

"A—al!" Claire protested in her nasal voice. "This is Merry Phelan. One of my bridesmaids."

"Meredith," she said in a self-possessed voice. "How do you do."

Quill shook her hand. "I'm awfully sorry about switching you to the Marriott."

"Not at all a problem. As a matter of fact, I'm off there now. Elaine and I are planning a little shower for Claire Thursday night, and I want to check over some details."

Santini saluted as she left the table. She gave Quill a wink, and proceeded demurely out the entranceway. Santini waited until she was out of earshot, then hunched over the table.

"So," Al said, "glad you could make it a little early, Quill. I've got a good opportunity in the park around five. A fund-raiser with this men's club. Crazy assholes wanted to meet in the dark, but hey, no problem. I'm adaptable."

"S.O.A.P.?" asked Quill.

Frank—or maybe it was Marlon—consulted a thick notebook. "Right. Men's organization. Acronym for the Search for Our Authentic Primitive. Chief is Elmer Henry. Mayor, and a Republican. He's fifty-six. Married, to Adela Henry, aged fifty-eight. One of the Walters family, Senator. Used to be money there but not anymore. First Brave is Harland Peterson, big farmer around these parts, net worth in the (he named a figure which astonished Quill), a Democrat, unfortunately, but maybe he can be persuaded. The sheriff, Dorset, is a member and so is the justice, Bristol."

"Stop already." Santini swallowed a scone whole and said through it, "How much time I got with them?"

"Half an hour. Our data suggests that the hearth and home speech should be appropriate."

"Got that one socked. Okay. So, Quill, dolly. I got more time for you than I thought. The bachelor party Thursday night's for twelve. You got that?"

"One of these gentlemen . . ."

"Ed," said Ed, giving her a toothy smile.

"Yes, Ed, gave us the count several months ago. But no guest list."

"In the interests of security," Marlon, or maybe Frank, said smoothly, "we'd prefer to be circumspect."

Santini snorted. "With that Cahill bitch sniffing around, you can bet we have to be careful. The thing is, Quill, dolly, we need to get her out of the way for the evening."

"Out of the way?" Quill repeated.

"Couple of these guys, they can't make it for the wedding. Christmas Eve and all. But they can make it Thursday. They want maybe to make a little contribution to the cause. You know what I mean?"

Quill, uncertain, nodded in lieu of doing anything else.

"You don't get it, do you?" He leaned forward and mentioned a Supreme Court Justice noted for his aggressive—and mean-spirited—decisions on Affirmative Action, a congressman who'd been indicted—but not convicted—twice for money laundering scams, and two names even Quill recognized as having been involved with illegal gambling activities.

"Senator," warned Ed.

"Yeah, yeah, yeah. So. We're giving these guys the best, right? Sirloin. Baked potato with all the trimmings, lotta good whisky, the works. But we don't want this Cahill broadie to give them the works, you catch my meaning?"

"Yes," said Quill. "But I'm not sure what I can do about it."

"She wouldn't do a thing about Tutti, either, Al," Claire complained.

"Your gramma's still coming? Shit!" Santini sat back with a shake of his head. "That's not till tomorrow, right? So we worry about it tomorrow. Hey!" He snapped his fingers. "That's from some book, right? Now, Quill. What are you going to do about Cahill? I figure it's your problem, see what I mean? She's a guest here, got that? And you're in charge of the guests."

"Could Claire take her to the shower at the Marriott Thursday night?"

"A-al!" said Claire. "It's my very closest friends at this shower!"

"It could work," said Ed. "Yes, Senator, it could work. You could give her an exclusive, Claire, couldn't you? Your father's notor—I mean well-known for avoiding interviews with the press. You could give her some safe inside dope, like where you and the senator will make your home, the place you're going to buy in Georgetown. Those sorts of things."

"Part of the political life, baby," Santini offered.

"All *right*. But I'm going to want something very, very nice to make up for this, Al. I'm warning you."

"S'all right. You get your nice little butt in gear, dear. Catch Cahill before she starts sniffing around about the party and nail her down. Quill, dolly, good work. You ever think about getting into the game, you let me know."

"Game?" asked Quill.

"Politics, baby. Politics. It's the only game there is."

"And that was it?" Meg exclaimed, much later, when they were sitting in Quill's room discussing her shortened lunch. "Myles didn't say, 'Let's keep in touch,' or better yet, 'You'll always have a special place in my heart'? 'It's awkward'? 'You're beautiful'? And 'She has presence'? That was it?! And you went straight from that to loathsome Al?"

"Well, sure there was the keep-in-touch speech, and the never-forget-you speech. But I think, Meg, he was relieved. I think I'm too complicated, or too independent. Or too—I don't know."

"You poor thing," Meg said with deep affection. "How do you feel?"

"Chagrined."

"Because of all the rehearsing," Meg said shrewdly. "You should know by now, Quillie, never rehearse. Other than chagrined, how do you feel?"

Quill swirled the last of her wine in her glass. "I think my heart's broken."

Meg shook her head, jumped off the sofa, and marched to the

small kitchenette where they sometimes prepared meals. She didn't have a kitchen in her rooms, which were one floor down from Quill's. The last thing Meg wanted to see at night, she'd told Quill and Doreen, was a stove or a refrigerator.

"No paper towels?"

Quill wiped her cheek with her hand. "Cloth ones."

"Here." Meg tossed her a dishtowel. "Are you sorry you broke it off with him?"

"He broke it off with me!"

"Do you want to make up?"

Quill shook her head.

Meg sat down next to her and announced, "This is absolutely the last pat of the day," and rubbed her back.

Quill cried, Meg patted her back, and then the room was quiet. They sat on the cream sofa in front of her French doors, feet propped on the oak chest Quill used as a coffee table. Quill drank another glass of the cabernet. Outside the French doors, the snow knocked against the window like a soft white cat trying to get in.

Quill's easel stood in the corner, half-hidden by the tea-stained drapes. A half-finished charcoal sketch—Doreen, laughing with a cup of coffee in one hand. Quill looked at it and felt the familiar clench of muscles in her right hand.

"Meg. Remember that taxi driver?" she said suddenly.

"The one that picked us up at the train station ten years ago? The day we arrived in New York? Me off to Paris, to learn to cook, you off to paint great things?" She laughed. "'The great thing about dis job, goils? Ya never know where it's gonna take ya.'" She smiled. "And he took us for a ride, all right. That was the wildest taxi ride I've ever been on before or since. To this day, I don't know why he didn't get a ticket."

Quill sat bolt upright. "Traffic court!"

"He didn't take us to traffic court. He took us to that cool little apartment in SoHo. Actually, it wasn't all that little . . ."

"I have to be in traffic court tomorrow morning. Nine o'clock. And you have to come with me."

"Why do I have to come with you?" Meg demanded indignantly. "I'm not the one who got a speeding ticket."

"I didn't get a ticket. Dave Kiddermeister stopped me and told me I was going a little fast past the school. But he didn't give me a ticket."

"How much over the limit were you?"

"I don't know. He didn't write me a ticket," Quill said patiently. "It's some screwup. Howie Murchison's going to represent me."

"Howie? Over a speeding ticket you didn't get?"

"Well, there's this thing called a bench warrant or whatever."

"Quill." Meg's voice was ominous. "You know exactly what a bench warrant is. You used to get them all the time."

"I swear to God, Meg. I've reformed. No speeding. No unpaid parking tickets. Honest."

"If they pulled your driving record from New York City, you could be in big trouble."

"It's been years," said Quill, "and if I have to tell you one more time that I didn't get a ticket, I'm going to scream. I talked with Howie on the phone today and he said just to be safe I should bring a witness."

"A witness to what?!"

"My general honesty, I guess. I mean, what if Dave says he gave me a ticket? He won't. Or he shouldn't. It'll take two minutes, Meg."

"Not necessarily," Meg said darkly. "And if they want me to witness what kind of driver you are, you're in big, big trouble. And anyway, what can I say? That I've never witnessed you getting a ticket?! That's bull. I've seen you get parking tickets, speeding tickets, every kind of ticket."

"Howie just said to bring you so you can testify as to my probity."

Meg shrieked, "I'm your sister. They aren't going to believe a word I say."

"Well, you have to come anyhow."

"Well. Okay. Since you've got a broken heart. But you better get over this broken heart fast." She grinned suddenly. "Howie's divorced. And I think he's pretty neat."

"The last thing I want is to jump into any kind of relationship with anybody. I'm going to be an aunt. A professional aunt."

"A professional aunt?"

"Yep. You're going to marry Andy Bishop sometime next year and have zillions of children, and I'll sit and rock them to sleep and look melancholy, and everyone will wonder about my tragic past." She started to hum a version of "Melancholy Baby" that was so repellent Meg threw a pillow at her and stomped off to bed.

Quill slept and dreamed of empty canvases, stacked in abandoned warehouses.

CHAPTER 4

Meg threw back her head and caroled, "Top of the world, Ma!" Then conversationally, "You're going to get sent up the river. To the big house. Yep, you're looking at hard time."

"Oh, shut up." Quill twitched the modestly tied scarf at her throat. She wasn't sure about the scarf; her hair was red and the scarf was a brilliant gold and teal. She felt tired, after yesterday's confrontation with Myles. She felt conspicuous. She didn't know if her anxiety was over the way she looked or the fact that she was in the Tompkins County Courthouse waiting to be arraigned for a nonexistent traffic ticket. She'd never actually been in the Tompkins County courtroom before. She wasn't surprised at how intimidating high ceilings, butternut paneling, and the musty smell ordinarily common to attic closets could be. "Other voices, other rooms," she said obscurely. Then, "It's only a traffic ticket. And it's my first traffic ticket . . ."

Meg, startled out of her Cagney imitation, went "Phuut!" which in turn startled Howie Murchison, who'd been sitting quietly next to them.

"In Tompkins County," Quill amended. "And that means it's my first for seven years at least. And they take them off your what-do-you-call-it after three years anyway."

"Your MV104," Howie said with a faintly surprised look. "You've had priors, Quill? In some cases the court can pull your records all the way to the beginning. They don't dump old information. It just doesn't relate to most of the within-eighteen-months laws, so it isn't listed on current requests. You didn't tell me you had priors."

"She didn't, huh," said Meg. Her gray eyes, clear and limpid, met Howie's wary gaze head-on.

Quill pulled at the scarf around her throat again. "This darn thing is stifling me."

"I must say that suit and little bow don't become you," Howie said thoughtfully. "No offense, Quill, but I'm used to seeing you more—how should I put it?—loosely dressed."

"Loosely?" Quill demanded, slightly affronted.

"Casually," Meg supplied. "You mean casually dressed, Howie."

"You said to dress discreetly, Howie." Quill stuck her thumbs in the waistband of her tailored wool skirt and jerked at the material. "I don't understand why the heck this thing is so constricting. I haven't gained any weight since the last time I wore this."

"You wore that suit to interview for the graphics job at Eastman Kodak company," said Meg. "Which means you last wore that suit when you were nineteen. Which makes it a B.T. suit. Ha! That's why you're wearing it. For luck."

"B.T.?" said Howie.

Quill jerked the skirt over her knees and glared a warning at Meg.

"B.T.?" Howie repeated. "What's B.T.?"

"You haven't gained weight," Meg added. "It's just that a person sort of settles around the middle, Quill, after fifteen years. Or is it seventeen?" She counted on her fingers, her lips moving. "Nope, fifteen. You're thirty-four."

"Before Taxes?" Howie said, and sighed. "I don't get it. But then, I never get half of what you girls are talking about anyway."

"Girls?" asked Meg, eyebrows raised.

Quill wriggled her shoulders against the high-backed seat and slid down so that she couldn't see over the top of the bench in front of her. "Howie, is this going to be over soon? I've got so much stuff to do back at the Inn that I haven't even opened my mail for a week. Which is why I'm here in the first place."

He peered at her over his wire-rimmed glasses. In his late

forties, Howie had settled into a comfortable, slightly paunchy middle age that Quill found very appealing. His well-cut Harris tweed sports coat was worn at the cuffs, the knot of his striped tie was skewed to leave his shirt collar loose, and his black wing tips had been resoled at least twice, not, Quill knew, because he couldn't afford another pair, but because he didn't want to break in new shoes. Like Myles (now on his way to London, with that perfect-looking woman!), Howie had his own kind of stubborn integrity. "Hard to say. I haven't been up before Justice Bristol yet. As you know, I'm accustomed to being on the other side of the bench."

"Well, *I* voted for you, Howie," said Meg, with an emphasis that seemed to imply Quill hadn't.

"*I* voted for Howie, too," said Quill.

"Of course you did. So did John. So did Doreen and Axminster. So did Marge Schmidt. Why are you acting like I didn't vote for Howie?"

"You're the one that's acting as though *I* didn't vote for Howie."

"I am NOT. Howie was a *great* town justice. And he's Hemlock Falls' best lawyer."

"I'm Hemlock Falls' only lawyer," Howie pointed out dryly.

"Whatever." Meg's cheeks were still pink from the cold outside; she rubbed them vigorously and made them even pinker. "The thing is, Howie, with everyone so mad at the President and the governor, *all* the incumbents in *all* the elections in New York State got kicked out six weeks ago. Myles isn't sheriff anymore. You're not town justice anymore. And it's not your fault. It's not Myles's fault. It's nobody's fault. It's democracy. It's the voice of the people. Just read the newspapers. Of course," Meg continued sunnily, "the other fact is that you sentenced the mayor and the Reverend Mr. Shuttleworth and practically the whole male side of the Chamber of Commerce to three months of community service for public rowdiness. *That* may have had some . . ."

Quill, exasperated, poked Meg into silence. Hemlock Falls tended to lag behind fashionable trends, but eventually caught up to such contemporary issues as male emancipation. S.O.A.P's first meeting, in the back room of the Croh Bar on Main Street, had ended in a public display which violated town ordinance 2.654 (prohibiting total nudity and drunkenness in public) and 4.726 (vandalism). Outraged citizens unsympathetic to the Men's Movement (Adela Henry and the members of H.O.W. mostly) had demanded their pound of flesh. Howie had reluctantly bowed to the legal demands of the aggressive plaintiff's attorney Mrs. Henry imported from Syracuse just for the occasion, and sentenced S.O.A.P. members to several weekends of highway cleanup. Reprisals had been effected at the polls in November.

Meg tapped her fingers against the wooden bench and ruffled her short dark hair. "Is this Bristol ever going to show up? You said it'd take a few minutes. It's been more like an hour. We're booked for the holidays and the rest of the McIntosh family is coming in this afternoon and I've got to get back." She looked at her watch, scowled, and rose to her feet. "As a matter of fact, I should be at the Aga right now."

"You can't leave. You're my witness." Quill shoved her back into her seat.

"Quill, it's just a lousy ticket. I wasn't even there. You just want me here as a character witness, and Howie doesn't even think I need to be here, do you, Howie?"

"I'd like it. Just as a backup."

"And besides, you always get tickets. There's not a thing I can do about it. There's never *been* anything I could do about it." Meg began to edge her way out.

Howie stirred uneasily. "Maybe you ought to hang on a little while longer, Meg. This won't take long. It's a matter of routine. We'll plead Quill guilty, have her throw herself on the mercy of the court to get the fine down, and that will be the end of it."

"I didn't get a ticket," Quill said. "I told you. It's a frame. Meg? Where are you going?"

Meg paused at the end of the row. "Honestly, Quill, I'm busy. Mrs. Whosis is coming in this afternoon to begin planning the food for the reception and I told her I'd have some samples."

"Mrs. McIntosh," said Quill. "It's not Mrs. Whosis, it's Mrs. McIntosh. For the Santini wedding," she explained to Howie. "He's already here."

Howie nodded. "I've heard."

"Have you met him?"

"Mm-hmm."

Meg jiggled impatiently. "Right. I'm suggesting pork tender-loin in persimmon sauce. If Santini wants pasta, I'll black his little eye."

Quill, still feeling pitiful, gave her a woebegone look.

Meg edged back along the bench and hugged her. "You'll be fine. Howie, tell her she'll be fine."

"As long as there aren't any surprises, yes, Quill, you should be fine. You're sure about no priors?"

Quill made a face in the direction of the judge's bench. She had a sudden, passionate regret that Myles was out of her life. Then, just as passionately, she decided she could save herself.

"So, there." Meg avoided her sister's eye, edged her way along the wall to the aisle, waved, and jogged toward the back doors, looking both innocent and ingenuous in her wool leggings, scarlet knitted cap, and droopy scarf.

Quill sat back, unknotted the silk scarf at her neck, and relied it.

The courtroom was as cavernous as a church, and as sparsely populated. The jury box and the judge's bench were segregated from the spectator pews by low spindled railings. The prosecutor's desk, Howie had told her, was typically to the left in front of the raised judge's dais, the defense to the right. The desks resembled library tables; long, broad, and made of a hardwood stained an ugly coffee color. The whole arrangement was stark, putting Quill in mind of some strict and unforgiving religious sect.

Pictures of the incumbent President and the governor of the state of New York flanked an American flag on the front wall. Quill wondered where pictures of the new governor would come from in January when the new governor took office and what would happen to the old ones. Were former gubernatorial pictures destroyed thoroughly and with precision, like worn-out money sent back to the mint? Or did cartons and cartons of them get returned to the loser, who was probably in a severely depressed state to begin with and shouldn't have to deal with fading portraits of a vanished career? Quill had liked this governor, who'd forgone a presidential campaign because he didn't want a greedy, self-aggrandizing media poking around his family any more than they had already. As far as Quill was concerned, at least at this specific minute, a person's private history should remain private history.

A door to the left of the flag opened. A figure dressed in black judicial robes stumped into the room. Hemlock Falls' new justice, Bernie Bristol, was round and jowly and wore the dopey, happy look of a hound getting its ears scratched. An engineer retired from Xerox Corporation fifty miles away in Rochester, Bristol had bought a small farm south of the village in September, and run a well-financed campaign for the justiceship. Quill had met him, once, when he'd stopped by the Inn for dinner. He'd been rather endearingly innocent of enough French to order his entree. On the other hand, Quill hadn't been surprised to discover he was a lousy tipper.

"All rise!" roared Dwight "Run-On" Riorden, the bailiff.

"All what?" said Howie, nonplussed. He got to his feet, muttering, "This is justice court, for God's sake, and we're all supposed to *rise*?" and stepped into the aisle, ushering Quill in front of him.

"Murchison?"

Howie turned, his eyebrows raised in polite inquiry. A brown-haired man carrying an expensive leather briefcase walked rapidly past the two of them, clapping his hand on Howie's shoulder in passing. It was, Quill saw in mild surprise, Al Santini.

Quill smiled and asked if he was looking for Meg. His eyes ran over her without a flicker of recognition.

"Al?" Howie's voice was wary and tinged with surprise. "What brings you out this way?"

"Good to see ya, buddy." Al grinned, revealing teeth like a picket fence in need of whitewash. He looked different. Quill looked at him carefully. He looked—almost senatorial. His scanty hair was moussed to an illusion of fullness. His dark blue pin-striped suit (cut to conceal the concave chest and his little potbelly) was so determinedly well-pressed it seemed to wear him. His watery blue eyes flicked over Quill like a pair of clammy hands. "This the perp?"

"The perp?" said Howie.

"The miscreant. The malefactor. The culprit." Al delivered a professional grin. "And a beaut she is, too, Howie." He clicked his tongue against his teeth, banged the briefcase playfully against Howie's knees, and loped up the aisle.

"What the heck?" said Quill. "Howie! He's acting like he's never seen me before! He's been a guest at the Inn for three days! He . . ." She subsided, muttering.

Howie frowned. "Now what the hell is he doing here?"

Santini stopped just short of the bench and appeared to be opening shop. He thumped his briefcase on the prosecutor's side of the bench, snapped it open, and spread a sheaf of legal-sized papers on the desk top. Above him, Justice Bernie Bristol polished his gavel with a spotless white handkerchief.

Quill looked around the courtroom. There were five—no, six—alleged traffic violators besides herself. At least, she assumed they were alleged traffic violators; all were probably as innocent as she was. She gave a sudden sigh of relief. "Howie. We won't need Meg as a witness after all. There's Betty Hall. I didn't know that she got pulled in, too, but I know for sure she saw me get stopped. And she knew I wasn't speeding. I mean, she's been driving school bus part-time for months and ought to know a speeder when she sees one. She'll be glad to testify to the fact that I'm a totally law-abiding citizen. She'd parked her school bus right on the side of the road where I got picked up. She even gave me this sort of sympathetic wave when Davy pulled me over."

Howie pursed his lips. "I don't like this. No, I don't like this at all. Quill, about those other tickets Meg mentioned. The ones from New York?"

"Oh, dear." Quill fidgeted with her scarf. "Um. It's like this. I thought that all that stuff would have disappeared by now. I mean, it's been seven years."

"B.T," Howie said thoughtfully, "B.T. Meg meant . . . Before Tickets?" he hazarded. He looked at her over his wire-rimmed glasses. "You mean you've been getting tickets since you were nineteen? How *many* tickets, Quill?"

Quill twirled a piece of hair around her ear. "It's not the tickets, so much. More like the totals."

"The totals?" Howie's eyes narrowed. "You don't mean totals as in total wrecks? Tell me you're not referring to total wrecks."

"All this happened years ago, Howie. In another life. I drove a taxi while I was trying to make it as an artist. In New York City, for Pete's sake. And you can just imagine . . . I mean, Howie, most of them weren't my fault. Well, half of them weren't, anyway," Quill said generously. "Meg knows all about it. So did Myles. Kind of."

Howie, if he picked up on the past tense, made no mention of it. "*Half* of them? How many . . . ? Oh, boy." He rubbed his nose. "I just need to know one thing. You haven't had so much as a parking ticket in the last seven years?"

"Not so much as a broken taillight," Quill said virtuously. "I mean, Deputy Dave did issue a warning last week—but that's all, honest."

Howie smiled. He had a very attractive smile. "Then we'll find out what's going on here. It's probably nothing. Can you handle Run-On's conversation for five minutes?"

"Sure. I mean, if anyone would know what's going on, he would."

Howie raised his voice slightly and called, "Dwight?"

Dwight "Run-On" Riorden had combined courthouse maintenance with the duties of bailiff ever since the Tompkins County Board of Supervisors had decided neither was a full-time job. Dwight wore a suit coat over his coveralls and white athletic socks with black lace-up oxfords, a mode of dress which seemed to accommodate both occupations. He gave Howie a high sign and ambled over. "Ms. Quilliam? Mr. M.?"

Quill extended her hand. Dwight's palm was calloused. "Hi, Dwight. I haven't seen you at Marge's diner on Sundays for a while."

"Nope. Been working weekends, Ms. Quilliam. Mr. Hotshot Bristol there got his knickers in a twist over the state of the courthouse. Day after the election returns come in, Mr. Murchison, Bristol there wants to know how long's it been since it's been painted. Long enough, I say, and it's going to be a sight longer. Don't have a budget for painting walls that don't need paint. The boiler now, I tell him, that boiler she could use a valve job. Place where I'm going to be judge got to look better than this, he tells me. The hell with the boiler, he tells me. The hell with you, I tell him. 'Course, after he goes to judge's school you'd think the son of a gun would know better than to tell people he's a judge. He's not a judge, he's a justice. But no, he's an elected official of the people, he tells me, and things been too slack around here. But judge or justice those walls don't need paint. So I tell him that and he tells me—"

Howie interrupted. Most people talking to Dwight interrupted. Those who couldn't made a practice of avoiding him. "Dwight, when did Bristol get back from judge's school?"

Responding like a rudderless boat to a brisk breeze, Run-On's conversation tacked amiably in a different direction. "Before Thanksgiving, it must a been when we got that couple inches of snow. Didn't think I was going to have to get the blower out till after Thanksgiving, but some years I just don't—"

"Is this the first justice court session he's held?"

"Nossir, held four Fridays ago, it was, just after Thanksgiving. You were on that cruise and then out to your sister's in Rochester, and everybody knew they couldn't get hold of you so nobody tried."

"I just got back yesterday," Howie agreed absently, his attention on the back entrance to the courtroom. "There were a lot of phone calls waiting for me. Thought most of the callbacks could wait. . . . Riorden, who are those people?"

"Them?" Run-On craned his neck. "That's press. Media people. Judge Bristol told me to be sure and save seats for them, so I did. I roped off seats by the fire extinguisher, although I roped off enough for a dozen, judge said, and it don't look like to me that there's more than four, counting the guy with the camcorder. Hey!" His furry eyebrows rose in mild excitement. "Hey! That's Nora Cahill! She's on the news from Syracuse when I eat my supper."

Quill waved hello. Nora ignored her. Maybe, thought Quill, there was some kind of cream she used that gave her complexion that flawless even tone. If there was, she wanted some.

A somewhat embarrassed-looking figure in trooper gray edged in behind Nora Cahill's camera crew. "There's Dave Kiddermeister, too," Quill whispered, as the deputy eased into the courtroom. "You know, Kathleen's brother. She's one of our best waitresses. Davy's the officer that flagged me down. And, Howie, I wasn't speeding, honestly. What the heck's going on?"

Howie took her arm and pressed her into her seat. "Stay there. Stay quiet. Don't say anything unless I ask you a direct question. And when I do ask you a question answer yes, no, or I don't know."

Quill bit her thumbnail nervously.

"Bailiff!" said Judge Bernie Bristol. "Can you come up here?" He took a deep, happy breath and thumped the gavel. "This court is now in session." Bristol thumped the gavel again and kept on thumping with an air of mild pleasure. After some seconds, Al Santini reached up, removed the gavel, and laid it to one side.

Run-On Riorden ambled back up the judge's dais and laid a stack of files in front of the justice, who regarded them with confusion.

"The people call Sarah Quilliam," Al Santini prompted after a long moment.

Howie rose to his feet. "Your Honor," he said, in dramatically sarcastic tones, "I was not aware that my learned colleague had been elected to the bench. I object to this disruption of proper courtroom procedure. It is the right and proper role of the bailiff to perform the roll call."

Quill blinked, her anxiety somewhat allayed; she'd never seen Howie in court before. He was impressive.

Bernie took a moment to digest the objection, then turned anxiously to Al Santini. "Well, I guess I object, too, Mr. Santini."

Al spread both hands in a deprecatory gesture. "My apologies to the court, Your Honor."

"Oh, that's okay," Bernie said generously. "No harm done. Let's see." He shuffled through the files, took the topmost one, stared at it, set it down, stood up, and hitched up his judge's robes. He was wearing the kind of red plaid trousers popular with stockbrokers at Christmas parties. He drew a small black notebook from his trousers pocket, shook out his robes, sat down again, and opened the notebook up. The silence stretched on, broken only by little hisses and sighs as Bernie read aloud under his breath. Howie cleared his throat. Al Santini sighed elaborately. Quill, feeling obscurely uneasy again, looked over her shoulder. Nora Cahill, the Syracuse anchor, was standing behind her, microphone at the ready.

"There it is, right here, got it," said Bernie.

The man holding the camcorder behind Quill switched it on.

Bernie squinted a little in the sudden flood of light. "You are Sarah Quilliam, of One Hemlock Road, Hemlock Falls, New York?"

Quill looked at Howie, who nodded.

"Yes," said Quill, much more loudly than she'd intended.

"You are charged with violation of section 11.74A of the Vehicular and Traffic Code." He beamed at her. "That's passing a stopped school bus, Miss Quilliam."

"A stopped school bus?" asked Quill, bewildered.

"One moment, Your Honor." Howie folded his arms and regarded Al Santini with a steady and disapproving eye. "The violation listed on Miss Quilliam's traffic ticket is 9.32C, speed in excess of five miles over the posted limit . . ."

"Well, according to the deputy over there, she was only going a couple miles over the limit and there's no news in that," said Bernie, clearly in the spirit of helpfulness.

"Of course there's no news in that," Howie said evenly. "And if there's a new charge, Your Honor, neither I nor my client has been notified . . ."

"Oh, yeah, she has. She's been notified. Got sent a letter after we got the computer readout on the camera. Sent the ticket through the mail. This school bus thing is valid, you know. Because of the camera."

"The camera?" said Howie. "What damned camera?"

"Counselor, Counselor," Al Santini said reprovingly. "The hidden intersection cameras. You're familiar with those, Murchison."

"You mean the cameras they've put up in New York City to catch people running red lights at intersections?"

"Uh-huh," said Al.

"There's one in Hemlock Falls?"

"Put up last week. Came out of the sheriff's budget. Lot of traffic violators out there, Murchison, so Judge Bristol kept it very quiet. Have to keep the streets safe for the kiddies. These little towns are laboring under the burden of high taxes paid to Albany and have little or nothing to show for it in the way of improvements to local government. When monies are made available to the hundreds of towns like Hemlock Falls across this great state of ours for the express purpose of saving lives, of making the streets safer for our little ones—I say it's money well spent."

Howie cast a sardonic glance at the running cameras. Nora Cahill smiled at him like a cat who'd had baby birds for breakfast. Quill took several deep breaths and retied the bow around her neck.

"Your Honor," Howie said, "I make a motion to dismiss."

Bernie cast a benign eye around the courtroom. "Do I hear a second?"

"A second what?" asked Howie.

"A second to the motion," Bernie explained with a kindly air. "If I hear a second, I have to consider dismissal, don't I?"

Howie spread his hands and looked up at the ceiling. His lips moved.

"Well," said Quill, more to break the stunned silence than anything else, "there was a school bus there, as a matter of fact. Betty was in it. She saw me, and she knows absolutely without question that I was not speeding. Didn't you, Betty?" Quill turned in her seat. Betty gave her a thumbs up.

"Quill, keep quiet," Howie said, between his teeth.

"Let the record show that the defendant has admitted passing the school bus and that the driver Betty Hall can identify her," Al Santini said loudly. "Judge Bristol, I believe you were going to continue with the charges?"

"Um . . . ya. The state of New York provides a minimum fine of seven hundred dollars and seven days in jail and a maximum fine of eight hundred dollars and one hundred and eighty days in jail for this offense," Bernie read aloud. "How do you plead, Miss Quilliam? Not guilty? Guilty? Or guilty with an explanation?"

Quill said weakly, "Well, guilty with an explanation, sir. I—"

"QUILL!" Howie shouted. "Be quiet! Your Honor, I demand a recess. I demand an examination of the judicial process involved in these proceedings."

"I believe my colleague is in contempt, Your Honor," Al Santini said smoothly.

"What?" asked Bernie.

"Contempt. He's in contempt," Al muttered.

"Stuff it, Santini," Howie said.

"That's no way to talk," Bernie Bristol said reprovingly.

"Your Honor, there is a motion to dismiss before this court."

Howie, Quill noticed, turned dark red when he was angry. "My client has not been notified of this most serious misdemeanor."

"She open her mail?" asked Al Santini. He waved a certified mail receipt under Howie's nose. "These electronic tickets get sent by certified mail." He turned back to the bench. "Your Honor? I'm going to ask for the maximum penalty here. To keep this kind of menace off the roads and pathways of our fair state."

"Menace?" said Quill.

"And to keep the money rolling in, too," Bernie added in a helpful aside to the steadily whirring camera. "Lot of financial opportunities being missed with these kinds of cases."

Howie ran his hands through his graying hair, which didn't much affect his hairstyle but added to the appearance of frenzy. "On what *possible* grounds could you ask for a maximum penalty here, Santini?! God knows why I'm even participating in this dog and pony show. Your Honor, if a ruling is not made on my motion to dismiss, I am going to file a protest with the O.C.A."

"I told you we should have repainted," Judge Bristol said to Dwight Riorden. "Now we'll have OSHA on our necks."

"Let me explain, Your Honor." Howie gave an exasperated laugh. "The Office of Court Administration is a disciplinary body—"

"Shall we get back to the case at hand, Counselor?" Santini laid a thick file in front of the judge. "I have here in evidence the defendant's MV104, dating back fifteen years to a multitude of V&T charges in the city of Manhattan, Your Honor."

"Um . . . ya," said Judge Bristol.

"Oh, dear," said Quill. "Oh, dear, oh, dear, oh, dear."

Howie cast an accusing glance at Quill, and said loudly, "I object!"

"A perusal of this document will demonstrate without question that Ms. Quilliam is one of the many, many reckless drivers at liberty in the state of New York—"

"I object! Objection!"

"—endangering the lives and physical well-being of our citizens."

"Your Honor!" Howie roared. Quill, impressed, hadn't realized he was so excitable.

Santini raised his hand for silence. "Your Honor, at the least, the very least, I request that you commit this woman to the county jail. She is a virtual felon—"

"Your Honor!" Howie, suddenly cold (and, Quill saw, very, very angry), folded his arms and lowered his head, like a bull about to charge. She put a hand on his arm. His voice was tight. "Go on, Santini. Hang yourself."

"She has been identified by the bus driver, and has a driving record which clearly places her in the ranks of the reckless. All the conditions for the severest penalty have been met, and I request the maximum sentence."

As if recognizing a cue, Bernie Bristol thwacked his gavel. "Seven days . . ." he said directly into the rolling camcorder.

Howie clenched both hands. "Your Honor! I must warn you that I will immediately contact the Office of Court Administration to file a complaint!"

". . . and seven hundred dollars for the much-needed budget of the state of New York. Bailiff? Escort the prisoner to the jail house, please." He adjusted the collar of his judge's robe and smiled at Nora Cahill. "You get all that? You want me to do it again?"

CHAPTER 5

The drive from the Tompkins County Courthouse near Ithaca had taken about twenty-five minutes, which meant, Quill thought, that it must be about eleven-thirty, although she wasn't certain. Deputy Dave had taken her watch.

The Municipal Building at the end of Main Street housed the Sheriff's Department and Town offices. The jail was on the west end of the building facing Main, so that Quill could see most of Hemlock Falls through the barred window. The sun was pale gold through a light snow, creating a veiled and misty landscape worthy of attention by Turner, if Turner'd ever gotten to America to paint, which he hadn't. And if he weren't dead. Which he was.

Most of the stores lining Main Street were cobblestone. Marge Schmidt's diner, Esther West's dress shop, and a few others were of white clapboard with black trim. The contrast was pleasing, even, Quill thought gloomily, from this vantage point. Four inches of new snow covered rooftops and bushes and made feathery cones on the wrought-iron standards of the streetlights. The snowplows had left the curbs knee-high with pillowy drifts. Through the heavy gauge wire screen, Quill could see Esther West in a bright red ski jacket, mounting a pine wreath on the front door of her shop. Esther finished hanging the wreath and walked the three storefronts down to Marge's diner and went in. A few cars drove by. Quill started to count the squares to the inch in the screen. Some minutes after Esther disappeared into Marge's diner, Mayor Henry, portly in a black and green ski suit, ran out of his office, crossed the street to the diner, and charged inside. Then the street was quiet.

Quill sighed, coughed, wound her hair around her finger, and sat on the bare mattress of the fold-out cot. She debated her chances of getting a cup of coffee. She'd been in the cell before, having interviewed incarcerated suspects in several murder cases in years past, and it was as utilitarian and boring as ever. Caffeine might keep her awake.

Open bars on the cell's fourth side faced the solid door to the sheriff's office. This door was half open, and she could see Davy Kiddermeister's feet propped up on his desk. His socks were sagging. Quill's own feet were cold and bare except for her panty hose, since Davy'd taken her boots and then had been unable to find a pair of prison slippers. Quill loved her boots. They were crushed leather with a fleecy top. They'd been soaked with snow and mud on the outside, but the inside always kept her feet warm, no matter how poor the weather was. Quill sighed again, chewed on her hair, and stared at the ceiling. Perhaps she should have called Meg, although Howie had assured her she'd be out before lunch. A flash of red in the street caught her eye and she went back to the window.

Like two fireplugs on either side of a skinny poplar, Mayor

Henry, Esther, and Marge stood in the middle of Main Street staring at the Municipal Building. Quill untied her silk scarf, a bright teal and gold, and wagged it back and forth. Esther clutched Elmer. Elmer pointed at the jail window, his mouth moving soundlessly. Marge socked Elmer in the arm, then all three waved together, tentatively. Quill waved the scarf in response. Esther semaphored back, knocking the mayor's knitted hat sideways and poking him in the eye. There was an excited colloquy, then Marge stumped to her Lexus, the mayor and Esther on her heels. They piled in. Marge peeled out from the curb, slush spraying from beneath the wheels.

"Coffee!" Quill shouted futilely through the barred window. "Bring coffee."

"You need anything, Ms. Quilliam?" Davy Kiddermeister stood outside the cell, his thumbs hitched in his belt loops. Davy was blond and fair-skinned. In winter, the tips of his ears were perpetually chapped.

"No, thanks, Davy," said Quill. She sighed and twiddled her thumbs. "Has Howie had any luck finding that judge? The real one, I mean?"

"Mr. Murchison's down to the courthouse right this minute, paying your fine. I told you that, twice. Not that I mind saying it more than once," he added hastily. "No, ma'am."

"Seven hundred dollars," Quill murmured darkly.

Davy shuffled. He was able to shuffle, Quill noted, because he had boots. She, on the other hand, didn't.

"I really hated to lock you up like this, Ms. Quilliam, but the law's the law."

"Then how's about my boots? Honestly, Davy, why can't I just have my boots? They aren't exactly lethal weapons."

"Sheriff Dorset'd have my guts for garters if I hadn't processed you in right, and prisoners can't have shoes or belts or anything like that. Says so in the manual."

"Where is Sheriff Dorset, anyway?"

"Out," Davy said vaguely, "with that senator."

"Al Santini is not a senator." Quill explained with restraint, "He lost the election. He's an ex-senator. Which, if I'm not mistaken, is why I'm here at this very moment."

Davy, who clearly had something on his chest, ignored this and said earnestly, "I just hope that you won't, you know"—Davy's ears turned an even brighter pink—"tell Kathleen that I treated you bad or anything like that. You want something, I'll get it for you. Just lemme know. Unless it's your boots. Can't give you your boots."

Quill felt an attack of tartness coming on. "Kathleen is perfectly capable of deciding that her brother is a Nazi all on her own. She's not only our best waitress, she's the one with the most sense." She sat on the cot and sank her chin in her hands. She wondered if she'd be in here if Myles had been reelected sheriff. Nobody knew much about Frank Dorset, except that he lived at the very edge of Tompkins County and farmed pigs. Myles, she thought, wouldn't have let things get to this point.

"I've been thinking maybe of getting out of law enforcement, like Sheriff McHale did," Davy said with remarkable prescience. "Stuff like throwing you in jail just isn't right, to my way of thinking."

"If you think at all, David Emerson Kiddermeister," said Marge Schmidt, entering the cell area with a great stamping of feet and a rush of snowy air, "which I doubt. The men in this town have all gone crazy. Look, Esther. It's true. Every word of it. There she is!"

Esther, Marge, and the mayor crowded next to Davy and stared at Quill like owls on a fence. Esther patted a stiffly lacquered curl over one ear and chirped in distress.

"I don't know as how you all are allowed in here," said Davy. "Prisoner's only allowed one visitor at a time."

"Stuff it." Marge planted a thick palm in Davy's chest and shoved him aside. "You all right, Quill? Getcha anything?"

"Coffee," said Quill, "I'd love some coffee. And something to do. A book, maybe?"

"How long they send you up for?" asked the mayor. "Are you going to need a lot of books? I could set up a fund-raiser, maybe."

"She isn't going to be here that long," Esther said stoutly. Esther, whose taste in clothes seemed to have been formed by watching old movies starring the McGuire sisters, adjusted her patent leather belt and added, "Are you?"

"Seven days," said Davy. "Judge says she's supposed to serve the whole time."

"He can't do that," said Marge. "I knew that little squirt Bristol never shoulda been elected. And it's your fault, Mayor. You and your nekkid friends running all through the woods like a bunch of assholes."

"Maybe the judge *can* do that," Esther gasped. "I mean—if she did what she did, she could be in here for years. Did you do it, Quill? I mean, we heard that you ran over a little child, but which little child? And the child couldn't have died, because we would have heard about it."

"I ran over a little child?" said Quill. "What? What?"

"You got it wrong, Esther. You always do. She didn't run over a little kid." Elmer sighed, regret all over his round face. "She *almost* ran over a little kid. Came this close." He held a pudgy thumb and forefinger minimally apart.

"I passed a school bus," said Quill. "A parked empty school bus. There weren't any little kids within forty blocks of that school bus."

"Well, there had to have been little kids within forty blocks," said the mayor reasonably. "The whole of Hemlock Falls isn't forty blocks, so there must have been little kids around somewhere. But you—"

"I did NOT run over a little kid!"

"You heard it wrong, Elmer, you hopeless little shit." Marge put her hands on her considerable hips and surveyed the cell and the shoeless Quill with a suspicious touch of satisfaction. "Just look at this. Cold, hungry, and practically bare nekkid. I'm going to go down to the library and check out a couple of books for Quill, here. Esther, you find some slippers in that shop of yours, and then give Betty a call. She can run over here with some hamburg and a thermos of coffee." She fixed a malevolent eye on Davy. "And don't you touch a drop of my coffee, David Emerson Kiddermeister. I ain't subsidizing any damn fool that had a part in this. And speaking of damn fools, where's that useless son of bitch sheriff?"

"You talking to me?"

To her fierce annoyance, Quill jumped and her breath came short. Franklin Douglas Dorset, newly elected sheriff of Tompkins County, didn't look at all like Travis Bickle, he only sounded like him. He looked, as Meg had stigmatized him at the start of his election campaign, like a canned asparagus. He unzipped his quilted winter jacket and regarded the group crushed in front of the cell with speculation. Dorset was tall; his skin, hair, eyes, and clothes a uniformly nondescript pale brown. His hair was thick, standing almost upright, and his shoulders, chest, and hips were of similar circumference, so that if you had an imagination as food-oriented as Meg's it was possible to imagine Dorset as one of the more cylinderlike vegetables. Quill thought he looked more like a bleached-out Elvis Presley than an asparagus.

Meg also claimed Dorset had the brains of a boiled onion. Quill, after one look at his flat brown eyes, wasn't sure about that.

"Deputy?" said Dorset. "There some good reason why all these people are in here?"

Marge drew breath. Quill waited confidently for the explosion. Blessed with the psychic drive of a Patton tank, Marge could flatten sumo wrestlers with a single glance from her turretlike eye.

"Guess we better be getting along," Marge said meekly. "I'm bringing her coffee and a book, Sheriff," she added. "And somethin' to put on her feet. If you don't mind."

"What I mind," said Sheriff Dorset, lifting a corner of his lip, "is you taking that intersection at Route 15 and 96 at seventy miles an hour last Sunday at 4:32 p.m., Marge Schmidt. That's a three-hundred-dollar, three-point V&T violation."

"Route 15 and 96?" Elmer asked alertly.

"Maybe it's there," Dorset said with relish, "and maybe it isn't. I'll see you folks sometime, right?" He held an imaginary camera to one eye and pretended to click it.

Quill watched Marge leave, followed by a studiedly careless mayor and a nervous Esther. She said to Dorset, "You mean you can move the darn thing?"

"The hidden camera? Bet your cute little ass. No use in a town this size if you can't."

Dorset unclipped the keys to the cell from his belt with a flourish and opened the cell door. His gaze flicked over her carelessly, avoiding her eyes, and concentrating on her breasts. He stood slouched, one hip thrust out. "Deputy here says you want to go home. Says you're a little scared. Can't say as I blame you."

Quill thought carefully about her response to this. She probably wouldn't get much more than seven years jail time if she punched

Franklin Douglas Dorset right in the nose. On the other hand, her feet were cold and she was going to die if she didn't get a cup of coffee. "Ahem," she said, in a noncommittal way.

"Tell you what. Senator out there wants to have a little talk with you, then he figures you pay the fine, you've served a little time, it's all settled, you can go back up to the Inn." Dorset smiled ingratiatingly.

Quill didn't say anything.

"Well, ma'am?"

"What kind of talk?" she asked suspiciously.

Dorset jiggled the keys. "Whyn't you come right out here and see?"

Dorset behind her like an ugly sheepdog, Quill marched into the sheriff's office and into a glare of lights, cables, and Nora Cahill's camera crew.

"Sarah Quilliam was released at 12:22, having spent all of two hours and forty-seven minutes of her seven-day sentence in jail," said Nora Cahill in her professional anchor voice. "Senator? Do you have a comment?"

Quill's stockinged toe caught on a piece of curling linoleum. She pitched forward. Al Santini grabbed her elbow and pulled her upright. Howie Murchison draped her down coat over her shoulders, grabbed Quill's other elbow, and pulled her toward the door.

"Sarah Quilliam is a wealthy businesswoman and Hemlock Falls' third largest employer," Santini said into the camcorder's little red light. "The level of this fine is a joke."

Ex-Senator Al Santini and Sheriff Dorset smiled for the camera. Howie looked pained.

"Here're your boots, Ms. Quilliam," Davy whispered apologetically. Quill grabbed them and pulled the left one on, hopping around the linoleum on one leg. They were still soggy with snow and mud.

Nora Cahill shoved the microphone in Quill's face. "Do you have a comment, Ms. Quilliam? Do you think this criminal charge will affect business at your upper-crust Inn? And how do you feel about Senator Santini's efforts to reform small-town America?"

Quill, who thought of herself as a generally equable person, felt the last shreds of her temper fray and snap. She grabbed the right boot by its wet, muddy top and swung.

"And he's going to press charges?!" Meg said indignantly some twenty minutes later. "That lunatic! That creep! I would have whacked him right in the balls."

Quill, wanting nothing more than to sit quietly for two minutes and warm her feet, looked at the kitchen with the nostalgic affection common, she supposed, to the recently paroled. She never wanted to see Al Santini or Bernie Bristol or Frank Dorset again in this life. She wanted to stay in the kitchen forever. The cobblestone fireplace was hung with dried bay leaf, braids of pearly garlic, and sheaves of lemon thyme. A fire burned briskly in the grate. Meg's collection of copper pots gleamed reassuringly from one of the oak beams running overhead. The air was filled with the scents of baking bread, orange sauce for the game hens, and freshly ground coffee. Admittedly, the view from the mullioned windows at the kitchen's west end was not quite as picturesque as that from the county jail; the herb gardens out back were still producing parsley and brussels sprouts. Sometime yesterday Mike the groundskeeper must have cleared them of snow. The mulched beds were consequently muddy with well-manured straw, but they looked beautiful to Quill. "Free," mused Quill, feeling warmly toward the mulch, "I'm free."

"The son of a bitch," Meg continued.

"Do you kiss your mother with that mouth, Miss Margaret Quilliam?" demanded Doreen, who had insisted that Quill completely change her clothes. "Lice," she'd said. "And I ain't sayin' a word more."

She tapped Quill on the shoulder. "The senator got a powerful lot of mud up his nose, or so I hear. But that don't make it right for Meg here to cuss him out. Jail! The good Lord give me a stummick to hear this. Jail!"

"Actually, I was aiming at Nora Cahill. I didn't mean to get Al Santini, although I'm glad I did. And why are you mad at me, Doreen?"

Doreen darted a beady, somewhat proprietary eye around the

kitchen. Six of the kitchen staff scrubbed vegetables, stirred sauces, and washed pots with unconcern for Doreen's cool reception of the fact that Quill had spent two hours and forty-seven minutes in the county jail. In her middle fifties, Doreen had been head housekeeper at the Inn for almost six years and regarded both Meg and Quill as sometimes satisfactory but frequently recalcitrant daughters, and everybody knew it.

"I'm ashamed of you," Doreen said severely. "The whole town's talking about it."

"It's not that big a deal! It was a setup! A mistake!" Quill sank her head in her hands. "I suppose Axminster's going to run a story in the *Gazette*."

"Huh," said Doreen. She scratched her nose vigorously.

"Isn't anyone glad to see me?" Quill asked somewhat plaintively.

The kitchen got very quiet, although, thought Quill, the kitchen was never really quiet. Even at two o'clock in the morning, the Zero King refrigerators filled the air with a gentle hum. And at one o'clock in the afternoon, four days before Christmas, with the rest of the McIntosh family due that evening and a wedding due at the end of the week, the Inn's kitchen was filled with the clank and clatter of *sous*-chefs at the Aga, the oceanlike hum of the lunch crowd in the dining room, and the slam-whack of doors opening and closing.

Quill thought about the sound of doors closing: storeroom doors, cupboard doors, oven doors—all of it far preferable to the unique sound of a cell door being shut and locked. But at the moment, the kitchen was quiet only in relation to the usual people noise: Usually Meg alternately shrieked at and sang to the Cornell interns; Doreen recited the latest depredations of departed guests on the Inn towel supply; Frank, the assistant chef, called out food orders to the hapless Bjarne; the other workers whistled, gossiped, or hummed. At the moment, everyone in the kitchen was dead silent, out of sympathy, Quill had assumed, for her recent incarceration. Now she wasn't so sure.

"Oh, for Pete's sake." Meg, shaping meringues into swans, paused and waved the palette knife in an accusing fashion. "Anyone would think you'd spent three days in solitary instead of three hours chitchatting with Davy Kiddermeister."

"I was not chitchatting with Davy Kiddermeister. I was in jail. A prisoner. And I was cold. I told you. They took away my boots."

Doreen made a surreptitious note on a pad she kept handy in her apron. Quill had seen the pad. It had a little logo of a mouse with a reporter's hat and five large capital W's running down one edge for Who, What, Where, When and Why. Doreen had ordered it from the Lillian Vernon catalog soon after she married Axminster and they bought the *Gazette*. Axminster had proved surprisingly good at publishing the weekly, although Quill suspected that Doreen's nose for gossip had a lot to do with it. That, and her savings from her wages as the Inn's housekeeper. Doreen was notoriously thrifty. Doreen caught Quill's eye and shoved the pad back in her pocket. Doreen's gray hair frizzed around her high forehead like a ruff on a grouse and her nose was beaky. Spurious attempts at innocence increased her resemblance to a startled rooster.

"Axminster's going to run a story about this, isn't he?"

"It's publicity," Doreen offered placatingly. "Publicity's good for business."

Meg snorted, "Publicity! If you'd just told Howie Murchison about those priors, none of this would have happened. What I want to know is, how come when the Inn gets publicity, it's always bad publicity? At least this time it isn't a corpse. I hate it when the headlines involve a corpse."

"They better not, missy," Doreen said darkly.

"Better not what?" asked Quill.

"Involve no corpse."

Meg grinned to herself and added a wing to the swan's body with meticulous care.

"What are you talking about? I didn't kill anybody!"

"Passin' a school bus, you might of, is all," said Doreen.

The silence intensified.

"I didn't pass a school bus!" said Quill. "I mean I did, but it was a parked school bus."

"That's when you're supposed to stop," Doreen said tartly. "When the school bus is."

"It was a parked, *empty* school bus!"

"Empty?" said Frank, the assistant chef. "You mean you didn't almost run over a little kid?"

"No!"

"That's what we heard," Bjarne said apologetically.

"I told you guys," said Meg.

"Told them what?" said Quill.

"I told them you didn't almost run over a little kid. You would have confessed to me." She winked.

"There is," Quill said stiffly, "evidence that I didn't run over anybody."

"Evidence?" asked Doreen.

"A videotape. From that damn hidden camera that started this whole mess. They showed it in court. All it showed was my car passing that school bus!"

"They show the whole thing?" Doreen asked alertly. "Stuff like that can be faked, ya know."

"All right, all right." Meg gestured widely with the palette knife, spattering egg white. "Doreen, you know gossip in a town this size. Quill didn't run anybody over with anything." She shook her head at Quill. "You're right, I should have stayed with you this morning. Next time you get arrested, I will. Sisters forever!" She began to hum an Irving Berlin tune so old Quill didn't even know where she'd picked it up. "Sis—ters. Sis—ters. Dah-dah-dah-sisters . . ."

"Thing is," Frank said earnestly, "if you didn't almost run over a little kid, what else would bring someone like Senator Alphonse Santini all the way to Hemlock Falls to prosecute a little traffic case?"

Quill rose from her seat behind the counter. "He's here for the wedding! He is not a senator. He's an ex-senator. Clearly he's turning even his wedding into a media circus! And he's running so hard for reelection he's going to need oxygen infusions before New Year's. As to why he picked on Hemlock Falls first, beats the heck out of me. Maybe because he's getting married here. You heard what Nora Cahill said—this is part of a whole campaign to reform small-town America. And he's started here. If anyone's a hit-and-run driver, it's him. I mean it's he. Whatever. I'll bet you a week's pay that right now he's off to the next town and the next victim, trailing his pet little media person and her camcorders behind him. He'll be jailing innocent people over in Covert next.

Or maybe Trumansburg. And he'll come back here to get married, and I'll kill him."

"The guy's a jerk," Meg said loyally. "If the McIntoshes weren't spending all this money on his wedding, I'd do more than shove a few handfuls of mud up his nose."

"Gee, thanks, Meg," said Quill. "Food first, sisters second." She paused, cleared her throat, and said huskily, "I can't believe you guys thought I did something as terrible as almost hitting a little kid."

"Somebody circulating that rumor again?" John came through the swinging doors from the dining room, a sheaf of lunch orders in his hand. At his seemingly casual comment, everyone busily resumed work. Quill had always thought his chief asset as business manager was his unflappability. She decided now that it was his easy air of authority. He smiled at her. "Glad to see Howie sprang you from the slam. I was about to call out the cavalry."

Quill gave him an unwilling smile.

"Mr. Raintree? This rumor that's been going around about Quill's jail time . . ." Frank began.

"You're too smart to believe that one, Frank. And even smarter enough to stop anyone who spreads it. Quill? You have a few minutes to spare? Mrs. McIntosh would like to go over some of the wedding plans."

"Sure." Quill latched on to the proffered diversion with relief. "Where is she?"

"Office. I'll meet you there in a second. Kathleen's busy with customers out there. The RV conventioneers from the Marriott snowmobiled over here in a huge group. I told her I'd turn these lunch orders over to Frank for her."

Quill hesitated, waiting for him.

"You go on ahead, Quill. I just need a few minutes with these guys."

Quill pushed her way through the swinging doors slowly enough to hear John say, "Everyone in this kitchen is going to listen to this once, and only once . . ."

The doors whispered closed. Behind her, John's admonitions rose and fell. Phrases like "innocent until proven guilty" would be hurled next. Not to mention, "going through a tough time at the moment." Quill folded her arms and glowered, startling a guy in an unzipped snowmobile suit at table fourteen into spilling Meg's pumpkin soufflé onto his T-shirt. Mindful of a public television special on psychic well-being she'd seen recently, Quill took deep breaths, strove for inner calm, and exhaled noisily, further alarming the gentleman seated at fourteen.

Quill concentrated fiercely on the McIntosh wedding, clearing her thoughts of a persistent sense of injustice. Mrs. McIntosh would want to know if they could accommodate the extra eighty people who'd somehow sprung up at the last minute.

She still wasn't sure how they were going to handle the entire McIntosh reception without opening the terrace, and there was no way to open the terrace because it was December and too cold for anyone except the S.O.A.P. diehards. She mentally rearranged the mahogany sideboards, the breakfront, and the tables. She waved absentmindedly at Kathleen, who was moving gracefully among the tables like a skater on a pond, and thought about taking out just one more wall. The sturdy building was used to it, and she'd been convinced they needed the extra space for a long time anyway.

When they had purchased the Inn seven years before, Meg and Quill had decided on twenty-seven guest rooms, a Tavern Lounge to seat a hundred, and an equivalent number of seatings in the dining room. They'd remodeled with that in mind. John had added a conference center for possible corporate business when he'd signed on with them two years after they had opened, over Quill's protests. The past summer John had encouraged them to open a small, boutique style restaurant in the Sakura mall which almost ran itself.

Neither Meg nor Quill had anticipated the sudden spurt of success of the last year or so resulting from John's management. Not only had the number of business parties increased—but so had the private. The McIntosh wedding would be the largest Meg and Quill had ever planned, and it would be the first of many, if the current trends held.

She felt John come into the room behind her and said, "If we could just take out the wall between here and the foyer, I know we could seat those extra eighty people."

"I think we should stick with the buffet."

"I hate to stand up when I eat. And so does everyone else."

"Well, by all means. Let's call Mike and get that wall down, the place recarpeted, and the walls repainted by Friday."

"Oh, ha." She paused. "I don't know, you're probably right about the spacing." She scanned the room. Mauve carpeting covered the floor. The tables were covered with deep dusty rose cloths in winter, to make the room seem warmer. The east wall gave a view of the snow-filled gorge. Sunlight sparkled off the icicles formed on the granite by the waterfall, a welcome change from the gloom of the day before. The contrast between the blue-white iridescence of the winter outside and the warmth of the room had a lot to do with the animation of the people eating Meg's food, she thought. *They're happy, they're full. This is a business that gives people a little peace of mind. And I like it.* She pushed the thought of Myles, and a home and children a little further into her subconscious.

A plump blond woman at the foyer entrance waved agitatedly in Quill's direction. "I almost forgot about Mrs. McIntosh," she said suddenly. "Poor thing!" She tucked her hand into John's arm. "Let's go relieve her agitation."

"That," murmured John, "will be quite a trick without Prozac."

On the way through the foyer to the office, Elaine McIntosh circled them like a retriever asked to herd sheep—plucky but easily distracted. She was a pretty, plump, beautifully shaped woman who wore well-tailored trousers and plain blouses trimmed with a bit of lace on the collar or the cuffs, high-necked and long-sleeved.

Quill had discovered that Elaine's physical appearance, combined with a more or less permanent state of soft-spoken distress, brought out odd impulses in men. Even John, who was as reserved around women as the Pope, fussed over her. He settled her on the couch in Quill's office, buzzed the kitchen for tea, and pulled the McIntosh wedding file from the drawer in Quill's cabinet with a minimum of words and a maximum of composure. With a cup of hot Red Zinger in her hand and John's solid height next to her on the couch, Elaine exhibited all the aplomb of a woman who owned a large amount of property over the San Andreas Fault. This was an improvement over her usual state of mind, which was that of a periodontophobe waiting for a root canal.

"There's two things," she said breathlessly. "The first is, I just wanted to thank you again for the use of this lovely, lovely building. It's so antique! It's so historic! You know, Claire—I mean, her father—well, our money is plumbing fixture money and Alphonse is so . . ." She waved helplessly.

"Fatheaded?" Quill ventured under her breath.

Mrs. McIntosh twisted her rings in agitation. "Ritzy," she finally managed. "The Santinis are bigwigs. My husband Vittorio gets so mad when I say that. He says money made in plumbing fixtures is as good as anybody's, but you know, it's not!"

"Of course it is," Quill said indignantly. "My goodness."

A brass plaque set near the fireplace in the Inn's foyer read "Est. 1693," the implication being that the Inn building with its copper roof and weathered shakes had been there for three hundred years. And most people, Quill knew, thought that antiquity conferred prestige. Quill never passed the plaque without a mild sense of guilt over the aristocratic implications; three hundred years ago, the Inn overlooking the Falls of Hemlock Gorge had been a one-room log cabin owned and operated by a lady of dubious virtue called Turkey Lil. From the War of 1812 on, the Inn had been added to, until it reached a sprawling twenty thousand square feet mid-century. Subsequent owners had adapted the Inn to fit various purposes, and it had been a girls' school, a rest home, and even, briefly, the home of the deservedly unknown Civil War General C. C. Hemlock. The Inn was a lot of things, but it wasn't, in Mrs. McIntosh's parlance, ritzy, aristocratic, or even prestigious. Merely old.

"And the second thing?" Quill prompted.

"It's Vittorio, my husband." Mrs. McIntosh apologized and Quill got the impression she was apologizing for the marital relationship as well as the existence of the man himself. "Actually it's Vittorio's mother, Tutti."

"Tutti?" asked Quill, leaning forward so she could hear better. Elaine McIntosh became almost inaudible when stressed, and since Elaine seemed to be stressed all the time, no one at the Inn had been entirely certain whether the McIntosh celebration was a wedding or an anniversary until Mrs. McIntosh confirmed the plans in writing last August. A secondary frustration was that no one knew why the McIntoshes—who were clearly Italian—had a Scottish cognomen; Meg had given up altogether on being able to figure that one out. "Has she decided not to come after all?"

Elaine gestured. Her eyes filled with tears. Quill, who'd been seriously alarmed the first, second, and third time Elaine's eyes had filled with tears over a crisis reached automatically for the box of Kleenex on her desk and handed it over. John, rarely demonstrative, put a sympathetic hand on her shoulder.

Elaine, hand stuffed against her nose, shook her head and wailed, "No! No!"

"She *is* coming," guessed Quill.

Elaine nodded, gulped, and folded the Kleenex into a neat oblong. "She's coming. And she had a vision. Tutti's famous for her visions. She's always right."

"A vision? You mean, as in a psychic vision."

"Yes! About . . . you know."

Quill, who'd been experiencing some mild concern about her level of tolerance—an essential trait of any innkeeper—for some hours since she'd allowed Alphonse Santini to provoke her into battery, made a conscious effort to be calm. "Your mother-in-law had a vision about the wedding?"

Elaine picked up a fistful of Kleenex. "She said . . . she said . . . he was going to leave Claire. At the altar. That the wedding's not going to come off. That I've been pushing. That it's my fault. That he really doesn't want to marry Claire."

"Of course he does," soothed Quill. "I mean, all grooms are supposed to be a little anxious before the wedding."

"The thing is, I just know everyone thinks that Claire's marrying him because . . . you know . . . plumbing fixture money. Not the same!"

"Oh, Elaine, Al loves Claire. I'm sure he'll make a good and reliable . . ." She tried to think of a polite substitute for demagogue and gave up. There were limits to her policy of honesty. "You've spoken with him, John, about the bachelor party. He seemed . . . you know, didn't he?"

"Al Santini?" said John. "Oh, yeah, Quill. Very you know."

"But you don't understand!" wailed Elaine. "Tutti wants to call the whole wedding off!"

"With all due respect for your mother-in-law, how can she?" Quill asked gently.

"You don't know her," Elaine said tragically. "You just—what's that?"

A soft tap came on the office door.

"Our receptionist, I think." Quill called, "Come in, please," with a guilty sense of relief. Dina poked her head around the edge of the door, her eyes large. A low-pitched wailing from outside accompanied her. "Excuse me. Quill? You'd better come."

"What's that noise?"

Dina glanced nervously over her shoulder. "It's Mrs. McIntosh. The mother-in-law. Claire's grandmother. She says to call her Tutti. She's standing in the middle of the foyer. Prophesying."

CHAPTER 6

"There will be three knocks!" cried Tutti McIntosh. "Three knocks on the door! And then . . . blood, *blood*, BLOOD!" The hairy little dog in her arms yapped twice. Tutti rather absentmindedly set the dog down on the Oriental rug. With a pugnacious scowl he squatted and piddled on the celadon and ivory rose medallion in the center.

"Oh, Tutti, dear!" Elaine McIntosh burst into tears.

Quill, nonplussed, stood for a moment to assess the situation. Claire's grandmother was plump and wide, with the frilly softness of a crocheted doll over a telephone. She had dimples, soft white hair, and very pink cheeks. The dog was some sort of pug. Tutti was wearing a fur coat the same color and texture as her little dog—a burnished red that was close to Quill's own hair color. Her prophecy wail was low, windy, and dirgelike, which made it easy to hear Dina's perplexed explanation.

"She came in. Saw the plaque that says 'Established 1693.' Closed her eyes. Spun around for a second saying 'prophecy' a couple of times and then started hollering about three knocks on the door and blood, blood, blood, blood, *blood* . . .”

“Stop,” said Quill.

Dina gazed consideringly at the little old lady for a moment, then said indignantly, “I didn’t do a thing to her.”

“Of course you didn’t,” Elaine McIntosh said in a helpless way. “She does this all the time!” She grabbed her mother-in-law’s wrist and shook it gently. “Tutti. Tutti! TUTTI!”

“What!” Mrs. McIntosh demanded in a suddenly pragmatic tone of voice.

“Are you all right?”

“I’m fine, dear. Thank you.” Mrs. McIntosh regarded Quill, John, Dina, and Doreen—who had appeared at the dining room entrance rolling her mop-bucket—with cheerful equanimity. “How do you all do?”

“Lot better since that caterwauling stopped,” said Doreen. “What’n the hell was that all about? You woulda thought . . .” Her suspicious gaze fell on the carpet. “Dog pee!” she murmured. “Dog pee. On my carpet.”

“Tatiana didn’t do it,” Mrs. McIntosh said immediately. She bent to pick up the pug, who backed away, snarling ferociously. She sang, “Good doggie, good doggie, good—OW!” Then she dropped it.

“Outta the way,” Doreen snarled. She jerked the bucket forward, the water sloshing. Tatiana stood defiantly over the small pool on the rug and yapped.

“G’wan,” said Doreen, brandishing the mop. “You little bastard.”

“Doreen,” John said mildly.

Tatiana’s yaps ascended the scale and increased in pitch. Dina clapped her hands over her ears. Doreen bent over, pushed her nose into Tatiana’s and roared, “SHUT UP!”

Tatiana’s little pink mouth closed. Her button eyes bulged. She panted, yipped once, rolled her eyes up into her head, and spasmed. She rolled on her back and lay upside down, all four legs in the air, motionless.

“My God,” breathed Dina. “It’s dead!”

“Huh,” Doreen said, pleased.

Quill clapped her hands over her mouth.

"She's not dead," Tutti said briskly, "she's fainted. Actually, she just wants us to think she's fainted. She's faking. Does it all the time." She nudged Tatiana with her toe. "Up, darling. Up. Up. Up."

Tatiana, still upside down, opened her eyes and gave Doreen an evil look.

"Come to Mummy!"

Tatiana rolled to her feet, gave a standing jump, and landed in Tutti's arms.

"Wow!" said Dina. "That's a valuable dog, Mrs. McIntosh. I mean, jeez. Did you see that, Quill? John? How did you train her to do that, Mrs. McIntosh?"

Doreen, on her knees scrubbing at the damp spot on the rug, looked up at Tatiana with a steady considering stare. Tatiana stared steadily back.

"Um, Doreen," said Quill. "Maybe we could all just kind of forget this. Mrs. McIntosh, I'm Sarah Quill—"

"Sarah Quilliam," she said with a gracious air. Her voice was high and sweet. "The *noted* painter. I am very, very pleased to meet you. I've seen your work in the galleries in New York. Such an eye for color, my dear! Such sensitivity! *You*, of all people should understand the aura here. You feel it, too, don't you?"

"Well, actually," said Quill, "I don't . . . feel what, Mrs. McIntosh?"

Her voice dropped an octave. "The Coming Disaster. I felt the vibrations as soon as I walked in that door. This marriage must *not* take place!"

"Tutti!" Elaine wailed.

"Where's Claire?" Tutti demanded briskly.

"Claire?" asked Quill. "Um. Yes. Claire."

"The bride," John said helpfully.

"Oh! Of course! Come to think of it, I haven't seen her today. Have you, Dina?"

"Nope."

Mrs. McIntosh gestured, her bracelets clanking. "I must see her. As soon as she arrives. There is danger here, I tell you. Three knocks at the door, and then blood, blo—"

"Mrs. McIntosh!" Quill said firmly.

"Claire took the Caddy to pick up her father at the train station, Tutti," said Elaine. "They should have been here by now, but with the snow coming on so fast, they must have been delayed."

"I told Vic to take the train," said Mrs. McIntosh. "It's more comfortable. It's safe. And a lot cheaper." She adjusted the large diamond brooch on her scarf with a virtuous air. "I just hope he doesn't get into an accident coming from Ithaca. Norton almost ditched my limo twice on the way up from Boston."

"They'll be fine. Vic's a wonderful driver." Elaine looked a question at Quill. "Now, Tutti, why don't I take you up to your room?"

"What a good idea! We've put you in the Provençal suite, Mrs. McIntosh. I'm sure you'll be very comfortable up there. And would you like a tea? We've got fresh scones and Devonshire cream. And our hot chocolate is very good."

The little dog in her arms barked.

"And I'm sure we can find a biscuit for, um . . ."

"Tatiana," Mrs. McIntosh supplied.

"Of course, um . . . good doggie," Quill said inadequately.

"We don't hold with dog pee here," Doreen said in an ominous way. "I don't do dog pee. Windows. Terlits. Refrigerators. I do all that. I don't do dog pee."

"Of course you don't!" Mrs. McIntosh said sunnily. "Now, if this very good-looking young man could escort me upstairs, I think I could use a little rest. It's Mr. Raintree, isn't it?"

John inclined his head gravely.

"Are you married, Mr. Raintree?"

"No, Mrs. McIntosh. Not yet."

Mrs. McIntosh took his arm and twinkled at him. "Call me Tutti! Everyone does. And I'd adore it if you could meet my granddaughter. She's single, too."

Quill watched them proceed up the winding stairs to the upper floors. Tatiana, flopped over Tutti's furry arm, regarded Doreen unblinkingly with her shoe button eyes.

"I didn't know you had two daughters, Mrs. McIntosh," said Dina.

Elaine took a deep breath. "I don't. She doesn't either. Have another granddaughter, I mean. Oh, Quill, what am I going to do? You see what I mean?"

"Well, I think your mother-in-law is *cool*," Dina said in a reverent tone. "I mean, is she really, like, psychic and all? Did you see how she knew John's *name* before anybody, like, introduced him?"

Quill tapped the nameplate under the "Reception" sign, which read, YOUR HOSTS: SARAH QUILLIAM/MARGARET QUILLIAM/JOHN RAINTREE.

"Honest, Quill, she walked right in here and started prophesying right away. She didn't have a chance to read a thing! Besides, John could have been anybody. Like, another guest or something."

"I don't think so," Quill said repressively. "Elaine, why don't we go back to my office and rework the plans for the reception? We're essentially doubling the number of guests, is that right? It's going to put a bit of strain on the kit—"

The knocker on the Inn's oak door sounded once, twice, and a third time, echoing impressively in the foyer. Dina screamed. Doreen raised her mop like a club, grasping the handle firmly in both hands.

"My God," said Elaine. "Oh, my God." She backed against the newel post to the stairway, quivering.

The knocks on the door were succeeded by a series of thumps and bangs. Quill marched across the foyer and flung the door wide. A gust of cold air blew snow across the Oriental rug. An extremely cross male voice ordered Quill to get the goddamned luggage.

"Vic!" cried Elaine. "You made it! I was so worried!"

"Roads were a goddamned pain," he snarled. "Claire? Will you get your ass in here, for Chrissakes?"

"Quill, this is my husband, Vittorio," Elaine fluttered.

Vic grunted. This was the first she'd seen of Vittorio McIntosh. And there was blood all over his hands.

"I hadn't even heard of him before, other than the name on his gold card," Quill said to Meg and John in the kitchen a few hours later.

"Well, I have," said John. "The fortune is privately held, but a conservative estimate would be in the area of fifty million. And Nora Cahill's information was sound. There have been rumors about his links to organized crime for years."

"He was bleeding?" asked Meg.

"Of course he was bleeding!" Quill, exasperated, bit into a left-over pâté puff. It was soggy. "That's why I had to give Dina an aspirin. He'd barked his knuckles on the door knocker trying to get in out of the snow. He said it was locked."

"The door's never locked until lights-out," said Meg.

"If you ask me, Mrs. McIntosh—I mean, Tutti—locked it when she came in," Quill said gloomily. "That old lady's a corker. And she sure doesn't like our Alphonse. Did John tell you what she did to him at dinner?"

"No!"

"Hot coffee," said John.

"All over his trousers," said Quill.

Meg grinned. She was sharpening her kitchen knives. She tested the blade of her favorite paring knife with her thumb, then asked, "What's Vittorio like?"

"Well, I'll tell you," Quill said crossly. "He could be Alphonse Santini's older uglier brother."

"That bad, huh? Dang." She counted through the knives laid out on the counter. "I'm one short."

"Check the dishwasher," John suggested.

"They know better than to put my good knives in the dish-washer."

"He called me dolly twice," Quill said loudly, feeling ignored. "Why is it, Meg, that women are just nicer than men?"

"Nicer? You think Nora Cahill's nicer? I mean, here Santini's her sworn enemy and she ends up in cahoots with him just like that. All for a good story."

"It's a lousy story," Quill said firmly. "Back to my point. Women are nicer than men. If you put one hundred women in a room with one hundred men, eighty percent of the women would be nice versus . . . versus . . ."—she waved her hands in the air—"twenty percent of the men. Would be nice."

Meg and John exchanged looks. "So!" Meg said brightly. "The Santinis and the McIntoshes will all be gone and it'll all be over in three days. Unless it keeps on snowing. You mind if I switch the television on? I want to get the weather report."

"No you don't," Quill said indignantly. "You just want to see if

Nora Cahill's plastered my face and my boots and my ugly coat all over the eleven o'clock news."

"I do not!" Meg made a deprecatory face. "Well, maybe a little. But I also want to be sure that the weather's not going to interfere with the food order getting here from New York in time. I grabbed Elaine after dinner and we finally reworked the buffet menu."

"Are we going to hire extra help?"

Meg, clicking though the channels of the small television set built over the Zero King refrigerator, nodded in an abstracted way. "Yeah, but I can't do much cooking—so it's a lot of fresh stuff: caviar, crab, shrimp. Dull, dull, *dull*!"

"And expensive," Quill said.

John agreed, then said, "There it is. The Syracuse channel."

Meg shrieked. "You're on! You're on!"

Quill stuck her fingers in her ears and hummed loudly, but try as she might, she couldn't keep her eyes shut. So she saw, although she didn't hear, a full color videotape of herself in her ugly down coat, hair every which way, a scowl on her face, sock Nora Cahill in the nose with her boot.

The station cut to a commercial.

"I need a haircut," said Quill.

"You need a new coat," said Meg. "Don't turn it off! Her commentary's next."

"That's not Nora Cahill," said Quill.

"It sure isn't," said Meg. "It's some guy."

"She told me she was on vacation," said Quill, with hope. "Maybe she just forgot about the story. What kind of story is a small-town traffic ticket, anyhow?"

". . . that news flash repeated," the male anchor said soberly into the camera. "The body of Syracuse television newswoman Nora Cahill was found under the traffic light of an intersection in the central New York village of Hemlock Falls. Sheriff Frank Dorset has refused to release details of the death pending investigation. No further details other than the report of the death are available at this time. KSGY-TV will be the first to bring you periodic updates on this tragic event. And now, for a look at the weather. The word is snow . . ."

"She was killed? Here?!" shrieked Meg. "Right here?!"

John reached up and switched the television off.

"You don't suppose . . ." said Quill. Her mind leaped to the last time she saw Nora, in angry conversation with Alphonse Santini. Except that it wasn't the last time she'd seen Nora. The last time, the very last time, struck her with the force of a fall on thick ice; she'd been wiping her cheeks free of the muddy spray from Quill's boots.

"Car accident," said John. "Had to be, in this weather."

"They would have *said* car accident," Meg insisted. "And that bozo Dorset refusing to release details? It doesn't sound good at all. Poor Nora! Maybe we should poke around a little bit, Quillie. You know, a lot of people must have had it in for that poor thing."

"No," said Quill. "No investigation. No murder inquiry. We are out of that business and into the Inn business. Full-time. This time I really mean it."

"Things have been so quiet lately," Meg complained.

"Quiet for you, maybe. I don't need to remind you that while you were peacefully chopping away in your kitchen I spent practically the entire morning in jail." *Except*, she thought, *for the part where I tried to whack. Nora with my boots.*

"Three hours," Meg muttered. "Big deal."

"You try it! God, I feel awful. I mean, the last time I saw her, I tried to break her nose."

"Oh, Quill. You were really provoked. Anyone would have tried to—um . . ."

"Um, what? I feel like a jerk. I'm a swine. I don't know why I ever agreed to run this place. All I've seemed to do is create one huge mess after the other. It's not worth it."

"Of course it's worth it," Meg said stoutly. "We have a terrific business, great guests . . ."

"Oh, *right*, Claire the cranky bride, Elaine the water faucet, Vittorio the mysterious Scottish-Italian, *and* let's not forget his psychic mother. And who has to deal with all this craziness while you retreat to this chrome and stainless steel haven? Me, that's who! And poor John has to run around cleaning up after all the messes I create."

"Quill, you are hardly responsible for Alphonse Santini and his choice of prospective in-laws," said John. There was a faint grin behind his eyes.

"She's hysterical," said Meg. "And about time, too. I was wondering when all of this would hit her."

"'Three knocks,'" Quill repeated with what she felt to be justifiable bitterness. "'Three knocks and then, blood, blood . . .'"

Three knocks sounded at the back door. They tolled through the kitchen like the bell announcing the arrival of the Ghost of Christmas Yet to Come. Like Scrooge, Quill felt like flinging the covers over her head, but the only thing at hand was a dish towel. She clutched Meg. "Sassafras," Meg said, patting her arm, "or comfrey. Herbal teas'll help you get right to sleep."

"I'll get it." John walked unhurriedly to the back door and snapped on the outside light. There was a murmur of male voices, John's voice louder than the others, an argumentative note to it. The door slammed and he stepped back into the kitchen. His dark hair was sprinkled with snowflakes.

"Quill," he said, so quietly that she had to strain to hear him, "get upstairs and lock yourself in your room. No questions. Just do it. Meg, get Howie Murchison on the line as fast as you can."

The back door rattled. A cold eddy of outside air curled around Quill's feet.

"Move, Quill!"

"But, John, what in heaven's name is going on? Why should I lock myself in my room?"

"Sarah Quilliam?" Frank Dorset pulled the hood of his dark blue parka away from his face. Davy Kiddermeister shuffled behind. Their snow boots left muddy tracks on the floor.

"You know very well who she is," Meg said tartly. "Have you come to apologize? It's about bloody time."

"You're under arrest, Ms. Quilliam, as a material witness to the murder of Nora Cahill. You have the right to representation by an attorney for your defense. If you do not have an attorney, the court will appoint one for you. You have the right to remain silent." He grinned, his teeth sharp and yellow. "And I sure as hell hope you do. Nothing worse than a yapping female behind bars."

The drive to the Tompkins County Sheriff's Department had taken about five minutes, Quill figured, which meant it must be about eleven-thirty. She wasn't sure. Deputy Dave had taken her watch.

She was sitting under the halogen lights in the sheriff's office huddled in John's parka. She'd been too dazed to find her own coat, and she missed its comforting warmth. The room felt too small. The linoleum—which had been installed at some point in the dim and faraway sixties—was as cracked and peeling as it had been that morning, although there was a fresh smell of disinfectant. Metal filing cabinets lined one wall. There were two metal desks, of the type found in every state and federal office Quill had ever seen: battleship-gray, incredibly heavy, with tarnished strips of chrome along the desk top edge. She sat behind the larger one, in the black Naugahyde chair that still, she thought, held a faint scent of Myles McHale. Frank Dorset balanced one buttock on the edge of this desk and leaned into her face. She pushed her feet along the floor and edged back, hitting the green-painted wall. Dave Kiddermeister sat at the adjacent desk, holding a small tape recorder.

"You want to go over this again?" Dorset asked. His voice was calm. Silky.

Davy cleared his throat. "She might better wait for Mr. Murchison, Sheriff."

Dorset twisted his head over his shoulder, so that Quill couldn't see his face. "Your shift about up, Deputy?"

"Nossir." Quill could hear both embarrassment and determination in his tones. "I mean, yessir, it is, but I should prob'ly stay here. You might need a wit—"

Dorset interrupted like a knife shaving beef. "That wasn't a question."

"Sir?"

"I said get your ass out of here."

Quill, who recognized that she was too mad to be scared, said, "I'll be fine, Davy. Don't worry about a thing."

"Thing," Dorset repeated softly. "Not a thing." He said loudly, "Deputy!"

Quill jumped.

Davy shuffled reluctantly to his feet.

"Leave the recorder, son."

Davy put the tape recorder near Quill's left hand, then shrugged himself into his anorak. "I'll be around, Sheriff. Just down the street at the Croh Bar."

Dorset grunted. The clock on the wall filled the silence with a soft and steady tick-tick-tick. She heard Davy close the outside door, then the crunch of his feet in the snow in the parking lot. His car door slammed. The engine turned over. He drove out of the lot and out of hearing.

Dorset leaned close. He smelled like peppermint toothpaste, sour sweat, and damp wool. "Ms. Quilliam? One more time. When did you last see Nora Cahill?"

"Right here. About twelve-fifteen this afternoon."

"She got back to the Inn around five-thirty this evening."

"Well, I didn't see her," said Quill.

"I can spit from one end of that place to the other. And you didn't see her? Not once? All evening?"

"It was a busy night, Sheriff. In case you hadn't noticed, we've got a full house."

"Huh."

He was so close she could see flecks of red on his canine teeth.

"Did you have pizza for dinner?"

His right hand came up, palm out. He shoved it into her left shoulder so hard that she spun and smacked her cheek against the wall. He grabbed the teal scarf at her throat, twisted it, and pulled her forward. "You listen," he hissed, "to me. You get that? You *lis*ten"—he whipped the scarf back and forth, pulling her from side to side—"to *me*! Are you listening?"

"Yes," Quill said calmly. "I'm listening."

He released the scarf with a swift, upward movement that jerked her chin backward. "I want you to sit there. Sit right there." He swung himself off the desk and turned his back. He whipped around so suddenly that she jumped. "You sitting? You sitting just nice and quiet, like?"

Quill nodded. It was an effort to keep her face still. She wanted to gasp for air. She took slow, shallow breaths through her nose. She felt as if she were suffocating.

"Good."

The tall metal cabinet was padlocked. Dorset pulled his ring of keys from his belt and opened it, and took out a small, hand-held videocassette viewer from the top shelf. He began to hum in a high nasal whine, an insinuating, minor-keyed tune that Quill had never heard before. He set the viewer on the desk, then scrabbled inside the cabinet for a tape. He turned, shoved the cassette into the viewer, and plugged the cord into an outlet on the wall. He swayed a little as he moved, humming.

Quill took a long, quiet breath.

He whipped his head around. "You sitting? Nice and calm, like? You little, little thing." He leaned across the desk, shoving his face against her cheek. He whispered, "Watch. This." Holding his head against her, he reached out and turned the viewer on.

The tape was black-and-white. Flickering. Grainy. The tape from the hidden camera. The LED flashed the date and 09:15, 09:16, 09:17. P.M. P.M. P.M.

The remote switched on, triggered by the approach of a car headed west on main. The car slowed, stopped, the headlights casting a dim field across the snowy street. Someone opened the driver's door and got out. Nora Cahill, her sharp nose prominent for a moment, bent down in front of the headlights to knock the snow from her boots.

A second figure emerged from the darkness. Tall. Slender. Wearing a long down coat and a round fur hat.

My God, thought Quill. She knew that coat. And that hat. And she hadn't been able to find them half an hour ago.

There was a pause in the tape. Quill strained her eyes. The other person, the one who was not Nora—*the one*, thought Quill, *who is not me! Not me!*—pulled an envelope from the depths of the coat and handed it to Nora. She thumbed through the contents.

"Money," Quill said involuntarily. "Money."

"Yowser," Dorset said in his soft silky voice.

The tape jumped, flickered, and resumed its steady whirr. Nora stuffed the money in her purse, tossed the envelope to the ground, and turned.

The dark figure stirred. Swung. And struck.

Nora fell, faceup, the headlights illuminating her face. Her lips moved. Silently. Quill shuddered and closed her eyes. She heard a click. The tape stopped. She opened her eyes to see Nora, frozen in time, her hand lifted in a last gesture, the fingers splayed out like claws, mouth open, eyes open.

"Dead," said Dorset.

"How?" asked Quill.

"You should know."

Quill shook her head.

Dorset pulled at her coat. John's coat. "When did you last see Nora Cahill?"

"This is ridiculous," said Quill. "Look. The time on the monitor. 9:23 p.m. I was at the Inn this evening."

"You got somebody besides your sister's gonna swear where you were between five after nine and nine-thirty? 'Cause that's all the time it'd take to hop down the road and off that broad. Maybe less. Haven't found a witness yet could swear to a time frame that tight in court. We blow this tape up, we're gonna see your cute little face right there."

"You will not," snapped Quill. "And somebody stole my coat. They must have."

He leaned close again, and blew out once, twice, against her cheek. Quill felt her stomach roil. "Just. Tell. Me," he coaxed. "Just me." He sat up suddenly, like a dog that hears the approach of an intruder. He laid his hand on her shoulder and squeezed it painfully tight. Quill heard a car door slam, then the sound of two—no, three people outside. There was a banging on the door, and then Howie, Meg, and John came in, the three of them abreast, like the cavalry in the kind of movies they didn't make anymore.

"Hi, guys," said Quill, dismayed to hear the quiver in her voice.

Howie glanced briefly at her, then turned his attention to Dorset. Meg, for once completely silent, came to the chair and stood to her right; John took up a position on the left. Meg reached down and squeezed Quill's hand hard.

"What's the meaning of this, Dorset?" Howie asked mildly.

"Should be obvious. I have a warrant for the little lady's arrest as a material witness to the murder of Nora Cahill this evening at 9:23. The good news is that she won't be charged with murder until the coroner's report comes in. Should be some time tomorrow. The deceased was taken to the county morgue not forty-five minutes ago."

"Can I see the warrant, please?"

Dorset pulled it from his shirt pocket. Howie unfolded it and read intently.

"This is absolutely ridiculous, Sheriff," Meg snapped. "Quill was at the Inn all evening. She was never out of my sight."

"Never?" said Dorset. "Never's a long time. I may as well tell you now, I've got affidavits coming from a couple of people up to the Inn."

"Who?" Meg tightened her hand on Quill's shoulder. "What kind of—Quill, *what's the matter with your shoulder*!?"

"Gave me a bit of trouble," said Dorset.

Meg's face turned white. John took an involuntary step forward.

"You watch it, Raintree," said Dorset. "I've read your record."

Quill stood up and grabbed John. Meg regained her breath and shrieked, "You hit my sister!"

"Meg, I'm fine. Let's not get too excited here, okay?"

"QUILL, for God's *sake*. What the *hell* do you mean, gave you a bit of trouble? Who the hell do you think you are?"

"Deputy'll bear me out on that."

"The hell he will," stormed Meg, who'd apparently lost the variety of curses usually at her disposal. "Get out of my way, you son of a bitch. I'm taking my sister home! Howie?!"

Howie folded up the warrant and tossed it on the desk. "I'd like to see this videotape."

"File a request with the judge."

"And this physical evidence found at the scene?"

"Envelope from the Inn. Says so right at the top. Decedent's name written in the accused's handwriting on the front."

"Who identified the handwriting?"

"File a request with the judge."

"Did the medical examiner give a preliminary cause of death?"

Dorset grinned. "Nope."

"He must have had some idea."

"Didn't say a word to me."

"You didn't ask him?"

"Didn't have to. Pretty much could see for myself."

"She was stabbed," Quill said tiredly. "With what seemed to be one of the knives from our kitchen."

Meg's hand jumped. Quill didn't think it was possible for her to get any more pale, but she did. "Oh, no, Meg! I saw the videotape. He showed me. It's right there."

John's right hand shot out like a snake. He pulled the cassette from the viewer and turned toward the door, seemingly all in one motion.

"Hold it," snarled Dorset. He snapped open his holster and drew his pistol. Meg screamed in furious indignation.

Howie said, "Put it away, Sheriff. John?"

"No," John said.

"You have to. Give it back."

"You're going to leave it with this bastard? There's no telling what he'll do with it."

"It's the law," said Howie. "I'm sorry."

"Is Quill coming back with us?"

Howie looked at the sheriff questioningly.

Dorset shook his head.

"Don't be a fool, Dorset. I'll get in front of a real judge tomorrow and she'll be out by nightfall."

"File a request with a judge."

John set the videotape on the desk. "This is some kind of setup, Howie."

"That's clear. The question is, why? Dorset, I'd like a few minutes alone with my client."

"Sorry."

"What the—" Howie calmed himself with a visible effort. "You can't deny her counsel."

"When she's accused of something, I can't, you're right about that. But she's being held as a witness. I got thirty-six hours before I have to let you talk to her at all. Now, tomorrow? Tomorrow after she's been accused of this murder, you can have all the time you want with her." His eyes flicked over Quill's breasts. John made a fierce noise.

"Wait for me in the car, will you, John?" said Howie.

"Murchison. This is bullshit. Absolute bullshit."

"I know. It's better if you wait for me in the car. Trust me. Please."

John shook his head and buttoned his coat. "I'll walk back to the Inn."

"You sure? It's cold out there."

"I need it." John paused in the doorway and looked back. Dorset shifted from one foot to the other under the stare. John opened the door, slid out noiselessly, and was gone.

Quill cleared her throat. "There's nothing we can do, is there, Howie?"

Meg's face was fierce. "What do you mean?! Of course there is! You're not going to leave her here!"

"I don't have much choice, Meg."

"Choice? What do you mean, choice? She's got to stay in here? Overnight?!"

Quill tried a laugh. A little weak, but a laugh nonetheless. "You didn't think a day in jail was so awful this morning, Meg."

"That was different. I thought it might teach you something about traffic tickets."

"Oh, you did, did you?"

"Well, yeah! You can't just go around thinking you're above the law. You can't—" She bit her words off in mid-sentence. "So she has to stay here? Then I'm staying, too."

"No, you're not," said Dorset.

"I am *not* leaving my sister in the Tompkins County jail overnight and that's that."

"There's only one cot in the cell," said Quill.

"So one of us can sleep on the floor."

"Which one? It's concrete. And cold."

"Concrete." Meg set her chin. "So what? I don't trust this creep."

"Meg, I'll be fine. Come by in the morning with some hot coffee, will you? And a toothbrush and stuff like that. I'll be better off if you're on the outside." She forced herself to smile. "Honest. You can nag Howie into getting bail set for me as early as possible. Okay?"

Meg scowled.

"Please, Meg. We'll get this all straightened out in the morning."

"What do you think, Howie?"

The lawyer's steady gaze had never really left Dorset. "I think," he said easily, "that Frank here ought to remember the number of friends I have on the State Supreme Court."

"Sure thing, Counselor."

"I want to see where she's going to be for the night."

"Suit yourself."

Dorset slouched through the metal door labeled LOCK UP. Meg put her arm around Quill's waist and, with Howie leading the way, they followed Dorset into the cell. The overhead light was harsh, the cell as bare as it had been that morning.

"She'll need another blanket," said Meg.

Dorset grunted and returned to the office.

Meg glared after him and turned to Quill. "And a nightgown. You can't sleep in that skirt and sweater."

"I'll be fine," said Quill, who had no intention of taking off her clothes within thirty blocks of Frank Dorset. She gave Meg a warning pinch.

Meg stared back at her, reached over, hugged her, and whispered, "Use it. If you have to. Even if you don't." She slipped the paring knife she'd been sharpening in the kitchen into Quill's hand. Quill slid it into her skirt pocket, then sat on the cot.

Dorset returned and tossed a thin wool blanket through the open door, then gestured Meg and Howie out of the cell. He clanged the door shut and locked it. Despite herself, Quill shivered.

"I'll take the key," said Howie.

"The hell you will."

"The hell I won't. Is there a duplicate?"

"Deputy carries one."

"I'm just down the street, Dorset. If you need to get her out before I'm back in the morning, call me."

"Fuck you, Murchison."

Howie's voice never rose above its mild tone of inquiry. "I don't know what the hell you're planning, Dorset. You know as well as I do that, at the very least, I can have this arrest tossed out because you prevented me from seeing my client privately. I'll tell you this. No matter where you are in the next few days, I'll prosecute you to the fullest extent the law allows—and maybe a little more than that. This woman has friends. She and her sister have a national reputation. You step an inch over the line, and it'll be safer for you in jail than out."

"You don't scare me, Murchison."

"Then you're a fool. Give me that key."

"Howie," said Quill, "don't. For one thing, what if there's a fire?

For another, he'd be a real idiot to assault my, um—virtue—after you and John and Meg have witnessed all of this. You guys go and do what you have to do to get me out of here—okay?"

"You're sure, Quillie?" Meg, pale, rubbed her face with both hands. "I really think I ought to stay with you."

"I'm sure. I'll be all right. Just go away and do what you have to do to get me out of here."

"We'll be back in the morning," said Howie. "I'll drive to Ithaca tonight, get Judge Anderson out of bed, and be back about six. Try and get some sleep." He frowned. "Dorset? Watch yourself."

At first Quill was grateful for the overhead light. The cell block was very quiet. Outside it had started to snow again, and the whisper/slide of a heavy fall brushed against the barred window. She lay back on the thin mattress, pulling the blanket over her shoulders, wriggling her stockinged feet through the folds at the bottom, trying to warm them. Meg's paring knife made a lump in her pocket, and she ended up sticking it under the pillow.

She fell into a broken doze, jerked awake every now and then by the relentless overhead light when her eyelids blinked half open. Eventually, she slid into heavy sleep.

She woke to whispered voices.

Confused, she sat up, swung her feet to the floor, and encountered cold concrete.

". . . in there right now," came a murmur, "trust me . . ."

A response, derisive.

". . . show ya . . ."

The metal door swung open. Dorset's lanky figure shambled through the flood of light from the office. Quill blinked, blinded by the overhead light. Dorset whistled as you whistle for a dog. There was someone behind him. Shorter than Dorset, about Quill's own height. Shapeless in her down coat. Face concealed by her fur hat.

Suddenly, the overhead light went out.

She flung her hand up, shading her eyes against the glare from the office door. The man? woman? behind the sheriff stepped back, arm upraised. Light flashed against steel. The arm came down, once.

Dorset screamed.

And again.

Dorset twisted, hands scrabbling for the unknown face. Quill willed her eyes open, strained against the dark.

The knife came down a third time, hard. Blood came from Dorset's mouth and nose. He cried, "Uh! Uh!" and fell in a clatter of boots and keys, arms outstretched.

The door to the office slammed shut. The cell was totally dark. There was a fumbling in the dark. The cell door clicked open. Quill shoved herself against the cold wall and grabbed the paring knife from beneath the pillow. She held it steady, blade out. There was the sound of dragging, then a shove and a grunt. Dorset's body rolled against her feet. She gasped and flung herself away, bruising her hands and knees on the iron bed frame.

A clatter and rattle of something dropped. The cell door clanged shut, and the lock clicked. The door to outside opened; the down-coated figure slipped through. Quill went to her knees and fumbled along the floor. She felt the knife, the butcher knife.

"Sheriff? Sheriff?"

"No," said Dorset. "No. Help. Help."

There was a horrible gurgle, like waste bubbling from a clogged pipe.

It didn't take him long to die.

CHAPTER 7

"Drink that tea right up," Doreen said with rough affection. "It's a mercy that bozo didn't come after you, too."

Quill, freshly showered and in a white terry cloth robe, drank half a cup of the Red Zinger and sat on her couch. Meg moved restlessly around the room, successively picking up a small ceramic vase, a replica of a Chinese horse, then a crystal swan, and putting each one down again. "You can't pin down the time of the murder any more exactly than about dawn?" asked Meg.

"John said he didn't stop to look at the time when he heard me scream, and Davy didn't give me my watch back until you and Howie came with the order for release." Quill looked at it. "But it's eight-thirty now, in case you were wondering."

"Oh, ha."

"Howie must have gotten that judge up in the middle of the night. I can't believe you guys came back for me before the sun was up."

"Anderson was pretty annoyed at Howie."

"You went with Howie to Ithaca?"

"What did you expect me to do? Go to sleep?! Besides, the roads were awful and I didn't think he should go alone."

"Well, thanks."

"I didn't do a darn thing, except ride shotgun." Meg sat next to Quill with a thump. "Are you sure you're okay?"

"Yes. The worst was not being able to help him. And not being able to see."

"And he didn't say a word about who did it?"

"He couldn't," Quill said dryly. "Not once the blood started to . . . never mind."

"I don't know why you're wasting perfectly good sympathy on that bozo. It's a mercy whoever killed Dorset didn't kill you, too," Doreen reiterated.

The snow had stopped and sunlight streamed in through the window. She looked old. Quill sighed. Myles had told her once that each murder had more than one victim, that every violent death resulted in little murders of the living.

"Quill survived because the murderer wanted Dorset's killing to be pinned on her," said Meg. "If John hadn't been sitting outside her cell window and seen him take off, there wouldn't have been a thing Howie could have done to get Quill out of jail. The knife that killed him was from our kitchen, her fingerprints were on it, and a spare key was found inside the cell under the mattress, proving that Quill could have locked herself in and tried to blame the murder on person or persons unknown."

"Somebody did some good thinking ahead." Doreen scowled. "John didn't see who it was, either?"

Meg shook her head. "Too dark. And he couldn't exactly walk in and ask Dorset what the heck he was up to, could he? He wasn't after any visitors to the sheriff's office. John was worried about Quill and was planning on standing guard outside the cell window all night. And a good thing, too. Otherwise . . . otherwise . . ." Meg trailed off.

"Otherwise," Quill said cheerfully, "I would still be locked up, although without a corpse in my bed. I just wish the killer hadn't taken off with the key to the cell door, or that I'd know the other key was under the pillow. It seemed to take hours before John located Dave and let me out."

Meg drummed her fingers on her knee. "Wait until we find that creep."

"When are we going to have time to find that creep, Meg? We've got Santini's bachelor party tonight, not to mention the terrace party for S.O.A.P."

"And who is going to catch this killer?"

"They're sending the state troopers to investigate. Until we find another sheriff, they'll be in charge of it."

"We gotta do somethin'," muttered Doreen.

Quill set her teacup on the oak chest and got to her feet. "What we've got to do is keep the Inn running smoothly. I'm going to get dressed and meet you guys in the kitchen."

"It is a full day," Meg admitted. "The rest of the Santini wedding party is checking in this morning, and that nutty Evan Blight is checking in this afternoon."

"You don't know that he's nutty," Quill said.

"That's true. I don't know that he's nutty. But he's written a nutty book. Do you know what state of mind you have to be in to write a book?"

"No," said Quill, "and neither do you."

"I know that I have to be in a custard frame of mind to make custard. And dough is my world when I bake brioche. I," Meg continued, jumping up and waving her hands, "am one with the *pig* when I am in a roasting sort of mood."

"I see things are back to normal," John said, tapping at the door and walking in. There were dark circles under his eyes. Andy Bishop, the local internist, was right behind him, black bag in hand.

"Therefore," Meg shouted triumphantly, "Evan Blight is a fruitcake because it's a fruitcake sort of book he's written. Andy! My love!"

Andy Bishop skied in winter and played tennis in the summer and was always faintly tanned. He was slender, well-knit, and a mere head taller than Meg, who stood five foot two with shoes. He gave her a sunny, intimate smile, and then looked with concern at Quill.

"How are you feeling?"

"A little stiff and a lot sleepy. Otherwise, fine."

"Let me just do a few physicianly things, then I'll let you alone."

"Andy, I'm fine. Who called you, anyway?"

"Let's just say I was in the neighborhood. Hey!" Meg wound her arms tightly around his neck and gave him a noisy kiss on the cheek. "Thanks, sweetheart, but you have to let me do my medical thing, here." He looked down at her. "Are you okay? I'm not going to have two patients on my hands, am I?"

"You are going to have no patients," said Meg. "I'm giddy with relief, I think. And Quill's okay, at least physically. And who did call you? Not that *I* wouldn't have, sooner or later. Probably sooner."

"Doreen. Due to a little case of frostbite."

"John!" Quill leaped to her feet, penitent. "Are you okay? I didn't even think! And I had your parka!"

John made a slight movement in protest, and Andy went on smoothly, "As I said, I was in the neighborhood. Sit right there, Quill, and let me take your blood pressure and your temperature."

"Do it," said Doreen, forestalling protest. "You might check her for nits, while you're at it, Doc."

"DoREEN!" shrieked Meg.

Quill held her arm out while Andy wrapped the blood pressure cuff around it and made an inquiring face at John.

"I'm fine," he said.

"Everybody's fine," Andy said absently. "Ninety-three over sixty,

Quill. I wish I had your metabolism. You're looking a little thin, though. Lost any weight recently?"

"Mmm," said Quill.

"At least five pounds," said Meg. "Courtesy of that rat, the ex-sheriff McHale."

"Meg," said Quill, "don't."

"Well, he is a rat, If he'd stuck around the way he was supposed to, you never would have ended up in the clink. It's all," Meg said obscurely, "his fault."

Myles, who was lousy at entrance lines, cleared his throat in a perfunctory way. He stood at the open door, his khaki raincoat rumpled, his battered leather bag in hand, a day's worth of stubble on his cheeks.

The silence was profound.

"Quill," said Andy, "I don't like this pulse rate at all."

"Well," said Doreen, "*I* can get back to work, I guess." She punched Myles on the shoulder as she passed. "Don't tell anyone it's good to see ya." John grinned, slapped him on the back and shook his hand, and followed Doreen out the door. Meg snapped Andy's doctor's bag shut, handed him the blood pressure cuff, and pulled him toward the hall.

"I haven't finished the physical," he protested.

"Is she anywhere near sick?"

"Well, no. A little shocky, maybe, but . . ."

"Then you're being persistent." She eyed Myles with enormous goodwill. "Not that I have any objections to persistent men. On the contrary. See you for breakfast, Sis."

"Don't call me Sis," Quill said automatically.

The door closed to a second, uncomfortable silence.

Quill sat down on the couch and covered her face with her hands. She held herself very still, then said between them, "Did Howie call you? Or John?"

"No." She heard him set his suitcase on the floor, then the rustle of his raincoat as he tossed it over a chair.

"There's coffee in the kitchen."

"Would you like some?"

She nodded. He crossed the carpet with his quiet, measured step. The coffee gurgled into the cups. He set it down and she felt the heat of the cup next to her knee, which was wedged against the oak chest she used for a coffee table. Myles settled next to her. He smelled of foreign places, of cigarette smoke, and—faintly—of fatigue.

"Were you on a smoking flight?"

He laughed. "Are you going to take your hands away from your face?"

Quill shook her head no.

"Why not?"

"If I do, I'll cry. If I start to cry, I won't stop. And I've got a busy day ahead. My hands," she explained, "are sort of holding my face on."

"I see."

"Did you . . ." Her throat was clogged and she stopped to swallow. "Did you hear what happened?"

"Just now. Downstairs. From Dina. Of course, having had experience with Dina's reportage before, I'm taking a lot of it under advertisement. I take it you didn't run over a little kid."

Quill shook her head.

There was a different note to his voice, a note she'd only heard once before, the day she'd been shot. "And you weren't raped by Frank Dorset."

"Good heavens, no." Quill took her hands away from her face.

"And the séance this afternoon isn't your method of determining who killed Nora Cahill and Dorset."

"The what?" Quill sat up straight and took a healthy swig of coffee. "Séance. Tutti," she said darkly. "Oh, *swell*." She looked directly at him for the first time since he'd come back. "I suppose you heard all about Nora Cahill and the videotape and my missing coat and hat."

"Your coat? You mean that ratty—er—cherished sort of down thing you wear in the winter?"

Quill nodded, then gave a coherent account of the last two days.

Myles asked a few questions, then said, "I think I have the gist of it." He got up and put on his raincoat.

"Where are you going?"

"I'm going to have a little talk with the mayor. To inquire about the availability of the sheriff's job."

"Myles!" She set her cup down and rose to follow him.

"Later, dear heart. After this mess is cleared up."

The door clicked shut behind him. Quill slipped off her robe and began to dress.

"Wow, you look fabulous." Dina made a credible attempt at a wolf whistle as Quill came down the stairs into the foyer. "Where'd that sweater come from? And I love the lace at the throat. Medieval. You look medieval." She wriggled her eyebrows. "And happy. Sheriff McHale came down the stairs about ten minutes ago and he looked happy, too." She sighed. "I sure feel better. Sheriff McHale said that of course you didn't stab that creep Dorset when he tried to— you know—that somebody else did it. Stabbed Dorset, I mean."

"Nobody tried to you-know. Especially Dorset."

"But Davy told Kathleen who told me that Dorset tried to . . . and *somebody* stabbed him."

"Somebody sure did. But it wasn't me. I. Whatever."

"Well, Sheriff McHale will find out who did it. And who killed Nora Cahill, too. Unless you and Meg find out first, like you've done before. Although, really, all either one of you has to do is ask Tutti. She's going to find out this afternoon, you know."

Quill, who was absolutely famished, stopped on her way to the dining room and turned around. "Which reminds me. What's this about a séance?"

"At one-thirty. Just after lunch."

"I didn't ask when it was. I asked what about it?"

"What about it?"

"Is it Claire's grandmother? Mrs. McIntosh?"

"You mean Tutti? Yep. And Tatiana."

"Tutti and her dog? The dog's psychic, too?"

Dina looked uncertain.

"Who's attending?"

"You mean who's going to be at the . . . ." She quailed at Quill's expression.

Quill reminded herself that Dina was one of the brightest Ph.D. candidates at the limnology department at Cornell University. The fact that she knew far more about freshwater ponds and copepods than real life had stopped astonishing Quill, but it didn't keep her from occasional irritation.

Dina said (meekly enough to make Quill feel badly about her momentary ill temper), "Tutti invited Tatiana, Claire, Mrs. McIntosh—the one that's Claire's mom, that is—Mayor Henry, and that Mr. Blight."

"Evan Blight? I didn't have him listed for check in until this afternoon."

"Well, he showed up this morning. Said he'd been out all night under the hunter's moon and wanted the amenities of a civilized existence before he returned to the primitive glory of the woods . . . that's what he *said*, Quill, honest to God."

"It's not what he said, it's about where he was. Out all night? Where?"

"In the gorge. Mayor Henry picked him up at the Ithaca airport, I guess, and they went off for one of those S.O.A.P. meetings. Anyhow, when the mayor brought him in this morning, I told him that you were in jail for murder and that's why you couldn't meet him yourself." She smiled sunnily. "I remembered what you told all us employees about being meticulously courteous to guests, and being in jail was a pretty darn good reason you couldn't meet him."

"I suppose it was," said Quill. She reflected briefly on the fact that she'd spent the best part of the previous night in the cold embrace of a corpse, survived with seeming equanimity the unexpected (and emotionally cataclysmic) return of her lover, and that it was twenty-four-year-old Dina Muir who was going to drive her to hysterics. "And after you'd welcomed a best-selling writer with the news that his host was in the slam for murder one, what did he do? I mean other than ask about the availability of rooms at the Marriott?"

"He had a reservation here. John made it himself. Well, he walked in with Mayor Henry and, Quill, you know me, I'm not one to gossip, because gossip is *tacky*, but my goodness, they smelled!"

"They smelled? Like what?"

"Like . . . like . . . I don't . . . dirt."

"They smelled like dirt?"

"Yep. And the mayor looked like he hadn't shaved since the elections, and of course Mr. Blight has that ratty—sorry—that long beard, and there were all kinds of twigs in it."

"Dina. I'm starving. I want my breakfast."

"You want me to hurry up," Dina said wisely. "So they came in smelling like—you know—and Tutti was bombing around waiting for that icky Claire to come downstairs for breakfast, and Tutti started prophesying the minute she saw Evan Blight. He said she—Tutti, I mean—had the spirit of the ancient wise women, and like that. *He* was very impressed." She added with a slight tone of injury, "I mean, you and Meg dismiss things you can't hear or touch or see awfully easily, Quill, if you don't mind my saying so. So she got him to come to the séance."

"What did she proph—never mind. I don't think I want to know. Where is this séance going to be held?"

"The Provençal suite. Where Tutti's staying. Quill?"

"What."

"Could I? I mean, I definitely, absolutely did NOT ask Tutti to invite me, but I did say that I was pretty good at taking care of little dogs."

"You mean you want to go to the séance?" Quill thought about this. Prone to breathless exaggeration as she was, there was always a strong foundation of truth to Dina's stories. And if Evan Blight and the men of S.O.A.P. had been rattling around the woods last night, she wanted details. Even details from Beyond.

"Sure. I don't mind if you take the time. Ask Kathleen if she'll cover the desk for you."

"Great. Look. You have a good breakfast."

"Thanks."

Quill walked through the foyer and into the dining room.

At nine o'clock on a Thursday morning in December, the Inn had very few breakfast guests. She hadn't been expecting Claire McIntosh (who normally rose around eleven), or Elaine (who never seemed to sleep at all, but roamed the halls in agitated fits), or Al Santini, but she wasn't surprised to see them at the table overlooking the gorge. Vittorio sat with them, looking ill-tempered.

She *was* surprised to see Marge Schmidt and Betty Hall. Their Hemlock Hometown Diner did a brisk business in the mornings, beginning with the dairy farmers who came in after milking at six a.m., and ending with the early coffee breaks at ten-thirty of the business people on Main Street. Quill wondered who was covering the shop for them, then figured Marge had probably left out the coffee urn, cups, some of Betty's fry cakes, and a coffee can for cash.

Marge waved her over. Quill, whose stomach was now positively demanding breakfast, gave a cheerful wave in response and kept on going toward the kitchen. Marge placed two fingers between her lips and whistled, then pointed to the empty chair at their table.

Senator Santini jumped and looked nervously over his shoulder. Claire sent a sullen glare in Marge and Betty's direction. Elaine twisted her napkin into a tortured shape then dropped it on the floor. Vittorio shoveled Gruyère scrambled eggs into his mouth and didn't react at all.

Kathleen came bounding through the swinging doors from the kitchen, and Quill stopped her with a gesture. "Could you bring me some breakfast? I'll be at table five with Marge and Betty."

"Sure thing. Meg's whipped up a bunch of stuff. Raspberry crepes, eggs Florentine, some of that Breton sausage. And fresh grapefruit juice."

"Great."

"Uh—Quill? Could I talk to you a second before you talk to Ms. Schmidt?" Kathleen gazed at the carpet and rubbed at a spot with one toe. "Hmm. I thought Doreen got that out. She sure hates that little dog."

"What is it, Kath? If I don't get some breakfast I'm going to fall over dead."

"Yeah. Sure. Look, Quill. About David."

"Your brother?"

"He was just following that jerk's orders. Dorset, I mean. And now that Myles is back . . ."

Quill checked her watch. As far as she could tell, Myles had been back in Hemlock Falls for approximately forty-five minutes. And apparently the whole town knew it.

Kathleen took a deep breath. "Could you maybe put in a good word for him? For Davy, I mean?" She made a face in the direction of Marge and Betty's table. "There's a lot of folks around here that are pretty upset with him. That hidden camera wasn't his idea, you know. It was Dorset and that judge."

"Justice, not judge," said Quill. "There's a big difference. You mean Bernie Bristol."

"Davy," Kathleen said desperately, "didn't have a thing to do with it. And when the camera caught people speeding, well, what's he supposed to do? Just ignore it? He was only doing his job." She darted a look at Marge and away again.

"Marge got a ticket?" Quill guessed.

Kathleen nodded miserably. "Yesterday afternoon. And, of course, everyone's furious with what Dorset tried to do to you—"

"They are?" said Quill, pleased.

"And since you ki— I mean, since Dorset's dead, it's Davy that everyone's blaming, and if you sort of, you know, were publicly nice to him, maybe at the bank this Friday when everyone's in cashing their paychecks, or at the diner on Sunday mornings when everyone's in for brunch—"

"Kath. Wait a second. I didn't kill Dorset."

"Nobody cares if you did," Kathleen said warmly. "People are *glad* that you did. The guy was a sicko."

"*I* care if people think I killed him. Davy knows. I didn't even have a weapon. I mean, he searched me, the jerk, before I went into that cell."

"Bjarne said there was a paring knife *and* a butcher knife missing from the kitchen. And you were arrested in the kitchen last night. And Davy says Meg and Howie and John went to see you *after* he searched you. He took a statement from Howie, and Howie admitted that all of you went into the cell together and that Meg found an excuse to send Dorset out of the cell. Davy says any one of those three could have slipped you the weapon and be an accessory."

"Howie admitted what? Excuse me? Meg asked Dorset to find a blanket for me. That was no excuse. It was cold in there."

"Yeah, yeah. So. Anything you can do for Davy. Without getting yourself into more trouble, of course."

"Kathleen, I am not a murderess. Murderer. Whatever."

"Yes, ma'am. Would you like your breakfast now?"

"I would. And why are you calling me ma'am? The only person

who calls me ma'am is Meg, and that's when she's so mad at me she wants to throw me in a snowbank."

"Nobody liked him, ma'am. Dorset, I mean. People are glad you took care of it. You're *due* some respect, Esther West says."

"Aaagh," said Quill. "Bring me a *lot* of sausage, okay?" She crossed to Marge and Betty's table and sat down.

"You look okay," Marge said after a short, sharp scrutiny.

"I feel fine. A little tired, though." Quill reached for the carafe of coffee and poured herself a cup. "I hope you two aren't going to congratulate me on killing Frank Dorset."

Marge chuckled. "That's what everyone's saying down at the diner," she agreed. "You didn't get a look at the fella who did it?"

"Hey," said Meg. She set a platter of food in front of Quill, then sat down at the last empty place setting at the table. "Marge, Betty. Mind if I join you?"

"Not if you quit using frozen spinach in the Florentine dishes," said Betty Hall. Her thin face split in a grin.

Meg flushed. "Dang. I didn't think this crowd would notice. I didn't have time to set up the sourdough pancakes last night, which is what I'd scheduled for the special this morning, and the only thing I had on hand was frozen spinach. Let me get you some oatmeal. I got a delivery from Ireland earlier this week, and it's wonderful stuff. I created a brown-sugar sour cream seasoning for it I think you'll like." There was a brief, professional discussion between the two chefs, involving the length of time needed to really scramble eggs. Twenty minutes under slow heat seemed to be the consensus. Quill ate her breakfast. Marge watched Quill tackle the eggs Florentine and waited a bit before asking again if Quill had seen the murderer's face.

"No. I'm not even sure what gender the murderer is." Quill, who had a number of reasons for believing the murderer was male, had decided to keep those facts, and the problem of her furry hat, to herself, at Myles's request. Everyone, he'd said, should know about the coat. The more people the better.

"Male," said Betty. "Fact."

"I'm not so sure." Quill thought of the videotape from the hidden camera, with the killer dressed in her coat and hat. Dave and

John had both searched the sheriff's office for it with no luck. It'd been tossed into a fire by now, she was certain. "Whoever it was, man or woman, was about my height." Quill had a sudden afterthought. "Unless he, she, it wore heels."

"He," said Betty. "Ninety-nine percent of serial killers are white males between the ages of twenty-five and forty-nine. Fact."

"What about that woman in Florida?" asked Meg. "The one who murdered six guys in a row."

"She had an extra Y chromosome. Fact."

"But this guy . . . woman . . . person . . . isn't a serial killer," said Meg.

"There's been more than one murder, ain't there?" demanded Marge.

"I suppose so," Meg said hesitantly. "But—"

Marge burped. "There you are. Betty's right. Adela Henry gave a whole report on this serial killer business to the committee just last week."

"What committee?" Meg asked.

"S.T.S. The H.O.W. committee for Stop the Slaps. Wimmin united against domestic violence."

"I'm all for that," said Quill. "But this wasn't a case of domestic violence, you know. It was a case of murder for gain."

Meg cocked her head alertly. "How'd you find that out?"

Quill explained about the exchange of money on the videotape, a fact both she and Myles wanted public.

"And the tape is missing, of course," said Betty. "Dumb male bastards."

Quill pointed out that if a woman was the murderer, a woman could have swiped the tape as easily as a man, then shut up when all three of her tablemates glared at her. Betty pointed out that of course with a guy like Sheriff McHale around, it just went to show you. Quill got so indignant over the implied slur on her feminism that she shut up altogether.

"So what happened, exactly?" Marge demanded.

"I'd fallen asleep on that cot, and I think it must have been the voices that woke me up."

Marge's eyes narrowed in a calculating way, which for some reason irritated Quill profoundly. "You heard their voices?"

"Uh-huh. One was Dorset. But as soon as they came in the cell block, the lights went out. The killer stabbed him, then shoved him through the door to my cell and rolled him in next to me. Then the killer relocked the cell door and took off, taking the key with him."

"Dorset musta weighed all of a hunnert and seventy pounds," said Marge. "Musta been a man, to wrestle all that deadweight."

The Breton sausage, one of Quill's favorites, stuck halfway down her throat. She swallowed carefully, then said, "He didn't die right away."

"Hung on awhile, did he? He musta said somethin' about who killed him, then."

"He whispered for help." Quill set her fork carefully on her plate and folded her hands in her lap. "His throat was cut. I don't think . . . he couldn't get anything else out."

Marge pursed her lips. "Hmm." Then, "Lemme pour you a little more coffee." She did so, then pulled a small notebook from the pocket of her bowling jacket. "You got times on this? And did you get any impression at all of the murderer's weight?"

"Marge!" Meg said suddenly. "Are *you* investigating this case?"

Marge shifted her large shoulders and scratched her neck with an abstracted air.

So that's why I was irritated, Quill thought with guilty surprise. *Petty old me, I don't like the competition.* She sat back, frowning. This feeling had something to do with Myles. And she didn't like what it said about her own motives for failing him in their relationship. If she had. Marge nudged her, and she blinked, startled.

"Thing is," said Marge, "Adela dropped to the diner this morning, early, with the milk crowd, and said she'd about had it up to here with town guv'mint. I mean, she'd just heard on that police scanner she carries around in her purse about you offing Dorset—"

"I did NOT—" Quill began hotly.

"Well, I see that now, don't I," Marge said equably. "Anyways, she's all hot for me to run for mayor."

"You, Marge?" said Meg. "But Elmer's mayor. I mean, to tell you the truth, you'd be an absolutely super mayor, and I wish we'd thought of it before the November elections, but there you are. Elmer's mayor. Duly elected and sworn in."

"That's as may be," Betty said mysteriously, "that's as may be. Anyways, let Marge go on. Go on, Marge."

"Right. What H.O.W. needs is some good P.R. Public relations, like. So, I figger we find out who killed Nora Cahill and Frank Dorset, this'd be just about the best P.R. we could get."

"So all of H.O.W. is investigating this?" asked Meg.

"Thought maybe you two'd give us and Adela a hand," said Betty, "seein' as how you have so much experience in the detective line."

"But," said Quill, "Myles—I mean, Sheriff McHale is back."

"Don't we know it!" said Betty. "And a damn good thing, too. Marge was thinking maybe now you'd put some of that weight back on."

Marge, whose nineteenth-century German forebears seemed to have passed on a genetic predisposition for substantial poundage, nodded judiciously, her three chins folding and unfolding.

"Thing is, Adela didn't know the sheriff'd be back when she laid out the campaign this morning." Betty hitched forward and hissed conspiratorially, "See, what we have here is Marge for mayor and Adela for justice. What d'ya think?"

"Marge would make a terrific mayor," Quill said promptly. "I'll go door-to-door for Marge anytime."

"Me, too," said Meg. "But Adela for town justice?" She rolled her eyes. "Sheeesh. Remember the year she was judge at the geranium competition and she brought in those Dutch imports and said they were hers and she tried to arrange a boycott of Esther's shop when Esther blew her in?"

"Yeah," said Betty. "I'd forgot about that."

"And don't forget what happened after the Jell-O Architecture Contest."

"Um . . . yeah," said Marge.

Meg swallowed most of Quill's grapefruit juice, burped, and added, "That lady is mean."

"Well, Bernie Bristol's crooked," Quill said flatly. She gazed with a ruminative air at Alphonse Santini, who was saying good-bye to his bride at table seven with a remarkable degree of indifference. Of course, practically anyone contemplating marriage with the whiny Claire the day after tomorrow was going to have to be equipped with indifference to whining. "But why do we have to choose between mean and crooked? Why can't we find a town justice who's fair and honest? Like Howie Murchison."

Marge snorted, leaned over her eggs, and rumbled, "The point of H.O.W. is, see, that it's the wimmin who are going to run this town."

"Oh," said Quill.

"And Adela's right. If the wimmin find this killer and make the streets safe again, then it's the wimmin the voters are goin' to put in government."

"By and large, I agree with you," said Quill. "Except that Adela Henry's a witch."

"She's right, Marge," Betty said without officiousness. "We'll have to think about this. In the meantime, are you with us, Quill?"

"Well, sure," said Quill. "I guess so. Except that I really think Howie'd make a great—"

"Lame, girl, lame." Marge patted her shoulder with one elephantine hand. "Now, what's the next step in this investigation?"

"Me?" asked Quill. "You're asking me?"

"You solved three murders before this," said Betty.

"Who better?" asked Marge.

Meg went, "Whoop!" and finished the last of Quill's sausage. Quill, both flattered (at the tribute to her investigative skills) and annoyed (Meg had eaten most of her breakfast—and who was it that had spent a sleepless night with a corpse, anyway?), looked over her shoulder. The McIntoshes had gone. More important, Alphonse Santini had gone.

"Okay, guys, I'll tell you my theory. I had a lot of time to think about it last night, while John was looking for Davy to get me out of that cell. In the videotape of Nora's murder, a figure dressed in my coat waited for her by the intersection. The figure was tall for a woman, short for a man. That coat was down and really huge. I don't know if you remember seeing me wear it."

Betty hooted. "Everybody in town knows that coat. That's the ugliest winter coat I've ever seen in this life. I dunno how many times I seen you walking into the bank in that coat and wonder why the heck—oof!"

Marge, who'd given Betty a substantial poke in the midriff with her elbow, rumbled, "Go on, Quill."

"So if you had a little potbelly, it wouldn't show when it was zipped up."

"A nine-month pregnancy wouldn't have shown with that coat," Meg remarked. "I know you loved that coat, Quillie, but, honestly, it was an *ugly* coat. I'm glad it's at the bottom of the gorge, or wherever it is that the murderer put it. Same for the hat." Meg yawned.

"Shut *up*, Meg. Now this is mere supposition at this point, because that tape has disappeared, but I think the only person it could have been was Alphonse Santini."

"The senator?" gasped Betty.

"Of course," said Meg. "You said the person dressed in your coat gave Nora a fistful of money."

"And took it back," Quill reminded them. "And I'll get to what happened to the money in a minute. Nora Cahill told me the day before she was murdered that she had 'more dirt on that guy,' meaning Santini, and that she'd love to publish it, but she didn't yet have enough proof. *And* she told me she was close to finding out something that would really nail him. Finally, I know for a fact that Santini hated her anyway. He blamed that whole H.O.W. fund-raiser debacle on her. I saw him reading her the riot act right after H.O.W. stopped throwing forks and spoons at him. I think what happened is this: Nora was blackmailing Santini, and he'd been paying her off right along. She said herself she was the only media person to get invited to his wedding—and she was just a Syracuse anchor. I mean, if he's going to invite anyone, why not Sam Donaldson? Or Barbara Walters? He could have cried all over Barbara Walters and it would have given him an enormous advantage in the next election. He's a national figure. One of them would have come."

"But Nora showed up at the courthouse when you were arrested for running over that little kid," Marge objected. "Why should she do that?"

"I didn't run over a little kid," said Quill.

"But it was the start of his 'national' campaign to rescue small towns," Meg said. "Nora wouldn't want to miss that. Although it was so clearly *phony*."

Quill smiled gratefully at her. "Just so."

"I get it," said Marge. "There's no reason why Nora'd pass up a good news story, even if she was blackmailing Santini."

"We probably," Quill said a little stiffly, "will always disagree about whether my little traffic ticket was a good news story. Anyway, I think that Frank Dorset recognized Santini in that tape and wanted that money for himself. He went right along with that trumped-up disguise that Santini meant to look like me, and put me in jail on bogus charges."

"That makes sense," said Meg. "I mean, Howie was raving all the way to Ithaca about the high-handed way Dorset was handling due process. He didn't see why or how Dorset was planning to get away with it. But, of course, he was trying to blackmail Santini, too. He was probably planning on taking that blackmail money and hightailing it out of town."

"And Santini showed up at the sheriff's office . . ." said Quill.

"Pretended to give Dorset the cash . . ." added Meg.

"And whammo! Cut his throat. Shoved him into my cell. Wiped the knife and tossed it in after Dorset's body . . ."

"And tried to pin the second murder on you."

"Holy crow," said Betty.

"You two are damn good," grunted Marge. "So how do we go around proving this?"

"We need hard evidence," said Quill. "Something factual, like DNA or hair samples that will link Santini to the scene of the crime. We have to find my coat and that videotape. And, we have to get an eyewitness to place Santini at or near the sheriff's office around five o'clock this morning."

"If the fella's smart enough to stay in the Senate for three terms, he's smart enough to burn that stuff," said Marge. "Or bury it."

"It's a lot harder than you think to dispose of things like that," said Quill. "Where is he going to burn it? Our fireplaces? We can sift through the ashes and find fibers, bits of plastic from the tape—whatever."

"I'll do that," said Betty. "He don't know me from a hole in the ground, and I worked cleaning house in high school before I learned to cook. I'll walk around here with a bucket and look like I'm cleaning fireplaces. I'll get a sample from each one in the place."

"Label them and put them in Baggies," Meg advised. "And as soon as you find something suspicious, call Sheriff McHale. Otherwise, we'll contaminate the chain of evidence."

"I'll tell Doreen what you're doing," Quill offered. "And, although Meg and I have a strict rule about invading the privacy of our guests, this is an emergency. Santini's in the Adams suite, room 224. And his bachelor party's tonight in the dining room, so he's going to be occupied with that from eight o'clock on. If there's anything hidden in his room, tonight's the best time to search for it. What I'm afraid of is that he's buried the stuff, or thrown it into the gorge."

"It stopped snowing late last night," said Meg. "Andy could ski the parts of the park that lead from here to the Municipal Building and look for turned up dirt."

"Likeliest spot's the gorge," said Marge. "I could take Miriam and Esther and we could hike down there."

"Why don't you three look in the park instead of Andy," said Betty. "We want this to be a victory for wimmin."

"It counts if *we* tell the men what to do," said Marge. "My goodness, partner, what would we do without Mark Anthony Jefferson at the bank buyin' and sellin' every time I tell him to? I'd be worth squat if I didn't work with male bankers."

"Good point," Meg said seriously. "So it's all right if I ask Andy to go ahead and search?"

"Long as Doc Bishop reports back to you," Marge said generously. "Be my guest."

"There's one last thing," said Quill. "The witness to Santini's presence near the sheriff's office."

"He sharin' a room with that lemon-faced fiancée?" asked Marge. "'Course, she'd probably alibi him, anyhow."

"No," said Meg. "Claire's in the Pilgrim suite on the ground floor. Santini's in the Adams suite on two. Claire's father didn't think Tutti would approve if the two of them shared a room, so they aren't."

"So he's by himself. That helps some." Marge sniffed. "Witnesses, huh? Who'd likely be out in a gol-danged blizzard in the middle of central New York in December that might have seen him?"

Quill made a diffident noise and offered, "S.O.A.P."

"Hot damn," said Betty.

Marge swung her head like a turret on a tank. Her eyes gleamed. "Speak of the devil, here comes one a them now."

Mayor Elmer Henry bustled into the dining room, accompanied by the swish-swish-swish of his Gore-Tex ski pants. He caught sight of the four women as soon as he entered, waved weakly, and veered toward the table like a boat in a low wind.

"'Lo, ladies," he said stiffly.

"You look a little pooped, Elmer," said Marge. "Little frostbit, too. Have a good time in the woods last night?"

"I have no idea what you are talking about. Quill? I'd like to speak to you about our meeting this evening."

"Of course, Mayor. Would you like to go to my office?"

"Sure. Ladies? Good to . . . um, 'bye."

Quill let him go ahead. She turned and nodded violently to Meg, who mouthed "Find out about last night," waved to Marge, and had to trot to get ahead of the mayor before he stamped into her office.

"No, I won't sit down. This won't take but a minute or so." He took a couple of deep breaths, whether because he was hot in his snowsuit or out of breath from racing away from the twin terror of Marge and Betty, Quill wasn't sure.

"John told you we've set you up on the terrace?"

"What? Oh. Yeah."

"We're bringing in some of the heating pots from Richardson's apple farm. Your members should be a lot warmer than they were, um, last night."

Elmer had soft brown eyes, rather like a cow's, Quill thought, or the more amiable breed of dog. He fixed them on her and asked earnestly if she was all right.

"Oh. You mean about this business with Dorset. Yes, Mayor. I'm fine."

"Talked to McHale just now. Seemed to think I . . ." Elmer

flushed. "Quill, you gotta believe me when I tell you I had no idea what these fellas were up to."

"You mean Frank Dorset and Bernie Bristol?"

"And that scum Santini." He shook his head. "And to think that a United States senator . . . well, by God, I never would have thought it, or I wouldn't have done it."

"Done it? Done what?"

"Authorized the purchase of that dang hidden camera. Cost the town plenty."

"How much is plenty?"

"Pretty near fifty thousand dollars—"

"Fifty *thousand*!" gasped Quill. "Good grief. Where'd the money come from?"

"Discretionary budget," he said gloomily. "Pret' near emptied it for the next year. Means no town celebration this summer, that's for certain. And here," he said indignantly, "and here this Santini is tellin' me how much money the village is going to make from this and how we'll have money comin' out our ears and look-it. The traffic fines all come from the townspeople anyhow. I did some figuring and it comes out even worse. I'd be a sight more popular if I'd just gone ahead and raised property taxes. And now, after this—ah—unfortunate incident last night . . . Well. I'm sorry, Quill. If I'd ever thought this would happen in a million years, I never would have done it. You can," he said hopefully, "yell at me if you like. I cert'nly deserve it."

"The town's going to do a lot more yelling when they find out how much you paid for that camera," said Quill, who was, in fact, awed at the amount. "Wow."

Elmer nodded miserably. "They're talking special election anyways, you know. The women. On account of what happened to you. If they find out I spent that money, I'll be out on my ass—sorry, but you know. Just like what's her name from England. Thatcher, that's it."

"Oh?" asked Quill, not sure if the mayor was allying himself with Labor or the Conservatives in that debate.

"Word of this gets out, I ain't going to have a friend left in this world."

"I won't tell anyone, Mayor. I mean, the episode's over, as far as I'm concerned."

"Myles thought as you might not need to mention any more than you had to, if I came and told you I was sorry," he said ingenuously.

Quill, who had been experiencing warmer than charitable feelings about the six-foot-tall, baritone-voiced sheriff since his sudden reappearance in her life that morning, set her teeth. "He did, did he?"

"Knows you pretty well, I expect."

Quill reflected on this and had to laugh a little. Myles certainly seemed to know her better than she knew herself. She realized she didn't mind that as much as she used to. "I suppose he does."

"You glad he's back?"

She smiled.

"My," he said. "I can see that you are. I am, too. I'd sure like things to be the way they were before the November election. Myles back in office and Howie, too."

"A lot of people would have preferred a different result from the general election, Elmer. If there's nothing else, I'd better talk to Meg about any preparations for your meeting. You're sure you don't want Meg to cook anything?"

"The guys are cooking a whole steer in the woods," Elmer said proudly. "On a huge spit. Mr. Blight himself had the idea. You met him yet?"

"Not yet."

"He's amazing. Just amazing. He's gonna join us at the sayance this afternoon with Mrs. McIntosh. There's going to be a whole pile of us there. All the McIntoshes, Santini, and, of course, Mr. Blight. I thought maybe I'd get a chance to ask about the special election, you know, in case these spirits of Tutti's really know anything. I'd be happy to ask anything you want to know on your behalf."

"The senator will be there? Then you sure can," Quill said flippantly. "Ask them who was in the woods last night. Ask them who murdered Nora Cahill and Frank Dorset. Tell them," she said, inspired, "that you know for a fact the murderer was seen."

"You're kiddin'," said the mayor. "Who seen 'im?"

"Just tell them that several of us in town know," said Quill. "Tell them the word is getting around."

"You're up to something."

Quill reached over and patted his hand. For the first time in three days she was the pattor instead of the pattee and she was glad of it. "What we both know, Mayor, won't hurt either one of us. As long as it reaches—or in your case—doesn't reach, the right people."

The mayor sighed. "Or the wrong ones. You watch it, Quill. You don't want this person comin' after you."

CHAPTER 8

"What do you mean you can't tell me what the mayor wanted?" Meg stood in the middle of her full team of *sous*-chefs, looking like a pony among Percherons. "And you're going *where*?"

"Don't yell, Meg."

The Finns found this funny. The Canadian and the kid from Texas smiled at the Finns. The Frenchwoman—Lisette—frowned and went, "Pssstah!"

"If Meg doesn't yell, it's a day without sunshine," Bjarne explained.

"Orange juice. A day without orange juice is a day without sunshine," Lisette said. "They are confused in their English. Plus, they are watching too much television."

"That's what's confusing me, Quill, your English. I mean, I'm not hearing this. You're off to Syracuse *again*, when we have two huge parties—no, three, counting H.O.W. tonight. A rehearsal dinner tomorrow and a wedding on Saturday? And it's because of what the mayor said that you can't tell me?" Meg picked up a wooden spoon and threw it across the room. It bounced off a copper sauté pot and clattered to the floor.

"In-di-GEST-tion," sang the Texan, which sent the Finns off again.

Meg glowered at them and jerked her chin at Quill. "Check into my storeroom. I've got to get some sherry to braise the shallots."

Quill followed her meekly. She liked the storeroom, which was cool and quiet. It was a large room, slightly smaller than the kitchen, lined with shelves of root vegetables, flours, sugars, vinegars, oils, the raw ingredients from which Meg created the foods that had made them famous. The wine cellar was directly below the storeroom and had been the single most costly item in their extensive renovations of the Inn seven years ago. Meg took the key to the cellar from its hook on the wall, unlocked the cellar trapdoor, and stepped backward down the ladder to the wine vault.

"Any bodies down there?" Quill asked.

"Yours will be if you bug out on me during the busiest week of the year." She snapped the light on, and Quill could see her shadow moving along the bins. Meg muttered, "Damn it, I don't want the sauternes. If Doreen's dusted these bottles again I'll have her guts for garters. So," she hollered up, "tell me."

"The sherries are along the north wall. Next to the burgundies."

Meg's head reemerged. She looked both dusty and cross. "Tell me what Elmer said." She set two bottles of pale dry sherry on the storeroom floor, climbed out, and slammed the trapdoor shut. "Was it a clue?"

"I think so. Nora intimated that she was onto a hot story involving Santini. And now that I think back on it, she was trying to warn me about this small town campaign of Santini's. You know, persecuting innocent citizens with bogus tickets."

"Ya-ta-ta, ya-ta-ta. So?"

"So I think we may be looking at kickbacks. I can't tell you any more than that."

"Kickbacks?" Her eyes widened. "You don't think the mayor is involved in anything illegal?"

"Of course not. I think he's a dupe."

"Adela'd agree with you there."

"My guess is that Nora was on track with the story, and I want to go to Syracuse to talk to her editors at the news station."

"Won't it keep?" Meg wailed.

"If I don't go now, when would be a better time? Tomorrow,

with Claire and Elaine and Tutti getting more and more frantic about the wedding? At least tonight they'll all be at the shower Meredith is holding for Claire in the lounge. Saturday, the day of the wedding, not to mention Christmas Eve when all those editors at the station will want to go home? Sunday, which is Christmas Day? Besides, if I wait much longer, the station will have cleared out her desk, and unless they've reassigned the story, what evidence there is may be destroyed or sent home to her parents or whatever."

"Look." Meg set the sherry bottles down with care, primarily, Quill thought, so that she could gesticulate without disturbing the sediment. She thrust her hands through her hair, tugged at it, and said with exaggerated patience, "Tell Myles. Have him go to Syracuse."

"I can't." Quill bit her lip. "I would really like to, but I can't."

"Why?!"

"Because I told the mayor I'd keep his secret."

Meg went, "Tuh!"

"Meg, I gave my word!"

"Then take Myles with you. Just don't tell him what the mayor told you."

"That's hairsplitting, Meg."

"You're right." Meg picked the bottles up and carried them tenderly out of the storeroom into the kitchen. "Myles swallowed his pride and came back here for you. Not because he heard you were in trouble. Not because he thought you'd welcome him with open arms. But because he loves you. Can't you at least call him and tell him where you're going?"

"It's not even noon. It's an hour round-trip to Syracuse and back. And it won't take me too long to talk to the editors. I'll be back before four."

"You are driving? In this weather?" Bjarne walked to the windows overlooking the herb garden. "You see this sky?"

"Blue," Quill said promptly.

"Those wispy clouds at the edges? Like mushy potatoes with too much cream? Very bad. Very, very bad. In a few hours, perhaps, there will be snow."

"Perhaps? Or for sure?" Quill hated driving in snowstorms.

Bjarne shrugged.

"I'll be back in less than four hours, Bjarne. Will it hold off until then?"

"It may not or it may."

"Great," said Meg. "I just hope the heck we get those food deliveries." She gave Quill a fierce hug. "Go do your thing. If Myles calls, do you have a message?"

"We're meeting for dinner at six. He won't call."

"Take my ski parka. And my hiking boots. And my hat."

"And make sure the gas tank's filled, ya-ta-ta, ya-ta-ta."

She went upstairs to her room and dressed for the drive, in a long sweater, ski pants, and long underwear. She rummaged through her bureau drawer for her "Investigations" notebook, unused since her last foray into murder, and slipped it into her shoulder bag.

She went back downstairs, and walked through the busy kitchen to the coatrack. The sleeves of Meg's parka were too short, but otherwise it was a comfortable fit. Quill added her own scarf and pulled out a pair of snow boots from the wooden box piled with odds and ends. She left by the back door to get her Olds from the garage.

The air outside was very cool and humid. A thin stream of water ran from the eaves, where the direct rays of the sun had melted the snow built up in the gutters. Mike the groundskeeper had shoveled the paths free, and she could see the Inn pickup truck, plow blade glinting in the sunlight, clearing the driveway to the road below their hill. The Olds would start easily in this weather. It always did. It was past time to get a new car, thought Quill, just like it was past time to get a new coat, but she was reluctant to give the Olds up. It was heavy, with front-wheel drive that gave her a lot of confidence in icy weather. It had also had its transmission replaced three times in its seventy-five-thousand-mile life, but the mechanic had assured her that this last install would last the life of the car. Quill skidded down the walkway to the outbuilding where they garaged their cars and maintenance equipment. She tugged on the latch of the overhead door, and it slid open, the bright day outside flooding the inside so that, for a moment, she saw the figure standing by the Oldsmobile as a blur of scarlet and tangled hair.

Despite herself, she gasped and jumped back, her heels skidding in the slush. Her voice was unexpectedly harsh. "Get out of there!"

Robertson Davies? Wearing my coat?

She raised her hand to her forehead, shielding her eyes from the sun. "Mr. Blight?"

"Yes?" The voice was unexpectedly gentle. Somehow, Quill had expected a gravelly rumble or a stentorian shout.

"Um. How do you do? I'm Sarah Quilliam."

"You are."

This was a statement. Not a question. Quill wasn't certain whether this was acknowledgment of her existence or mere inattention to the requirements of the spoken word.

"Mr. Blight? I'm sorry. I don't mean to be rude, but . . . where did you get that coat?"

Evan Blight stepped vigorously into the sunlight. The picture on the book jacket had smoothed out the wrinkles in his sun-beaten face and not really done justice to the impressive beard. There were bits of things in it—small sticks, a clot of scrambled egg, and possibly bird droppings, although Quill wasn't certain. Her down coat concealed the rest of him, but Quill had the impression he was thin and wiry. He could have been anywhere from sixty to ninety.

"Ms. Quilliam! Delighted. Delighted!" He grabbed her hand and shook it. His own was hard, muscular, and calloused, the fingernails blunt and dirty. "The irony implicit in the heart of the Flower series. The sardonic comment on the state of humankind! I saw the 'Chrysler Rose' in a traveling exhibit in New Jersey. Wonderful. Wonderful! There is a strong streak of the primordial male in you, Ms. Quilliam. The thrust of brushstrokes! The intensity—if I may say so, the *masculinity* of the color—wonderful! Wonderful!"

Quill felt an immediate (and cowardly) impulse to tell Evan Blight she was proud of her breasts and really missed sleeping with Myles McHale. She suppressed these politically incorrect (and socially inappropriate) responses and thanked him, in as hearty a voice as she could manage.

"You have read my Book," he asserted. "There could be no other explanation for the quality of your work. How pleasing to see the effects of my own small efforts to stem the tide of corruption of our basic, most natural drives."

Quill, who had recently read a most interesting book on the way that men verbally dominate social and business conversations, interrupted firmly, loudly, and with a terrific feeling of guilt. "Mr. Blight?"

"Call me Evan. Not Urban, if you please, which was the highly charged response to a review of my Book by the female reviewer of the *San Francisco Chronicle*. I was not offended. No, not offended. Was Hannibal offended by the piteous mewings of the Romans when he swept down on Trebia? I think not. Was the Khan himself dismayed by the pleas of the reindeer people as he led the mighty charge against their tents?"

He paused, either for breath or agreement, and Quill said hastily, "That coat, Mr. Blight. Have you had it long?"

He looked down at himself. "This coat? A gift of the forest, my dear." He shrugged himself out of it with a decisive movement. "But your softer flesh clearly is more in need of it than I. The garment you yourself are wearing must have clothed you as a child."

"It's my sister's," said Quill. "She's shorter than I." She took the coat, holding it by thumb and forefinger. He was wearing a baggy, hole-at-the-elbows gray cardigan, a knitted vest underneath that the color of a bird's nest, tweed trousers, and a pair of sensible boots. He shivered in the cold air. "Oh, dear, Mr. Blight. Don't you have a coat of your own?"

"Nature's embrace is all that I need."

Any forensic evidence that might be in the folds of the down was already tainted, and Quill handed it back to him with a resigned sigh. "Here. Take the coat back and get into the car. I'll turn the heater on."

Blight accepted the down coat with an intolerant air, although what he was intolerant of, Quill couldn't imagine, since he'd been wearing the coat only moments before. He lowered himself into the passenger seat of the Olds with the tenderness of the arthritic.

"Why don't I drive you around to the front of the Inn so you can go inside?" Quill suggested. "Then I'm afraid that I will need my coat back, Mr. Blight."

"I am moving toward a profound Change," he announced, "an experience of a unique and perhaps Life Enhancing Kind. The Inn's My Destination."

"You Bester," said Quill, who occasionally read science fiction. She curbed her irreverence (but he *would* speak in capitals!) started the Olds, and backed carefully out of the garage. She pulled into the circular drive leading to the Inn's front door.

"Ah," said Mr. Blight. "They await."

"They sure do," said Quill, eyeing the crowd outside. "My gosh. It's all of S.O.A.P. and Alphonse Santini. And Vittorio McIntosh."

"They are waiting for Me. I am scheduled for an Address. Stop here, please."

Quill braked. "An address? You mean a speech?"

"On the link between the generosity of Nature and the generosity of the human spirit."

Quill thought this through. The crowd of men, seeing Mr. Blight in the passenger seat, began to murmur and shift, like crows in a cornfield. "Is this a fund-raiser for Alphonse Santini?"

Evan Blight's eyes were deep-set, gray, and, Quill realized, very, very sharp. "That is *very* acute of you, my dear. Not what one would expect of the softer sex. Not what one would expect at all." He maneuvered himself out of the down coat and opened the passenger door. "I leave you now for whatever may be your Destination."

"Syracuse," Quill said absently. "Channel Seven. My coat, Mr. Blight. Where did—um—nature present this to you?"

"At the base of the Root," said Blight. "Near the seed of the tree."

"Beg pardon?"

He clasped her wrist with strength. "Each Conclave of Men has a Center. A Totem. A Signal which—er—signifies the heart and thrust of male power. There is one such Totem here. Perhaps more. I will discover *that* in future."

There was only one even remotely totemic item in Hemlock Falls, which also happened to be five minutes swift walk from the sheriffs office. "The statue of General Hemlock? That's where you found my coat?"

He patted her cheek. Quill hated anybody patting her cheek.

"Let no man gainsay the occasional wisdom of women." He pulled himself out of the car, slammed the door shut, shouting, "Farewell! And on to Syracuse." And turned to meet his fans.

"Aagh!" Quill muttered. "And aaagh again." Alphonse Santini must have heard Blight shouting out that she was headed to Syracuse. Most of the village must have heard Blight. She returned the wave and drove down the road to the turnoff for Route 96. She turned south instead of north, toward Buffalo, on the off chance that this would confuse Santini and discourage anyone from following her.

The only problem with this particular diversionary tactic was that it took her twenty minutes to get to an exit to turn around to head south, and she lost nearly an hour before she was on Interstate 81 to Syracuse.

She lost another half hour trying to find the proper exit to Genesee Street, where the television station was located. For some years in the late eighties Syracuse had been a dying city, its major employers having fled the punishing New York State taxation system for the better business climate in the South. But lately there'd been a resurgence, and a great many streets were undergoing repair. Quill passed work crews red-faced with cold, flagmen who seemed to have been recruited for the amount of ill temper they vented on drivers, and innumerable, irritating, annoying orange cones, which blocked each shortcut to Genesee with fiendish regularity.

By the time she reached the KSGY parking lot, the wind had risen and Bjarne's mashed potato clouds were thickening the blue sky. Quill parked in a space marked KSGY EMPLOYEES ONLY ALL OTHERS WILL BE TOWED!

She'd worked out a cover story. It was risky, but, as she'd told Meg, time was running short. What she hadn't told Meg—or John—or anyone—except Myles—was that Howie wasn't all that certain she was in the clear. The way in which she spent the next twenty years, he'd suggested, was dependent on how believable John's testimony would be to a jury. Nothing would be gained at the moment, Howie had added, by ruminating on the fact that the new governor had promised to reinstate the death penalty once in office.

Quill took a deep breath, got out of the Olds, and sloshed

through the inadequately plowed lot to the lobby. A middle-aged security guard sat behind a glass-walled kiosk. Quill pulled off her knitted cap, smiled, and rapped on the sliding glass window.

The guard raised her eyebrows and slid the panel open. "Can I help you?"

"Hi. I'm Sarah Cahill. Nora's sister." She bit her lip and thought about twenty years in jail.

The guard looked at her face sympathetically.

"I'm not too certain about whom I should see regarding Nora's personal effects. Has—um—any of the family arrived yet to take them? I've been out of the country and haven't had a chance to talk to any of our relatives."

"I thought your folks had passed on," said the guard. Her name tag read: "Rite-Watch Security, Rita."

"You must be Rita," Quill said warmly. "Nora's told me so much about you."

"She did? I on'y met her the two times."

"She said that the one who'd been here before . . ."

"Paula?" The guard looked smug. "I guess so!" She shook her head briefly. "You know how many jobs Paula's gone through on account of that mouth? I told her. We all told her. But there you are. So Miss Cahill remembered me, huh? Well, I remember her. Poor thing. Poor, poor thing. And you're her sister, huh?"

"We were quite close," said Quill. "I'm sure she's told you all about me, too."

"Yeah. Yeah. Look. I doan want to hurt your feelings or nuthin', but she never did say much about any of the family."

"Given her schedule," said Quill, "I can understand." She sighed, "All the same, it hurts."

"Poor thing," said Rita, "poor, poor thing. Well. I'll tell you. Mr. Ciscerone packed up all her stuff and said to wait sixty days and if nobody showed up, to ditch it."

Quill, who was beginning to feel genuinely sympathetic on Nora Cahill's behalf, said, "And no one's come yet? No one except me?"

"Nope. You hang on. I'll get her stuff for you." Rita reached through the open panel and patted Quill's hand, then disappeared through a door at the back of her kiosk. Quill shifted nervously from foot to foot. Nero Wolfe always told Archie Goodwin to conduct his investigation based on his intelligence guided by experience. There was never any indication that either detective felt terrible about pulling the wool over various people's eyes. Quill tried hard to feel she wasn't taking advantage of Rita's warm heart and didn't succeed.

Rita reemerged from the back with a large cardboard box and set it on the ledge of the kiosk. It was stuffed with papers, disk files, a Rolodex, a flower vase with four dead daisies, a photograph of Nora with two other women on a beach, and a stack of magazines. Quill made a cursory examination. The computer disks were parts of software packages; the papers mainly office memos, clippings from magazines, and letters from fans and critics of Nora's show.

"Nora was really proud of an investigation she was conducting just before she—you know . . ." said Quill. "Did Mr. Ciscerone mention that? Nora would have been so happy to know that it had been reassigned."

Rita shrugged. Quill, under pretext of neatening up the box, lifted the magazine pile out. Bingo. A set of keys, marked "spares."

Quill reached over the box, hand extended. Rita got out of her chair and shook it. "Thank you so much! I feel a little closer to Nora, now that I've talked to you. I'll just take these, shall I?"

"Gotta sign for 'em," said Rita. "Hang on." She produced a manifest, marked an empty line with a large X, and handed it to Quill. She signed the first name in an illegible scrawl and the last, Cahill, in readable but sloppy script.

"Thanks, Rita. I'll be off."

"Poor thing," said Rita. "Poor, poor thing."

Back in the Olds, Quill turned the engine on and turned up the heat. There was no address book—presumably the police had taken it—and the Rolodex was almost empty. It wasn't going to do a bit of good if she had the keys to Nora's apartment and car without her home address; no celebrity—especially an investigative reporter—was going to risk an open listing in the city phone book.

Quill turned to the papers; there, under a calendar for the coming year marked "compliments of Mac's Garage," she found a letter from Nora's HMO, addressed to 559 Westcott St. Quill hesitated a moment; it was getting late. She didn't want to risk returning to Rita to ask directions to Westcott. But it couldn't be too far; Nora had mentioned being able to walk to work.

Nora hadn't mentioned the fact that Syracuse was an old city, by American standards, and the streets a bewildering labyrinth, twisting around buildings that didn't exist anymore, truncated due to the building of newer roads, blocked by renovations to entire city blocks. She found Westcott after a series of frustrating dead ends.

This whole area, Quill realized, was oriented to nearby Syracuse University. Most of the students had gone home for the holidays, and the parking was relatively easy. She pulled up at the curb next to a row of storefronts that gave her a pang of nostalgia for her days in SoHo in New York: a pizza parlor with the phone number painted on the window in screaming red letters; a small gallery, filled with student work; a boutique clothing store; a business sign for a company called Oddly Enough. She scanned the store numbers and found a door marked 559. She fumbled at the entrance, going through three of the four keys on the ring before she found the right one. Inside, scanning a row of metal mailboxes she found N. CAHILL #3.

The single door at her right was marked 1. Quill mounted the steep stairs. At the top of the landing, #3 was on the left.

The interior of the apartment belied the student atmosphere. Nora had corner rooms, with windows on two sides overlooking Westcott and Argyle. The style was Euro-Tech: Berber carpeting, a black leather couch, plain wrought-iron shelving, and a display of hand thrown pottery. A very nice copy of a de Kooning hung on the wall over the couch. The kitchen was through an open archway on the east wall; the two closed doors on the south wall probably led to bedrooms. The first Quill opened was to a room with a sofa bed and a desk. A window looked out over the back of the building, letting in dim gray light. Quill glanced out; light snow was falling, like spume from a breaking wave. She hesitated, a hand on the overhead light switch, and decided to work in the dimness as best she could.

There was a place on her desk where Nora's PC had been,

marked by cables and an extra battery. Quill flipped through the file case of computer disks. They were all pre-formatted and, as far as she could tell, unused. Were they really empty? Quill wasn't sure. If she were an investigative reporter, she wouldn't label files. She slipped the disks into her shoulder bag.

The desk drawers were filled with stationery, envelopes, a folder of bills neatly marked "paid" with the date of payment, used check registers, and a few bank statements. Nothing unusual, except for the fact that Nora's affairs were so orderly. That was suspicious itself.

The front door opened into the living room, and someone walked in.

Quill swallowed so hard she choked. She stepped to the office door. A man in a suit stood in the center of the living room, behaving much as she had done, casting swift, appraising glances around the room.

Quill's visual memory was good; where Meg could separate flavors into component parts of recipes, Quill's artist's eye, like a good cop's, could categorize age, background, and dress. The man in the living room was from somewhere around the Mediterranean; her guess would be Northern Italy. He was wearing a medium-priced suit with a cut at the edge of this year's fashions. Like his haircut. There were a lot of guys like this one on the streets of New York, lawyers on their first job, mid-level bankers, entry-level stockbrokers.

Quill stepped into the living room. "Excuse me." She kept her voice as well under control as she could, but thought she could hear a nervous quaver. She scowled to cover it.

The guy in the living room didn't jump. This made Quill uneasy. Any friend of Nora's would have assumed the apartment was empty.

"Hi. You're Nora's sister, Sarah?" He stuck out his hand. "Joseph Greenwald."

Well, south of Northern Italy, Quill thought. Very south.

"Rita at the station thought you might be here."

Quill looked at him.

"Nora told me quite a bit about you two as kids." He grinned. Like a shark. "You don't know who I am?"

Quill cleared her throat. "I can't . . . that is, Nora never mentioned you."

"No? We've been dating almost a year. But she was pretty goosey about letting anyone know about us. Even you. Her favorite. Sister."

"Why?"

His eyelids fluttered. "She thought the single-minded career woman bit would keep the station focused on her performance. Was she as determined to make it big-time when you two were kids?" He shook his head, clicked his tongue against his teeth, and said admiringly, "That Nora. God. She was one focused lady. I miss her, you know? What a shame. What a rotten shame." He took a step toward her. Quill dodged and moved left, out into the living room, toward the front door.

"Rita said she'd given you the box of Nora's things from the office. If you don't mind, I'd like to take a look. Have you been through it yet? There was a picture of the two of us that I'd like to have, as well." He glanced around the living room. "It's why I came here. To pick it up. She used to keep it on the shelf right here. But it's gone. Was it with her stuff from the office?"

"I haven't had a chance to go through it." Quill added cleverly, "If you leave me your address, Joseph, I'd be happy to mail it to you."

"I'll see you at the funeral, won't I? Could I get it from you there?" He frowned at her expression. "You have been making the arrangements, haven't you? The police wouldn't tell me a damn thing. Just told me anyone could walk off the street and claim they'd known her and I had no proof that we'd been dating." His voice sounded bitter. "She was right on her way to being famous, you know. So anyone could take advantage. People are scum. Just like whoever killed her is scum."

Did Nora have a sister? Suddenly, Quill felt like the worst kind of liar, the most offensive kind of intruder. She was exploiting a tragedy.

Joseph Greenwald sat down on the couch. He looked sad. He also looked as if he had been there before. "The police must have told you if they have a lead on who did it. They'd let family members know."

"I haven't really heard anything," Quill said cautiously.

"You want to sit down? I'll make us some coffee." His expression was wistful. "I haven't been able to talk about her to anyone yet. She didn't want anyone to know about us."

"Was there a reason she didn't? I mean, other than the fact that she thought it'd be better for the station not to know she had a personal life?"

"God, I don't know. I teach ninth grade math at the University High School. Nora knew a lot more about the real world than I did."

"You never went to law school?" Quill asked. "Or banking? You were never interested in banking?"

"Me? Heck, no. I like kids. I've always liked kids. That was the one area Nora and I never did agree on. I wanted to get married and she—Say, are you sure you wouldn't like me to make you a pot of coffee?"

"No. Thanks." Quill, feeling more traitorous every minute, was positive that her cheeks were red. "I've got to get back to the, um, hotel."

"Where're you staying?"

"The Hyatt," said Quill. There had to be a Hyatt in Syracuse. Every large town in America had a Hyatt.

"I didn't know we had a Hyatt," said Joseph.

"Could you give me your phone number?" Quill said desperately. "I'll be sure to call you about the . . . you know."

"The funeral. Yeah. You have a piece of paper?"

Quill drew her Investigations notebook out of her purse and took out a pen.

"It's a local area code, 315. And it's 624-9123."

Quill wrote this down. After this was all over, she could call and explain and apologize. He might forgive her. By the next millennium. "I'll let you know as soon as everything's been completed." She shoved the notebook back in her purse, dislodging the computer disks she'd stolen from Nora's desk. She laughed, "Ha-ha!" stuffed them clumsily into the depths of the purse, and held out her hand. "Goodbye, Joe. I'm so sorry."

"Yeah. Can I drop you off at the Hyatt? It must be new. Of course, you know us teachers. Never pay much attention to anything outside of test scores."

"It's really more toward Rochester." She shook his hand. "We'll keep in touch."

She clattered down the stairs, her purse banging against the wall, warm with embarrassment. No detective she'd ever read in any of her favorite fiction, from Philip Marlowe to Dave Robicheaux, ever got embarrassed in the middle of an investigation. And they were sensitive guys. She'd have to work at being tougher.

She pushed outside to the sidewalk. The snow was falling faster now, and the temperature had dropped. She slid on the sidewalk. The Olds' windshield was covered with a thin coat of icy mush. She scraped it free with her bare hand, and removed the flyer some enterprising entrepreneur had stuck under the wipers with a click of irritation. She balled it up and wiped futilely at the glass, then turned and opened the driver's door. She glanced up. Joseph Greenwald stared at her through the living room window. She forced a smile, waved, and caught herself just before she tossed the flyer in the street. *"Red-haired, early thirties," Greenwald would tell the cops. "Said she was Nora's sister. No, we've never met. But Nora told me a lot about their life together as kids. And I tell you this, Officer, Nora's sister was no litterer."*

The Olds started, as always, with a cough and reliable roar. Quill buckled herself in and took a right off Westcott onto Argyle, from Argyle to Genesee and from Genesee to the entrance ramp of 81 north without really seeing anything at all.

She became aware of the intensity of the snow when she almost hit the car in front of her.

Its taillights flashed. Quill braked automatically, and the Olds skidded on the rutted slush, narrowly missing the car on her left. There was a blare of horns, a shout, and the Toyota next to her swung wide. She swerved into the skid and came to rest against the ramp curb. Behind her, a line of cars slowed, and inched by her stopped vehicle, an occasional hollered curse adding to her misery.

She pounded the wheel and yelled, "Ugh. Ugh *ugh*, UGH!"

It snowed harder as she watched, moving from a veil to a heavy curtain in minutes. She waited until her heart slowed and her breath was even, then inched out into the traffic. She made it to the expressway. The snow was thick, gluey, and treacherous. Her windshield wipers were on full speed, but the snow fell faster than the blades were moving. Quill hunched forward in the classic posture of the snow-blind driver and followed the taillights ahead of her.

She switched the radio on, punching the buttons until she hit the Traffic Watch.

"Seven to eight inches expected before nightfall," came the announcer's excited voice. "Most major thoroughfares have been closed to all but emergency traffic. High winds are expected to pick up as a front moves in from Canada. Our travel advisory has become a snow emergency. The sheriff's office has ordered no unnecessary travel, I repeat, no unnecessary travel."

Why, thought Quill, *do these weather guys always sound as though we're about to be bombed by Khaddafi?* Half of her anxiety about driving in snow came from the we-who-are-about-to-die-salute-you tone of this guy's voice.

She drove on, keeping her speed under thirty, and told herself that somewhere on the continent the sun was shining, the roads were dry, and the outside temperature wouldn't kill you if you fell asleep in it. She imagined a map of the United States, with the sun shining everywhere but this little stretch of Interstate 81 north. She pretended that all she had to do was drive a few miles more, and she would break into clear roads and blue skies.

The line of cars in front of her exited at the off ramp at 53. She looked in the rearview mirror. There were a few sets of headlights in back of her, not many. The snow whirled and spun like a immense bolt of cotton, now obscuring the road altogether, now whipping aside to reveal snow as high as her knees.

She switched the radio, found Pachelbel's *Canon,* which she'd come to loathe, then a mournful harpsichord version of Claude-Marie deCourcey's *Spring Fate.*

"Oh, humm," Quill sang. "Hummmm hummm." She shivered, despite the fact that the heater was going full blast.

She checked her watch. Three-thirty. At the rate she was traveling, she wouldn't be home before five. When it would be dark.

"This is stupid," she said aloud. She'd take the next exit, find a motel, and call Myles, then Meg, and tell them not to worry, she'd be back home in the morning.

The miles crawled by. On her left, headed south, two exits went by. The next one northbound would be 50. It was on the outskirts of the city, and her chances of finding a motel right off the ramp were not good, but at least she'd be close to the ground, near a gas station or a diner, where there would be light, and the warmth of human beings, and an end to the white that so ruthlessly wrapped the car.

She checked the rearview mirror. The traffic was gone, the road almost empty but for a pair of headlights traveling at speed in her lane. She slowed again, to under twenty-five, and signaled a move into the far right-hand lane. The headlights moved, too. They were high above the ground, shining eerily above the piled snow, plowing through the drifts like a fish through water. *Four-wheel drive*, Quill thought glumly. *I should have taken the Inn pickup.*

She turned her attention to the road in front. The Olds was lugging a little, the snow was halfway up the hubcaps. Her headlights were almost useless, bumping above the snow as often as they were obscured by drifts.

High beams flashed in her rearview mirror. She ducked, swerved, and cursed. She regained control and then the Olds jumped forward, like a frightened horse.

"No," said Quill.

The high beams filled the car, drenching the inside with light. Quill slowed to a crawl. The truck behind her was pushing now, its bumper locked into position. Quill leaned on the horn, the noise whipped away on the flying wind, driven on the snow. She blasted the horn once, twice.

The headlights behind her dimmed and flared in answer.

The truck backed off. Quill remembered to breathe. The headlights filled her mirror again, and she peered frantically out the windshield, looking for a place to stop, to let the bastard pass. The truck didn't hit her again, just hung there like a carrion bird, the headlights hovering.

The world was filled with snow.

The dark was coming.

She looked at her watch. A quarter to five. The exit to 96 had to be coming up next. She searched the side of the road. A green sign crawled by. Two miles. If she could just make it two miles.

The lights from behind filled her vision.

She squinted. She drove on. She rubbed her right hand down her thigh, pushing hard against the muscle to calm herself. Her gloved hand brushed the flyer she'd dropped in the seat beside her. "Pizza," she said, just to hear the sound of a voice. "Oh, I wish I had a pepperoni . . ."

She smoothed the paper out.

FREE DELIVERY!

"Lot of good that'll do me."

CALL 624-9123—ANYTIME!

"624-9123, 624-9123," Quill chanted, fighting a hopeless battle against the choking fear.

It's a local area code, 315. And it's 624-9123, Joseph Greenwald had said.

And then, from days ago, Nora Cahill's voice: *No offense, but if you tell me you've got your love life socked, too, I'm going to hit you with a stick. I haven't had a date for eight months.*

She got mad.

"You idiot!" she yelled. "You bonehead! You twink!"

I could pull over to the side, wait for him to come up to the car, and hit him with . . . what?

The tire iron was in the trunk. And she wasn't sure she could use it on flesh and bone no matter how mad and scared and stupid she was.

HEMLOCK FALLS, 10 MI., the green sign said.

Quill thought about the exit ramp. At this juncture of 81, the exit ramps were on a gentle upward slope to 96, which ran along a drumlin left by glaciers. So the snow wouldn't be any higher at the exit than it was now—more than likely less, since the wind would blow it downward. And the highway department always started plowing 96 here first, at the boundary of Tompkins County.

Unless the blizzard was too much for even the plows.

"Nah," said Quill.

Then . . .

"It's just like the West End at rush hour," she said aloud, to reassure herself. "And you remember the West End at rush hour. Oh, yes, you do. In your short—and unlamented career as a taxi driver . . ."

She gunned the motor. The Olds leaped forward. *Thank God,* she thought, *I never got a lighter car. Thank God . . .*

She signaled left and instead swerved into the center lane.

The truck behind her faltered, moved left, and spun briefly out of control. She had time. A little time.

She could barely see the signposts now, between the dark and the snow and the wind. The tiny mile reflectors flashed white-white-white as she hurtled by, the front-wheel drive giving the heavy car purchase in the drifts, her speed preventing a skid. She'd be all right until she had to make that turn.

The pickup behind her straightened out, barreled forward, and nudged her bumper with a thud.

The mile marker for the exit flashed.

Quill bit her lip, pulled a hard right, spun, drove into the skid, and gunned the accelerator. The Olds fishtailed. Quill let it ride, keeping her hands off the wheel, her foot off the brake.

She broke through the barrier of snow at the ramp's edge.

The upward incline slowed the Olds, steadied it.

She waited.

Behind her, the pickup roared and tried to turn to follow. The engine whined. The pickup bounced, the height and weight of the truck throwing it into a spin from which it couldn't recover— and she heard the squeal of the transmission. He'd thrown it into reverse. His engine screamed and died.

"Fool," Quill said, and slammed her foot on the accelerator again.

The tires bit into the powdered snow and held.

She drove up the ramp, the Olds' rear end slamming against the guardrail, now to the left, now to the right. She clenched her hands to keep them from the wheel and braked, gunned, braked, gunned, the car rocking back and forth until she broke through onto 96 . . .

"And thank you, *God*!" she shouted.

The road was plowed.

CHAPTER 9

Quill had approached the Inn at Hemlock Falls at least two thousand different times over the past seven years, in every season, at practically every time of the day and most of the night.

It had never looked more welcoming.

Warm golden lights shone through the mullioned windows as she drove carefully up the driveway. There was a pine wreath at each window—as they had every year at holiday time—wound round with small white lights. Mauve taffeta bows shot through with gold were wired to the wreaths. Hundreds of the small white lights sparkled in the bare branches of the trees clustered near the gorge, casting jewel-like twinkles over the snow.

Mike the groundskeeper had been busy; white snow was piled in neat drifts on either side of the drive. The asphalt was powdered with at least a half an inch. He'd be out again with the plow later, when the snowstorm finally quit.

The Olds was lugging worse than ever. Quill took the left-hand path to the maintenance building out back in low gear, with a vague idea that this would save the engine. She hit the button for the overhead door opener, then pulled in and stopped. The engine died with a cough.

"Good *girl*," she said foolishly, patting the dash.

She was surprised to discover that her legs were weak. And she had trouble opening the driver's door. She got out, then turned back and opened the rear door to take the red down coat to Myles.

It was gone.

"Damn." She punched the light switch and the garage flooded with light. The coat hadn't fallen to the floor in that hairy ride down 81 and it wasn't under the seat. The box with the contents of Nora Cahill's desk at the office was gone, too.

"Damn and damn again." She slammed the rear door shut.

Joseph Greenwald. She hoped he was up to his eyeteeth in snow. The computer disks from Nora's home office were still in her purse. Quill hoped her quota of luck for the week hadn't run out; she'd made quite a dent in it with Route 96 being plowed at just the right time. If her luck held, those disks would contain Nora's investigative files.

She marched to the Inn's back door, her adrenaline charged from annoyance, stripped off her winter clothing, and hung it on the coat pegs. She ditched her boots and walked into the kitchen in her socks. It was overly warm. There were six *sous*-chefs busy at the Aga, the grill, and the butcher block counters. To her surprise, Meg was seated in the rocking chair by the cobblestone fireplace, smoking a forbidden cigarette.

"Hey! I thought you'd be up to your ears in work. How come you're sitting down?"

Meg threw the cigarette into the open hearth with a guilty air and bounced out of the rocker. "Hey, yourself! I was just beginning to worry. You're more than an hour later than you said you'd be and that storm Bjarne predicted is a doozy."

"In Helsinki, this is spring," Bjarne said. He whacked at a huge tenderloin with the butcher's knife, and whacked again.

"I thought you'd be run off your feet, Meg."

"You're kidding, right? Santini's closed the dining room so that he and his eleven pals can eat tenderloin in lofty seclusion. Ten pals actually. One of them got held up by the storm. Listen. I spent the day with Tutti McIntosh, and I've got something really interesting to tell you."

Quill interrupted, "Santini paid the table minimum? For all twenty tables?"

"Claire's doting dad did, I think. Anyhow, everyone's eating away and they're all taken care of. The mayor and his soapy friends ordered cold stuff, except for their roasted cow which they did somewhere in the woods themselves, and I made all that this afternoon. And the H.O.W. ladies each brought a dish to pass. That's where Tutti is now, surrounded by the entire protective brigade of—"

"John's not going to like that. Guests aren't supposed to bring their own stuff."

"I like it," Meg said firmly. "I've got enough to do with this rehearsal dinner for twenty tomorrow night. And then the wedding. Thank God the truck got here just before the snow. We got all that stuff unloaded. And then Tutti was with me in the kitchen all afternoon. I'll be glad when this is all over and we can put up our tree and close the place down for two days. By the way, Myles called and said he won't get here until midnight or after. The snow's caused the usual numbers of crises, including some damn fool wrecking his pickup truck at the 96 exit to 81 and you'll never guess what Tutti did—"

"At the moment," Quill said crossly. "I just don't give a hoot." She settled on a stool at the butcher block counter. Exhaustion overtook her like a dam bursting. She could just sit here and go to sleep. She yawned. "Can you tell me the fascinating news about Tutti later? I have to speak to Myles about that pickup." She glanced casually at Meg. "It sounds like the one that tried to run me off the road."

"Oh, yeah? Well, you can go pound on the driver personally tomorrow. The truck's been towed to Bernie's garage and the guy's at the hospital with a broken arm. Andy says he's not going anywhere soon. Let me tell you what happened *here* this afternoon."

"Oh, yeah? That's all you have to say when I tell you I was almost murdered right there on 81 by a crazed guy who very probably is involved in Nora Cahill's death, not to mention Frank Dorset's?"

"You're here all in one piece, aren't you?" Meg said callously. "Honestly Quill, sometimes you exaggerate as much as Dina does. It's either that or the other extreme—like failing to mention your absolutely awful driving record to Howie Murchison, which is when all this nutty stuff started. Try to be a little rational for once, will you?"

Pressure always upset Meg. In some remote part of her mind, Quill tried to remember this, and failed. "I am perfectly rational!" she shouted.

"Perfectly rational people don't shriek their heads off at a little mild criticism from a beloved relative. No, they don't. Wait until you hear about the séance this afternoon."

Quill slid off the stool. "I'm numb with cold. I'm sweaty with the aftermath of fear—"

"The what?!"

"And I'm going up to my room and call Myles and tell him about the evidence I just uncovered in this murder case, because it's practically solved, Meg, and then I'm going to take a hot, hot, hot shower, wash my hair, nap, and be gorgeous for poor Myles when he finally gets off road duty."

"Practically solved the murders, huh?" Meg shouted after her as she shoved open the swinging doors to the dining room. "Quill! Don't *go* that way!"

Quill took two steps into the dining room and encountered the affronted glares of Alphonse Santini, a well-known Supreme Court Justice, an equally well-known Democratic senator, and Vittorio McIntosh, among others.

They were all in black tie.

Quill was jerked out of her fatigue into the present. Sweat streaked her face. Her knitted cap had made a tangled mess of her hair. She'd been wearing black long Johns under her snow pants, and she was suddenly aware that rather than resembling leggings— which they were not—they looked like long underwear. Which they were. And there was a hole in her argyle socks.

She retreated to the kitchen.

Meg looked smug. This, Quill reflected later, was the straw that broke the camel's back, the monkey wrench in the machinery, the penultimate push. Actually it wasn't the smugness as much as the pious comment that accompanied it:

"You *never* listen to me. You'd never get into half the trouble you do if you'd just listen to me."

Quill washed her hair in the shower, drained the tub, filled it with water as hot as she could stand it, and threw in four capfuls of Neutrogena Rain Bath Shower and Bath Body Gel. She had, she realized, told Meg (and any interested person within forty feet of the kitchen) that in the past two days she'd a.) been thrown in jail for a bogus traffic ticket, b.) renounced her lover, c.) been humiliated on television, d.) been thrown in jail on a trumped-up murder charge, e.) been assaulted and sexually harassed by a human asparagus, f.) witnessed a murder, g.) spent the night with a corpse, and finally, been terrified almost to death by a high-speed chase in a snowstorm. Meg's tart rejoinder ("There's no need to get hysterical about it!") made her so mad that she'd upended an entire canister of whole wheat flour on the kitchen floor. The Finns thought this was hilarious. "Americans," Bjarne said with a pleased air, "how I love this country."

A knock on the bathroom door roused her from the gloomy contemplation of her soapy knees. "Yes?" Quill shouted.

There was a bout of furious yapping, a thump, and a muttered "Gol-durn it."

"Doreen?"

"Yap-yap-yap-yap," came Tatiana's voice, in a furious fusillade, "yap-yap—"

Crash!

"YAP!!"

"You git, before I turn you into earmuffs!"

There was another crash, as of a mop hitting a hardwood floor, and a ferocious growl. Doreen wouldn't dare deep-six the dog. Would she? Quill waited for a canine gurgle. Maybe that growl had been Doreen. Maybe a short dog drowned in a tall mop bucket didn't have time to gurgle.

"Doreen?"

"It's me," came Doreen's familiar foghorn voice. "You decent?— OW!"

Decent, she thought. *How decent is a person who yells at her sister?*

"I'll be right there." She sloshed out of the tub, pulled on her terry cloth robe, and opened the door.

"Doreen. You look really nice."

The housekeeper was dressed in a long velvet skirt, a metallic gold turtleneck with blouson sleeves, and sandals with rhinestones at the toes. This gave her a charmingly old-fashioned (if gaudy) appearance. She was carrying a mop. Quill smiled at her. "You ought to wear soft shapes more often. But why the mop?"

"You'll see," she said with a glower. "'Bout this outfit, Stoke bought it for me. I think it makes me look like I'm plugged inta a outlet. Say, Quill. The girls, I mean the organization members, sent me up to see if you're comin' to the meeting."

"The H.O.W. meeting?" Quill stepped barefoot into the room,

the sash to her bathrobe trailing. "Boy, Doreen, I'm just so—OW!" Tatiana, who'd been hiding under the couch, retreated as soon as her needle teeth got Quill's ankle.

Crash! Doreen wielded the broom with prompt efficiency. "Durn thing," Doreen said glumly. "She'll do that. Ain't hit her yet."

"It doesn't seem to me that you try very hard." Quill nursed her ankle with one hand and hobbled to the couch. "Why is she up here?"

"She follers me around. Why it is, durn'd if I know."

"Is Tutti here?"

"Yeah."

"She's not at the shower for Claire, is she?"

"Heck, no. She's in the H.O.W. meeting. Where *you* bin, anyways?"

"To Syracuse. Why?"

"Big hoo-ha here this afternoon, I can tell you."

She remembered suddenly: séance. And Meg anxious to tell her about it just before Quill lobbed verbal fireballs at her over the tenderloin. "Did something happen at the séance?"

"You bet it did. That Tutti's amazin'. She ought to be on TV. You know how many serial killers that one'd catch if she went public?"

"What?! What serial killer?"

Doreen gave a patient sigh. "This one that killed that Dorset and that poor Nora Cahill. He spoke to us. Right there in the Provençal suite next to the fireplace. We don't have to worry about him. He's dead. Deader than a doornail. Which is how come he come back from Beyond to speak through Tutti. You shoulda heard him. You know how Tutti has that nice sweet voice? Well, it was like somethin' from that movie where the devil was in that Linda Blair and turnt her head right around like a screw cap. Ol' Tutti's head turnt around—"

"All the way?" Quill asked sarcastically.

"No, ma'am. Just partways. Then this here voice comes out. Low. Ugly-like. A man, of course." Doreen's voice, although hoarse, was generally clearly feminine. She pitched it several octaves lower than usual and growled, "I DONE FOR 'EM. I DONE FOR 'EM BOTH."

"Yap!" went Tatiana, "yap, yap!!"

"See, the dog's a familiar, like. Tutti don't do her sayance without her. Good girl," Doreen cooed suddenly. "Good girl. She got two mice in the storeroom today, too."

Tatiana made a noise like a Norelco shaver. Quill shifted back nervously. "Did Tutti say anything else?"

"You mean he, the murderer. Oh, yeah. RABBIT! RABBIT!"

Quill opened her mouth, then closed it. Nobody knew about her rabbit hat. Except Dorset, and he was dead. Except herself, and she didn't do it. Except the murderer, who had worn it.

Tutti?

Impossible. She was too short. Too round. And the murderer was a male—Quill wasn't entirely sure how she knew that, except that she'd been no more than three feet away from him while he slashed Frank Dorset's throat. The sound of his breath, the way that he walked on the videotape. And the arms, she thought suddenly. The arms extended way past the sleeves of her coat. So the murderer was a man. She trusted her painter's eye that far. And Tutti, for reasons known only to herself, was letting the murderer know she knew.

But why? To stop Santini from marrying Claire? If she knew about the rabbit hat, she knew enough to turn Santini in to Myles. It didn't make any sense for Tutti to warn a man who had killed twice already.

"Alphonse Santini was at the séance, wasn't he, Doreen?"

"Yep. Shook him up some, I'll tell you that."

"I'll bet it did."

What did Tutti know? And how had she found out? More important, a man who had killed twice wouldn't shy away from killing again. Now that Tutti had revealed her hand, she was in danger.

Unless Tutti were protected, there'd be one less guest at that wedding, Quill thought, and it wouldn't be Alphonse Santini.

"Is the senator still in the dining room?"

"Yep."

"Doreen. You've got to get back to the H.O.W. meeting right away. I believe Tutti's in danger."

"Nah, Tutti said the murderer's dead. That no matter how long the sheriff—Myles, I mean—searches for him, he'll on'y find him in the next world."

"Or at her daughter's side at the church." Quill shook her head to clear it. "Doreen, you don't believe all this séance hooey."

There was an all-too-recognizable glint in Doreen's beady black eyes. "Tell you the truth, I was feelin' kinda psychic myself, the longer that there sayance went on. Anyhow, Tutti's holding another one for the wimmin of H.O.W., to help us find out ways we can get these men off our backs and into their proper role, she says." Doreen took a deep breath. "You comin'?"

"Of course I'm coming! We don't want a third corpse in Hemlock Falls. What time is it?"

"Nine-thirty."

Two and half hours until Myles came. "You get down there right now. And stick to Tutti like glue, you hear me? Don't let Alphonse Santini come within a country mile of her."

"If you say so," Doreen said doubtfully.

"Is everyone as dressed up as you are?"

"Not them boobs in the S.O.A.P. meeting. Members of the organ'zation have the sense to dress with respect. So you get dressed with respect. I'll see you down there." She turned and marched out the door, mop slung over her shoulder. Tatiana poked her blunt little nose out from under the couch and eyed Quill with suspicion.

"Go on," Quill said encouragingly. "Go find Doreen."

Tatiana rolled her upper lip over her teeth and advanced sideways, like a mongoose stalking a cobra. Quill jumped up on the oak chest. "Beat it, Tatiana. Go hunt some ghosts. Better yet, go bite the senator."

The prospect of senatorial flesh between her jaws apparently appealed to Tatiana. She cocked her head, trotted off, and Quill climbed down from the chest. She was so tired she felt as though she were swimming through mud.

She pulled on a stretchy ankle-length velvet dress over her head, swept her hair into a knot, and slid on a pair of black sandals. "The well-dressed host," she muttered, spraying herself with musk perfume, "goes to meet her fate."

She heard the drone of Tutti's voice halfway down the hall. The conference room was only three years old, and John had designed it for several purposes. Wood panels on the walls opened up to reveal whiteboards and film screens. The long credenza on the south wall opened up into a serving bar. And the long mahogany table in the center of the room could hold more than twenty people in a pinch.

Quill knocked on the door and opened it in a single motion. The room was dark, except for a single lamp at the head of the table. It was a lava lamp in the shape of a globe, the viscous red liquid churning like the contents of somebody's stomach. Tutti's round face hung over the lamp like a wrinkly white moon.

"Nnnnnnnnmmmmmmmm," she hummed.

"Nummmmmmmmmmmm," responded the members of the Hemlock Organization of Women.

"Shut the damn *door*," somebody called out.

Quill flipped on the light. Doreen sat at Tutti's left, Marge Schmidt at her right. Tatiana barked from the safety of Tutti's lap. Tutti herself blinked owlishly and smiled. She was dressed in a fuzzy angora sweater, a long plaid taffeta skirt, and an emerald necklace that weighed more than her dog.

"Sorry," said Quill. "I hope I'm not interrupting anything."

"Of course you are," Miriam Doncaster said testily. "What *is* it, Quill? We were just about to hear the truth about what goes on in that dratted men's group."

"I won't keep you. I have something to ask you guys. It's important, but short."

She walked to the head of the room. The women of Hemlock Falls looked back at her: Esther West, in a black chiffon cocktail dress with rhinestone earrings; Betty Hall in purple lamé, a red bow in her hair; Marge in a size twenty-two Diane Freis after-dinner suit that cost more than Quill's automobile when it was new. Even Adela Henry looked vulnerable in the sudden flare of the overhead lights.

Quill felt a wave of affection so strong she blinked back tears.

"You okay, honey?" Nadine Wertmuller (Hemlock Hall of Beauty) snapped her gum in concern.

"Yep," Quill said a little huskily, "I'm just tired, that's all."

"PMS," said somebody. "Gets me like that, too."

"I want to ask your help." Quill tugged at a tendril of hair.

"Some of you were at the séance this afternoon. By now, most of you have heard what went on. And I believe that Tutti's been given a warning."

There was a swell of excited comment, like wheat rippling in the wind.

"Tutti was right—or rather, her—um—spirit guide was. The man who killed Nora Cahill and Frank Dorset is connected with rabbits."

"Those bums at S.O.A.P.," yelled Nadine. "Torturing animals in the woods!"

"Oh, no!" Quill flung her hands out. "The killings don't have anything to do with S.O.A.P. Sheriff McHale is very close to obtaining evidence that will convict this man."

"You find something in Syracuse?" asked Marge.

Quill made what she hoped was a noncommittal "hmm." Tutti regarded her with the set, unblinking gaze of her dog. "I found something that I think will be useful in bringing this person in. But until the case is wrapped up, I believe that Tutti is in real danger."

"Surely not!" Tutti protested.

Meg, dressed in jeans and a clean T-shirt (which meant that the kitchen was closed), appeared at the open door. She caught Quill's eye, wriggled her eyebrows, then folded her arms and leaned against the door frame. Quill straightened her shoulders and continued firmly, "I'm afraid so, Mrs. McIntosh. I *know*," Quill said, scanning the room, "that no one at this meeting is implicated in these murders. I saw the murderer myself."

Meg went, "Phuuut!"

Quill ignored her.

"Jeez," said Betty Hall. "You think you should announce it like that?"

"If we were weren't close to bringing him in, and if I didn't trust everyone in this room, I'd agree with you. As it is, I wonder if we could assign a guard for Tutti, just until Sheriff McHale gets back from this snow emergency. Would some of you volunteer to keep an eye on her at all times?"

"Of course we will," said Esther West. "My goodness, do you think she'll be attacked? Right here at the Inn?"

"It's possible."

Meg cleared her throat, rolled her eyes, and yawned.

"How long do we keep this watch?" asked Miriam.

"Midnight," said Quill, with a sangfroid unimpeded by Meg's giggle. "There's something else. Marge and Betty, how did the search go today?"

"Quill?" Adela Henry rose to her full thin, elegant height. "If there is to be a disclosure of the activities of the investigatory subcommittee, perhaps I should chair this meeting."

"Well, sure," said Quill.

"What subcommittee?" Miriam demanded.

"H.O.W. shall solve," Adela said grandly, "the murders of Nora Cahill and that disgusting Frank Dorset." Her eyes flickered. "And then we shall seek to replace the lamentable town government with a mayor of quality. A town justice of integrity, a sheriff of—"

"Be *quiet*, Adela," said Miriam. "What's going on here, Marge?"

"Quill, Meg, Betty, and me have been looking for that down coat of Quill's. It's what the guy wore when he stabbed Nora and Frank Dorset."

"And I've been looking for the videotape from that there hidden camera that shows him doin' it," said Betty. "I checked each one of the fireplaces in the Inn today, Quill, and I didn't find a thing."

"So that's why you dragged Esther and me all over the bottom of the gorge today, Marge Schmidt," said Miriam. "I'd like to have died from the cold, too. Why didn't you tell me?"

"I'm tellin' you now, or Quill is. What's next, Quill?"

"First, who wants to guard Tutti?"

"My goodness," said Tutti, her cheeks pink. "And to think the spirit guides led us to this, Tatiana!"

"We want the big ones, like me," said Marge with satisfaction. "That means you, Shirley Peterson, and you, Trish Pasquale. We'll stick to you like debentures in a bear market, Tutti."

"And the rest of you have to turn this Inn inside out," said Quill, "discreetly. And you should work in pairs, for protection."

"What are we looking for?" asked Betty.

"A videotape that's mini-sized, you know, about half the size of the ones you rent from the video store. It's the tape of Nora's murder. And a hat."

"A hat? What kind of hat?" said Esther.

"My rabbit hat."

"You mean that horrible old thing with the earflaps you wore all winter last year?" asked Esther.

"The murderer disguised himself in it," said Quill.

"Disguise?" somebody muttered. "Heck, you show up in that thing at a school picnic and half the little kids would fall over from fright."

"I always thought the hat was one of the reasons the sheriff dumped her," said somebody else.

Quill maintained her aplomb. "Just two caveats ladies. Don't be so obvious that the other guests suspect anything. And if you do find the hat or the videotape, don't pick either one up. One of you guard it, the other one should come and find me. Or the sheriff."

"Well, I'm ready," said Miriam. "Esther, you come with me. We'll start right away."

"What about the guest rooms?" asked Doreen. "You want I should get out the master key?"

"There's only one room I need to search," said Quill. "And I should be the one to take the risk."

Meg started to whistle the theme from *The Bridge Over the River Kwai.*

"Tutti," said Marge. "How'd you feel about a game of bridge?"

"Fifty cents a point? We'd love it. Wouldn't we, Tatiana?" The dog gave her a skeptical glance, hopped off her lap, and followed Doreen and the other H.O.W. members out the door. Tutti pulled a deck of cards from her capacious handbag and shuffled them expertly. Quill strode toward the hall. She felt great.

"Colonel!" Meg snapped to attention and saluted.

"Cut it out, Meg."

"You're right. I should be addressing you as Inspector Alleyn. He always gathered the suspects in the drawing room and exposed the murderer. Nope. Sorry. Wrong again. It's Holmes himself and the Baker Street Irregulars."

"Why are you bugging me, Meg? I've had a tough day. And you didn't tell me what went on at that séance."

"You didn't give me a *chance* to tell you about the séance!"

"Tutti's clearly in danger, and you didn't do a thing about it."

"I most certainly did," Meg said indignantly. "Why the heck do you think she was in the kitchen with me all day? I mean she's a sweetie, Quill, and I learned a great new recipe for homemade pasta, but this is one of the busiest days of the whole darn year!"

"Oh," Quill said.

"I mean, really. How irresponsible do you think I am? You never look at anybody the way they really are, Quill. You look at them the way you think they should be."

"I do?"

"Yes, you do. You make up your mind first and then you decide what's happening. Have you ever known me to boot an important clue like the one Tutti rolled out this afternoon?"

"No, Meg."

"And don't we usually solve these cases together?"

"Yes, Meg."

"So how come you came in all hissy this afternoon and picked a fight with me?"

"Because I was scared out of my mind!"

"Then why didn't you tell me? Honestly, Quill, it does nobody any good if you keep your emotions buttoned up. It doesn't do any good with me, that's for sure. And look what happened with that lunch with Myles. You were so busy keeping a stiff upper lip that you didn't even talk to each other. And look what almost happened. If Miles hadn't taken the risk to come back . . . restraint is all very well, Quillie. But not when it screws up your emotional life."

Quill stared at her. "You really think so?"

"I really think . . . what the *devil* is that noise?"

"The bachelor party, I suppose. Meg, I was scared out of my mind, but only partly from being almost run off the road."

"Somebody really did? Quill!"

"Somebody really did. But that's not what's bothering me."

"My Lord, Quill. Did you report this man? Are you hurt? It's a good thing you have that big heavy car."

"I'm pretty sure that the truck's at Bernie's and Joseph Greenwald is in the hospital. Do you think you could call Andy and verify that he's going to be in overnight?"

"Joseph Greenwald?" said Meg.

"There's a funny look on your face."

"He showed up here right after you left for Syracuse. Good-looking guy? Looks like a Philadelphia lawyer?"

"He showed up here?"

"Tried to check in, but of course there wasn't any room. So I sent him on to the Marriott."

"Well, I'll be dipped, as Nora Cahill once said."

"That's not the reason you should be dipped. The reason you should be dipped is that he's an attorney. And he asked for Alphonse Santini at the desk."

"Wow. Meg, I think we should interrupt that bridge game."

"I think you're—Quill. If that's the bachelor party I hear, it's getting really out of hand. We'd better check that out first. It sounds like a riot."

Quill had heard sounds like that before: whoops, yells, screams of laughter, cheers, the thump of running feet. "Pamplona, Meg. The summer I spent in Madrid? With the foreign exchange group?"

The thrumming of running feet drew nearer and shook the walls of the solid old building. Marge burst from the conference room. Tutti, with a perplexed expression, trotted after her, her bridge cards in her hand. Her two other guards peered over Marge's shoulder.

"What'n the hell?" asked Marge.

The door at the end of the east end of the hall led to the Tavern Lounge. It shuddered, rattled, and for a moment seemed to bow outward from a massive weight on the other side. It burst open, to reveal Mayor Henry, naked but for a loincloth, with red stripes on his cheeks and his forehead painted stark white, dragging Claire's bridesmaid by the hand.

"Meredith!" called Quill. "Are you all right?"

"Let *go*, you geezer!" Meredith said irritably.

"Lances UP!" shouted the mayor.

"Lances UP!" came a male chorus in response.

"Lances UP, UP, UP!" yelled Evan Blight.

The members of S.O.A.P. stampeded through the hall like maddened buffalo. Most of them dragged a person of the opposite sex by the handiest protuberance: an arm here, a collar there, three or four by the hair, for those participants of H.O.W. and the bridal party whose hair was long enough for the S.O.A.P. snatch-and-grab technique. One of Harland Peterson's Norwegian cousins—a blacksmith notable for the breadth of his shoulders and the strength in his back—carried Esther West over his shoulder. She looked thoughtful. Her screams were perfunctory.

Evan Blight himself—womanless—cried, "On, men, on! Remember Romulus! Forward, in the name of Romulus. Lances UP! UP! UP!"

Meg and Quill shoved themselves against the wall. Marge and the rest of the bridge party beat a prudent retreat into the conference room, to reemerge as the sounds of the raid faded on the nighttime air.

"They left the back door open," Marge observed.

"I'll get it." Meg walked down the hall, turned around, walked back, and said crossly, "You didn't see Andy with those idiots?"

"They weren't carrying any lances," Tutti observed after a moment.

"Heck, no," said Marge. "The 'Lances UP!' part of this is pret' obvious. But who's this Romulus guy?"

"Um," said Quill. "The Sabines. He needed wives for his troops." She went to the west door, opened it, and peered out. "It's okay," she reported. "It's turned into a snowball fight." She paused. "And the women are winning."

Myles was late. Quill stood at the French doors to her balcony and watched the clearing sky. The storm left a swathe of tatterdemalion clouds. Stars emerged through the misty remnants like lilies floating up from the bottom of a pond. A chilly breeze sprang up. The moon came out. And Quill waited, a cup of coffee in her hand, until she heard him at the door.

CHAPTER 10

Sunlight crept across the lace coverlet Quill's grandmother had brought from England almost a century ago. The fabric lay in folds at the foot of the bed, and the sunshine threw the rose design into sharp relief. The years had aged the lace from white to cream. Quill, propped against the pillows, thought about how the lace had traveled for over ninety years, to end up here, covering her bed.

She was facing the large mullioned window that kept her bedroom light and airy, even in the depths of winter. The glass was old, perhaps even older than the lace, and her view of the snowy fields outside was distorted, wavy, as though she were underwater.

Myles walked in carrying a tray of coffee and fresh brioche. A pink rose nodded at her from a crystal vase, and the scent of the flower mingled with the odor of fresh yeast.

"Wow." She smiled at him. "You didn't go downstairs dressed like that?"

"Undressed like this?" He grinned. "The bread and the rose were outside the door. Doreen must have left it for you. Or Meg."

"How late is it?" asked Quill. She accepted a cup of coffee and held it steady as he climbed back in beside her.

"Ten o'clock."

"Oh, dear. I should get downstairs. The florist from Ithaca is bringing the flowers in this morning and they're going to decorate for the wedding. Meg's going to be all wrapped up in the kitchen. And John hates doing that stuff."

She set her coffee on the nightstand and stretched, then turned and burrowed into Myles's shoulder. "Well. Here we are again."

His hand, large and warm, smoothed her hair. "I wouldn't have given odds that I would see you again, like this. Wrapped in lace. With your hair tumbled down your shoulders."

She didn't answer right away. "So what about this blonde?"

"What blonde?"

She drew back her hand to punch him, and he caught it, kissed it, and clasped it in his own.

"Meg said that you're wasted as sheriff here in the village. That if it hadn't been for me, you would have taken a job like this global thingy a long time ago."

"That's probably true."

Quill sat up, indignant.

"But it would have been a stopgap. Until I found a village like this again. With someone like you in it."

"That's a . . . a . . . perplexing sort of statement."

"Is it? It's what I want. You. A family. A town small enough to know. A town large enough to be comfortable in. I'm forty-seven, Quill. And I'm tired. Not of life. But of the kinds of ambition that drove me when I was younger. I want a certain . . . orderliness to my daily life. That might be the wrong word. I don't believe that I want to see much more of humanity in the raw than I have already. I've had enough."

There was a puckered scar on his stomach from shrapnel, a dimpled hole in his right shoulder from a gunshot wound. Quill traced these marks with one forefinger. "In a way," she said at last, "I haven't seen enough."

"Mmm."

"Was that surprise?"

"I suppose it was. I think you're right."

"I love you." Her voice was husky. She cleared her throat. "I'm not whining, you understand. But why do women always have to choose? Between life outside and making a home?"

"If I were younger, you'd met me before I'd been satisfied I'd seen enough, maybe you wouldn't have to. We're at different stages, Quill. I don't want you to give anything up."

"I don't want you to give anything up, either." She sighed. "I wish I were a clone. Had a clone. Whatever."

His arm tightened around her shoulder. "Let's take it one day at a time. Now, I gather from what you said last night that Greenwald gave you quite a chase."

"Green . . . oh! The jerk in the pickup truck. You're sure my coat wasn't in it?"

"Positive. I've sent a couple of troopers out to search 81, but it doesn't look good. He dumped it before the rescue trucks got there. But the coat wouldn't be enough, Quill. It's circumstantial at best, unless we find either Nora's or Dorset's blood on it, and even if we do, we'd need harder evidence to convict."

"But you do think it's Santini?"

"I'm not willing to make that leap yet. What's his motive? Guesswork's hazardous in this business, Quill. So far, you're operating on mere surmise."

"Surmise." Quill made a face.

"Intuition? Feeling? What do you want me to say? You don't have any facts. You think that Nora Cahill was blackmailing Alphonse Santini, but you have no proof. And without that fundamental fact, Quill, the rest of the motive falls apart. Why would he kill Dorset? I admit that the videotape you said you saw—"

"I did see it."

"I know you did. But who is a jury going to believe? You can't convict a man of a capital crime on hearsay, Quill."

"But I have proof. Or at least I think I have proof. I didn't get a chance to tell you everything last night . . ."

He smiled.

She blushed, then went on, "But I took some disks from Nora's apartment."

"Quill." He stopped himself, then said with obvious patience, "I won't talk to you about breaking and entering. You know all about that already. But I have told you about the importance of the chain of evidence. And if you've entered the victim's apartment unlawfully and gathered it unlawfully . . ."

"Stop." Quill held up her hand. "I know all that. I told the H.O.W. members last night that if they found anything not to touch it, but to call you first."

Myles grabbed his forehead with both hands, in a gesture reminiscent of Meg. "You sent thirty women from a feminist organization careening through this Inn looking for evidence against Alphonse Santini?"

"The wedding is tomorrow. Then, he'll be gone. I feel awful about poor Claire. And I'm worried about Tutti."

Myles shut his eyes for a moment. "You don't have to worry about Tutti."

"Why not?"

"I'll let you know after I call New York this morning. I'd like to know something right now, though. Was it the H.O.W. search that kicked off the riot?"

"It wasn't exactly a riot," Quill said a little guiltily. "They didn't find anything, anyway. They all went home to nurse their bruises after that snowball fight. And besides, Myles, you're forgetting the hard drive."

"The hard drive?" He shook his head. "We're talking about you breaking into Nora's apartment again? You mean the hard drive for Nora's PC?"

"Yes! You have her laptop in custody, or whatever, don't you?"

"Yeah. It's been entered into evidence. We do."

"And her laptop was collected in a proper and legal way, wasn't it? Almost every newer PC backs up files automatically. There's bound to be a copy of whatever is on those disks in Nora's hard drive. So it doesn't matter if you can't submit the disks in evidence. You've got the hard drive. All the disks will do is give us the right kind of lead. I hope. They aren't labeled."

He rubbed his chin. "Hmm. You might be right. You still have the disks?"

"Right in my purse. And I can use John's PC to go through them. If you don't mind."

"I don't mind. I've got two murders to solve." He raised an eyebrow. "And I need all the help I can get. But first, I need a shave."

Quill kicked the covers off and jumped out of bed. "Last one in the shower's an unemployed sheriff."

"Eleven-thirty," said Meg. "I thought you two were never coming down."

"Don't be vulgar." Quill settled onto the stool at the butcher block counter and raised her cheek for Myles. He bent down and kissed her. Meg beamed.

"You two want some lunch?"

"He's off to apply a rubber hose to Joseph Greenwald," Quill said. "But I'd love some lunch."

"I'll get something at Marge's later," said Myles. He left, and the kitchen seemed suddenly empty.

"Crab cheese soup?" Meg asked.

"Sounds great. The dining room booked for lunch?" •

Meg glanced at the agenda posted on the wall. "Most of the wedding party's out skiing."

"Not Tutti," said Quill, alarmed.

"No, not Tutti. She and Doreen and Elaine are in your office hassling the florist about the flower delivery. The senator and one of the aides—it's either Frank or Marlon or Ed—are still upstairs making phone calls. Which is a lot better," Meg said cheerfully, "than any of them hassling me about the reception. Claire and the bridesmaids and the groomsmen are out skiing. There's a plot afoot to make Claire drunk, so she can actually go through with the wedding. Or maybe the plot's to make the senator drunk. Either way, nobody innocent's going to get hurt, if the nuptials do come off."

"Meg," Quill protested. "This is a tragedy shaping up. You're not being very kind."

"It's a tragedy all right," Meg said tartly, "but not the kind you think." She ladled a portion of the crab soup into a small crock and set it in front of Quill. "How sure are you that the senator's behind these murders?"

"Who else could it be?"

"Lots of people. Maybe this Joe Greenwald. Maybe . . ."

"Maybe who?"

"Maybe Tutti."

Quill put her spoon down. "That's ridiculous."

"Is it? Maybe she's setting Al up. Wouldn't you try to get him out of the way if he was going to marry your granddaughter?"

"I wouldn't commit two murders to do it. And if she's going to kill people, why doesn't she just go straight to the source of the problem and kill Al himself? You've been smoking funny cigarettes, Meg."

"Okay. So Tutti as murderer is a ludicrous idea. I'd just like to point out—"

"That I'm engaging in wild surmise?"

"Well, yeah."

"I've already been informed of the dangers of engaging in wild surmise. So let's change the subject."

"You want to change the subject because you want to solve this case all by yourself."

"Well, I do," Quill admitted. "But not all by myself. I've got a partner."

"Sure you do. Me."

Quill swallowed a spoonful of soup. Then another.

Meg's face changed. "Not me. Myles."

"Do you mind?"

Meg's eyelids flickered. "No." Then, "Yes. Yes, I think I do. This is a real reversal, Quill. Normally it's you looking out for me."

"I'm looking out for you!"

"Then that's not what I mean. I mean normally it's been the two of us. Together. Now it's not." Meg ran her hands slowly through her hair.

"So you do mind."

"It's just . . . different."

Quill couldn't think of anything to say to this. Except that just when you seemed to have one relationship problem solved, another popped up in its place. Meg drummed her fingers on the butcher block, pulled the agenda from the wall, and started making notes with a dull pencil. Her face was flushed.

After a moment, Quill said, "This is terrific soup." Then, "How many for the rehearsal dinner tonight?"

"Twenty. And it's a fabulous menu, Quill. I'm having the best time. I've made a brandied fruit compote, a squash soufflé, and the pièce de résistance—potted rabbit." The flush on her face had faded to two bright red spots.

"Rabbit." Quill bit her lip and chuckled. "Is this an unsubtle signal to the senator?"

"Is what a signal? What?" Alphonse Santini banged through the swinging doors into the kitchen. Both women jumped. "So you heard already? I think it's a sign, too. Like, I shouldn't be getting married again. I mean, one ball and chain in a lifetime's enough, you get my drift. The old lady's loaded, but still. Shit."

"It's Tutti that's—er—loaded?" Quill asked casually. "I thought it was Vittorio, her son."

"In that family, where the money comes from isn't the issue. It's who's got the balls. And in that family, it's Tutti."

"Then how come . . ." Quill began. She stopped. She couldn't very well ask Santini to his face why Tutti—if she was the driving force in the McIntosh family—was permitting a marriage to go forward of which she clearly didn't approve.

"Then how come what?" Santini moved restlessly around the kitchen, snapping his fingers. He stuck a finger in the soup crock, licked it off, and moved to stick it in again.

Meg took two long strides forward and moved the crock out of reach. "Is there something specific we can help you with, Senator?"

"This dinner tonight. The rehearsal dinner, we got a problem."

Meg raised her eyebrows politely. "With what?"

"Can't have the rehearsal in the church. It's drifted in and the plows can't get to it until later today. So we'll want to push the dinner back, see, and have the rehearsal here, about nine o'clock."

"How far back?" There was an ominous note in Meg's voice.

Quill slid off the stool and said hastily, "It really isn't necessary, is it, Senator? There's been such a lot of disruption around here lately, it'd make life a lot easier for everyone if we just kept to the original schedule." She grabbed him by the arm, guided him back to the dining room, started to ask him how his dinner had been the night before, realized that the reenactment of the rape of the Sabines had probably altered his view of the hospitality offered by the Inn, and blurted out instead, "Why did you send Joseph Greenwald to burglarize Nora Cahill's apartment?"

"Huh?" His eyes narrowed to slits. "You out of your mind, throwing around crap like that? Joe Greenwald?" He grabbed her by her upper arms and thrust his face close to hers. "Joey doesn't even work for me," he hissed. "And if he did, which he doesn't, what the hell were you doing in that broad's apartment?!"

Quill regarded him as steadily as possible with her heart pounding and her hands damp. "I'm onto you, Senator Santini. So are a lot of other people. If I were you . . ."

His grip tightened. He was stronger than he looked. "Well,

you aren't, you little bitch. And let me tell you something . . . Goddammit." He dropped his grip abruptly. "I never should have gotten into this. Married to a whining cow. For what? Money. Goddamned money."

"Alphonse!" Tutti's voice cut across the dining room like a sledgehammer. She stood in the doorway to the foyer, erect, her face stem. Quill had the sudden, eerie feeling that the genial, sweet-voiced grandmother who believed in spirits had been replaced by a refugee from a *Godfather* movie.

Santini dropped his hands and backed off. "Sorry, Gramma."

Sunlight flashed off the rhinestones in Tutti's spectacles, obscuring her eyes. There was an uneasy silence. She resumed, in tones approaching her normal voice, "I thought you were planning on skiing with Claire, Alphonse."

"Yeah, yeah."

"Don't yeah, yeah me." The whiplash was back.

"Tutti?" Elaine fluttered behind her, a moth against her mother-in-law's stolidity. "The flowers are here. Shall I tell them to bring them in? Quill?" Her voice trailed off into its usual inaudibility. She was wearing yet another long-sleeved blouse with lacy sleeves and high collar, and looked fragile, despite her substantial curves.

Quill stepped away from Santini. "I'm sorry, Elaine, I wasn't paying attention. Would you like me to talk to the delivery people? Are the Cornell students here to do the decorating? They are? Then it shouldn't take too long to have the whole dining room looking wonderful."

"The church," muttered Elaine. Her eyes teared up.

"We'll put the flowers for the church on the terrace. They won't freeze and they'll keep just fine until morning. Then we'll whip over to the church and get them up."

Tutti gave a discreet little cough. "We'll see you at dinner tonight, then, Alphonse." The benign grandmother was back. Alphonse snarled at the three of them and stamped off, presumably, Quill hoped, to cool off skiing down the slope of the gorge.

"Well, dear," Tutti said briskly. "Let's get those roses up."

"You'll have to excuse me, Tutti, Elaine. But I have some pressing business in the office," said Quill. She badly wanted to go through the computer disks, if only to save Claire and her female relatives the embarrassment of having Alphonse Santini hauled off to jail at the church door.

Tutti fixed her with a gimlet eye. "My dear. I have no wish to be more direct than necessary. But my family and I have spent a great deal of time—and money—at your Inn. I would appreciate it if you would help in the arrangement of the flowers." Her rose-leaf cheeks crumpled in a smile. "It won't take very long at all."

The dining room was decorated in less than two hours. And it was because Tutti, Quill realized, had the instinct, if not the outright talents, of a second Napoleon. "Except there *were* two, weren't there? Or three?" she murmured aloud.

"Three what, dear? No! Redo that swag, young man. I want all the roses facing out. And the drape needs to be loosened just a little. That's it. That's too far. Put it back. Good." She clapped her hands. "I want this mess cleaned up and all of you gone. Five minutes." The crew went to work with a will.

Quill turned slowly in a circle. "It's not just good, Tutti. It's beautiful."

"It is, isn't it?" Her faded blue eyes sparkled. "I never had a formal wedding myself, my dear. I took a great many pains with this one."

"The rose swags were designed by . . ." Elaine leaned forward and whispered a name most of America knew into Quill's ear. "But he wouldn't come here to direct it himself, of course. So Tutti said she'd do it."

"Why wouldn't he come himself?" asked Quill. She caught the exchange of glances between the two older women.

Tutti said tactfully, "Well, it's the family, dear."

"Nonsense," said Quill. "Shaw was right, you know. Good manners don't have anything to do with whether you treat a shop girl like a duchess, good manners have to do with whether you treat a duchess like a shop girl."

"I'm afraid I don't quite understand, dear," said Tutti.

"Just that plumbing money is morally neutral. It's what you do with it that says whether or not you have taste. And this is wonderful."

Quill looked around the dining room again and was delighted.

It must have cost the earth, but the florist had delivered outdoor roses in the depths of December. The vibrant peach-orange of Sutter's Gold, the full glorious yellow of Faust, the paler yellow of Golden Fleece were all mixed in glorious confusion with the rich reds of Frenshman and Dickson's Flame. An ivy of a deep, pure green twined around the rose bouquets, interspersed here and there with full-leaved fern. The rose garlands hung from the long windows, swung gracefully from the center chandelier, and twined down freestanding vases in the corners.

"It smells like June," Quill said. "It's amazing."

"Now," Tutti said briskly. "The crate's arrived with the table linens. Elaine, dear, if you'd go find that nice groundskeeper . . ."

"Mike," said Quill.

"Mike, and ask him to wheel it in here, we'll set out the tablecloths for this evening. Then tomorrow, Sarah, we'll use the white damask and the linen napkins. But tonight is a quiet, family celebration, so we don't need to be as formal." She smiled at Quill as Elaine left in search of Mike. "I had a chintz sent directly from England. It has a wonderful Chinese yellow background with aquamarine accents. It just makes these roses."

"Tutti," Quill began. She hesitated. "I thought . . . Forgive me, I don't mean to be rude. But do you want Claire to marry Alphonse Santini?"

"Of course I do. It's time we had a little political connection in the family. At least, one that we can count on." She twinkled at Quill's expression. "You can't count on money alone, my dear. Blood ties are everything."

"Oh," said Quill. "But, Tutti. What you said about the rabbit. At the séance. You know who killed Nora and Sheriff Dorset. I don't understand. I don't understand at all."

"You think Alphonse was responsible?" Tutti took a small muslin handkerchief from her purse and patted her cheeks. "That's warm work, decorating. Well. My little messages to Alphonse were more in the nature of letting him know who's the head of the family. Not, my dear, that that's any of your business. As far as I'm concerned, if Claire wants him, she can have him. As long as he treats her well. As long as he understands the rules."

"But murder, Tutti. If you know something, you really have to tell the police. Have you met Sheriff McHale? He's wonderful. A wonderful sheriff, I mean. And you won't find it difficult to talk to him at all."

Tutti began to laugh. It was a warm rich laugh, and it made Quill think of her father's mother, a round woman with a joy of life that was infectious. Quill touched her arm. "I don't want to upset you. But I'm almost sure that the senator is behind these murders. And since Sheriff McHale's been here, every single murder that's been committed in Hemlock Falls has been solved. All this beauty," Quill said. "I just hope it's not wasted."

"We'll be fine, my dear. Just fine." Her pink cheeks got a little pinker. "There's Dina. Yoo-hoo! Here we are, dear."

"'Scuse me, Quill?" Dina, unusually tentative, crossed the dining room with a hesitant air.

"Now, Dina, did you call that young nephew of mine?" Tutti asked fondly. She pinched Dina's cheek. "He's first-year law, Cornell," she said to Quill. "The poor boy doesn't have time to find himself a nice girl, so when Dina came to the Welcoming—those of us with the Gift don't call it a séance—it's so—Fox sisters, if you know what I mean. We call it a Welcoming. So, you called him?"

"Your nephew Anthony, Mrs. Mc—I mean, Tutti. No. There's this botanist I've been dating—"

"Botanist!" said Tutti. "What kind of living does a botanist make? Now a young lawyer . . ."

"Well, there's one to see you," said Dina. "A Mr. Greenwald."

"Oh, really?" said Quill. "I certainly would like to see him, too, Tutti."

"Joey? Here? How nice!" Tutti beamed at them both. "He's engaged, though, to my brother's third daughter, Christina. A beautiful girl."

"Where is he, Dina?" Quill asked grimly.

"I put him in your office." She gave Tutti an apologetic glance, leaned forward, and whispered in Quill's ear, "Meg said that's the guy who tried to kill you!"

Quill nodded.

"Shall I get a gun or something? John's got that rifle he uses for rabid woodchucks and stuff."

Quill shook her head. "How does Greenwald look?"

"Pretty banged up. His arm's in a sling and his face is purple."

"Oh, dear."

Quill marched after Tutti and found her fussing over Joseph Greenwald, who was, to Quill's guilty satisfaction, looking very banged up. He rose to his feet as she came in. Quill folded her arms and glared at him.

"I see you've met," Tutti said comfortably. "Sit down, dear." She settled herself behind Quill's desk and waved at the couch.

Quill sat.

"I received a phone call from Joseph this morning, after your sheriff had a little interview with him down at the Municipal Building."

Quill blinked at her.

"Joseph is a young member of a law firm that has represented my family's interests for years," Tutti said.

"Then you absolutely need another law firm, Tutti. This man tried to run me off the road last night. In the storm."

"Why in the world would he want to do that?" Tutti cocked her head. One white curl fell charmingly over her left ear. She patted it back into place. "If Joseph was following you, and I say if, it was because perhaps you had something that belongs to me."

"Belongs to you?"

"What are those little things called, dear? You know, they stick them into those machines all the young people have these days."

"Computer disks?" Quill, perhaps because she'd had a late night, was feeling a little faint.

"That's it. Computer disks." She turned to Joseph, who had resumed his seat next to Quill on her couch. "Now, Joey. What's the number of that New York State statute you were telling me about?"

"The breaking and entering statute? Or the fraudulent impersonation statute?"

Tutti turned her blue gaze onto Quill. There was a scene in *Jaws* that had scared the dickens out of her as a little kid. The one where Bruce the shark pulls along the boat, and his flat black eye hypnotizes Robert Shaw. "Either one," said Tutti, with a click of her white teeth. "Either one."

"I have no idea what you're talking about." Quill kept her hands still and her voice steady.

Tutti pulled out a jeweled compact, a lipstick, and frowned at herself in the mirror. Then she reapplied the lipstick, put the compact away, and said, "Rita the security guard does. The boy from the pizza parlor who stuck the flyer under the windshield of that battered Oldsmobile of yours does. On the other hand—if you said that you'd met Joseph on Interstate 81 headed north—there wouldn't be anyone who could gainsay that—or prove it, either. You see, dear." She leaned forward. "No witnesses." She sat back. "We'll wait here."

"It's not going to do you any good." Quill stood up. "You know about computers, Mr. Greenwald."

"Some."

"What type did Nora Cahill use?"

He shrugged.

"I can give you a hint. Those software disks you found in the box of her office equipment? It was the latest edition of Microsoft Word. Practically every PC with the power to run that software automatically backs up files. Even if Nora erased it, the likelihood of one of those disk doctors being able to recover it is pretty high. And you know who has her laptop?"

"Who?" Tutti demanded.

Joseph Greenwald rubbed his forehead. "Mrs. McIntosh, ah, McHale's got it."

"The local sheriff?" she asked sharply. "How much trouble can we get from a local sheriff?"

"He's not just any local sheriff."

Quill got up. "If you two will excuse me, I have some work to do."

Tutti jerked her chin at Greenwald.

"If you don't mind, Ms. Quilliam, we'd like to recover our property despite the—er—circumstances."

There was a long silence.

"They're in my room," Quill said finally.

"Go with her," snapped Tutti. She got to her feet with a groan. "This arthritis is acting up again. I'm going to have a hot bath before the dinner." She patted Quill's arm. "I hope we see you there, my dear. In one of those lovely velvet gowns like the one you wore last night." She patted Quill's cheek. Quill had to restrain herself from biting her.

"And you gave them to her?" Meg asked, several hours later. She was standing at the Aga, an egg whisk in one hand and her copper sauté pan in the other. A brown sauce was bubbling in the pan. It smelled rich, earthy and winey. Quill, dressed for the evening in bronze silk, nibbled at a piece of sourdough bread.

"What else could I do? I can just see poor Howie trying to defend me on felony charges of breaking and entering."

"It's a misdemeanor, I think. Depending on what you swiped. Whatever. Tell me I was right. She *is* the murderer."

Quill cut a piece of Stilton from the wheel Meg had set out for the rehearsal dinner. She added it to the bread.

"Will you stop?" Meg said testily. "You're wrecking the display."

"Okay. You were right. But you were right for the wrong reasons. I can't believe you care about the quality of the food you're going to serve to a family whose business is organized crime. And a sweet little old lady who's capable of knocking off six people before breakfast."

"It's not whether you win or lose, it's how you play the game," Meg said obscurely. "And you don't know that they're members of organized crime."

"Ha!"

"Or that Tutti's the Godmother."

"Ha, again. It should be obvious to the meanest intelligence."

"What's obvious to the meanest intelligence is that you're still no further in discovering who killed Nora and Dorset and why."

"If we could just find some hard evidence," said Quill. "The videotape. Or my coat. Even my hat, which has got to have blood on it."

"Whoosh." Meg shuddered. She dropped the whisk, startled. "Darn it, do you hear that? You don't suppose it's those idiots from S.O.A.P. again?"

Quill listened: muffled barks and equally muffled curses, followed by the crash of a mop against the floor. "Tatiana," she said. "From the dining room. Maybe she caught another mouse. And

that's Doreen whacking along behind her. She seems to have taken
a liking to Doreen."

"That'll shorten her life." Meg dipped a spoon into the sauce,
tasted it, scowled, and dumped it down the sink. She rinsed out her
copper bowl and began to reassemble the sauce. Tatiana's barks
came closer, accompanied by the thump of tennis shoes against carpet. There was the *skritch-skritch-skritch* of canine claws against
the dining room doors. Quill pushed them open. Tatiana burst in,
barks at an hysterical pitch.

"You did catch a mouse," Quill said. "Ugh. Good girl."

Doreen stamped in behind her. "That ain't a mouse. It's a hat.
Your hat. And there's blood all over it."

CHAPTER 11

"Catch that dog!" Meg screamed.

"I'm tryin'!" Doreen thwacked the mop on the floor. Tatiana
raced around the kitchen, the rabbit hat flapping in her jaws. Bjarne
jumped, cursed in Finn, and leaped out of the way, a serving of
squash soufflé held high above his head.

"Wait!" Quill commanded. She grabbed a leg of potted rabbit
(despite Meg's agonized cries of "My dinner!") and crouched down
on the floor. "Here, doggie, good doggie."

"Don't you dare give that dog my good food, Sarah Quilliam!"

Tatiana came to a halt next to the boot box at the back door.
She sat down, the hat dangling from her jaws. Her little black eyes
glared malevolently over the bedraggled rabbit fur. She growled.
Doreen growled back.

"Don't, Doreen." Quill inched forward, the roasted rabbit held
temptingly in one hand. "Gooood dog."

The back door opened. Tatiana whirled. John walked in. Tatiana leaped past him and into the night.

"No!" Meg, Quill, and Doreen yelled simultaneously.

"Good grief," John said.

"The hat!" Meg shouted.

All four of them dove out the back door.

The sun was setting in a modest blaze of pink. Shadows crawled across the snow-covered garden. The air was damp and still. The dog spun in circles on the snowy path, apparently chasing its tail. The hat sat in a sodden lump near a stalk of brussels sprouts, on top of a pile of cow manure. Quill snatched it up. "My hat," she mourned. "It's a mess."

"You shut up," Doreen said to the dog. "Get in there. Now!"

Tatiana considered this command for a long moment, her head cocked to one side, then followed the four of them back to the kitchen. Quill put the hat on the butcher block counter.

"That is a bad thing to do to a hat," Bjarne observed over Quill's shoulder. "Shall I give the little dog a treat?"

"You can give the little dog a kick in the butt," Doreen growled. "Here. Gimme that." She snatched the scrap of fat from Bjarne and held it out. "C'mere, you."

Tatiana sat down, scratched her neck ruff furiously with her hind leg, stretched, grinned, then accepted the piece of fat with a contemptuous air.

"Where did she find it, Doreen?" Quill took a long-handled fork and turned the hat over. "It's a mess."

"Outside somewheres." Doreen took a Kleenex from her apron, sneezed, and wiped her nose. "We went out for walkies . . ."

"For what?" asked John.

"Walkies," Doreen said impatiently, "so she could do her business. We went on down to the park and she run off in the woods and come back with this."

They stared at it. The hat was fashioned after the style affected by World War II Chinese generals. The inside of the crown and the earflaps were lined with rabbit fur. The flaps could be drawn up over the top of the hat and fastened together with a button, or worn down over the ears and fastened beneath the chin.

It shed rabbit hair, continually.

"Why d'ya ever buy the durn thing?" asked Doreen.

"It's warm," Quill said defensively. "And I've never been all that fashion conscious."

"I know corpses more fashion conscious than you," Doreen agreed. "It sure is some mess." Snow, blood, cow manure, and dog saliva matted the hat from crown to chin strap.

"There's blood all along the inside," John observed. "The murderer was wearing this hat on the videotape, Quill? And in the cell block, when he knifed Dorset?"

"Yes. And I agree with you. There shouldn't be any blood inside the hat. At least, I don't know how it could have gotten there."

"Maybe it got knocked off in the cell block in the struggle with Dorset," Meg suggested. "You said he was bleeding pretty badly."

Quill shuddered at the memory. "It's possible. I couldn't see all that much. I didn't want to see all that much. But it's possible."

John threw a glance at the kitchen clock. "I've got to get to the dining room to seat the McIntosh party." He shrugged himself out of his parka, pulled off his sweater, and put on the tweed sports coat he normally wore throughout the day. "The van from the Marriott's out front with the overflow guests. I told the driver to come in here for some food." He poked at the rabbit hat with a tentative finger. "You might want to put this somewhere before he comes in to eat."

"I'll give Myles a call and tell him the dog's found it." said Quill. "Let's stick it in the storeroom, in the meantime."

"I've got a crazy suggestion," Meg said irascibly. "Why don't we try serving this meal in the meantime."

"Murders come and murders go, but food goes on forever?" said Quill. "Okay. Okay! You're right. John and I will get out to that rehearsal dinner and grin, grin, grin at the horrible senator."

Meg eyed her potted rabbit with satisfaction. "At least the condemned is getting a hearty meal. If you two are going to serve it, that is."

"You go on ahead, John. I'll just give Myles a call."

Quill dialed the familiar number from the kitchen phone. The sheriff, Deputy Dave informed her, was out, talking to some computer guy at Cornell about Nora Cahill's laptop. He'd be back around seven-thirty.

Quill left an urgent-please-call message with Davy, who said that he hoped there were no hard feelings over her recent incarceration.

Quill said certainly not, and Davy, emboldened, offered the information that Bernie Bristol had resigned his justiceship in the wake of the unfortunate publicity surrounding Nora Cahill's death. The mayor, Davy told her, was practically on his knees to Mr. Murchison to return as justice, who had told him, the mayor, to go fly a kite.

"So there's a bare possibility," Quill said to John a few moments later in the dining room, "that Adela will get that justice job."

She smiled as Claire and Tutti walked in, and said out of the corner of her mouth, "And if she is elected, I hope her first job is to arraign Senator Santini. For murder."

Having caught at least her fiancé's name in this murmured speech, Claire said, "A-al's not *here* yet," in her nasal whine, and slouched over to the table by the window. Quill pulled a chair out for her and commented on the beauty of the rose garlands as Claire sat down.

"They're all right, I guess," Claire said listlessly. "Where's Mummy?"

"Still getting dressed, dear." Tutti beamed at the tablecloths. "Sarah, you have an eye. What do you think?"

"They're wonderful," Quill said sincerely. For whether or not Tutti was, as she suspected, the head of a large criminal organization of Italian (and Scot) descent, she clearly had taste. If not on her own, at least taste that she was willing to purchase. The tablecloths shouldn't have worked with the natural flowers and the mauve carpeting, but they did. The print was of brilliantly colored roses. They splashed across the tables; the pattern was tiny, the colors vivid. The heavy linen napkins were aquamarine, the china a creamy white rimmed with platinum. Claire sat in the middle of this splendor with a sallow face and a discontented mouth.

Meg came out of the kitchen and toward the party. She was dressed in her chef's coat, a specially made tunic that had been a present from Helena Houndswood, the celebrity chef who had visited the Inn two years before. The tunic was made of fine white wool, with full sleeves that ended in neat narrow cuffs at Meg's wrists. Her cheeks were pink from the heat in the kitchen and her gray eyes serene. Quill was swept with affection and then wondered, briefly, at her own emotions. She jerked a little in surprise: despite everything, the two bodies, her night in jail, the discontented bride in front of her, she realized that she was happy.

She took Meg's hand in her own and brought her to the table. "For those of you who haven't met her yet, this is our chef, Margaret Quilliam."

Polite applause swept the table.

"I'd like to welcome you to the Inn," Meg said. "Our partner, John Raintree, will be serving chilled champagne in a moment, so that Quill and he and I, in fact all of us here at the Inn at Hemlock Falls, can toast Claire and the senator, and wish them the very best."

"Hang on a second," said Marlon. "I want to get this on tape!" He took a mini-camcorder from the case sitting by his chair, then circled the table, the camera whirring. Meg straightened her collar uncertainly. Quill ducked out of camera range.

"But Al's not here yet!" Claire said.

Quill exchanged a glance with Meg. "Why don't I go upstairs and see if he's still in his room. I do know that he went out skiing fairly late. He may just have gotten back."

"Tell Elaine and Vittorio to come down, too, will you, dear?" Tutti, who was looking especially grandmotherly in pink lace over gray satin, gave Quill a decisive little nod.

"I'd like to tell you what we'll be serving tonight," Meg went on. "For the first course, I've developed a clear game soup seasoned with a combination of herbs we grow right here at the Inn."

Quill went into the foyer. The chair behind the reception desk was empty. Dina had left that morning to go home for the holidays. Mike had filled the Oriental vases near the cobblestone fireplace with fresh pine, and the scent filled this small area. Quill drew a deep breath. It was like being in the woods. The fire was low in the fireplace, and she bent to put a fresh log on it. The odor of burning apple wood joined that of the pine.

"It smells wonderful in here." Myles came in the front door. Snow powdered the shoulders of his heavy anorak and the heels of his boots. His face was red with cold. Quill went to him and put her warm hands on his cheeks. He kissed her. She put her arms around him, inside his jacket. She could feel his heart beating against her hands.

"Davy said you called. Is anything wrong?"

"We found the hat. Or rather, Tatiana found the hat. My hat."

His eyebrows drew together.

"Oh, it's Tutti's little dog. Apparently, Tutti dragooned Doreen into taking it, I mean her, for her constitutional in the park. The dog ran off and came back with the hat. I stuck it—the hat, I mean—in the storeroom." She looked around vaguely. "I don't know where Tatiana is. Doreen's stuck with her, I suppose. Anyway, the hat's there whenever you need it. How did the interview with Greenwald go?"

Myles's gray eyes narrowed. "The guy's slick. You're sure that no one saw him after you on the interstate?"

Quill shook her head. "Positive. The snow was awful."

"Greenwald didn't come right out and say it, but he intimated that a couple of witnesses could place you at Cahill's apartment."

"He's right. I wasn't very careful, I guess."

"Quill, you shouldn't have gone there in the first place."

"True, true, true. Sorry. I'll know better next time. It turned out to be useless, anyway. Greenwald practically blackmailed me into giving him those computer disks. As a matter of fact, he did blackmail me. He threatened me with impersonation and breaking and entering. So I gave him the computer disks."

"Hmm. It doesn't matter. You were right about Nora's hard drive. The computer boys in Ithaca found—"

"Sarah, my dear. Can you encourage my daughter-in-law to join us? We're waiting that delicious dinner on her and my son."

"Tutti." Quill pulled away from Myles's arms. "I haven't been up there yet. Have you met Sheriff McHale?"

Joseph Greenwald, his dinner jacket slung over his shoulder to accommodate his broken arm, appeared behind Tutti. Ed—or maybe it was Marlon—joined him and stood on her right.

"How do you do, Sheriff?" Tutti's eyes gleamed behind her glasses. "You've met my boy Joseph. And this is my boy Marlon Guppa."

Myles nodded and said, "Ma'am," which made Quill want to giggle.

"I'll be back in a minute with Elaine, Tutti. Myles, Meg's set aside some food for you in the kitchen. I think she put it in the storeroom."

Quill ran lightly up the stairs to the Adams suite on the second floor. She knocked, received no answer, then knocked again. She called out Santini's name, then took her master key from the chain around her neck and let herself in.

She turned on the overhead light. Doreen had been in to clean, and the room was neat. Quill and Meg had managed to save the chestnut floor in this particular set of rooms, and the yellow, striated wood gleamed softly in the lamplight. The suite was two rooms. In the living room, a Queen Anne style sofa sat in front of the small fireplace next to a wing chair covered in a Williamsburg print. The coffee table held a filled ashtray and a half-empty glass. Quill picked up the glass and sniffed. Scotch. So the senator had been in the room after Doreen had cleaned. She searched the small secretary that stood under the window. The stationery with the Inn logo was there, and a partially filled pack of matches, but that was it. No briefcase, no notes, no documents.

She went into the bedroom. The king-sized bed was covered with a wedding-ring quilt. The cherry rocking chair next to the four-poster held a crumpled envelope. Quill picked it up. It was empty. The return address was for the Golden Pillar Travel Agency. Typed on the front of the envelope were the words: "Enclosed, please find your ticket! Thank you for your business." It was addressed by hand to Marlon Guppa.

Quill opened the armoire: empty.

Maybe Santini'd stopped off at the Croh Bar in town after skiing and forgotten the time. She'd known quite a few Hemlockians to stop off at the Croh Bar and forget what day of the week it was. Except that he wouldn't take his suitcase, his clothes, his briefcase, and the contents of an envelope from a travel agency to go skiing, or drink at the Croh Bar, or go anywhere at all in Hemlock Falls.

Poor Claire.

Poor Myles.

She picked up the phone by the bed and dialed the kitchen. Meg answered, her voice impatient.

"Is Myles there?"

"I was just about to feed him. I will feed him and my twenty guests if you'll get off the phone!"

"Tell him it looks like Santini's skipped town. I'm in his room and everything's gone."

There was a short silence. "Wow," said Meg. "Sorry I snapped. Well, there's one good thing. At least I won't be serving a murderer."

Quill thought of Tutti and her two "boys." "I wouldn't be too sure about that."

The McIntoshes had taken a pair of adjoining rooms on the same floor as the Adams suite. Quill let herself out of Santini's room and walked down the hall to 246. She mentally rehearsed a few lines: *Elaine, Vittorio, I'm so sorry, but the senator seems to have skipped. Very probably with the cash from the murder of Nora Cahill in his pocket. And to avoid prosecution for two murders.*

She raised her hand to knock and heard the sound of angry voices; Vittorio's harsh and bullying, Elaine's soft and tearful. Quill turned away. She'd go downstairs and give the room a call from the front desk. Vittorio's voice rose; there was the sound of a blow. Elaine cried out.

Quill's reaction was instant and unconsidered. She whirled and pounded on the door. The voices within stopped, except for the soft sounds of Elaine's tears. Quill pounded on the door again. Vittorio jerked it open and pushed his angry bulk into the hall. "What the hell do you want?"

"Tutti was a little concerned and asked me to come up and find you. Dinner's waiting."

"Beat it."

Quill placed her palm against Vittorio's shoulder and shoved him out of the way. She walked into the bedroom. It was chaotic: clothes were draped over every available surface, cosmetics littered the small dressing table under the window, and three suitcases lay open on the floor. It was the bedroom of an untidy child.

Elaine sat on the edge of her bed, rubbing her wrist. She was in a silk full slip, pale pink. She looked at Quill with swimming eyes.

Vittorio came partway in and half-knocked, half-slammed the open door with his fist. He was wearing a dinner jacket. The smell of a heavy aftershave—*Polo*, Quill thought—floated across the room.

"You coming down, Lanie?"

She sat very still.

"Elaine!"

She stirred. "Yes, Vic. I'll be right there."

"You. It's Quilliam, right?" He jerked his head toward the hall. "I told you to beat it."

"I'll just give Elaine a hand."

He gave a short, unpleasant laugh. "Suit yourself."

"Close the door on your way out," Quill said softly.

Elaine jumped when it slammed shut. Quill sat down next to her on the bed and gently lifted her arm. "This is why you wear the long-sleeved blouses?"

"He doesn't mean it," Elaine said, so quietly that Quill had to bend her head to hear her.

Quill touched her wrist gently. "That's already pretty red. And the ones farther up look old. It must have been going on for a while."

Elaine dabbed at her eyes with a Kleenex. "My makeup's a mess. And I've got to get down there to the dinner." She got up and crossed to the dressing table.

"Elaine, there're lots of people that can help you. There's even a group in the village, attached to the hospital. It's a shelter. The woman that runs it is terrific. Why don't you let me give her a call?"

Elaine dabbed at her face with a powder puff, then reapplied her eyeliner.

"Meg's good—um—friend is our local internist. He's a pretty good listener. Would you like to talk to him?"

Elaine picked up a red lipstick, set it down, and selected a gloss. She turned and went to the closet and took out a long filmy dress in pink. Full sleeves. High collar. She bent to step into the dress.

Quill's stomach lurched. She pinched her own knee hard, then managed to say lightly, "I didn't know Vittorio smoked."

A faint smile crossed Elaine's face. She pulled her slip away from her chest and looked down at her breasts. "He quit for almost twenty years. This business with Al got him started again."

"What business with Al?"

She shook her head.

"Can I get you some antibiotic cream?"

"I'll be fine."

"You shouldn't let those burns go. And you shouldn't irritate them with cloth." Quill's voice rose; she was shaking with anger. "Why don't you do something to help yourself? And if you can't, let me. Does Claire know?"

"Oh, no!" Elaine turned pale. "Claire worships her father."

"I'll bet." Quill rubbed her face with both hands. "What about Tutti? Could she be any help? Now that's stupid. He's her son."

Elaine zipped her dress up, slipped into a pair of pink high-heeled shoes, and took up a pearl-beaded purse. She looked at herself in the mirror, then took a double row set of pearls from the top of the dresser and fastened them around her neck.

"What do you think?"

"Elaine."

She smiled. "He won't do it anymore. He promised."

"Elaine, every battered woman in the world believes that. You've got to do something to help yourself."

"Oh, no I don't. You don't know Tutti. She'll fix it. She'll fix everything."

Quill walked to the dining room with her. Vittorio was seated at the head of the table. The chair at the foot, near Claire, was still empty. Quill seated Elaine at Vittorio's right. She was afraid to say anything. Even to do anything. She'd heard that abusers took revenge when they were confronted—not on people like her, who would fight back, but on their original victims.

Tutti, at Vittorio's left, cast a shrewd glance at Quill, and said, "Doesn't Elaine look wonderful, Vic?"

"Yeah. Great. How long are we supposed to wait to eat?"

"I'm sure Al will be here any minute, Daddy." Claire crumbled a piece of bread between her fingers. "He's late all the time. And you said he had some appointments, Marlon, didn't you? With that little creepy person? The mayor?"

"Yes, Miss McIntosh. But he should have been back by now."

Quill let her gaze rest on Marlon for a long moment. His dark brown eyes shifted under her steady gaze. "The sheriff's in the kitchen right now. Why don't I ask him to put out a call? If the senator's in the village, someone should know where he is. Maybe he got lost on his way back to the Inn."

Marlon jumped. "Oh. Hell. We don't need to do that, Miss Quilliam. He'll show up sooner or later."

"In the meantime," Tutti said firmly, "I would like to eat. Your sister's prepared quite a meal for us, Sarah. I can't wait. The senator will just have to eat leftovers."

"I'll let the kitchen know." She smiled. She hoped no one noticed how strained it was. She resisted the impulse to whistle a few bars of "Flying Down to Rio." "Enjoy your meal, everyone. And let us know if there's anything else you need . . ."

". . . like a bridegroom," she muttered as she walked into the kitchen. Myles, Meg, and John were sitting at the counter, all three of them eating potted rabbit. Quill put her hands on her hips and glared at them. "Myles, I thought you'd be halfway to the airport by now. You're not going to let him get away?"

"What's this?" John asked. "I just got here."

"Santini's skipped. As in beat feet, left town, took a powder?" Meg said flatly.

John whistled. "Wow."

Myles swallowed a bite of rabbit and said calmly, "You're sure about that, Quill?"

"I don't know what other explanation there could be, Myles. His room's empty. His suitcase is gone. There's an empty airline ticket envelope. If you ask me, he took that blackmail money from Nora Cahill and just . . . skipped, and Tutti set it up. Why aren't you after him?"

"Wow," Meg said again. "Does Claire know?"

"No. And they want to start eating."

"Oh. Good." Meg hopped off the stool. "Bjarne! Guys! We're ready."

Quill took Meg's place at the counter and absently began to eat the rabbit. "This is just great," she said. "I'm so glad everyone's reacting to my hot tip. Myles. Are you going to put out an APB on Santini or not? He's probably halfway to Argentina now, or wherever it is that international felons escape to." She put her fork down.

"I'm sorry. That sounded bitchy. It's just that this is so awful. Poor Claire's in there and I don't know which is worse, being jilted or being married to a murderer."

"There's no law or statute against refusing to get married. And the senator isn't our murderer. Santini couldn't have killed either Nora or Dorset," said Myles. "Santini was out with the mayor and Evan Blight the night of the murders, from about eight until well after midnight."

"When did you find that out?" asked Quill.

"This afternoon. One of the women involved in the—er—fracas with S.O.A.P. wanted to swear out a complaint against Blight and the mayor. It was a good opportunity to find out just what goes on at those meetings."

"What does?" demanded Quill.

Myles grinned. "Never mind. The alibi is supported by something else. Those computer files of Cahill's. It was a complete plan to sweep small-town America with a campaign called R.O.A.R., Return Our American Rights. You have the honor, Quill, of being the first candidate to kick this campaign off. Dorset, Bristol, and a number of other small town dignitaries from across New York State were involved."

Quill bit her lip. "So Santini didn't do it! Who, then?"

John got up suddenly, his face grim. "Your hat, Quill. Where is it?"

"The storeroom."

"Hang on a minute." John disappeared into the back and reappeared with the hat. He set it on the counter carefully, avoiding touching the bloody spot inside. "Take a look at this, Myles."

"Swell," said Quill. "Myles? Where are you going? You haven't finished your rabbit."

Myles stood up. His face was calm. "What you just told me about Santini being missing? It doesn't make sense. Tutti McIntosh was funding this whole R.O.A.R campaign. It was designed to put the senator back into his seat in four years. Al struck me as the sort of person who'd marry the devil herself for gain."

"Thanks for the pronoun," Quill grumbled. "So what do you think? Why else would Al skip out on his wedding?"

"We need Doreen," said Myles. "And that dog. There's hair, blood, and bone on the inside of that hat. And neither of our corpses had a head wound."

Quill's winter clothes were still damp from the day before. She drew on the snow pants, the ski jacket, and the knitted hat with a shiver. Doreen stamped impatiently outside the kitchen door. Her winter gear consisted of a leather flight jacket (courtesy of a former husband), several sweaters, stocking cap, and flannel lined jeans. For some reason, she'd stuffed Tatiana into a baby's sweater. The little dog pranced in the snow with more than its usual arrogance.

"She actually looks pretty chic," Meg muttered in Quill's ear. "You going to be warm enough?"

"I think so."

"Be careful. You, too, John."

Meg stood at the door until they reached the maintenance building. Quill turned and waved.

They set off on foot down the circular drive to the Inn and into the park near the gorge. It was going to snow again, and soon. Clouds drifted past the moon like passing sailboats.

John walked with his head down, hands thrust in his pockets. Quill walked next to Myles, skipping occasionally to keep up with his long strides. Doreen zigzagged back and forth, once in a while throwing a snowball for the dog.

Tatiana was the happiest of the group.

"Right about here, Sheriff." Doreen took a sharp left and plunged into a grove of pine. The way was narrow here, the paths clogged with snow. Quill grabbed on to the back of Myles's anorak to help her keep to her feet.

The dog stopped. Raised its head. Sniffed. Broke into shrill barks and leaped forward, plunging through the drifts. John broke into a run. So did Myles. Doreen and Quill trudged along behind.

"I smell smoke," said Quill.

"S.O.A.P." Doreen said briefly. "They cooked that durn cow here last night. You shoulda seen it."

"Did you see it?"

Doreen turned her head in the dark. The whites of her eyes gleamed. She said with a chuckle, "Me'n Marge? We follered that

Elmer and Harland last night. You shoulda seen them guys. Half of 'em buck nekkid 'ceptin' that bozo Blight. He's too smart to jump around in a gol-durned blizzard with no clothes on. But there they all was, jumping and hollering around this big old fire, with this big old steer carcass a-turnin' and a-turnin' over the fire on this here spit."

Which was where they found the body of Alphonse Santini, turning slowly over a dying fire, under the moonlit sky.

CHAPTER 12

"Thank the good Lord he wasn't skewered," said Doreen. She and Quill stood huddled together under the pine tree. It was cold and getting colder, but Quill would have had to be nearly comatose with the chill to approach the slow-burning fire. Myles and John kicked the slow coals away from the body. The remnants glowed like wolf eyes in the dark.

Myles squatted and examined the ropes that bound Santini. John knelt in the snow beside him. "You can see where the dog's scurried in the snow," said John. "Here and here. Do you think it was the head wound that killed him?"

"Most likely. Two shots behind the right ear. But I've been wrong before." He lowered his head in thought. Then, "Quill?"

"We're over here."

"You saw the videotape of Nora's murder what, once?"

"That's right."

"Think about it. Think hard about it. Pretend that you're going to paint the scene."

Quill edged nearer. Doreen bent and picked up Tatiana, who was for once silent. Quill closed her eyes.

"Anything you can remember about the figure in your coat and hat. The least thing, Quill."

"It was a man, I'm sure of that. His arms were longer than my sleeves. And he was my height, because the coat hit his leg where it hits mine."

"About five eight, then," Myles said to John. "Any idea of weight, Quill?"

Quill shook her head.

"Anything else?"

Quill went over the videotape in her mind. Nora getting out of the car. Nora bending over to brush the snow from her boots. Nora falling, her hands outstretched, her fingers spread in a final gesture of death . . .

"Dorset. Dorset did it, too!" she exclaimed. "That must have been how he knew."

"Did what?"

"Nora spread her fingers like this." Quill stripped her glove from her hand and held it up. Her first two fingers formed a V. "Vittorio! Myles. It's Vittorio! It must be. That would explain what Elaine said. And all that crazy stuff about Tutti and the séance."

"The séance wasn't all that crazy," Doreen grumbled. "I think there's a lot to it."

"Tutti must have seen that videotape. Nobody knew about that hat. No one except me, Dorset, and the murderer. And Elaine told me—that Vittorio's scum, Myles, just scum—but Elaine told me that Tutti would find a way to keep him in line so he wouldn't beat her up anymore."

"Those long-sleeved blouses," John said softly, "I should have known. Damn him."

"Tutti's got the tape, Myles. She must have. And all that stuff that the senator said? About how it didn't matter where the money came from in that family, it was who had the control? It's Tutti. And the weapon she has over her son is the tape!"

"Jeez," said Doreen.

"Brilliant, Quill." John clapped his hands together softly.

She could see Myles's smile in the dark.

"You've got it, dear heart. John, we need some time. I'd like you to stay with the body. I'm going down the hill to get the deputy and to call forensics. Quill, I want you and Doreen to go back to the Inn. I don't want you to do anything, you understand? Just keep an eye on that whole party, Tutti in particular. I'm going to bring in some people to search the Inn; if Tutti's using the tape as a hold over Vittorio, it's got to be there someplace. If anyone tries to leave, don't stop them, but call me, all right?"

"Another storm system's moving in," John said. "Why don't you tell them you've heard Syracuse is blanketed and it's moving this way?"

"We'll be fine," said Quill.

"We're goin' back, then?" asked Doreen.

"Yes. And bring Tatiana." She reached over to ruffle the little dog's ears. "We'll find something nice for her supper. After all, she found the bod— OW! Dammit, Doreen, can't you keep her from nipping?"

Doreen carried the dog back to the Inn, which was just fine with Quill, since she was wearing half-boots that left her calves exposed. Back in the kitchen, Doreen set her on the floor, and she promptly fell asleep.

"Put her in the storeroom," Meg said callously. "With some food and water. Better yet, give her back to Tutti. Maybe she'll bite Vittorio."

"Are they still eating?" Quill peered through the swinging doors. Everyone at the table seemed to be having a fine time. Two of the Cornell students that worked as waiters in their spare time stood at polite attention beside the mahogany sideboard. Tutti was holding court. Vittorio was leaning back in his chair, genially smiling at Marlon Guppa. Elaine, sitting painfully erect, was chatting with Merry Phelan. Even Claire was smiling, flirting in a gawky way with Joseph Greenwald.

"He looks like a murderer, doesn't he?" Meg said into her ear. "Vittorio, I mean."

"Claire doesn't seem to be too upset that the senator's not here," Quill observed. "Didn't anyone say anything about it at all?"

"Oh, there was quite a bit of discussion," said Meg. "Claire finally went up to the Adams suite with her bridesmaid and found that all of the senator's clothes and personal effects were gone. They also found that envelope you did, from the travel agency. So they came back down and Claire cried that she'd been jilted and

Joseph Greenwald poured her more champagne. After a second bottle of that Avalon Patriot's Red, Vittorio got up and proposed a toast. 'To the absent bridegroom,' he said. 'May he never return.' That got a big laugh, for some reason. Then Elaine started fluttering on about plumbing money, and about how the senator really wasn't their kind of people and good riddance to bad rubbish, and Vittorio told her to shut up. We should have known he'd done it the minute we saw him."

"But he hadn't done it then. Anyhow, I don't think anyone really looks like a murderer," Quill said in an uncritical way, "but Vittorio's going to get off scot-free if we don't find that tape."

"When will Myles get here with the search warrant?"

"Not for a couple of hours yet." Quill frowned. "I know the thing's here."

"Gol-durn it," Doreen exploded behind them. "You git!"

Tatiana whose brief nap seemed to have brought an unfortunate degree of vigor to her sixteen pounds, had jumped up on the counter and was worrying the rabbit hat. Quill turned around, regarded the dog, and pulled thoughtfully at her hair. "Hey, guys. I've got an idea. Meg? Can you ask one of the guys to bring another case of champagne?"

"For who? For them? Haven't they guzzled enough?"

"No," said Quill, "not nearly enough. Tell them this one's on the house Doreen? Can you keep that darn dog quiet?"

"Prob'ly."

"Good. I'm going to my office. Meg? When you give them that champagne, offer to videotape it. Get the camcorder from Marlon and bring it back with you. If he's drunk enough, he won't even notice that you have it. And then I want the three of us to go upstairs."

It took an interminable time for the McIntosh party to get through the extra twelve bottles of champagne. The Reverend Shuttleworth, who arrived for the wedding rehearsal, only to be told that the groom had failed to show, returned home in mild confusion. (Since mild confusion was a more or less permanent state of mind with Dookie, none of his family noticed.) Quill, Doreen, and Meg waited patiently on the second-floor landing for the party to wind down.

"They're comin'," Doreen said. "Hear that?"

There was a scrape of chairs, the kind of dismissive laughter that signals the end of a long party, a murmur of "good nights."

Tutti, Vittorio, and Elaine proceeded up the stairs. Meg moved the camcorder into position. Doreen set Tatiana on the floor. Quill stood at the head of the stairs.

"Now," Quill whispered.

"Git it!" Doreen roared at the startled dog. She held a mini-sized videocassette above Tatiana's head. The dog leaped for it. Doreen jerked the tape out of reach and ordered, "Git it! Git it!" The dog, irritated to a frenzy by the incomprehensible behavior of this bad-tempered human, barked like Joshua at the walls of Jericho. She leaped, and leaped again.

"They're looking up," Quill said from her vantage point on the landing. "Any time now."

Doreen let the cassette drop. Tatiana snatched it up with a triumphant "Yap!" Tutti, hearing the barks, cried, "Tatty! Come to Mummy!" Tatiana raced down the stairs, videocassette in her mouth.

Tutti caught the dog in her arms and grabbed for the tape. Tatiana wriggled and dropped it. Vittorio picked it up. His swarthy face turned pale.

"Goddammit!" roared Vittorio. "Ma! You told me you hid the goddamn thing."

Quill walked down the stairs. Doreen thumped down beside her and snatched the tape from Vittorio's hand. Meg followed, the camcorder rolling, the camera eye fixed on the group on the stairs.

"Give me that thing," Vittorio demanded. He swayed, caught himself with one hand on the banister, and blinked blearily at Doreen.

"Is it yours?" Quill asked sweetly. "I'm afraid the little dog went through your things when Doreen was straightening your room, Tutti. Where she unearthed this thing I don't know. It can't be yours, can it, Mr. McIntosh? It's marked, 'Property Tompkins County Police Department.'"

"Give it to me, you bitch!"

"Vic!" snapped Tutti. "Shut up!"

Quill took two more steps downward. "This is it, Mr. McIntosh? The videotape from Frank Dorset's hidden camera? The one that shows you killing Nora Cahill?"

"Yes, goddamit! Yes!"

Meg shut the camcorder off. "Well," she said sunnily, "I got it all. And the little dog, too."

Quill surveyed the wreckage in the dining room with a sense of satisfaction. It was a shame about the roses, of course. But it had taken less than half an hour that morning to strip the walls and windows of the wedding finery.

Mike the groundskeeper poked his head in from the foyer. "You want I should take the trash?"

Quill nudged one of the garbage bags with her toe. The scent of crushed roses was strong. "Yes. Thanks, Mike."

"I'll bring the tree in, then. You want it here?"

"I think so. Everyone's coming at eight tonight, so we have plenty of time."

"No problem. I got all the ornaments down and I'll bring 'em in first. Meg having that oyster stew again this year?"

"And Marge is bringing the pumpkin bread."

"Ahh!" Mike patted his flat stomach. "You didn't hear me say this, Quill, but I'd almost give up the holiday bonus for that pumpkin bread."

Quill stripped the rose-patterned cloths from the tables, bundled them into a box, and replaced them with the red plaid she used for the holidays. She set out the buffet plates, the flatware, and the punch bowl, humming "The Boar's Head Carol" under her breath, then "God Rest Ye Merry Gentlemen."

Mike brought the tree in, a fifteen footer he'd cut from the woods beyond Hemlock Gorge. It filled the windows overlooking the Falls. It smelled of snow, of cold fresh winds, of pine tar. The two of them strung the hundreds of tiny white lights that Quill had collected over the years, then stepped back to view the result.

"It'll look great at night," Mike said. "You want I should plug 'em in?"

"Degradation!" Evan Blight bellowed, so suddenly that Quill

nearly fell over. "Young man? Remove those artifacts of man's inhumanity to the arboreal immediately."

"Hello, Mr. Blight," Quill said. "Can I get you some hot chocolate? I'm afraid that breakfast is over."

"There was," he said a little pathetically, "a disturbance in the night."

"There was indeed. I hope it didn't keep you up."

"She most certainly did," he said with indignation. "Not to mention going through my personal effects."

"She?" said Quill. "You mean someone was in your room?"

"That . . . dog. That . . . perverse mutant of the noble wolf."

"Tatiana? Oh, I'm sorry. I guess in all the confusion last night, we sort of ignored her." Quill chuckled. "Tatiana isn't a dog that likes being ignored. But, under the circumstances, I hope you will forgive her."

"I understand from the Red Man that several guests were arrested."

Quill thought about this for a moment. "Do you mean John Raintree?"

"Yes! The Primal Savage. The nobility of him! It's a shame," Blight continued, "to see on him the wrappings required by our so-called *civil*-ization, although anything less civil . . ."

"Do you mean his clothes?"

"Why, yes. At any rate, I understand that the primal urge has been satisfied, the blood lust quelled."

"If you mean by that that Vittorio McIntosh has been arrested for three murders, the answer is yes, he has."

"And the motive. Lust, no doubt."

"No doubt at all. It wasn't. He killed for gain. He killed Nora Cahill because she was blackmailing him over evidence she'd gathered of his organized crime connections. He killed Frank Dorset because Dorset recognized him on the videotape and also tried blackmail. And he killed Alphonse Santini because Tutti told Santini about the murders—to guarantee to the senator that she had Vittorio under her thumb, and that she would call the political shots—and Santini was ready to turn all the McIntoshes in to the police." Quill reflected a moment. "So I guess he died a better man than he lived. Or something like that."

"*Cherchez les femmes*," said Evan Blight.

"If by that you mean that women were behind Vittorio's downfall, you couldn't be more wrong." Quill, sorry that she'd lost her temper, asked if he would like some lunch before he checked out.

Mr. Blight ran his finger through his beard in agitation. He circled the dining room. His beard was even wilder and untrimmed than before. He'd exchanged the shapeless gray sweater he'd been wearing for two days to an equally shapeless brown sweater. "As you see," he said grandly, catching Quill's eye on him, "I have donned my holiday garb."

"You were planning on staying over Christmas, then?"

The gray eyes blinked behind the fringe of tangled hair. "I would not be welcomed?"

Quill had the feeling, apropos of nothing whatsoever, that Evan Blight, world-famous standard-bearer for manly men, had nowhere to go. She sat down at the table she reserved for the Inn staff, and indicated the chair next to her. He shook his head warily, rather like a small goat approaching a large obstacle.

"Of course you're welcome," Quill said warmly. "We don't normally keep the Inn open over Christmas Eve and Christmas Day, but we'd love to have you join us. As a friend, Mr. Blight. Not a guest."

"The bountiful hospitality of Woman!" exclaimed Mr. Blight.

Quill held her hand up. "There's just one thing. Elmer Henry. Our mayor. And the gentlemen of S.O.A.P. You may not be fully aware of the—um—divisive nature of your beliefs, Mr. Blight. Especially now, at this particular time in the town's history. Perhaps you could soften your views, somewhat? I mean, in the spirit of the season. We need, Mr. Blight, to have the men and women of this town talking to each other again. And you could help, if you wished."

"Humpf."

"Humpf?" Quill sat back, frustrated.

"You would have me abandon a lifetime of beliefs? A value system carefully built up over years of study, years of effort, years of—"

"Bullshit," said Doreen. She marched into the dining room, clutching a pink, elastic object. Tatiana leaped beside her, jaws snapping for the straps dangling from Doreen's hand.

"Down, Spike," said Doreen.

Tatiana dropped to the floor obediently.

"Spike?" asked Quill.

"They was goin' to shoot her," Doreen said flatly. "On account of she betrayed that Tutti. And her name's Spike. Tatiana's no name for a dog."

Quill sighed. "Okay. I guess. But if she bites anybody, Doreen, that's it, do you hear me?"

"You'd think a lot better of this dog if you knew."

"If I knew what?"

"If you knew how she could keep this here Blight from wrecking our Christmas party tonight."

"The dog's going to do that?" Quill said, bewildered.

"The dog did it already. Look here." She thrust the pink elastic object at Quill. Beside her Evan Blight yelped. Spike yelped back.

"Good grief," Quill said. She unfolded it. "It's a minimizer bra."

"So it is." Doreen grinned in satisfaction. "Well, Ms. Blight. What you got to say for yourself?"

There was a long, long moment of silence. Blight tugged at her beard, pulled it slightly away from her chin, and winked at them.

"What do I have to say for myself? It's going to be a very Merry Christmas Hemlock Falls."

"We'll wait to turn the lights on," said Quill. "Myles might be here soon."

Meg gave her a hug. "He'll be here."

"I hope so. He took Vittorio straight to the FBI office in Syracuse. But you know how these things go. He might not make it at all."

They came early, her friends. Marge and Betty, Miriam, Esther, and all the members of H.O.W. Elmer Henry and Adela, Harland Peterson and his wife, Dookie Shuttleworth and the patient Mrs. Shuttleworth, Kathleen and her brother Davy; it seemed as if the whole village gathered together in the warm and capacious dining room.

They talked, and laughed, and sang carols, and listened to Evan Blight talk about the harmony of love.

Meg brought hot stew from the kitchen. Andy Bishop poured hot cider. One by one the ornaments went on the tree; the flying unicorn that Meg had given her years before, the bubbling lights from Marge and Betty, the beaded angel for the top of the tree from John's grandmother.

The sky grew dark. Snow began to fall, tapping against the windows like the tips of feathered wings.

John's quick ears heard it first, the roar of the Jeep as it came up the drive to the front door of the Inn. He switched the tree lights on, and it glowed in the window, a galaxy of stars, to welcome Myles home.

MARGE SCHMIDT'S INCREDIBLE
CHICKEN STEW

Marge has been very annoyed that her straightforward American cooking has heretofore been ignored in the Hemlock Falls adventures. Here is her recipe for the best chicken stew ever made. (She says!)

one large, cheap old chicken
two carrots, coarsely chopped
two stalks of celery, coarsely chopped
one large onion, chopped
two medium bay leaves
a tablespoon of garlic powder
a few pinches of salt
½ cup soy sauce
one package Knox herb soup
three potatoes, peeled and coarsely chopped
one ten-ounce package frozen peas
two cups Bisquick

Place chicken, carrots, celery, onion, bay leaves, garlic powder, and salt in a large stewpot. Cover with water. Add soy sauce. Simmer until chicken is tender, about an hour and a half.

Remove chicken from pot. Cool. Debone. Replace chicken in pot. Add Knox herb soup, potatoes, and frozen peas. Simmer for one half hour.

Mix Bisquick with one cup water. Drop the dough by large table-spoonfuls into simmering stew. It will make about fifteen dumplings. Cover and simmer for ten minutes. Uncover and simmer for another ten minutes.

Serves ten.

Claudia Bishop is the author of fifteen previous novels in the Hemlock Falls series, as well as the three-book series, The Casebooks of Dr. McKenzie. As **Mary Stanton**, she is at work on the fifth Beaufort & Company mystery novel, *Shadow of a Doubt*.

Claudia divides her time between a two hundred acre farm in upstate New York, and a small home in West Palm Beach, Florida. She loves to hear from readers, and can be reached at her websites, marystanton.com and claudiabishop.com.